THIGH SCRAPERS

SOME MEN PLAY THE GAME. OTHERS LIVE BY IT.

C.C. Cowan

CCP Publishing & Entertainment, Brooklyn, N.Y. 11236

C.C. Cowan/CCP Publishing & Entertainment
9602 Glenwood Road, #362
Brooklyn, N.Y. 11236
www.ccppublishing.com

Publisher's Note: This is a work of fiction. Names, characters, places, and incidents are a product of the author's imagination. Locales and public names are sometimes used for atmospheric purposes. Any resemblance to actual people, living or dead, or to businesses, companies, events, institutions, or locales is completely coincidental.

Thigh Scrapers/ C.C. Cowan. -- 1st ed.
ISBN 978-0980126570

Dedicated to Cozette, Charmaine, Rhukia

ACKNOWLEDGMENTS

Without the support of the following people this would have been a lot harder to accomplish:

Don Credle, Kevin Moss, Rodney Goode, James Johnson, R&B Group Vokal, Romaro Spivey, Stephen Felton, Adrian Rias, Marlyn J. Hunter, Ronald Benbow, Eddie Lampkin, Quinton Dukes, Antonio Watkins, Byron Sawyers, Matthew Womack, Reggie Freeman, Anthony Marshall, Kurtis Grant, Rodrick Tomlin, Gerald Readus, Christopher McMorris, Kenneth Carter, Benny Forest, Lee Stallworth, Keith L. Smith, Bruce Das Tate, Zoltin Williams and Don White.

A Very Special Thanks to Anlami Shaw (Cover Model).

THIGH SCRAPERS

SOME MEN PLAY THE GAME. OTHERS LIVE BY IT.

CHAPTER ONE

Another Terrible Night

Omar's eyes rolled to the clock on the nightstand; the neon red glare from the numbers read 3:56 a.m. He yawned, took a few minutes to focus running his fingers over his eyelids; he stretched. It had been another terrible night. He and Asia had argued again, but this time not over silly things. This time, not over him leaving the toilet seat up or because he had left an empty milk carton in the refrigerator again; it was far more severe. Being at home, in his bed, snug beneath his soft down-comforter made him feel better, but not her. For so long everything had been about her, what she wanted, what she needed. It felt good to be in control again.

Last night, Omar had fallen asleep with the belief that things would once again work themselves out in the morning. They always did. It had only been a few hours since they had gone to bed, but the way the streetlight peaked through the bedroom window provided the perfect backdrop for the end-of-an-argument makeup sex. He shifted himself in the bed slowly, careful not to wake her. He intended to snuggle close to her, to wrap his strong arms around her, to make her feel secure, to press his warm body against hers, to provide the comfort he knew she needed. He licked his lips as he prepared to guide his bulging morning erection against her round, voluptuous ass. It was to be a prelude to his apology. He had it all planned out. He would kiss her, hold her, caress her, lick her, and make everything all right between them.

It had become customary for them to have wild, passionate sex after one of their fights. Usually, they'd end up ripping each other's clothes off and screaming in butt naked ecstasy until it woke the neighbors. In the past year, Omar had to replace three headboards, two canopies, a futon, a dining table, and two chandeliers. Asia is an adventurous woman on some real Cirque du Soleil shit, and he wasn't much better. As far as he was concerned, this morning wouldn't be any different. In fact, a few things were about to be broken; a few more pieces of furniture and the emotional wall Asia had put up between them.

He slid his hand along the sheet, feeling for her. The coolness from her side of the bed startled him. He turned over quickly and gasped...

TWENTY-FIVE MINUTES AWAY

A young woman rested her face against the cold, hard glass in the backseat of a taxicab; her body was limp with exhaustion. She hadn't slept a wink.

As the cab arrived at her place, she was suddenly overcome by a feeling of relief-367 West 122nd Street never looked so good.

The driver watched as she lifted a large bag from the back seat. Although petite, she was strong. He popped the trunk and aided her in removing the rest of her luggage.

"Is anyone coming down to help you, Miss?" he asked.

The young woman rolled her eyes and replied sharply, "My name isn't Miss, it's Asia, and I don't need anyone to help me. Thank you very much!"

The driver's eyes widened.

"Would you like to tell me how much I owe you rather than standing there looking like someone just stole the medallion off your cab?" she snapped.

"That'll be thirty-five dollars," the driver replied, speaking softly for fear that Asia would once again snap at him.

Asia fingered through her purse.

"Are you sure that I can't help you with your things? They look pretty heavy." He glanced at the twelve concrete steps that led to her front door.

Asia cast her eyes on them as well then proceeded to unfold a few loose bills. "Okay, fine! Whatever!" she replied.

Although her snappy tone was less than appreciative, the eager cabby immediately hoisted the large bags from the ground. The lean, muscular frame that was once hidden beneath his baggy clothes became more noticeable as he carried the bags toward the steps. He was a fit man, in his late 30s, handsome, and trying to impress her. It probably would have worked too had he encountered her at any other time. Fire probably would have burst from between her thighs, but not this time. She was over men, over him, and overly exhausted. She cut him a fierce look. *I hope you don't think that I'm impressed with your immature attempt at playing Superman. Those bags are heavy and if you throw your back out, you had better not look this way.*

She sneered as he placed the last bag at the top of the steps.

"All done," he said, smiling as if he were waiting for some sign that she was impressed.

"Thanks," Asia said, flashing him a phony one in return.

"No problem beautiful, any time."

"Oh, trust me; it will only be this one time, I can assure you!"

Asia's behavior had left the cabby perplexed. He just stood there staring at her, feeling like a child who had been spoken down to by an evil parent. He pondered, what could make such a beautiful woman so darn uptight? He watched as Asia began dragging her things inside.

He mumbled, "Somebody has obviously done her wrong and now she's going to take it out on every man she sees."

"What did you say?" Asia snapped.

"Oh nothing; you have a good night ma'am. Maybe I'll see you around sometime," the cabby said, shaking his head as he headed back to his car.

The look on Asia's face changed immediately-from annoyed to utter disgust. She spoke to herself as she dragged the last of her things inside. "If I never see another man again in this lifetime, it'll be too soon, yet let alone a damn cab driver!"

She slammed the door shut, kicked off her shoes, and fell to her knees sobbing.

CHAPTER TWO

The Big Black Pendulum Swings Both Ways

Omar noticed a light coming from beneath the bathroom door and breathed a sigh of relief. He sat straight up, took a deep breath, and got out of bed. The impression his body made in the mattress faded slowly behind him.

Although there was a slight chill in the room, slipping into a robe was the furthest thing from his mind. His large, black endowment swung like a mighty pendulum as he made his way toward the bathroom. In the few seconds it took to walk across the room, he began recalling all the changes he had endured in his life just to make Asia happy. He had made so many sacrifices for a woman he never intended to spend more than a few horny nights with, much less fall in love with.

He stood in front of the door for a few moments staring at it - wishing it were an entrance to another galaxy, another world where men like him thought about the things they say before saying them. A place where arguments over silly shit could be avoided and where, if he had the chance to undo everything he had done, he would. If there were such a place, then she wouldn't be on one side of the door and he on the other.

Omar knew the door was no magic portal to the perfect relationship, but he hoped it could be the gateway to the end of their argument. He took another deep breath, gripped his crotch, and prepared to throw himself on the mercy of Asia's ample breasts.

"Sweetheart is everything okay?" he called out but received no answer.

"Baby, I know you're upset. I'm upset too. Let's talk about it." He pressed his ear against the bathroom door. There was still no answer. In fact, he didn't hear a thing. After waiting a few more seconds, he pushed the door open and discovered that the bathroom was empty. His eyes panned to the mirror over the sink where he found a message written in lipstick. *You're not the man I thought you were. I hate you!*

His stare intensified, and so did his desire to find her. He raced through the house calling out her name, checking every closet and room.

Within a few seconds, he had completed his search of the second level of his house but found no sign of her. He immediately dashed downstairs. She wasn't in the kitchen, dining room, or the study. As he entered the living room, he noticed an empty space on the wall where her picture once hung. A shard of glass cut into his foot, stopping him in his tracks. When he looked down, he noticed a smashed picture frame, picked it up and in disbelief headed back to his bedroom.

Specs of blood trailed all the way to his bedside; his foot was bleeding profusely. It didn't matter though. He had lost more than blood. He had lost his woman.

MEANWHILE IN HARLEM

Asia laid in bed chastising herself about all the emotions, money and time she had put into trying to sustain a relationship with a man who never really wanted one; a man who clearly proved that he could never be faithful to any woman.

She stared at a necklace he had given her; it dangled from a picture frame on her nightstand. Her mind became flooded with memories of how happy she was when Omar surprised her with it. That type of happiness seemed so unattainable now, primarily since she was back at square one, feeling alone and bitter. She resented him and his gifts. In fact, she vowed to never trust another man again. And she had just cause not to. Her recent discovery of Omar's secret lifestyle dealt her a painful blow that she never had any idea was coming; a blow that left her with three very real truths: that all men are selfish, that they are after only one thing, and that no matter how painful it was going to be, she would have nothing else to do with Omar's tired black ass.

She had placed him on a pedestal for too long, putting his needs before hers, always making sure that he was okay. Well, she wasn't okay. And whenever she spoke up about it, he'd whip out his dick as if it were some magic wand that was supposed to instantly make everything all right. Often it did, but that wasn't going to work this time. Not if she could stay away from the mighty pendulum in his pants.

It was clear that his endowment was the biggest obstacle in their relationship; he shared it with whomever he pleased, and she couldn't seem to resist it. It was also evident that he used that knowledge to do and say whatever he wanted to her. Yet, the pendulum swings both ways and the one in the middle of their relationship was not swinging in her favor anymore.

Tears rolled from her eyes. She removed the necklace from the frame and tossed it into the trash.

OMAR'S BEDROOM

The scent of Asia's perfume lingered on his sheets, jeering at him as he clutched a pillow from her side of the bed. He noticed a single strand of her hair dangling from the pillowcase as if she had left it there on purpose to taunt him.

He shook his head as he recalled their last words to each other. He called her 'needy, desperate, and stupid.'

She called him 'a selfish ass.'

He couldn't believe how they argued the night before. It was as though they were strangers; perhaps they were.

He stared at the broken picture frame he had placed on his nightstand. It had all happened so fast. One minute he was sizing her up for a roll in the hay; the next, he was spending more time with her than he had any intentions of doing. Maybe it was a good thing that she left.

I was getting tired of her anyway. She was always hanging around, nagging me about spending more time, getting married, moving in together. I told her when we first met that I wasn't looking to get involved in anything too serious, but she just kept pushing.

He continued to try to rationalize Asia's absence. *It's a good thing that she took a hike. It saves me the trouble of having to hurt her feelings later. Like I said, I never wanted to get serious in the first place.*

He recalled what his intentions were the night they met at the party. She was going to be just another notch in his belt, another dollar in his pocket. After all, men like him never fall in love.

CHAPTER THREE

Superman Is A Cartoon

How could I have been so stupid? Asia thought. *Was I so caught up in his bedroom eyes, chiseled body, and all his Hallmark Greeting Card flattering bullshit that I couldn't see what his real intentions were?*

Like so many women before her, she played the questions over in her mind, but couldn't come up with any logical explanation about why she allowed a man to use her the way Omar had. Now she was just another woman who had foolishly fallen for the wrong man. After years of denial, she had finally come face-to-face with the truth. Superman is a cartoon.

She began to question herself aloud as if it would help her to realize something she hadn't.

I'm a smart woman. I'm college educated. I have a subscription to Essence Magazine, and I watch Oprah. I even read The Secret in hopes that I could positively think my way into a better relationship. Well, a lot of good that did; I'm in a worse situation than I was before I knew what the Laws of Attraction were. Here I thought that I was luring my dream man into my life through the power of positive thinking when all the while I was setting myself up to be hurt. I still can't believe he had me saved in his phone as number seventy-three. No first name, no last name, just number seventy-three. Well, Mr. I-can-play-with-a-woman's-heart-anytime-I-get-good-and-damn-

ready, you are now saved in my phone as eighty-six, be-
cause you've been fuckin' eighty-sixed!

Asia had met vain men in the past, but they would usually cut and run once they realized she wasn't falling for their games, but Omar was different, he was serial with his shit.

Many men felt like they had to let me go when I didn't
fall for their smooth line, but Omar was good. I had no
clue what he was up to. If I had known he was such an
emotional charlatan, I would have put my nose up in the
air and walked away a long time ago. But no, I had to
stick around, buying into his lame excuse about the num-
bers in his telephone. When I confronted him, he said,
"Oh, baby, I know so many people, it's just easier to re-
member everyone by number, like I do with all my
clients."

Right...clients my ass! He was sleeping with every
woman he trained and then some. Furthermore, he was
leading a double life that I knew nothing about. I swear to
God if he's given me anything, I will kill him. For that
matter, I want the money back that I paid for "The Se-
cret" because the one Omar was keeping from me was far
greater than anything I learned reading that damned
book.

Asia was going through so many emotional changes that she didn't know what to do with herself. She needed someone to blame, and she did. She blamed her friends, her exes, other women Omar had slept with, even God.

How in the hell did I ever allow myself to become this
man's fool? I've read all the relationship books, watched
all the talk shows; this was not supposed to happen to me.

I'm not supposed to be some common stereotype. I'm not supposed to be! She burst into tears.

Asia was overwhelmed; disappointment held her hostage. She was ashamed not just for herself, but for all the other women who had suffered the same fate at the hands of a lying man.

"Knock, knock!" A voice said, spilling into the moment.

Asia's eyes rolled toward the door, brimming with tears as she noticed the face of a close friend.

"Pam?"

"Yes, honey, I'm here."

Tears ran into the sides of Asia's mouth as she became even more emotional. She and Pam had been friends for so long. They embraced.

"I didn't know who else to call," Asia said, resting her head on Pam's shoulder.

"It's okay; I'm glad you called me; I would have been angry if you hadn't."

"He hurt me so bad."

"I know baby, I know." She patted Asia on the back.

"Hey, stop this crying. Everything is going to be fine."

Pam pulled some napkins from her purse and handed them to her friend.

"I don't know where I went wrong, Pam. I thought that I was doing everything right."

"Honey, this isn't about you what you were doing. It's about that man's decision to take you for granted."

"I gave him everything I had. Now I have nothing left for me." She grabbed Pam's hand.

"Yes, you do. You have a good heart, you have your health, and you have God."

"What use is a good heart when it's broken in a million pieces?" Asia said, lowering her head.

"Honey, a man can hurt your feelings, but he can never break your heart. It's all just an illusion."

"Yeah, well, tell that to my heart."

"Listen, I know what you mean. But I want you to know that God can wipe that feeling and that man clean out of your system. He's seen your intention and knows your pain. He can take it away from you, too. All you have to do is ask Him." She reached for Asia's hand to pray.

"Yeah, well, you have to excuse me." Asia gently pulled away. "I don't think I'll be asking God for anything else anytime soon."

"What?" Pam's eyes widened.

"Tell me something, Pam. What type of God would let a man use a woman the way Omar used me? Before we met, I prayed and asked God to send me a good man and look what I got."

"I know, we've all prayed that prayer at one time or another, but-"

"Oh, please...but nothing!"

"Asia?" Pam was shocked at her friends' tone.

"I can't believe I actually thought that God would look out for me on this one. And why should I have believed it? I attend church every Sunday; I'm a good neighbor, I honor my parents; I even toss a little something extra in the collection plate when it comes around. So, why the hell did He let this happen to me?

Pam was stunned. She had never heard Asia speak that way. Her friend was usually the one talking about how good God is and how much He's done for her. Now she was blaming him for what she and Omar had gone through.

"Asia, do you honestly blame God for the way Omar treated you?"

She cut Pam a look as if to say yes, and then some.

"You know what? I don't believe that for a minute. I know you're hurt and you're trying to make sense of things, but blaming God isn't the answer."

"No, then what is?"

"Well, you can start by sucking it up, saying a prayer, and trusting that God is going to help you get past this."

"Oh, I am going to suck it up, and not because I believe that God is going to help me, but because I'm not going to let Omar break me. And, as far as getting past this, you have no idea."

"Honey, please, God loves you, and He will never abandon you. You know you can trust in that."

"Oh, please, God is of the male gender. Just like Omar and the rest of the dogs out there."

"So, what are you saying?"

"I'm saying I'll never trust another man again, or God for that matter."

Pam shook her head; the words that came out of Asia's mouth sent chills up her arm. However, she was determined not to give up. She began to pray.

"What are you doing?" Asia snapped.

"What does it look like? I'm praying."

"I told you that I didn't want to pray."

"I know, but that doesn't mean that I can't."

Pam sat next to her friend and continued praying. Asia fought the need to join in by staring across the room. The power of Pam's prayer tugged at her heart, but her stubbornness prevailed.

"Amen!" Pam opened her eyes. "So, have you spoken to him at all?"

"No, and I'm not going to." Asia's voice was layered with resentment.

Pam looked directly into her eyes searching for any sign that she'd be able to convince her not to go through with her decision.

"Why are you looking at me like that? Do you think I'm wrong for leaving him?"

"No, I would have left him too. But this is bigger than you just packing your things and leaving. When you do this, there's no turning back. I just want you to be certain that this is what God wants for you."

Just as Pam spoke those words, Asia's cell phone rang. She glanced at the number, and the look on her face became icy-her tears nearly froze on her face. She couldn't believe his audacity. He was calling her as if she would give him the time of day.

"Who is that?" Pam asked.

"It's him, the deceitful one. The one man I thought I could trust. The same man who had single-handedly caused me to consider having my vagina removed and sent to the moon for preservation against men and their bullshit." She turned off her phone.

"Honey, are you sure you're doing the right thing? You still have time to change your mind you know." Pam glanced at her watch.

"Yes, I'm sure," Asia replied, looking at her friend with tears in her eyes. "Thanks again for being here."

"Girl, please, I know what it's like to have your knight in shining armor turn out to be the biggest mistake in your life. I went through the same thing with Tony, remember?"

"Yeah, I remember. He was a mess." Asia chuckled slightly.

"That's right, and you were there for me, so I'm going to be here for you no matter what it takes." She touched Asia's hand.

"I just can't believe how many things he lied to me about. I should have seen this coming. I should have known."

"Women are always the last to know."

"Why are we so naive?"

"Maybe it's because we really don't want to know."

"What woman wouldn't want to know that her man is leading a double life?"

"I know, but sometimes knowing hurts worse than suspecting."

"There were times when I had my doubts, but then he would wrap those big strong arms around me and make love to me, and all of my doubts would go flying right out of the window."

"Believe me, I know. I don't think there's a woman in this world that hadn't a clue about her man doing wrong before she was hit in the face with it."

"How do we stop before we get in too deep?"

"I wish I had the answer for that, but I don't. All we can do is pray and hope that what we're feeling isn't true."

"I guess in my heart I knew that something wasn't right with him. I just ignored it."

"Honey, that's every woman's story. No matter how much we suspect, unless we've seen it with our own two eyes, our minds won't let us believe that it's possible."

Another voice spilled into the moment, "It's time, Ms. Coakley, are you ready?"

"Yes." Asia spoke softly. A tear fell from her eye.

"I love you, Pam."

"I love you, too." Pam hugged her and then stepped away from the bed.

Tears drenched Asia's face, but she was firm in her decision. She had made too many mistakes in the past, and she wasn't about to make another. There was a possibility that she would never be able to live with herself after this, but she was willing to risk it. And although she wasn't totally sure what the future held for her regarding men and relationships, one thing was for certain-she never wanted to see Omar's trifling ass again.

OMAR'S PLACE

Omar returned the phone to the base. He sat at the foot of the bed glancing around at all the material things he owned-the imported furniture, the expensive jewelry, the designer clothes-all of it paid for by women who were desperate to hold on to him. None would be so lucky though.

Well, I guess there's a first time for everything. He smirked and then shook his head as reality set in. He'd been dumped for the first time in his life.

His eyes rolled toward the mirror above his dresser noticing something he hadn't earlier, another message written in lipstick. His eyes widened as he read it. I hope you burn in hell for what you did to me. You're a damn liar. I know everything!

"Damn it!" he yelled, grabbing the sides of his head. Had Asia really found out the truth about him?

CHAPTER FOUR

Strictly Business

Ben, Omar's longtime friend, had been trying to reach him for a few days. Omar hadn't shown up to work, hadn't replied to any of his text messages, nor had he returned any of his calls. The fact that he hadn't heard from Omar in days prompted him to stop by. He had a spare set of keys to let himself in.

When he entered the house, an unpleasant odor immediately mugged his nostrils.

"What the fuck?" he muttered through his fingers. Something was wrong.

Omar was anal about the way he kept his place-he liked things clean and in their proper place. However, what Ben walked into was just the opposite. The house was in total disarray; clothes everywhere, unwashed dishes and rotting food were scattered throughout the kitchen. There were even flies, feasting on a trash that had been left uncovered. The place looked like a war zone.

The stench in the house was so overpowering that Ben removed a handkerchief from his pocket and pressed it firmly against his nose.

"I don't know what's going on, but Omar better have a good explanation for this shit." Ben moved slowly through the house, partially afraid of what he might find. While there could have been a million reasons about why Omar's place looked like a snapshot from Better Slums and Train Wrecks, a few stuck out in his mind.

Perhaps the place had been broken into and ransacked by burglars. Or maybe a hurricane had swept through Brooklyn and tore Omar's place apart. Neither really made any sense. What burglar would take the time to lock the front door after ransacking a house? Second, if there had been a hurricane in Brooklyn, Ben would have known about it. He called out Omar's name as he headed upstairs.

The putrid smell that was lingering throughout the house continued to assault Ben's nostrils as he approached Omar's bedroom. His eyes widened as he looked inside and found his friend's body lying limply across the bed. His eyes panned to the floor, noticing a trail of red drippings leading to Omar's bed. He froze in his tracks.

"No, no, no!" Ben squealed, rubbing his forehead. As he moved farther into the room fear gripped him, entirely. Suddenly, his legs felt weighted as if they were being held by some invisible restraints. His trembling jaw caused his teeth to chatter as he nervously scanned the room for intruders. There weren't any. While looking around, he noticed the bedroom was also unkempt. The curtains were drawn, and the room was dark. He glanced down at Omar's body, afraid to touch him.

"O!" he called out, shivering as he reached to touch his friend's arm.

Suddenly, Omar moved.

"What the fuck are you doing here?" he asked, causing Ben to leap back.

"Oh shit! Man, I thought you were dead. What the hell is going on?"

Omar rolled over to avoid eye contact with Ben. "Just leave me alone," he said, burying his face in a stack of pillows.

Ordinarily, Ben wasn't the emotional type but seeing how Omar had just scared the shit out of him; his dander was a bit stirred. "Leave you alone? Man, you better get your ass up and tell me what's going on with you! Why are you lying around like this?"

Omar ignored him.

"Get up!" Ben demanded, switching on the lights.

"Just leave me alone, Ben, please."

"I'm not going to do that." Ben said, as he pulled back the curtains and raised the blinds.

"Then just sit there and be quiet." Omar said, pulling the sheet over his head.

"Damn it, Omar! What's wrong with you?" Ben barked, snatching the sheet from the bed.

"She found out, that's what's wrong with me!"

"What?"

"You heard me. Asia knows everything, about me, about you, about everything we've been doing!"

Ben's mouth fell open as he lowered himself into a chair near the window.

"She won't answer my calls; she won't see me. I don't know how this could have happened."

Ben closed his eyes and took a deep breath.

"How did she find out?"

"I told you; I don't know," Omar paused. "I feel sick." He leaned over the edge of the bed preparing to puke in a nearby wastebasket.

"Okay, look, are you absolutely sure she knows?"

"Yes, I'm sure." Omar snapped.

Ben noticed the message written on the mirror, which confirmed that Asia did indeed know something.

"Okay, don't panic; we have to figure this out."

"Figure what out? We're screwed."

"Damn it, Omar!" Ben shouted. "I know this situation is jacked-up, but you need to pull yourself together! Stop acting like that woman is the one with the balls."

Ben didn't have much respect for women, and even less respect for men who cried over them. As far as he was concerned, Omar needed a good swift kick in the crotch to remind him that he had a scrotum. Unfortunately, his attempt at tough love wasn't sitting well with his friend.

Omar stared at Ben as if he was solely responsible for what happened between him and Asia. The look on his face was like that of a lion ready to pounce on its prey. Ben was no punk, though, and wouldn't be taken down easily.

"You do know that this is all your fault, right?"

"My fault?"

"Yes," Omar barked. "No woman has ever walked out on me. If I hadn't listened to you, she wouldn't have been the first. Now we're about to be exposed."

"Just calm down and tell me exactly what happened."

"I told you what happened; we had a fight."

"I know that; when?"

"Three, maybe four days ago."

"You're kidding me, right?" Ben walked into the bathroom, which was found at the far end of Omar's huge bedroom. He turned on the shower and pulled a few towels from the shelf.

"No, I'm not kidding."

"So, you've been laying here like this for three goddamn days?" Ben's tone reflected his annoyance. The more he analyzed the situation, the more upset he became.

He had warned Omar to keep his association with Asia strictly business, which he obviously had not done.

"I don't know what to do; this shit has my mind all messed up. Just look at me," Omar said, wrestling with his emotions.

"Yeah, I'm looking at you," Ben mumbled. His response was cold and not what Omar expected.

Ben slung a towel at Omar' face. "What the hell is wrong with you?"

"No, what the hell is wrong with you? This is bullshit. If you mess around and let this woman get to you, we could lose everything. I'm telling you now; I'm not going to let that happen. Now get up and get dressed."

"I'm not going anywhere."

"So, you're willing to throw all of this away just like that?" Ben glanced around at Omar's well-furnished abode.

"I don't care about any of this shit!"

"Well, you should care!" Ben urged, staring at the Cathedral-style ceiling in Omar's bedroom, "Look at this place, it's practically a damn' mansion."

"Yeah, well, you can have it," Omar commented blandly.

"Careful, don't spit in the face of the mother-fucker who gave it to you."

Omar's face contorted. What did Ben mean by that? Everything he has he's worked hard to get, from sunup to sundown, finessing some of the wealthiest and uptight bitches on the east coast to get what he wants. As far as he was concerned, no one had given him a thing.

Ben grabbed him by the arm and pulled him from the bed, guiding him toward the window.

"Look down there!" he commanded, "You drive a Mercedes S Class, and you're only 32 years old."

"So, what, it's just a car." Omar turned and headed back toward the bed.

"It's just a car, huh?" Ben halted him, this time guiding him across the room. He swung the doors open to a huge walk-in closet. "Look at this...Versace, Armani, Gucci, and Boss. You have more designer labels than Paris."

Omar sighed. "So."

Ben led him over to a large mirror that hung above his dresser.

"So, you have it made. You're young, good looking, and you drive a car that most men from your background can only dream about. Don't let this woman get you so caught up in what's between her legs that you can't see the value of what you have in front of you." He stared into Omar's eyes.

Omar broke the stare by lowering his head.

Ben clutched his face. "Look man; she's just a piece of ass. You didn't really care about her anyway, right?"

Omar leaped up, grabbing hold of Ben's collar. He drew his fist back. "Don't you ever talk about her like that again. I'm warning you!"

"Wow! Okay, it's like that now?" Ben's tone changed immediately.

Omar released his grip. "Look, bro, all I'm saying is-"

"I know what you're saying, and you're right." He sat on the edge of the bed and lowered his face into his hands.

"Of course, I am." Ben said, straightening his collar.

"Man, I have to find out what she knows. This shit could ruin us," Omar said. His eyes telegraphed a need for help.

"You know I'm not going to let that happen, right?" Omar nodded; they slapped hands.

"Don't worry; we'll figure it out." Ben said, placing his hands onto Omar's shoulders. "Now, can you go wash your ass, please?"

"What are you trying to say?"

"I'm not trying to say anything. I'm telling you your ass is funky!" Ben tooted up his nose, suggesting that Omar was a major contributor to the pungent smell that was lingering in the house.

Omar headed into the bathroom, but not before tossing a pillow at Ben for his smart remark. Just as he was about to shut the bathroom door, Ben spoke.

"Hey, I'm going to call your housekeeper. What's the number?"

"There's a card in the top drawer of the nightstand," Omar replied, staring at himself in the bathroom mirror. His eyes were puffy, and his face was covered with whiskers; it was so unlike him. He undressed quickly and stepped into the shower.

Meanwhile, Ben was standing near his nightstand, glancing down at a bowl of what used to be cereal, fermenting in what used to be soymilk. He shook his head. *Yeah, this damn housekeeper needs to get here quick, fast, and in a hurry.*

After making the call, he placed the card back into the drawer, but not before nosily thumbing through his things. He noticed a wallet size photo of Asia lying at the bottom of the drawer. He picked it up.

"I don't see what all the fuss is about," he muttered. "Like I said before, she's just another piece of ass."

He tossed the picture into the wastepaper basket with the bowl of days old cereal.

Ben had never been impressed with Asia; as far as he was concerned, she was an unwelcome thorn in his side and not good enough for his friend. No woman was for that matter. He and Omar had been inseparable for years. They had a bond that no one could come between and he didn't give a damn what Asia or anyone else thought about how close they were. He had taught Omar every-thing he knew about hustling: how to get laid and paid without ever committing to anyone. He had a three-step plan that he lived by, which was screw 'em, use 'em and forget you knew 'em...a philosophy he thought Omar had mastered as well. That is until Asia's persistent ass showed up on the scene.

It didn't matter now, though, because she was gone and as far as he was concerned, no longer a threat to his relationship with Omar.

IN THE BATHROOM

As the steaming beads of water poured from the showerhead, Omar closed his eyes and recalled the many times that he and Asia had showered together. He filled his hand with liquid body soap. The smell reminded him of her; he rubbed some on his chest slowly.

The warm pellets of water danced across his back as he imagined her hands touching him. He remembered how she used to lather the soap into thick, silky foam, and then slowly rub it all over him. The more he thought about it, the more aroused he became. Soon he was covered in soap and fighting the onset of an erection.

He had only been in the shower a short while, but a thick layer of steam veiled the bathroom. The frosted glass shower doors created the perfect cover for his private moment. He slid his hands down between his legs and drifted into thought. He imagined his hand belonging to someone else.

Leaning back against the wall, he spread his well-defined legs and moved his hands vigorously along the shaft of his manhood. The pounding of the hot water against his naked body heightened his senses. It had been three days since he'd been touched, kissed, or made love to. He was horny and way overdue. The steaming water dripped from his head like a mystic waterfall. His grip tightened with every stroke of his hand, working him up to near climax. He became even more excited when he looked down at himself and prepared to pop at any second. The pressure was building beneath his fingers, so much that he couldn't hold it any longer. All at once, his lips parted and...he...he...he heard a knock on the bathroom door.

"Hey, man, are you okay in there?"

"Huh, oh, yeah-" Omar flubbed his words. The sound of Ben's voice had forced him back into reality. "I'll be out in a minute."

"Are you sure, it sounded like you needed some help," Ben joked.

"Nah, I think I got it, bruh," Omar replied, wrapping a towel around his waist as he stepped from the shower.

Ten minutes later…

When Omar exited the bathroom, he was expecting to find Ben waiting for him. Instead, he found a note. *Hey, I had to run, meet me at nine o'clock at our usual spot. Don't be late, sexy.*

After reading the note, Omar tossed it onto the nightstand. He would meet with Ben later, but for now, he needed to focus on Asia. He wanted to know just how much she knew and then he'd work on making her believe otherwise. There was no way he was going to let her destroy his reputation.

He walked over to the dresser, stared into the mirror and began to scheme. *She has to pick up the phone sometime, and when she does, I'll get back in her good graces and then-* He chuckled at himself in the mirror. *All you have to do is pick up the phone and gotcha!*

Omar was a very handsome man; so much so, that at times he marveled at himself. Vanity was his middle name. While searching through his extensive underwear collection, he pondered whether to wear boxers or briefs. *When you can't decide, don't wear any*, he thought, shutting the underwear drawer.

He removed the towel from his waist, glancing at the clock on the nightstand-it was three fifty-five p.m. He noticed the date on a small calendar on his dresser as well.

It had been a little more than three years that he and Asia first laid eyes on each other. Time had flown by so fast.

He sat on the bed and began to reminisce.

Always expect the unexpected...

Omar Hicks was a highly sought-after personal trainer at a high-end fitness club called *Skyscraper Fitness*
which offered an unparalleled fitness experience at the top
of one of New York City's luxurious high-rises. It had
been a long day filled with disgruntled clients-new ones
that wanted special treatment, old ones that expected special attention, all of whom in his opinion, needed special
attention from a shrink.

All day long, dozens of women walked around the
gym, spending five minutes on one machine, two minutes
on another, not enough time on any of them. Instead, they
spent hours standing around complaining that they were
too fat to fit into clothes they had no business still having
in their closets in the first place. Some would need the
help of a magician to help them reach their fitness goals.

By the end of the day, Omar was mentally spent and
wanted nothing more than to head straight home, shower,
and dive into his bed. He had enough of the cackling and
longed for the silence of his abode. Unfortunately, that
wasn't going to happen.

The manager of the gym was throwing the annual
party to solicit new clients, to which every trainer was expected to attend. The party was closed to the public and in
the past had drawn upward of fifty new potential mem-
bers-all of them women with high disposable incomes.

Hundreds of women from all over would flock to the
Skyscraper Fitness Annual Extravaganza with hopes of
winning an exclusive membership. The Skyscrapers'

trainers were amongst the hottest and sexiest in the business.

However, it was all just fluff to Omar. At times he despised being looked at like a piece of meat, especially by women who had no clue what it would really take to get next to a man like him.

Ben caught up with him before he left. "So, are you ready for the big party?"

"Man, I'm not going."

"You have to go."

"See, that's where you're wrong. I don't have to do anything."

"Well, if you don't go, you know the boss is going to have your head."

"Yeah, well, my head is willing to risk it." Omar gripped himself.

"You really like stirring up shit, don't you?" Ben chuckled.

"Yeah, I guess I do."

Omar turned and left the gym. Ben just shook his head.

About an hour later...

Omar had made it home and was preparing a sandwich and protein shake for his dinner. He wasn't a fan of eating meat, so he piled lettuce, tomatoes, thinly sliced cucumbers, black olives, red peppers, and pickles onto two slices of twelve-grain bread. His mouth watered before the first bite. Just as he raised the sandwich to his lips, the phone rang.

"Hello? Hello?" Ben said. "Hello, are you there?"

"Yes, I'm here. Where else would I be?"

"Didn't you hear me talking to you; why didn't you respond?"

"I don't know. I didn't feel like it."

"You didn't feel like it?"

Omar laughed.

"I swear, sometimes I think you need to be admitted to an institution."

"Whatever!"

"Anyway, did you change your mind about the party?"

"No."

"No?"

"Man, you have no idea how much I hate these company parties, especially when they mandate our presence. I know all too well what's going to happen once we get there."

"What?"

"You and I are going to throw back a few shots, make a bet on who'll leave with the prettiest woman in the room. I'll win, and then you'll be mad at me for about a week."

"That's not true."

"Yes, it is," Omar replied, biting into his sandwich.

"Besides, the place is probably going to be crawling with a bunch of women who we've already slept with; or worse, women who neither of us would ever consider sleeping with."

They both laughed.

For every reason Omar offered up as to why he shouldn't go, Ben offered two to support why he should.

Ben was a social butterfly and would use any reason he could to get his hand around a drink and his arms around the waist of a beautiful woman, especially if it meant more business.

"So, what time do you want me to pick you up, playboy?" he asked, ignoring Omar's comments.

"Didn't I just tell you that I'm not going?" Omar retorted, staring at the phone as if Ben was becoming irksome.

"You say that now, but you know if the boss calls, you're going to be right here. So, save yourself the trouble of having to kiss her ass later and get dressed now." Ben chuckled.

"I don't think that's funny."

"Okay, okay, listen. I heard there's going to be a lot of women at this party that you and I have never seen before. And you know we have our little side hustle going on, so it could work out to our advantage."

"I don't care about that. I'm tired. So, you can have them all to yourself tonight."

"Right, like I need your charity," Ben retorted. He listened as Omar burst into laughter on the other end of the phone.

Ben had quite a reputation for being a ladies' man; in high school, he was voted most likely to get laid. In college, his frat buddies dubbed him the black Hugh Heffner because of the number of beautiful women who flocked around him. He was known for having a different woman on his arm each day of the week. He was handsome, fit, athletic, and never took no for an answer.

"Hey man, I thought we were boys. Now you're sending me out here to face these broads without any backup?"

"You know what, Big Ben, cut the shit. You've been picking up women at parties long before we knew each other. You don't need my help with that."

You're right about that, Ben thought. "I don't know, man, I just have a feeling about this party. I really think you should come out tonight."

"Sorry, I'm going to have to pass."

"Okay, fine, what are you going to say to the boss?"

"I don't know. I'll think of something to tell her when I get to work tomorrow."

"Okay, have it your way."

"I always do," Omar replied.

Ben didn't respond.

Omar chuckled and then hung up the phone.

Thirty minutes later...

Omar was lying across the bed watching CNN when his phone rang. He reached over and answered it cheerfully.

"Good evening."

"Hi, is this Omar?" A female voice spilled through the phone.

"Yes, it is. Who is this?" he asked flirtatiously.

"You're boss!"

"Oh." He began to cough. "Hi, um, what's up? I was just about to call you."

"Oh really; are you okay?"

"Yeah, I'm fine. Well, not really; I'm feeling a little hot and clammy and stuffy. I think I'm coming down with something." He began to sneeze.

"Oh, I see." She paused. "Well, if you're not here in an hour, you're going to be coming down with unemployment."

CLICK!

The humming of the dial tone pierced his ear. "Hello, hello...Damn it!" he scoffed, pressing his finger on the receiver and then immediately
calling Ben.

"Hello."

"Hey, did you rat me out to the boss?"

"What?"

"I was just told if I don't come to the party, I'm fired."

"I told you to get dressed and get your black ass here before."

"Yeah, well, how did she know that I wasn't telling the truth? Did you say anything?"

"Why in the hell would I do that?"

"I don't know; maybe you didn't want to hang out alone tonight."

"Look, man, just because you were being a punk about hanging out doesn't mean that I'm going to run off and tell the boss on you. I'm perfectly capable of taking care of myself."

"Sure, you are, Alfalfa."

"You keep on talking like that and I'm going to have to find someone to take your place in our little partnership."

"Yeah right, try it and see what happens."

"Just get your ass to the party, chump."

"Yeah, I've got your chump."

"Whatever!" Ben retorted and hung up the phone.

Omar crawled from the bed and headed into the bathroom.

An hour later...

As Omar's silver Mercedes pulled into the block, an over-head streetlight sliced across the hood of his car like a knife. He noticed a trail of cars in the driveway outside of his boss' house. He also noticed a group of women making their way
inside. They were dressed scantily, each one wearing out-fits that looked like band-aids. His disposition changed immediately.

"Perhaps it won't be a boring night after all," he murmured, glancing at them from his car.

Parking was limited, so he circled the block a few times, hoping to find a space not too far away in case he needed to make a mad dash. He parked quickly and then headed inside.

While walking through the crowd, he spotted Ben chatting it up with a male partygoer. He stood watching them for a few moments before making his presence known.

"Hey, you finally made it," Ben said cheerfully.

"Actually, I've been here a while; you just didn't notice me."

"Okay, well damn; shoot me." Ben chuckled.

Omar shot Ben a blank look.

"Seriously though, sorry, man. I really didn't think you were going to show up, but since you're here, I'd like you to meet someone. This is Flex...Flex this is-"

Omar cut in.

"Ben, can I speak to you for a minute? In private?"
Omar added.

"Sure. Flex, will you excuse me for a minute?"

"Take your time, man. I'll be at the bar."

Omar and Ben stepped away.

"What are you doing?" Omar asked.

"What do you mean? I'm talking."

"I can see that. Why are you talking to him?" Omar questioned with authority.

"Not that I need to explain myself to you, but he's a cool guy."

"Yeah, he's also a few other things as well."

"I know what he is, Omar."

"Do you?"

"Yes."

"Okay, so do you want everyone to start questioning our associations?" Omar gritted his teeth as he spoke.

"You know I don't."

"Then cut the shit and leave Mr. Bi-Sexual Chocolate where you found him."

"Aw! Are you jealous?" Ben joked, reaching for Omar's face.

Omar forcefully slapped his hand away.

"Hey, man, why are you so fuckin' uptight?"

"I'm not uptight, but I will be if you don't get your shit together," Omar threatened.

Ben stared at him and then walked away.

Omar watched as he made his way through the crowd, hating that he was at odds with his best friend. Ben had a warped sense of humor and took too many liberties at times, but he was still like an older brother to Omar.

The two of them had been through so much and Omar knew that he didn't deserve to be spoken to that way. He also knew that he needed to apologize. Just as he started to make his way over to Ben, someone grabbed him from behind.

"So, I hear you're the man to go to when a woman needs a little loving. Is that true?"

Omar smiled. "That depends on your definition of loving." He clutched the hands that enveloped him.

"Well, I'm looking for the type of loving that will set my soul on fire. Can you recommend anything?"

"Perhaps, how much do you know about fire?"

"I know a little," she replied, pressing herself snugly against his back. "Mmm, I just love a man with a nice hard behind."

"Yeah, well, you know what they say, 'if it's hard in back, it's even harder in the front'." He guided her hands across his crotch.

"Oh, my God!" she shrieked, pulling away quickly.

Omar grinned as he spun around.

"I can't believe you did that...that thing is alive!" she said, taking a step back.

"Yes, it is, and I think it likes you," he clowned, pulling her toward him. "How are you, Iris?"

Iris was the owner of *Skyscrapers Fitness* and Omar's boss. She was a beautiful, middle-age Mulatto woman, half-Black, half-Italian, with a petite frame and a smile that could melt the polar ice caps.

"I'm fine, Omar, and I'm glad you decided to come to the party."

"Did I have a choice?"

"Not really," she said, flirting with her eyes.

Although she was his boss and ten years his senior, she was undeniably attracted to him. Yet, as much as they often flirted with each other, neither one of them ever crossed the line. Perhaps it was because of their employer/employee relationship. Maybe it was out of respect for each other, or simply it was because Omar knew if he slept with her that things would get messy, so he ignored her advances.

"You're looking as handsome as usual," she complimented.

"Thanks, you look great as well," he retorted, fixing his eyes on her tight little frame. She was neatly tucked into an emerald green, strapless dress that made her look like a younger version of Susan Lucci.

"Damn, girl, you seem taller; are you growing on me?"

"I hope so." She smiled, snatching a glass of wine from a passing waiter's tray. Omar's eyes panned the curve of her backside. For a mulatto woman, she was stacked in the back, and since he was an ass man, he couldn't help noticing it.

"Damn, are you sure you're not all black?" he muttered under his breath.

"What?" Iris spun around.

"Oh, I said, wow, you really look nice in that...dress."

"Thanks," she blushed. "So, did you come to the party alone?"

"Yes, please don't start."

"Come on, Omar, when that woman leaped from the bushes at the last party, I didn't know what to do. She was at least two hundred and fifty pounds, dressed in pink lingerie and screaming that she wanted to be your love slave. I didn't know whether to laugh or call the police."

"Me either," Omar snickered.

"Yeah, well, as crazy as she seemed, I felt sorry for her."

"Sorry for her, what about me?"

"Oh, please. You were as much responsible for her making a fool of herself as she was."

"Me?"

"Yes, you! You slept with her, didn't you?"

"I plead the fifth."

"I'll take that as a yes," Iris said, sipping from her drink. "What did you think would happen when you slept with a woman who was recently out of a bad relationship and looking for someone to console her?"

"I don't know, but my first thought was to run her big ass over with my car, but since I'm a lover and not a murderer, I let Ben handle it."

"Ben?"

"That's right. He has more experience with those types."

Iris smiled.

"Till this day, I don't know what he said to her. He pulled her to the side, threw a car cover over her, whispered something in her ear, and in less than three minutes she was gone. I never heard from her again."

Iris shook her head.

"Are you ever going to let me live that down?"

"No, not until you realize that you were just as responsible as she was. Or, until you start playing by the rules."

"What does 'playing by the rules,' entail?"

"I don't know. Maybe, settling down."

"Yeah, well, I'm not looking to settle down."

"Why, because of Ben? Be your own man."

"I am my own man. If I choose to sleep with a woman without any commitment after that, that's totally up to me. I don't need anyone's approval."

"True, but one of these days you just might get caught out there."

"I don't think so."

"Yeah, well, don't say I didn't warn you."

"It'll never happen, I'm too slick," Omar chuckled.

Iris stared at him over the rim of her glass as she sipped her drink. She was unimpressed with his jejune sense of humor.

"Listen, I see someone I need to talk to. Enjoy the party." She cracked a half smile and then walked away.

Omar stood there shaking his head. Once Iris was out of sight, he began scanning the room for Ben, who was nowhere to be found.

He didn't mind, however, because there were dozens of pretty women in the room; many he had yet to engage. He noticed a few of the fellows checking him out as well. So, he decided to have a little bit of fun, making up with Ben could wait. He began moving slowly about the room, scrutinizing each woman as if with x-ray vision. There were so many to choose from-big, tall, short, skinny, thick, thin, white, black and Latina. There were even a few Asian sisters in the mix. The lyrics to a song by the *Mary Jane Girls* popped into his mind, causing him to smile.

He noticed a guy standing across the room staring at him. Omar winked and the guys face lit up as he made his way toward Omar, who turned and walked away as if disinterested.

A few other guys were checking him out as well, but clearly for a different reason. They were straight and sizing up the competition. But Omar was the man, Beast of the bush, King of the freakin' jungle. And far too confident to compete with chumps.

He turned his focus back to his mission, to catch the prettiest, most financially set fish in the bowl. He moved about the room like a lion, slow, deliberate, and stalking. He didn't care what the other guys at the party thought of him. He wasn't there to mingle with them; he was there to stake his claim on the best piece of ass in the house.

He could have any woman he wanted, and he knew it, but his decision wouldn't be a rash one. He checked out each potential lay, taking stock of her hair, eye color, bust size, style of dress, body language, and most importantly the heels on their shoes. All of which would play a significant role in his decision about which one would be worthy of his company for the evening.

After a while, he became so preoccupied counting each woman's flaws that he nearly failed to notice the most beautiful woman in the entire party. As she passed him, his eyes stretched in disbelief about how beautiful she was. In fact, she was startling, so much that all the other women vanished in her presence.

When she walked, her hips swayed like a device used during hypnosis. Within seconds, he summed up the cost of her entire wardrobe, estimating it at an easy four grand. He was instantly entranced as she made her way to the backyard.

He waited a few minutes and then followed. Omar was no dummy, though. He understood patience was a virtue, and the key to a smart man getting what he wants in life, and he wanted her.

She sipped from a beautiful martini glass...

The light from the Chinese lanterns caused the rim of her glass to sparkle, and so did her eyes. She pulled on a cigarette and then blew a line of smoke into the air as if drawing a line between herself and everyone else at the party. She was perched on a lawn chair like an exotic bird. Her long black hair framed her oval face perfectly. Her posture spoke volumes and so did the harsh look in her eyes. Clearly, she wasn't interested in mingling with anyone. Unfortunately, not everyone noticed that. One of the trainers approached her.

"Hi, I just have to tell you that you look stunning in that dress. Vera Wang, right?"

She looked him up and down.

"I can tell that you're into fashion; I am too."

She stared at him as if she wanted to shove him off the seat.

"Come on, don't look at me like that; I don't bite, unless you want me to," he said, waiting for a response while she bumped the ashes from her cigarette.

She didn't respond though.

"Okay, well, I'm not going to leave until you tell me your name," he insisted.

She clutched her purse.

Omar watched attentively, waiting for the gavel to fall. She took a short drag of the cigarette and then dropped it in his drink. Omar fought to hold back his laughter and gasped as his peer continued his pursuit.

"Okay, now that you've ruined my drink, are you going to tell me your name?"

"Sure, it's Tiffany."

"Really, like the singer?"

"No. Like the little blue box," she replied.

He smiled, feeling like he was finally making leeway.

"You know, since I was a little girl, I've always loved Tiffany jewelry. In fact, I'm wearing a piece right now. Do you like it?" She touched a small locket that hung around her neck.

"Wow, that's definitely Tiffany! It's great!"

"Yeah, that's what I thought you'd say."

"What do you mean?"

"I mean this locket isn't from Tiffany; it's a knock-off, just like that watch you're wearing, and those shoes and those shades."

"So, you're just going to call me out like that?"

"Oh, please. I didn't have to call you out. That loud suit you're wearing has been doing a good job of that. Now if you don't mind, get out of my face."

"Oh, I see. I'm not dressed fancy enough for you, huh. You're one of those materialistic black women that only date men for what they have right?"

"Look," she took a deep breath. "I'm not a materialistic woman at all, okay. And for that matter, I'm also not impressed with men who layer themselves in designer knockoffs to impress women who probably wouldn't be interested in them in the first place."

"Oh, really?" he sneered.

"Yes, really; so why don't you go back over there with your Rolaid watch before I call the knockoff -police, and have you arrested."

The guy's face cracked immediately. It was as though she had reached into his pants, snatched out his nuts, and flung them across the lawn. He quickly scurried away. A few other unlucky souls suffered the same embarrassment. One by one, she sent their egos plummeting to the pavement. One guy even made eye contact with Omar, as if to warn him not to make the same mistake that he had.

Omar was unscathed, though. Neither of his predecessors was as charming, nor as good-looking as he was. He knew the rules of engagement like the back of his hand and was undoubtedly more than prepared to confront the feisty beauty. He licked his lips once more and prepared to make his introduction.

CHAPTER FIVE

Pay Attention Little Boy

The memories had made Omar smile. He removed a can of shaving cream from the medicine cabinet. He turned on the faucet and began mixing the powder with cold water. He stirred it into a thick, smelly paste and then set the bowl on the edge of the sink. He winked at himself in the mirror before applying the cream, careful not to spill any.

Asia hated it when he dropped shaving cream on the tiled floors. He remembered that about her.

He glanced at himself in the mirror and recalled the first time he saw her.

I was feeling a little Louis McKay...

She was even more beautiful up close than she was from a distance. For a moment, he was having second thoughts about approaching her. Not because he feared being shot down, but because he sensed there was something different about her. He took a few more seconds to read her body language and then he made his move.

"Of all the women here tonight, you are the finest. What does a man have to do to get to know you better?" he asked.

She ignored him.

"My name is Omar," he said, extending his hand. Asia had no use for the same, lame pickup lines she'd been hearing the entire night and couldn't care less if his name was Omar or Obama. She was just a few seconds from telling him to take a long walk off a short pier. To her, he was just another overly confident idiot trying to invade her space. She shifted herself in her seat, turning her back to him, slightly.

"So, do you want my arm to fall off?"

Her eyes widened. Oh, no he didn't! Did he just recite a line from *Lady Sings the Blues*? She turned around slowly, prepared to rip him apart. Her attack was stalled when she noticed how well he looked in his slacks. His waist was small and his legs strong and muscular. As if he controlled the elements themselves, a slight breeze caused his shirt to press against his chiseled torso, displaying a ripped midsection and an endowment she couldn't help but notice.

"I'd try to guess your name, but I'm not any good at it," Omar said, smiling as he also noticed her staring at the imprint of his appendage.

The look on her face changed immediately. He could tell by the glimmer in her eyes and the shift in her posture that she was impressed.

"I'm sorry; my name is Asia." She extended her hand to shake his.

"It's nice to meet you, Asia. Can I ask if you're here alone?"

"No."

Omar's eyes telegraphed his disappointment.

"It's not what you think. I came with friends who, incidentally, must have forgotten that I'm here. What about you?"

"Oh, I'm here because a buddy of mine begged me to come and because my boss is the one throwing the party.

"Wow, in that order, huh?"

Omar smiled.

"So, do you mind if I keep you company until your friends return?" he asked.

"Help yourself."

"Are you from around here?" Omar inquired, noticing that she wasn't wearing a wedding band.

"No, I live in Harlem. What about you?"

The small talk was cute, but Omar's plan was to give out as little information about himself as possible, especially since his interest in her extended no further than the length of his dick.

"I'm from Brooklyn. Although now that I know that you're from Harlem, I'm kicking myself for never considering Manhattan as a place of residence."

She chuckled.

They talked for hours. Neither Asia nor Omar showed any interest in getting to know anyone else at the party. Asia seemed pleased with the conversation her new friend was offering. Omar did as well. They shut out the world, or at least everyone else at the party. At one point, they moved to a more secluded area of the backyard to get to know each other better.

Her skin glistened under the moonlight, causing Omar to realize further how flawless she was. At times, during their conversation, he would lose focus and begin to stare at her. The first time it happened his eyes were fixed on her breasts as if he had never seen cleavage before.

She summoned him back to reality.

"Uh, excuse me, are you listening to me?"

"What did you say?"

"I asked if you were a native New Yorker; come on, pay attention."

"Do you know my mom used to tell me that same thing when I was younger?" She sneered.

"Okay, I'm sorry. Yes, I'm a native New Yorker, what about you?"

"Apart from living in Texas for the past two years, New York has always been my home."

"So, do you have family in Texas?"

Asia turned to admire a nearby flowerbed, ignoring his question.

Omar's eyes were cast on her behind. She had a body that would anger Greek goddesses.

"Where exactly in Harlem do you live?"

"If I tell you that, I'll have to kill you," she said, flashing a smile that lit up her face.

Omar took it as a flirt and began calculating the distance between her home and his. He smiled and then moved closer to her.

"What part of Brooklyn do you live in?" She backed away.

Wow! Smart move, Omar thought. Clearly, this woman wasn't just some ignorant chick from the streets. If she were, they'd be on their way to her place where he'd begin waxing her ass. Instead, she redirected the conversation away from her place of residence, to his.

"I live in Clinton Hills; have you ever been there?"

"No, I haven't."

"Perhaps I can show you around sometime."

Omar tossed out the invitation in hopes that she would take the bait. If she did, a quick lay would be inevitable. In his sex-driven mind, they could be in bed in less than an hour. All she had to do was say yes. His attention shifted to the curve of her hips again.

Asia was growing annoyed with Omar's repeated entranced state. She snapped her fingers, to once again, draw him back from his daydream. "Omar!"

"I'm sorry, Asia. I'm having a little attention span problem."

"And you think sharing that makes you, what, more attractive?"

"No, it only happens when I'm in the presence of a beautiful woman."

Is this guy serious? I can't believe he had the nerve to drift off again, Asia thought. Omar was becoming so unlike a man she would ever consider dating.

That night, he ran some of his best lines, but Asia wasn't buying any of them. She wasn't going to his place no matter what he said. She was a firm believer that you can teach a person how to treat you. In fact, she's lived by the quote ever since her last boyfriend left her in pursuit of the wind. It had taken her many years and several Iyanla Vanzant seminars to pull herself back together, so she wasn't about to be a sucker for a pretty boy with a pocket full of one-liners. Moreover, he was starting to sound like all the other jerks she and her girlfriends had been on dates with; fast talkers that say the right things, flash the perfect smile but have only one thing on their minds. Sex!

She folded her arms and began telling him precisely what she thought about smooth talking, pretty boys with short attention spans and ogling eyes.

Omar shrugged off her icy rant. As far as he was concerned, she was just playing hard-to-get, a game she'd surely lose.

CHAPTER SIX

Just So We're On The Same Page

After shaving, Omar tried to reach her again, "You mean to tell me that you don't even think enough of me to return my calls, Asia? How the hell am I supposed to make it right, huh?"

Omar spoke into the phone, wiping the excess shaving cream from his face. "I know that you're there listening; just give me a chance to explain," he begged.

The beep from her answering machine pierced his ears. He slammed the phone down and flung the towel across the room.

Asia was stubborn and he knew it. He recalled the first time he experienced just how stubborn she could be. It was on their first date...

Well, Well, Well, Anyone for Chess?

The look on Asia's face was blank as he returned to the table.

"Are you okay?" he asked.

"I'm fine."

"That's good. Listen, I apologize about all the interruptions. My clients can be a bit manic at times."

"I see. So how long have you been a trainer?"

"For a few years now, but I'm still trying to perfect my craft."

She rolled her eyes over his body, thinking, *your look perfectly crafted to me.*

Omar noticed the way she was looking at him but didn't let on.

"Maybe you can train me one day," she said with a hint of flirtation in her voice.

"Perhaps," he replied, playing it cool.

"Are the women you train built like me?"

"I can't say that they are," Omar smirked, thinking, "I've trained men who aren't built like you."

"I heard that gym is really expensive. I was only able to work out there because a friend of mine gave me a few passes."

"Well, you get what you pay for. Wealthy clients who can afford top-notch personal attention for Master Trainers. They pay well."

Yeah, that would explain the expensive car and fancy clothes, Asia thought. She sipped from a glass of water.

"What about you? What's your field of expertise?"

"You're an observant man; why don't you guess?"

"Okay, well, I noticed when we walked in that you were admiring the drapes and the artwork, so I'll take a stab in the dark and say...interior design."

"You're quite perceptive," Asia said, clapping lightly.

Omar sat back as if he had performed a great chess move.

"Oh, don't get too cocky just yet. Let's see if you can guess what I'm thinking." She stared across the table as she licked her lips seductively.

Omar's chest filled with confidence, "Oh, this one is going to be easy. You're thinking about how badly you want to kiss me." He grinned.

Asia just sat there without saying a word.

Omar was such a shark and Asia was a new fish in his bowl. He would say anything to get next to her and he did.

"Wow, I can't believe this."

"Believe what?"

"That I'm on a date with the most beautiful woman in the world and she's actually speechless."

His words caused her to stare through him like a sheet of glass.

"What is it?"

"Come on, Omar, the world? Please." She rolled her eyes.

Not only did his comment cause her to question his sincerity, but also his constant flattery was starting to sound more contrived than she cared to listen to. "You know, if you want to get to know me, why don't you try being honest?"

"Excuse me?"

"I'm just saying, don't you think that all of these lines you're using are a bit immature?"

"Immature?"

"Yes, and some of them are downright unbelievable. In fact, you might have better luck convincing me that you're Denzel Washington's long-lost brother, rather than trying to convince me that those lines are actually sincere."

He was stunned. No woman had ever spoken to him that way.

"I'm sorry," he said, sitting back in his seat.

She looked at him as if to say, yes, you are! But Asia was unaware that the person sitting across from her was a master at the game he was playing. And he was about to prove it.

"If I've offended you, I apologize. It wasn't my intention. It's just that I find you so utterly attractive that I babbled without thinking. I'm a fool and I'm sorry."

Damn! Sideswiped.

His apology was as unexpected to her as a snowstorm in Vegas.

"The truth is that I'm not really any good at this."

"Explain."

"Well, I've never been really good at knowing what to say to a classy woman like you, never mind liking one as much as I like you. It's hard to relax and be myself."

She stared across the table, thinking, you're damn right, I'm classy; too classy to fall for your juvenile games and your pimp-daddy flirts. So, if you want to come at me, you had better come correct, or I will chew your ass up like a stick of gum and spit you out when I'm done. She flashed him a phony smile.

He flashed a sincere one in return.

"So, tell me Omar, are you being yourself right now?"

"No, I mean, yes."

Asia sneered.

"What I'm trying to say is most women won't allow me to be myself. They look at me and only see one thing."

"Oh, really and what is that?" she asked, all the while answering the question in her mind. *Who could blame us?*

"They see the same thing that I see the potential to be made love to by a man who looks like a goddamn gladiator and then whisked away into a world of marital bliss by a pelvis-thrashing warrior whose sole purpose in life will be to send their vaginas into cataclysmic convulsions. And after years of having settled for men who wouldn't know the difference between making love and eating a breakfast burrito, who can blame them? With my luck, though, you're probably just another handsome face with very little to offer otherwise."

She fought the urge to laugh but was unsuccessful.

"What's so funny?"

"Nothing, continue." She said, sipping from her glass to prohibit any further laughter.

"As I was saying, I'm six-three, two hundred and forty-five pounds and I wear a size fourteen shoe."

Did he say he wears a size fourteen shoe? She took the measurements in her head. Oh my God!

The water Asia sipped slipped down the wrong pipe and she began to choke.

He leaped up.

"Are you okay?" he asked. "Raise your arm above your head?"

"I'm fine."

"Are you sure?" He began patting her on the back.

"Yes, I'm fine," she said, almost snapping at him.

The truth was, she wasn't fine; she was broken and needed to be fixed. Asia hadn't had a man in years; all because she's been saving herself for Mr. Right; so long that she barely remembered what it felt like to be touched by a man.

Put my arm above my head. Sure thing, I'll put my arms above my head and my legs too, if you'll take me right here, right now, in this restaurant, on this table, in front of all of these people; I don't care; just take me, take me, take me, now!

Her eyes began to water as she imagined Omar taking her right there on top of the table.

"Are you sure you're all right?" he asked, moving closer.

"I'm fine, Omar, really."

Good, he thought. *Don't get it twisted; I'm concerned about you, but I'm not about to break one of my golden rules. Never show a woman how much you care, even if she's choking. If you do, she can potentially use it against you later. He wasn't about to have that happen.*

Since she wasn't passed out or bleeding half to death, there was no need for him to continue to hover over her. He returned to his seat.

A few seconds later...

A waiter made his way over to their table.

"Wow! That looks good," Asia said, turning her focus to the two large platters of food the waiter was carrying.

"Yes, it does. I love lasagna," Omar said, spreading a cloth napkin on his lap.

Asia did the same and prepared to say grace.

Omar dug right in.

"Aren't you going to say grace?" she asked.

"No, I don't believe in that?"

Asia's neck snapped back. "Excuse me?"

"Oh, I don't subscribe to the notion that there's some magical being living in the clouds that I have to thank every time I get ready to eat. I believe everything I have in life I have because I worked hard for it, including this meal." He pressed his fork into his plate.

Asia was so disturbed by his statement that it kept nipping at her until she had to comment on it.

"What type of Black man has the luxury of not believing in God these days?" she asked, lifting her fork to her mouth.

"The kind that would never discuss religion over dinner," he replied, winking at her as he politely switched the subject.

Asia sneered.

"I see you like your lasagna traditionally prepared."

"Yeah, you can have that vegetarian stuff; I love meat." She moaned as she rolled the food around on her tongue.

Omar smirked.

"Is my eating meat a problem, Omar?"

"No, if you're not concerned, I say go for it."

"What should I be concerned about?"

"Well, with all the health alerts about Mad Cow Disease, I just thought-"

"Mad what?" Asia's face contorted. She had never seen a live cow in her life, much less a mad one. She couldn't care less.

"You know, Mad Cow Disease. It was all over the news a few years ago; that's why I stopped eating red meat."

"Yeah, well, red meat offers a relevant nutrient for a proper diet. You should know that Mr. Universe," she said, rolling her eyes at him playfully.

He appreciated her humor.

"Are you a vegan?" she asked.

"No, I just try to eat healthy to maintain my boyish good looks."

Asia ignored his ego trip and lifted another heap of lasagna into her mouth.

"Is that a problem for you?" he questioned.

Asia set down her fork, patted her mouth with a napkin, and then stared at him. "It's not a big deal that you don't eat meat, Omar, as long as you eat something."

The heat of her suggestion raced from Omar's ears straight down to his groin. He reached for a slice of bread trying to avoid groping himself. She reached at the same time; their hands touched, their eyes met, and then something happened. She pulled away, quickly.

"What's wrong?" he asked.

"Nothing. I just realized I really don't need the extra carbohydrates."

"Right!"

She fumbled with her napkin.

Omar sat back with a smug look on his face. He knew that she was making that up. The feeling that Asia felt was like 10,000 volts of electricity shooting through her fingers and straight to her vagina. He sensed it and decided that it was his turn to flirt.

"Listen, just so that we're on the same page, you did say that you love meat, right?"

She was still reeling from the volt of sexual electricity that had shot throughout her body. Her entire system was shaking and there was something going on beneath her skirt. Something a woman shouldn't feel in public.

"Is everything okay?" he asked.

"Everything is fine," she replied, trying desperately to compose herself. She was attracted to him and she knew it. The problem was she didn't want him to know it, not yet anyway.

She regained her composure quickly. She was not going to let him get too cocky, too quickly. In fact, she was about to throw a monkey wrench into his little moment of self-assuredness.

"So, Omar, how long have you been married?"

"What! What makes you ask that?" He sat straight up in his seat. This time he was the one who nearly choked.

"I just figured that a good-looking man like you must have a special woman in his life. Since you're not the playa type, I assume that you must be married, right?"

"Right, I mean, wrong. I mean, wait!"

Asia loved it. She had him stammering like a drunk. He was so caught off guard by her question that he spilled a chunk of lasagna onto his lap.

"Damn!" he scoffed.

Asia had successfully knocked him off his pedestal. A look of confidence settled on her face as she continued her meal. She sat there thinking, *'On the same page,'* *yeah, right, in your dreams!*

Omar sat across the table, clearing the food from his lap, wiping away the stain with his napkin.

"We will not be on the same page until I'm good and ready." Asia spoke softly under her breath.

"What did you say?" Omar looked up.

"Oh, I said, this lasagna is great; next time, I'll try the spaghetti."

"Oh." He turned his focus back to the stain.

Asia enjoyed seeing him squirm. He was so cool, so together, it tickled her to see him fidget. She continued with her investigative questioning.

"So, okay, you're not married, but how many children do you have?"

"What?"

Asia had struck a nerve again. Omar set his napkin on the table and stared at her. The look on his face was serious.

"I'm sorry, did I say something wrong?"

"No, it's just that I'd like to have children one day, but I've yet to meet a woman who possesses the qualities it would take to mother my child."

Asia played his words over in her mind, thinking, *who does he think he is, Jesus?* She had a problem with a few of his statements that night, first the one about not believing in God, then the one about women not being good enough to carry his child, and now the one he was boldly making by shifting his attention to a young waitress as she passed their table. Asia noticed the young waitress smiling as he returned the gesture.

Her lips grew tight as she watched.

Suddenly, he became preoccupied with finishing his meal. He pretended not to notice her scowling across the table.

Omar was fully aware that Asia was annoyed. He recognized the look on her face as he had seen it so many times before. It was jealousy. And if it wasn't clear to him before, he was now certain of it. Asia is interested in him. Why else would she be getting so upset?

"Hey, eat up. I have a surprise for you." He said, glancing at his watch.

Yeah, I have a surprise for you, too, and if you keep smiling at that waitress, you're going to get it sooner than you think, Mr. Size Fourteen Shoe, she thought, cutting her eyes at him on the sly. She wasn't up for any bull crap, certainly not from a guy that doesn't believe in God. In her mind, he should be glad that she was still sitting there with him.

She shot a menacing look toward the waitress who was watching Omar from across the room, causing her to scurry away. Although she wasn't willing to admit it, she wanted him badly.

After dinner, they headed farther uptown. The night they met at the party, Asia had mentioned how much she loved concerts, so Omar managed to get his hands on two tickets for a *Mary J. Blige* concert. His original intention was to take Ben, but since he was trying to lure Asia into bed, he thought the show would help him appear more sincere about getting to know her better.

When they arrived at the Beacon Theatre, they noticed a huge crowd waiting out front. Asia hated crowds but was excited about seeing Mary J. Blige. She pushed her feelings aside for the evening.

Omar grabbed her hand and guided her through the sea of people, saying hello to nearly a dozen women as they headed toward the entrance of the theatre.

"Aren't you Mr. Popular," Asia said, glancing around at all the women Omar had spoken to.

"What makes you say that?"

"Probably the fact that you spoke to more than a dozen people while walking from the curb to the lobby door, all of which happen to be women. Are they your exes?"

"No; they're my clients."

She smirked, not believing a word he said. In her mind, if all those women were his clients, then she's the real Queen of England and the woman on the throne now is an imposter. Since neither was true, she rolled her eyes discretely and didn't put much stock into his explanations.

Inside the lobby, Omar spotted another woman he knew.

"Melinda, is that you?"

"Oh my gosh!" The woman shouted as she spun around and noticed him. As she raced toward him, her large bouncing breast became his focal point. Throwing her arms around his neck she planted a kiss on his face.

"Girl, what are you doing here?" Omar asked, eyeing Asia nervously.

"What does it look like, silly?"

Asia mumbled and then looked away.

"Don't tell me you're working here now. I thought you owned a hair salon in Queens?"

"I did, but the landlord sold the building and I was forced to close down."

"Oh, I'm sorry to hear that."

"It's okay, I still have a couple of clients that come to my house to get their hair done, and of course you know I still do my own hair, too." She patted her head proudly.

Asia's eyebrow rose.

"Okay, so this is just a side gig for you?"

"Yes, I'm working here part-time just to make a little extra money until I can find another location. You know how that goes."

Yes, I do." He flashed an even wider smile.

"So, how have you been; what have you been up to?

"I'm fine, baby," he said.

Baby? Asia's lips tightened.

"Yeah, I can see that," Melinda replied, staring at him as if she could eat him alive.

Asia cleared her throat.

"Oh sweetheart, I'm sorry. Melinda, this is Asia...Asia this is Melinda."

"It's nice to meet you," Asia said, smiling.

Melinda didn't return the sentiment.

Asia sensed that something was up, so she wrapped her arm in Omar's in an act of possessiveness.

"Anyway, how's Ben?" Melinda asked, cutting her eyes at Asia.

"Ben's great...baby, are you okay?"

"I'm fine," Asia smiled.

"That's good, but it's unusual to see one of you without the other."

"Things change; a man can't always hang out with his boys, you know."

"Yeah, I guess. If you must settle, then hey, what can I say?"

"Settle?" Asia mumbled. *Believe me honey, he's not settling. I've graduated at the top of my class with a 4.0 GPA and a Master's in Business Finance. I'm 27 years old, own my own home, have a 401k balance that would make your eyes pop out of your head, haven't fallen into the trap of having kids by a man that I'd eventually have to call 'my baby's daddy.' If he's settling, it's because he's wasting his time standing here talking with your ignorant ass. If you ask me, he'd find it more stimulating conversation talking to a doorknob.*

Melinda cast a shady smile in Asia's direction.

Asia squinted; she didn't appreciate the cattiness, and she wasn't going to put up with it much longer.

Omar sensed that Asia was growing annoyed, so he decided to move the conversation along.

"So, Melinda, how's your friend?"

"Which one?"

"The one that was crazy about Ben."

"You mean the top-heavy one with the blond hair?"

"Yeah, how is she?"

"She's fine. She's actually going to school to become a mortician."

"She's what?" Omar burst into laughter.

"You know...the person who fills you up with bombing fluid when you die."

Asia couldn't believe what she heard. Melinda's ignorant description made her completely lose faith in the public-school system.

"What made her go into that field?"

"I don't know. You know she's always been crazy."

"True, true, but she's nice, though."

"Yes, she is. That's why I never understood why Ben never really took her seriously. Tell me the truth; did he have another woman?"

"Ah, Ben is Ben; I really can't speak for him." Omar skated around the question.

"Well, thank God birds of a feather don't always flock together." She batted her eyes suggestively.

"Speaking of flocking," Asia cut in, "This lobby is getting crowded. Baby, don't you think we should go inside now?"

"Yeah, you're right." Omar handed Melinda their tickets. She smiled and grabbed hold of his fingers while removing the tickets from his hand.

At that point, Asia was tired of the childish games. Although she and Omar weren't officially a couple, the flagrant disrespect had gone too far. Her first thought was to snatch Melinda by the hair and begin beating her down, but since that would lead to her missing the concert, she decided to handle it another way. She smiled and allowed the ignoramus to escort them inside.

The auditorium was well lit, and the seats were filling up quickly. As they walked slowly down the descending aisle, Asia grew more excited. She loved Mary J. Blige and expected a good show.

"Okay, sexy, here are your seats." Melinda brushed her breast against Omar's arm.

"Oh, honey, these are great seats, thank you," Asia said.

"Only the best for you, baby," Omar replied.

Melinda rolled her eyes as Omar and Asia fell into a stare.

"Anyway, Omar, it was good seeing you. We'll have to get together soon, for old time sake." She turned and brushed her big behind against his crotch.

"It was nice seeing you, too," Omar said, stepping aside quickly. Glancing around, he noticed Asia brooding just a few feet away.

Melinda leaned in to give him a hug, gripping him so tight he could have popped out of her back.

"Oh, my gosh!" Asia squealed.

"What's wrong, babe?" Omar spun around.

Asia was frantic and pointing at Melinda.

"What is it?" Melinda replied, harshly.

"There's a spider crawling in your hair," Asia said, shaking as she pointed at Melinda's head.

"What, where is it?"

All at once, Melinda started running up and down the aisle, screaming. She started crying and shaking her head like a crazy person. Everyone in the auditorium took notice. People were standing on their seats and while others were leaning over the balcony to get a closer look. A couple of ushers rushed to her aide.

"What's wrong?" a chubby male usher asked.

"What is it?" another female usher asked.

"There's a spider in my hair. Get it out!" she screamed.

Every eye in the auditorium was on them.

"Wait, I don't see anything. Where is it?" the female usher asked.

"Right there," Asia pointed.

"Where is it?" the male usher asked.

"Are you blind? It's right there!" Asia continued pointing.

"I don't see anything."

"Me either."

Asia moved closer, "I see it."

"Oh my God, get it out of my hair," Melinda screamed, louder.

"How? What do you want me to do?" Asia asked.

"I don't know; kill it!"

Asia raised her purse high into the air and began slamming it against the top of her head, repeatedly. She must have whacked the spider twenty times in a matter for five seconds.

"Did you get it?" Melinda slurred. She was delirious from the pounding of Asia's purse against her head.

"I think so-" Asia said, placing her purse beneath her arm. "Okay, yeah; I killed it. One of you are going to have to remove it, though."

"I'm not doing it," the female usher said.

"Okay, I'll do it," the male usher volunteered. Melinda lowered her head as he reached into her disheveled mane, pulling out something that looked like a large dead tarantula.

"Is that it?" Melinda asked.

"Yeah, that's it," Asia confirmed.

"This isn't a spider," the male usher said.

"It's not?" Asia's eyes widened.

"No, it's the track from her hair extension."

"Oops! My mistake," Asia said as she turned to enter the row.

All at once, there was a roar of laughter from the huge crowd of onlookers. Omar couldn't believe it. Melinda turned beet red with embarrassment.

"Look, Melinda, I'm really sorry about this." Omar said, attempting to apologize for Asia's terrible faux pas. Before he could finish his sentence, she snatched her hair track from her co-worker's hand and bolted out of the auditorium.

Omar stared at Asia as he joined her at their seats.

Omar laughed, "Wait, you did that on purpose didn't you?"

"I don't know what you're talking about," Asia said, smiling.

"No? Why are you smiling then?"

"It's just this place, baby. I can't get over how unbeweavable our seats are."

Omar laughed. "Wait; don't tell me you did that on purpose. Did you?"

Asia smiled, and the house lights dimmed. She chuckled under her breath as the show began. Omar didn't know whether to laugh or be concerned, but that was just the start of things. The evening was about to get a lot more interesting.

When Omar picked up the tickets, he had no idea who the opening act would be, nor did he care. Mary J. Blige was such a major headliner that anyone else would pale in comparison in his eyes.

The curtains opened and their attention was immediately locked on the large neon display above the stage. Asia's mouth fell open.

"What, what is it?" Omar asked, following her stare.

"This can't be," she said, staring as the overhead lights illuminated three guys ascending from beneath the stage.

Suddenly, a voice ripped through the theatre: "Reb-732, C-Blanx, Blaq Beard, are you ready, let's go!"

Asia leaped up and so did every other person in the theatre as the nineties singing sensation, Vokal executed a flawless choreography that caused a simultaneous roar to spill from the crowd.

Omar pumped his fist in the air as six scantily dressed women swarmed the stage, surrounding the members of Vokal as they performed their new hit single, *On da Pole*.

"Man, I haven't seen these guys in years," Omar commented. "Where have they been?"

Asia didn't respond. She was too busy melting beneath the pounding bass line of Vokal's chart-topping single.

"Damn, I love this song. I have it downloaded in my cell phone," Omar said.

Asia glanced at him and then back at the stage. Torrey, aka Reb-732, riffed his way through a dynamic intro that sent the audience into a frenzy. He was sharply dressed and worked the right side of the stage as if it was his own little piece of the world.

Camaron, aka C-Blanx, took ownership of the left side of the stage. His smooth voice wrapped around the screaming audience like a stream of warm caramel as he joined Reb-732 in a lyrical display that sent chills through every person in the auditorium.

Omar and Asia clapped with excitement.

Then it happened; the third member of the group took center stage. Tai, aka Blaq Beard, took position under the center spotlight. Every woman in the audience screamed at the top of their lungs as he delivered a vocal performance likened to the late, great Donny Hathaway, setting the microphone on fire. He unleashed a quick and powerful vibrato that ricocheted throughout the room like a bolt of lightning. Everyone went crazy-men, women, and especially Asia. So much, she began calling out his name.

Omar watched as she jumped up and down, shouting like a schoolgirl.

"Baby, you're calling him as if you know him," Omar said, smiling as if to poke fun at her.

"I do know him; we go way back."

"Right!" Omar chuckled.

"What is that supposed to mean?"

"It means, everyone claims to know someone after they make it big. Let me guess, he's your play cousin, right?"

"Whatever; I'm just excited to see them. I didn't know that they had a new song out," Asia said.

"I heard something about them planning to do a new CD, but I didn't know it would be so soon," Omar replied.

The members of Vokal had a reputation of being able to sing women out of their clothes. Omar knew it, and from what he had already heard that evening, they still possessed the ability.

There were women all over the place dressed in tight-fitting clothes and screaming at the top of their lungs when the group hit the stage. A few even threw their panties up on stage.

Omar scanned the room in shock at how bold some of the women were being. The only other time he had seen such a display, was when women threw their panties at him.

While performing a medley of their hits, Tai slipped into a low growl and stepped toward the edge of the stage, causing Asia to lose her mind. The lower his voice dropped, the more frantic she became.

Tai noticed her from the stage and his eyes widened. So, did hers.

So did Omar's as the crooner moved purposely toward the edge of the stage, singing directly to her.

Asia blushed as he blew her a kiss between verses. The crowd watched in amazement while Tai performed vocal acrobatics that sent every woman in the place into a sexual frenzy, Asia included. The look on Omar's face was one of total disbelief as Asia appeared to be having a secret orgasm. She was so worked up and Mary hadn't even taken the stage yet. After the first song, Tai asked the musical director to lower the sound while he searched for a lucky audience member to join them on stage.

Omar was bowled over when Asia was selected.

"Do you mind?" Asia asked.

"No, I don't mind. If you want to do it, go ahead."

Omar watched as Asia slid past him. He didn't think that she would do it. She didn't seem like the type.

Asia was standing on the stage, blushing as the stagehands placed a chair under the middle spotlight. Tai escorted her over to the seat.

The next thing Omar knew, the music was cued back up and the group was performing a song entitled "*Ride.*"

Within seconds, they were gyrating and pumping their midsections toward the audience like a bunch of horny rock stars.

Omar was taken aback, not because of the performance, but because Tai had somehow switched positions with Asia, who was now giving him a lap dance. Omar attempted to play it cool while the heat of anger brewed in his gut.

As he watched, his forehead wrinkled with agitation. He wasn't used to someone else getting so much attention; nor was he aware that Asia would participate in such an act.

After their performance, the group had invited Asia back to their dressing room.

"Oh, my goodness, baby; they invited us to come back to their dressing room after the show. Isn't that great?" Asia smiled.

"You're kidding, right?" Omar's tone was sour.

"No, I'm not. I'm quite serious."

A look of discontent settled on his face.

"What's wrong with you?"

"Nothing!" Omar responded quickly.

"So, can we go backstage after Mary finishes?" She gripped his fingers in a show of affection.

"I'll come with you backstage, but I'm not going into their dressing room."

"Why?"

"Because, I'm not."

"Please."

"No."

"Oh, come on, I'll owe you one."

Bells and whistles went off in Omar's head. He had just hit the jackpot. Owe him one she would indeed, and he had every intention on collecting on it later.

"Okay."

"Great, thank you so much." Asia beamed with excitement. "You're going to love them; they're really great guys."

"Ssh! Mary is about to come out," he said, cutting her off in mid-sentence.

She just stood there staring at him with her lips parted, thinking, *did he just Ssh me like I'm some screaming toddler in a highchair? She rolled her eyes at him, Okay, you stand up there with your big head acting like you're running something now, but you better believe I'm going to deal with you later buster.*

Just then, Mary J. Blige's voice yanked her attention back to the stage, but Asia wasn't through-not by a long shot.

CHAPTER SEVEN

Surprise, Meet My Ex

The concert was amazing. Mary sang her heart out, Asia screamed her lungs out, and Omar spent most of his time trying to figure out what connection Asia had with the bearded crooner.

As they headed backstage, he tried to put the pieces together.

At the end of a long corridor, two massive security officers standing outside of Vokal's dressing room greeted them.

"I'm sorry, you're not allowed back here!"

"I'm a friend of the group, and they invited me to come back after their set."

"Yeah, that's what they all say."

The next thing that anyone knew, the door to the dressing room swung open and a voice spilled from inside, "It's okay, Troy, let them in."

Asia smiled at the two burly security guards as they stepped aside.

Omar followed her inside, watching closely as she and Torrey, aka Reb-732, greeted each other as if they were long lost relatives.

"Damn girl, you look good."

"Hey, Torrey, my goodness it's been a long time."

"Yes, it has." He looked her over after hugging her, again. "Girl, I swear you are as pretty as you were the last time I saw you."

Omar couldn't believe the way this guy was checking her out as if he wasn't even standing there. However, he maintained his composure.

"Thank you; you haven't changed either-you're still as fly as ever."

"Well, you know-why fool with perfection if you don't have to?"

They chuckled.

"I hear that. By the way, you guys were great." Asia continued stroking Torrey's ego.

"Thanks, we do it all for folks like you, baby."

A voice spilled from another room.

"That's right," said Camaron. He was the baby of the group. He was known for being a man of few words, but the glare in his eyes spoke volumes when he entered the room.

"Camaron, hey!" Asia smiled. "My goodness, you still look the same, too."

"Well, you know, it's all this good living." He rubbed his belly.

"So, where is Tai?" she asked.

Just at that moment, Tai walked in, excited and shocked at what he would find.

"Hey, guys, Mary's going to do the feature on the track for us. So-"

"Hello, Tai," Asia greeted him softly.

Tai's eyes lit up, "Asia?"

Omar watched as they stared at each other. It was as if they were communicating with their souls. He filled in the blanks immediately.

"It's good to see you. What have you been up to?" Tai asked, further questioning her with his eyes.

"You know… this and that," Asia replied.

"I see. Well, it looks like you've been taking care of yourself." He looked her up and down.

"Well, if I don't, who will?"

Tai glanced at Omar.

"Oh, look at me being rude," Asia said, spinning around.

"Guys, this is my friend, Omar."

Omar extended his hand to shake Tai's but was rudely ignored.

"So, Asia, the last I heard, you were living in Texas. I never understood why you moved so far away," Tai questioned, as if Omar wasn't in the room.

She hesitated.

"Were you there on business?"

"Sort of."

"Oh, okay." Tai looked at her curiously.

"How's your grandmother?" Torrey asked, changing into a Gaultier jacket to match his glasses.

"She's fine," Asia replied.

"Hey, Tai, don't we have a concert to do out there next month?" Camaron asked.

"Yeah, maybe we'll stop by and say hello to your Granny."

It was clear to Omar that Asia knew the crooners well. What wasn't clear, was why the look on her face changed when they spoke of going to Texas.

Torrey sat in a reclining chair biting on the end of a toothpick.

"So, Asia are you still into riding?"

"Oh lord, no. I haven't been on the back of a motorcycle in years."

Omar's eyebrows rose. He had no idea she liked motorcycles.

"Well, you know, I have my bike out back," Tai said.

"No, you don't." Asia grinned.

"Yes, I do."

Asia glanced at Camaron for confirmation.

"Yes, he does. Now that we're making all this money again, that fool has his bike transported everywhere we go."

"Guess what he named it?" Torrey hinted.

"Oh, gosh, you named your bike?" Asia asked.

"Yeah, he did-after you." Torrey grinned.

Omar had enough. Although he wasn't jealous of Asia's R&B buddies, he was sick of the sexual undertone in the room.

"Asia, we should be going," he said.

"Okay."

"Hey, Asia, you know what today is. Don't you?" Torrey asked, walking into another room as he spoke.

"Yeah, it's Friday," Asia replied as she hugged Camaron. "See you later, baby."

She walked over to say good-bye to Tai. Before she could, Torrey reentered the room carrying a large cake and a bottle of champagne.

Asia blushed with embarrassment.

"That's right, you should be embarrassed; it's Tai's birthday. How could you forget?"

"Oh, Tai, I'm sorry; Happy birthday!" She leaned in to hug him.

He gripped her waist.

"So, are you going to stay and have some cake or what?" Torrey asked, casting his eye at Omar.

"I don't know," Asia replied, glancing at Omar as well.

Before Omar could say a word, though, Tai cut in, "Oh, don't tell me Kevin Costner over here is playing your bodyguard tonight." He moved toward Omar. "Listen, she'll be safe with us, why don't you run along and see if you can find out who killed Whitney."

Torrey and Camaron burst into laughter.

Omar, however, wasn't in the least bit amused. Tai had already offended him twice that evening, and he wasn't going to tolerate any more disrespect. He reached over Asia's shoulder and before anyone could blink, snatched him by the collar.

Torrey and Camaron leaped up immediately.

"Wait, oh my God, Omar, wait!" Asia shouted.

"Ooh, Asia, he's a bold one," Tai said, sarcastically.

"Yeah, bold enough to kick all three of your asses in your own dressing room," Omar snapped.

Tai chuckled.

"Wow and he's stupid, too," Torrey said.

Omar released Tai from his grip and turned his wrath toward Torrey.

"Guys, wait!" Asia shouted. Her voice alerted the two large security guards posted outside the dressing room.

"Is everything okay in here?" one of the guards asked.

"Yeah, everything's fine. Omar here was just leaving," Tai said.

The security guard took Tai's cue. "Would you come with me, sir?"

"Asia, let's go," Omar demanded.

"Go ahead, I'll be out in a minute; there's something I need to say to Tai."

"What? I'm not leaving you in here with this fake ass Barry White. Let's go." He grabbed her arm.

"Baby, please, I'll be right out. I promise."

Omar hesitated.

"Please, Omar!" Asia insisted.

"All right; I'll be out front."

"Thank you." She kissed him on the face.

"Don't be too long or I'm coming back in."

"I won't."

Just as he turned to walk away, she stopped him, "Oh, babe, take this with you, please." She said, shoving her small handbag into his hand as if it was some type of confirmation of her word.

Omar turned to leave the room, eyeing the members of his now, least favorite group on the planet. As he exited the dressing room, he tossed Tai a threatening look as if to say, *I'll see you again, motherfucker!*

Omar had a thing about holding purses.

Even though the world was suddenly full of men who thought it was trendy to carry Man Bags, he thought it was just another excuse for gay and D.L. men to explore their feminine side. How did he even end up holding her purse in the first place? All he remembered was Tai saying something slick and then reaching over Asia's shoulder to grab him.

"What the hell does she have in this thing?" Omar mused.

Asia's purse was small but heavy. Like most of the women he knew, she probably carried everything in it except the kitchen sink. He grew tired of holding it and tossed it inside the car.

Although Omar had enjoyed the concert, he wasn't particularly happy with Asia's behavior during the concert. The way she behaved when Vokal hit the stage, made him wonder just what type of woman she really was. That was his initial reason for being upset. The negative mood continued when she decided to stay behind while he was escorted out

of the theatre by security, leaving him standing outside holding her purse.

Normally, Omar wouldn't have been caught dead waiting for a woman outside of a concert, or anywhere else for that matter, but the scene with Tai provided the perfect opportunity for him to gain a little bit more knowledge about her. So did the fact that he had her purse. He peeked inside.

"Visa, MasterCard, American Express-Gold; Bingo!" He cracked a smile.

Asia had just been upgraded from a one-night stand to a 'financial regular'. That's how he and Ben refer to booty calls with no-limit credit cards.

After thumbing through her purse, he knew a little bit more about her. He also knew that he needed to step up his game, especially since the Barry White wannabe had his eyes on Asia as well.

A sly grin etched on his face as he decided which card he would play next.

Most women believe when a man is jealous of her association with another guy, it must mean that he really cares for her. Sometimes, that might even be true, if the man sees value in his woman and in their relationship. Not Omar; he couldn't care less. He wasn't interested in being anything more than a sexual confidant to any woman. The closest he had ever come to being jealous over a woman was when he planned it to gain greater access to her heart.

He used the jealousy card like an emotional fishing rod, casting it out whenever he felt like an overconfident woman needed to be reeled back in.

Since Asia was taking her time, it was the perfect opportunity for him to call Ben.

Five minutes into the call...

"Yeah, bro, can you believe it?"

"Yes, I can believe it, that's how women are," Ben said.

"Yeah, well, I thought about leaving her ass right here with the Johnny Gill knock-off."

"You should have."

"Nah, I won't give that punk ass the satisfaction of taking her home tonight."

Ben laughed.

"I can't believe she hasn't come out yet." Omar glanced at his watch.

"That's what you get, for giving away my ticket without asking me. She should ride off on the back of his motorcycle like Batgirl."

"That's cold man."

"Now you know how it feels."

"Okay, okay, I'll make it up to you later."

"You can bet your ass on that," Ben replied.

"What are you going to do now?"

"What else?"

"Play the jealousy card," they said in unison.

They each burst into laughter.

"Shit, I think she's coming out now." Omar scanned for her.

"Okay, well, let me know how it goes, playa."

"I will."

Omar ended the call, quickly.

The jealousy card...

After assessing Asia's fiery attitude and independent nature, Omar realized that he'd have a little more work to do than he had originally planned-which was okay, seeing how she was so fine.

A quick shift in his plans didn't mean that his goals were unattainable, but that he had slightly underestimated her. It didn't matter much, though, because to him, she was still just a woman. No matter how strong-willed she appeared, she was still subject to the same emotional needs and flaws as any other woman he had encountered.

In Omar's mind, every woman wants to know that she has what it takes to stir up a little envy in a man. For most, it was a sure-fire way to find out if a guy is interested or not; especially if she's unclear where the relationship is going. It was the oldest trick in the book, and so was Asia's attempt at making him jealous. What was she thinking, inviting him to the dressing room of a guy that she obviously had past relations with? She was playing a very dangerous game, and she had no idea what was brewing in his mind.

Asia cheerfully made her way through the sea of people and toward the car where Omar was standing holding the door for her. She slid inside.

He walked slowly to the driver's side, started the car, cut her a look of displeasure and then turned his focus to the road.

"What does that look mean?" she asked.

"What look?" he asked, playing stupid.

"The one you gave me when I came out of the theatre." She glanced at her purse as if he had possibly snooped inside.

She tried to read the look on his face but couldn't. She opened her purse and removed a tube of lipstick.

"Did I do something wrong?" she asked.

He sneered as she reapplied the color that had smudged from her lips.

Omar shook his head. For about five minutes, there was nothing but silence in the car. Neither of them said a word.

She watched as he cut through the evening traffic. She couldn't believe that he was ignoring her. She tossed him an incredulous look as if he was the one who had done something wrong.

It was unlike Omar to put up with bullshit, so he pulled the car over.

"Okay, Asia, what's going on?"

She didn't respond. She just sat there staring at him, thinking, *just look at him, sitting over there looking like the manifestation of a wet dream. I can't believe he's jealous. Well, he can be jealous all he wants, but it's not going to be that easy to wrap me around his finger. I bet if I'd let him, he'd wrap me around something else.*

Omar was doing some thinking as well. *Damn, she's stubborn. Instead of just telling me how much she wants me, she'd rather sit over there acting like she's God's gift to men. I should just reach over there, snatch her by the hair, and throw my tongue into her mouth. Then again, with all the mixed signals she's been sending me, she'll probably end up slapping me, or worse.*

"Damn it!"

"Excuse me?" her eyes widened.

"Sorry, I was just thinking out loud."

"Yeah, well that language isn't necessary."

"No, what isn't necessary is the cold shoulder I'm getting when all I tried to do is show you a good time.

"Really, by refusing to go backstage with me?"

"Backstage? Please, you're lucky I didn't snatch your ass off the stage. How could you let them pull you up there and grope all over you like that?"

"No one was groping all over me; we were dancing. It's called audience participation."

"No, it's called disrespecting your man."

"Yeah, well, I don't have a man," Asia snapped. Her nostrils flared as she spoke.

The game of mind-chess was getting serious. Until that moment, Asia hadn't shown much emotion. She had been as cool as Omar at every turn. Once again, it was not what he expected. He decided to shift gears.

"Damn, Asia, can't you see that I'm jealous!"

"Why? Tai is my ex. We don't have anything going on anymore."

"That's not the point! He's your ex and you shouldn't have been backstage with him."

"You shouldn't have threatened him."

"Oh, so now I'm the bad guy?"

"You were being rude, Omar!"

"I was defending your honor."

"Yeah, well, I don't need your help, trust me!"

"Yeah, you black women never do."

"What is that supposed to mean?"

"It means I'm a man, Asia, let me be that!"

"Even if it means potentially getting your ass kicked in the process?"

That was a low blow. If Omar were an insecure man, that statement would have probably felt like a punch to the nuts, but since he'd never had his ass kicked in his life, and certainly wasn't about to start, he absorbed it for what it was just another one of her tests.

He sensed that she was trying to see how far she could push him. He knew that there wasn't a woman in the world that respected a punk. Whether she was willing to admit it or not, the fact that he appeared jealous made her loins tingle. He knew it, she knew, and her vagina knew it; and he was about to turn the drama up another notch.

Omar put the car into drive and pulled away from the curb.

After a few seconds, Asia realized that her comment was out of line. Beneath the surface, she really did appreciate his willingness to defend her honor, but she felt it was also vital for him to know that she could take care of herself. Unfortunately, she chose the wrong words to do it.

"I just didn't want anything to happen to you," she muttered while folding her sweater onto her lap.

"What did you say?"

"I said, please don't drive so fast." She pressed her heels into the floor under the dashboard.

"Let me get this straight. First, you call me a punk and now you're telling me that I don't know how to drive?"

"No! I'm just asking you to slow down."

"I heard you the first time, Asia." He turned his focus back to the road.

"Good, then can you please slow down?" Her voice became like a gnat in his ear. He was an excellent driver and certainly didn't need to be told how to handle his car. He ignored her.

"Omar!" she said, reaching for his arm.

"You know, Asia? I enjoy spending time with you, but honestly, I can't be with a woman who wants to control everything!

"What are you saying?"

"I'm saying, I want to see you again, but I don't know about all of this bossiness."

"I'd like to see you again too, Omar, but-"

"No buts and let me make something clear to you-" Asia listened attentively. "I'm a good man and I'll do anything for a good woman. I'll even wait outside of a theatre while she reminisces with her boy band ex-boyfriend, but no woman is going to tell me how to drive my damn car, is that clear?" Omar's sternness excited her. He could see it in her eyes. Her legs parted slightly, and her lips cracked into a smile; probably because he was being assertive or because she thought he was jealous. Either way, she reached for his hand. He could feel her staring at him, as he watched the road.

Suddenly, the blaring sound of a police siren shocked them both.

"Damn it!" he scoffed, pulling over as the flashing lights grew nearer. Soon they were illuminating the inside of the car.

"I told you to slow down!" Asia said nervously. He glanced at her and then through the rearview mirror.

A large white police officer exited a squad car and made his way toward the car. Omar sized him up quick.

"Red Neck," he mumbled.

The cop tapped on the glass.

"Lower the window.

Omar grimaced."

The officer stood with one hand on his service revolver and the other on a flashlight, which he beamed directly into Omar's eyes.

"What's the problem, officer?"

"I was about to ask you the same thing, boy," he said, flashing the light into Asia's face and then into the back seat.

"Show me your license and registration, please!"

"Come on, is this really necessary?"

"Hey, smart ass! Did I ask you to speak?"

Asia touched Omar's arm.

"Was it really necessary for you to be speeding like a bat out of hell? No, but you were doing it, right?"

Omar gritted his teeth. He disliked cops, especially big, fat, ill-mannered ones. He took one hand from the steering wheel, slowly, and reached into the glove compartment to retrieve his registration. He handed the officer his license as well.

Asia could feel that Omar was ready to explode at any moment. It was obvious by the way his nostrils were flaring and the wrinkles on his forehead.

The officer continued to shine the light at Omar's face.

After a few moments, Omar had enough. He removed his hands from the steering wheel and prepared to confront the officer. Before he could, a horrible screech ripped from beside him, causing Omar to spin around.

"Asia, what's wrong?"

"It's coming! It's coming!" she screamed.

"What's coming?" he asked, confused.

Asia's outburst, with the sudden expansion of her waistline, added even more to his confusion.

"What are you doing?" he mumbled.

Asia pressed her back against the passenger side door, gapped her legs open, and continued to scream.

The officer looked inside.

"Ma'am, are you okay?"

"No, it's my baby, I think I'm about to deliver!" The officer's eyes stretched as wide as his huge nose. Omar's did as well, as Asia began blowing and panting, and panting and blowing as if she was about to give birth to twins.

It took a few seconds for Omar to catch on, but when he did, he leaped right into character. Within seconds, everyone was blowing; even the police officer started blowing. He was blowing so hard that his face became as red as his neck. It took all the restraint Omar could muster to refrain from bursting into laughter. He was about to crack when Asia cautioned him with her ✸ eyes.

"Omar, please, get me to a hospital," she begged.

"Okay, baby...Officer?"

The cop's disposition changed instantly.

"Don't worry, ma'am, we'll get you to a hospital; you just hold on."

The officer raced back to his car.

"What are you doing?" Omar asked, glancing in the rearview mirror to keep an eye out for the officer's return.

"I'm defending your honor."

"You're what?"

Asia began to explain.

"Oh please, I don't need you to do that. I can take care of myself."

"Ssh!"

"Don't Ssh me! What is this?" He reached for her belly, lifting her blouse.

"It's my sweater."

"Woman, are you crazy? What if he finds out?"

The squad car pulled up alongside them. Asia quickly lowered her blouse and resumed her performance.

"Follow me; I'll get you to the hospital, quick."

"Okay, great."

Omar raced through the traffic, as the unsuspecting officer cleared the way.

Asia laughed.

"You know you're crazy, right?"

"Yeah, well, you just drive, and I'll be whatever I need to be, for now."

When they arrived at the hospital, the officer raced inside to fetch help.

"Okay, Ms. Know-It-All, what are you going to do now?"

"Just follow my lead," Asia said.

Omar watched as two attendants raced toward his car. One was pushing a wheelchair.

"Asia, you're not pregnant. What's going to happen once we're inside?"

"You know what, Omar? Earlier you told me to let you be a man, right?" She cupped her hands beneath her belly.

"What does that have to do with anything?"

"Everything; just let me be a woman."

Huh? Omar had no idea what Asia meant, but he would find out later.

As the emergency room attendants approached Omar's car, Asia let out a scream that could wake the dead. The look on her face read, *I'm about to give birth to a brand-new camel hair sweater. Now get me out of this car, you freakin' idiots!*

She sat in the wheelchair, panting and blowing as if ready to deliver her sweater at any moment.

As they rushed her through the sliding doors of the ambulatory entrance, she maintained a dramatic posture the entire while.

Omar trailed behind them, feeling like he had been warped into an episode of I Love Lucy.

"I have to call Ben and tell him this shit." He spoke under his breath as he pulled out his cell phone.

"You know, you're not supposed to use that cell phone in here," a voice warned from behind him.

Omar spun around and saw a short, dark-skinned woman sitting behind the nurse's station. She rolled her eyes and spoke in a heavy Caribbean accent as she addressed him.

Omar didn't care too much for Caribbean folk with bad attitudes, so he ignored her.

"Hey, buddy, are you excited?" Another voice spilled into the moment. He spun around once more, this time to find the officer who had escorted them to the hospital standing just inches away from his face. He was breathing directly onto Omar's face. His breath smelled like onions and boiled bologna. Omar held his breath as the officer spoke.

"So, are you okay?"

"Huh, oh yeah, I feel fine." Omar squinted.

"That's good because becoming a dad is the best thing that could happen to a man. You get to teach your kid how to swim, play catch, fish, most importantly, how to respect the road!" The officer joked.

Omar cracked a phony smile, thinking, *I wish your dad would have taught you to brush your fucking teeth; damn!*

By the way," he slapped Omar on the shoulder, "my name is Officer Joe, if you want to name the kid after me."

Omar wasn't amused. He just stood there thinking, *Yeah, right, I wouldn't name a freakin' virus after you. And if you put your hand on me again, you're going to be laying on one of these gurneys waiting for someone to pull my boot out of your ass.*

The officer must have sensed Omar's irritation and headed back to his car.

Omar watched until the coast was clear. He shifted his attention back to Asia.

"Okay, now what?"

"Bring the car around front and wait for me in the parking lot," she whispered.

"What are you going to do?"

"Don't worry; just keep the motor running."

"Keep the motor running? Who do you think we are, Bonnie and Clyde?"

She looked away.

Omar shook his head as he headed through the sliding doors. His first thought was to leave her sitting right there but then decided against it. He wanted to sleep with her, and he wasn't about to pass up the opportunity, no matter what.

On the way back to his car, he made eye contact with a young woman who was walking across the intersection. She smiled, causing Omar to stop in his tracks.

Thirty minutes later...

Asia was still in the emergency room, watching as a young woman stood in front of the nurse's station demanding information about a relative.

"I can't believe this," the young woman scoffed. "How could you misplace a patient?"

"Ma'am, please calm down."

"Don't tell me to calm down. My sister was brought in here this morning. Now you're telling me that you can't find her?"

"I'm sorry, but we have a lot of patients here; just give us a few more moments, please." The nurse's Caribbean accent was layered with unwarranted arrogance. The more she spoke, the angrier the younger woman became; she erupted.

"No, you look! I can see that you have a lot of patients," she mocked.

"But you are not going to talk down to me, as though you're doing me a favor when I ask you to find my sister. Do your damn job or let someone else do it!"

An argument ensued as the nurse engaged in an unprofessional exchange. "Me don't need ya to tell me what me job is; me know what me job is, okay!" She slammed a stack of folders down on the counter.

At that point, the young woman had enough. She removed her purse from her shoulder, set her bags on the floor and stepped closer to the counter. The look on her face was serious; she meant business.

"You know, it's clear to me that you people have been getting these jobs out of the Cracker Jack box and that you have a problem speaking proper English, but my sister was admitted here this afternoon with complications with her pregnancy. So, forgive me when I say, I DON'T GIVE A DAMN how many other patients you have. Right now, I'm all my little sister has. So, you have exactly one minute to find out where she is, or else!"

It took all of three seconds for the nurse to find the chart.

"Okay, I found it. Let me check with one of the doctors to find out where your sister is, okay?"

"You do that," the young woman snapped. Asia chuckled in disbelief. *It was unbelievable how insensitive people who work in hospitals can be.*

The young woman turned and looked at Asia. "Is this place for real?" she asked rhetorically.

"Unfortunately," Asia replied. "It's no surprise that they can't find your sister. They're about to deliver my baby and I'm not even pregnant."

"What?"

Asia lifted her blouse.

The woman grinned.

"Don't ask!" Asia said.

"Girl, I won't. It's been a long day, full of nothing but surprises."

"Who are you telling? When I left home this evening, I had no idea I'd end up in the emergency room."

"I'm sure, and certainly not with a sweater beneath your blouse."

Asia chuckled as she removed a rhinestone clip from her hair, causing it to fall past her shoulders. She pulled the sweater from beneath her blouse, put it on quickly, and buttoned it all the way up to her neck. She stood up from the wheelchair.

"It's a shame; you never know what to expect when you come to a County Hospital."

"Tell me about it. I just ran into someone I thought I knew. But it was a good thing that he wasn't who I thought he was because I would have socked him right in the nose."

"Oh, really? Asia inquired.

"Yes, really. He's the reason my little sister is in this hell hole."

"Hmm, man problems?"

"Yes. Some women really need to start making better choices about the men they choose to lay down with. If they did, it would save them a world of trouble later.

"Girl, if I had a nickel for every time I told my girlfriends that same thing, I'd have more money than Oprah."

They shared a laugh.

"Hi, I'm Asia."

"Hi, I'm Collette."

"You know, Asia, I don't think there's a woman in this world that doesn't worry about her man being unfaithful."

"I know. It seems like the more we trust them, the more they give us a reason not to."

"I swear the next man I settle down with is going to be on life support, so the minute he starts to show his behind, I can pull the damn plug on him."

"Girl, you can't say stuff like that out loud. Let's try this again."

They shared a laugh.

"Hi, I'm Asia."

"Hi, I'm Collette."

"You know, Asia, I don't think there's a woman in this world that doesn't worry about her man being unfaithful."

"I know. It seems like the more we trust them, the more they give us a reason not to."

"I swear the next man I settle down with is going to be on life support, so the minute he starts to show his behind, I can pull the damn plug on him."

Asia's laughter caught the attention of one of the emergency room attendants. He walked toward her.

"Excuse me, where did the young woman go who was in this wheelchair?"

"Oh, you mean the pregnant one?" Collette asked.

"Yes, the pregnant one."

"Oh, they took her in already."

He stared at Asia peculiarly as if he were on to her. At that moment, the nurse began to summon for Collette from across the room.

"Uh oh, you're being flagged; that's my cue. Good luck." Asia said, touching her on the shoulder. "I hope everything works out with your sister."

"Thanks. I'll see you around."

Asia smiled and then headed slowly toward the exit. With each step that she took, she could feel the emergency room attendant watching her. She thought about looking back but quickly decided against it. Instead, she hastened for the exit.

OUTSIDE THE HOSPITAL

It was taking longer than he expected for Asia to break out of Alcatraz, so Omar used the time to handle some business. After shuffling around his appointments to see other women, he called Ben to chat.

"So, how long are you going to wait for her?" Ben asked.

"I don't know; I guess as long as it takes."

"You really want it that bad, huh?"

"Man, I just want to sample it, that's all."

"Yeah, well, let me know how it goes."

"I will."

Omar hung up the phone, turned on the radio and reclined in the driver's seat. It was getting late, but he didn't mind at all. The late hour almost assured that he'd be invited in for a nightcap once they arrived at her place, which is exactly what he wanted.

He decided to rest for a few moments, but just as his eyelids met, he heard the clanking sound of high heels against the pavement. He sat up just in time to notice Asia running toward the car.

"Start the engine!" She yelled.

He sat straight up and turned the key in the ignition.

She opened the door and quickly jumped in.

"Go, go, go!" she urged.

He tore out of the hospital's parking lot and joined the merging traffic.

Asia unbuttoned her sweater and tossed it onto the back seat.

"What the heck was all that?" he asked. The tone of his voice suggested that he wanted a detailed report.

"That was me saving your hide."

"Is that right?"

"Yes, if it weren't for my quick thinking, you'd probably have a one-hundred-and-fifty-dollar ticket right now, or worse."

"So, you went through all of this just to keep me from getting a ticket?" he smiled.

"Oh, please. Don't flatter yourself,"

Asia lowered the overhead mirror to check her hair and makeup. "I played pregnant because I didn't want to see another black man face down on the ground like a common criminal when he's not."

"Gee, thanks...I think." Omar turned away.

He smiled to himself, thinking how unusual it was for a woman to go through so much trouble for him.

"What are you thinking?" she asked.

"You really want to know?"

"Yes."

"Well, I would have preferred the ticket if it would have meant spending more time with you."

"So, you don't appreciate me breaking out of the hospital like a mental patient?"

"Of course, I appreciate it."

She began touching up her makeup again.

"No woman has ever gone through so much trouble for me."

"Well, I'm a different type of woman," she said, pulling a stick of gum from her purse. "Have some?"

"No thanks."

"Okay, well, thanks for the dinner and the concert. I enjoyed them both."

"I'm glad. "

He grabbed her hand and held it for the entire ride back to her place. He didn't want to admit it, but he was really starting to like her, a lot.

They arrived at her place quickly. Although he had very strong feelings about Harlem's gentrification, Omar was impressed by some of the changes in the neighborhood.

"So, this is where you live, huh?"

"Yes."

"Alone?"

"That's right."

Omar's eyebrows rose. The homes on Asia's block went for no less than a million dollars.

He parked in hopes of being invited in.

"Well, since you know that I'm not a criminal, are you going to invite me in for a nightcap?" Omar asked, flashing a boyish smile in hopes of winning Asia over.

She stared at him. *A nightcap? Please, you'll be lucky if I don't slap the taste out of your mouth before I get out of this car.* She wanted to do it but refrained. Omar had refrained as well. In fact, he wanted to kiss her all night but hadn't.

"Omar, I'm tired, maybe another time. Okay?"

"What are you doing tomorrow morning?"

"I'm going jogging."

"Good. I'll come with you."

"What? No!"

"Why, you don't want to see me?"

"Omar, don't get yourself into something you can't get yourself out of, okay?"

"Trust me, anything I get into with you, I plan to stay in."

Asia stared at him as he slid closer to her. His lips were parted and so were hers. He moved in slowly for the kiss he wanted so badly. Just as he did though, he heard the click of the latch and she stepped from the car.

"Meet me at 110th street at 6 am and don't be late."

"Damn!" he gripped himself. His eyes were glued to her backside.

She spun around. "Uh, do you think you can stop looking at my ass long enough to hand me my sweater?" She folded her arms and waited.

"I'm sorry, I was just-"

"I know, another attention span problem, right?" She shook her head. The look on her face read, *with a crack like that he'd never get a nightcap.*

"I look forward to our jog tomorrow. It's a good way to stay in shape, but I don't have to tell you that, right?"

Omar's weak attempt at flattery was starting to wear on Asia's nerves. She could see right through all the sweet talk straight to the depth of his intentions. He was after something and it wasn't a jog in the park.

She closed the car door and spoke to him through the opened window.

"Good night, Omar."

"Good night, Asia. Thank you for the eventful evening."

"You're welcome." Asia turned away.

"Oh, wait, I have something for you." He fumbled behind the passenger seat.

She sighed as she watched.

After a few seconds, Omar pulled a large plastic bag from behind the seat and handed it to her. When she opened the bag, she immediately fell into a blank stare.

"What is this?"

"It's a welcome mat, do you like it?"

"Omar, I don't know what to say." Asia said, fighting the urge to throw it at him.

"I know it's not much, but I thought you could use it since you did just buy your house."

Asia's disposition changed immediately; she was flattered that Omar had thought of her. Yet, although it was a step in the right direction, it wasn't a big enough step.

"I'm going to put this down in front of my door, right now."

Asia smiled, glancing back at the car as she headed up the stairs to her home.

She placed the mat on the landing in front of her door, cut Omar a flirtatious look, and then stepped inside.

He appreciated her flirt and blew her a kiss before she closed the door. After a few minutes, he jerked the car out of park and glanced at her door a final time before heading back to Brooklyn.

Meanwhile...

Asia was watching from her bedroom window until his car was out of sight. Once she was sure that he was well on his way, she lowered the shade and began to undress.

The light in her bedroom cast a silhouette of her naked body onto the pavement below.

A young man that happened to be walking by at the time noticed the shadow on the ground, glanced up at the window and awkwardly stumbled into a row of trashcans. "Damn!" he barked.

"Damn is right," Asia said, responding to the young man's comment, just as she had Omar's. Neither of them was appreciated.

She walked into the bathroom.

"I'm too smart to fall for some fast-talking wannabe playa who thinks he's going to add me to a list of broken hearts."

She ran the bathtub full of water.

"If he thinks I'm just another naive woman with low self-esteem looking for a man to make my day, he's sadly mistaken."

The foam from her favorite bubble bath rose high in the tub. "I'll give it to him, he's cute...actually he's gorgeous. If nothing else, he'll look good on my arm at parties."

She pinned up her hair.

"I can't believe he bought me that cheap welcome mat."

She immersed herself in the water.

"Did he really think I'd be impressed with such a lame gift?"

She closed her eyes.

"He's going to have to do a lot better than that if he wants to spend time with me."

She opened her eyes and stared at the ceiling, "So, Mr.   I-want-to-gawk-at-a-woman's-backside-all-night-long, you want a nightcap, huh?"

The soft white bubbles covered her entire body. She lifted one of her shapely thighs from the water and sponged it gently. A cunning look settled in her eyes and a devilish grin emerged on her lips. She chuckled and began her plot.

Male Privacy interrupted...

Omar sat on the corner of his bed, flicking channels on the television. He couldn't believe the night he had with Asia. She had been on his mind ever since they parted. So was the fact that he was horny as hell and had not been laid in days. It was so unlike him.

While it was true that he had about a dozen women that he could call, Asia was the one he desired. He flashed back to the moment when she stepped from his car. The image of her ass aroused him.

After a few minutes of being nagged by his hormones, he decided to relieve his tension.

Usually, Omar wasn't one for self-gratification, especially since he could have any woman he wanted, whenever he wanted. However, since none of them was the woman he really wanted, he'd have to make do.

He slid back on the bed, propped two pillows behind his head, pulled a bottle of lube from the top drawer of his nightstand, and proceeded to self-gratify.

He knew many women who would have loved the opportunity to stroke his ego. However, what he was feeling at that moment was just for Asia.

He continued gripping himself like a baseball player grips his bat, guiding himself toward ecstasy. The more he thought about her, the harder he stroked. He imagined her hand replacing his. The muscles in his legs flexed and so did the ones in his stomach. His abs tightened, his toes curled-he closed his eyes and pointed his chin toward the ceiling, stroking harder and faster, causing his manhood to slip repeatedly through his fingers like a slippery eel. The muscles in his ass tightened as he prepared to paint the ceiling, and then the phone rang. "Shit! Shit!! He snatched it from the night table and answered it abruptly.

"Hello!"

"I'm sorry, is this a bad time?"

Omar leaped up, kicking over a glass of lemonade that he had been drinking earlier. He searched frantically for something to cover himself.

"Ah, shit! Asia?"

"Yes, is everything okay?"

Omar behaved as though Asia had walked in on him. "I'm sorry; just give me a second, please?"

"If I'm disturbing you, I can call back another time."

"No, you're not disturbing me. I just kicked over a glass of lemonade, that's all."

He was completely discombobulated, pulling the spread from his bed and covering himself with it.

"I could ask you why your foot would be anywhere near a glass of lemonade, but I won't."

"Let me explain." Omar said.

"No, don't. What you do in the privacy of your home is your business; just like what I do when I'm all alone is mine."

Asia's voice dripped with suggestion, causing his eyebrows to rise. He didn't expect to hear from her so soon, and he didn't expect to hear all the suggestive breathing that she was doing on the other end. He wiped up the spill and moved to a chair near the window.

"Are you there, Omar?"

"Yes, I'm here," he said.

"That's good; now we're here together."

The sound of Asia's voice caused him to return to his bed. He turned off the television.

"What are you doing?" he asked.

"I'm just laying here talking to you," Asia said. Her tone, however, suggested otherwise.

He turned off the light in his bedroom.

"What sign are you, Omar?"

"I'm a Scorpio."

"Ooh, I love Scorpio men."

"Really, what do you love about them?"

"Well, they have magnetic personalities, they're sensitive, and they're passionate love-makers. Are you a passionate love-maker, Omar?"

"Yeah, I think I am."

He chuckled under his breath as he spoke, thinking, Please, I'm the Messiah of passion. "So what sign are you, baby?"

I'm a Pisces. Do you know anything about the zodiac?"

"Not really."

"Well, Pisces women are unworldly, caring, and very giving, especially of our hearts."

The entire time that Asia was speaking, Omar thought, *that's nice, but I hope you're equally as giving of that ass because that's all that I care about. I don't want to know what's your moon or your rising. The only rising I'm concerned with is the one taking place between my legs.*

She moaned, "So, what are you wearing, Omar?"

His antennas went up immediately. Was she trying to lead him into phone sex? If so, she was in for a rude awakening. He had never had phone sex and he wasn't about to start with her. Nor had he pegged her to be such a freak. Sure, she was a little arrogant and in need of a strong man to tame her lioness-like attitude, but never a phone freak. Omar knew that the situation had to be handled delicately, so, he played along just to make sure he knew exactly where she was coming from.

"You know what baby? I'm wearing some nice boxer shorts."

"Really, what color are they?"

"Black silk with white strips," he replied, lying. He was nude and the only thing he was wearing that resembled a stripe was his fleeting hard on.

"Is that all you're wearing?"

"Yeah, why? Should I be wearing something else?"

"No; I was just imagining how you must look, laying there with that muscular body of yours, wearing nothing but a pair of little shorts."

Omar smirked as he gripped himself. There was nothing little about his shorts, or what he'd fill them with had he been wearing some.

"What about you, what are you wearing?"

"Nothing," Asia replied seductively.

Omar's jaw dropped.

"Oh, really?" he said.

"Yes, really." She chuckled playfully. "There's just something about being naked that makes me feel so good."

"Damn, I wish I could see that," he muttered.

"What?"

"Oh, I said, I can believe that."

"I shouldn't be talking to you like this; I don't want you to get the wrong impression of me."

"It's okay; I'm not getting the wrong impression."

Omar searched around in the dark for the lube.

"Good, because it's not like I have a big strong man to hold me, you know?"

Now he was befuddled. She had been sending him mixed signals all night, talking about women should choose men wisely before sleeping with them. Now, she's implying that she's lonely. He didn't believe a word of it. What he did suspect, however, was that her only reason for calling him was that she was as horny as he was- which could work to his advantage.

"So, are you suggesting that you want me to come over?"

"No, I can't ask you to do that."

"Not a problem! I don't mind, really."

"That's sweet, but I'm just going to lay here and just enjoy being one with myself. I might even-"

Omar's mind began to race.

"You know, Asia, I like being one with myself, too, perhaps we can do that together. I can be there in no time."

Asia ignored his comment.

"No, we have to get up to go jogging tomorrow, re-member?"

"Yes, so I could come over now and then we can leave from your place in the morning."

"Ooh, Omar, these sheets just feel so good against my body," she teased, once again ignoring his comment.

Her panting caused him to pitch a tent under the spread, but she still hadn't answered his question.

"Baby, just let me come over there, please."

"Omar, it's too late."

"It's not too late, damn it!"

Omar stumped his toe as he raced around the room in search of something to slip on. He dressed and grabbed his keys.

"Baby, I'm on my way out to the car."

"Oh, Omar, have you ever done it in a car?"

"Oh, my God, no baby, but I want to, what about you?"

Just as he climbed into the car, he heard a dial tone.

"What the hell!"

He dialed her back but to no avail.

"Come on!"

He began to cuss under his breath that the call had dropped. He redialed the number, again, but still had no luck.

After redialing a fifth time, her voicemail picked up.

"Hi, this is Asia, I'm a little busy right now but when I finish, I'll call you back, okay, bye."

He slammed his hand against the steering wheel repeatedly before heading back into the house. He dragged himself back upstairs, grabbed the bottle of lube, and slung it on the bed.

"Shit, shit, shit!"

Suddenly, his face lit up and he smiled. Asia had played him, and he realized it. Yet, there was no way he was going to just lay there, rock hard.

He grabbed his phone, "Hello, Brenda?"

WORDS OF DESPERATION

Asia lay in bed dressed in her nightclothes, twirling a spoon around in a bowl of vanilla ice cream.

'So, what are you saying; do you want me to come over?' "Please, in your dreams." She chuckled as she mimicked Omar's words of desperation.

She sat the empty bowl on the nightstand, turned off the lamp, and curled up under her covers. In her mind, it would be a tough night of clenched fist and cramped abs for Omar, but for her sleep would come easy. She was still in control of her life and her body. No man was going to play with her head, nor her heart. Especially not some guy she met at a party and with whom she only had one date. She closed her eyes, hugged her pillow, and drifted off to sleep-alone.

CHAPTER EIGHT

Oh, Hell No!

Omar hadn't slept much. After speaking with Asia, he remained awake for hours. Clearly, getting her to agree to go to bed with him wasn't going to be as easy as he expected, but it was cool. He liked the challenge. So much that he was up all night plotting his next move. Just as he closed his eyes to rest there came a loud pounding on the door, startling him.

He leaped from the bed.

"I'm coming."

He slipped on a robe and angrily stomped his way to the door.

The knocking continued.

"I said I'm coming!" he yelled.

With one tug, he swung the door open and found Ben standing in front of him with both arms stretched across the doorframe. The look on his face was as though he had hit the lottery.

"Man, what are you doing here?" He released the door and headed through the foyer.

Ben followed him inside. "Oh, I need an excuse to stop by now?"

"Ben, don't start, please. It's too early in the morning." He rubbed his hands over his face to brush the residue of sleep from his eyes.

"What do you mean, early? It is after noon. The only folks sleeping now won't be getting up at all today."

"Damn it!"

"What's wrong?"

"Nothing, this chick just kept me up all night."

Ben smirked. "Well, where is she? Maybe she can keep me up, too." He said, glancing at the steps.

"Would you stop it?"

Ben chuckled.

Omar rubbed his head with his fingertips.

"Man, you look a mess," Ben said, grabbing a carton of orange juice from the refrigerator, with three eggs, tomato juice, a bottle of Tabasco sauce, and a can of ginger ale.

"I can't believe I slept so late."

"What's the big deal?"

Ben removed a glass from the cupboard.

"No big deal; I was just supposed to meet Asia at the park this morning.

"Oh, really, for what?"

"We were supposed to go jogging."

Ben cut his eyes at Omar on the sly, as he removed a bunch of spices from the cupboard.

Omar lowered his face into his hands.

"Don't tell me the woman's got you whipped."

"Oh, please, I'm not whipped. She asked if I would go jogging with her and I said yes. What's wrong with that?" He watched as Ben poured the ingredients into a blender.

"There's nothing wrong with it as long as she understands that you won't be settling down."

"I'll let her know."

"Good, because when you commit to a woman, you become subject to obligations. I know you don't want to be checking in and giving detailed reports about your whereabouts."

"Oh, hell no!" Omar barked.

"Yeah, well, that's what's going to happen if you're not careful. You'll be expected to remember birthdays, attend family picnics, holiday functions, and even accompany her to her girlfriend's parties occasionally."

Omar grimaced.

"If you're single, though, you can do whatever you want," Ben said, licking some of the Tabasco sauce from his fingers.

"You really think it'll be all of that, huh?"

"I'm just saying...I don't want this woman causing any problems for us."

"It was just going to be a jog in the park."

"That's how it starts out. Next, she'll be asking you to hold her purse and then-"

"Okay, I get your point!" Omar cut in. He wasn't about to tell his friend that he had already fallen victim to that stunt.

Ben pressed the setting on the blender.

"What the hell are you making?" Omar asked, frowning at Ben's concoction.

"This, my friend, is a sure-fire cure for hangovers. After a wild night, one glass of this and you'll feel like a new man."

"Yeah, well, I happen to like the man I am; besides, I don't have a hangover, so I'm not drinking that."

"Good, it's not for you anyway."

Ben chugged the greenish-brown glob straight from the blender. Omar squinted.

"Okay now that you've managed to upset my stomach, why don't you tell me why you're here?"

"Well, when you asked me why I was having such a good time at the party, I never told you. I've been working on something."

He removed an envelope from his jacket. Omar's face lit up as Ben handed him the envelope. He opened it and began to read the contents.

"Ben, is this for real? Don't fuck around, man."

"I'm not; they're as real as the bags under your eyes. Now go get dressed, I need to go see a guy about a camera before we head to the hotel."

Omar bolted upstairs, took a quick shower, dressed, and speedily headed downstairs where Ben was waiting. On the way out, he glanced at the telephone. The caller I.D.-displayed five messages. He ignored them and headed outside. "So, buddy, am I riding with you?"

"I thought we should take your car. I'm feeling a little sick right now," Ben said.

Omar laughed.

"I bet you do, and you're going to feel worse than that if you don't stop drinking that green shit."

They climbed into Omar's car and tore out of the driveway.

CHAPTER NINE

The Game of Cat and Mouse

"You know that you're going to have to handle that situation, right?" Ben commented, flipping through an assortment of CDs in Omar's car.

"I know."

"What do you plan to tell her?"

"I don't know. I haven't put that much thought into it."

"Well, you better handle it soon if you want to take things to the next level with me."

Omar sat quietly.

"Do you hear me?"

"I hear you; I hear you, okay!"

"That's what I'm talking about."

Ben turned up the volume on the CD player and started singing the lyrics to one of his favorite songs. "I'll stroke it to the east. I'll stroke it to the west-"

Omar shook his head.

"You need to take some lessons from this dude. He knows how to handle his business."

"Are you saying that I don't?"

"I don't know. Do you?"

Omar stepped on the gas. The cheesy lyrics bleared through the speakers, delivering an awful tribute to an unfaithful man's promiscuity.

While Ben danced in his seat, Omar's mind drifted back to Asia. She played him last night and he knew it. Still, he couldn't get her out of his mind. The game of cat and mouse was a bit junior-high school, but it excited him, nonetheless. And the fact that Asia was obviously a playa as well meant one thing-the rules of the game were about to change dramatically.

Omar was used to women eating out of his hands. In his mind, there wasn't a woman alive that could resist his charm or his third leg, but Asia's strong will was a bit of a surprise. Usually, he could talk a woman out of her clothes within minutes of meeting her, but not Asia. Somehow, she's managed to resist the power of his lure, but that only made him want her more.

"I'm telling you all I could think about was spreading her legs and putting this stuff on her."

Omar clutched the steering wheel with one hand and himself with the other.

Ben lit a cigarette.

"Are you telling me that she teased you and you still want to see her?"

"That's exactly what I'm telling you."

"Yeah, well, you better be careful," Ben warned.

"Please, man, she's harmless. I just wish that I hadn't overslept. I'd probably be tapping that ass right now."

Ben shook his head.

"Why are you shaking your head?" Omar asked.

"Never mind that; what reason are you going to give her for standing her up?"

"Who knows, I'll come up with some lame excuse like my best friend drunk some green shit and got really sick and…"

Ben shoved him playfully.

"What?"

"Don't put me in the middle of your mess. Just tell her one of your elaborate lies."

"Come on, bro. You know the truth is always a better alibi than a lie."

"You're right about that." Ben smiled, glancing from the window at the scenery.

"Women these days expect men to lie, so when they do, they're just digging a grave that's already there."

Ben nodded in agreement.

"Women are fools," Omar said. "They'll fall for anything."

"Yes, they will, my brother," Ben concurred.

"Man, all I want is for Asia to fall in my bed one time. I promise you I'll fuck the frost off her cold stuck-up ass."

"I heard how she disrespected a couple of the guys at Iris' party; is she really that cold?"

"Icy," Omar replied.

"Shit, if she's that cold, you might be better off sticking your dick in the freezer." Ben laughed.

"That's okay. Asia will do just fine." Omar glanced in the rearview mirror.

He turned up the volume on the and joined Ben in singing the chorus to the cheesy song.

"I stroke it to the east. I stroke it to the west. And I stroke it to the woman that I love the best. I be stroking."

Sticks and Stones may break my bones, but...

While parking, Omar's eyes were fixed on a large sign that hung over the storefront business. It read, *Joey's Pawnshop, We Buy and Sell Gold.*

"Man, don't tell me we drove all the way out to Passaic, New Jersey so you can go to a pawn shop."

"Okay, I won't tell you," Ben joked.

When they walked inside, Omar noticed a white male standing behind a counter at the far end of the store. He looked as if he could be in his mid-forties, had jet-black hair and a huge belly. His hairline was receding, and his face was scruffy; a real grease ball.

"Italian?" Omar whispered.

"As parmesan cheese," Ben replied. "Joey, how are you, baby?"

"I'm good, Ben. What can I do you out of?"

Ben chuckled.

The large white male stared at them as they approached the back of the store. The look on his face wasn't very inviting as he inhaled a large plate of sausage and peppers."

"What can I do for you, Ben?"

"You can make me a very happy man today." Ben said, casting his eyes on a photo that hung on the wall behind the counter. He recognized two of the mob bosses in the photo.

Omar glanced around the room while Ben conducted business. He had a funny feeling that something wasn't right.

"I told you, I can't do it for you."

"Come on man, stop playing with me. You told me the other day that it was a done deal." Ben's tone became less playful.

"What I told you the other day is not what I'm telling you now. Things change."

Ben chuckled and rubbed his chin, but the guy didn't smile or even blink. There wasn't even a hint of playfulness coming from him. Omar started to wonder, how in the hell does Ben even know this guy?

He turned his attention to a small television at the other end of the counter. "Hey, Ben, check this out. Your favorite movie is on."

Ben didn't respond.

"Ben! I said, Fight Club is on."

"Omar, would you give me a minute, please!" Ben snapped.

Omar took a step back.

"Joey, you said that you would do me this favor; now you're reneging?"

"I'm not reneging. The guys that I'm dealing with decided to go another direction."

"So, I rode all the way over here for nothing. Is that what you're telling me?" Ben retorted.

"If that's how you feel, what can I tell you? They changed their fuckin' minds; what do you want from me?"

"How can they change their minds at the last minute, Joey?" Ben's tone heightened.

"Look, buddy, I have things to do. So, if you don't mind, would you get the fuck out of here?"

Ben leered at him across the counter as if he could rip Joey's head off.

Omar tried to intervene.

"Ben, let's just go, man. We can get the equipment from somewhere else."

"So, it's like that, Joey?" Ben continued, ignoring Omar.

"I rode all the way to New Jersey for nothing?"

"What are you, deaf? I asked you to leave," Joey snapped, stepping from behind the counter.

"Ben, come on," Omar urged.

Once again, Ben ignored him.

"What, you want' a fuckin' problem?" Joey asked.

"No, no problem Joey," Omar quickly replied.
"Right, Ben?"
"Right, no problem at all, Joey."
They turned and headed out of the shop.
"That's right, listen to your buddy; you're probably fuckin' homos anyway."
Ben spun around slowly and stared at Joey.

Omar knew that Ben was about to do something he'd probably regret later. Ben had a short fuse and his wick had just been lit. He could hear the clicking of the muscles in Ben's hands as he balled his fingers into a massive fist.

"Ben, let's go!" Omar demanded.
Ben walked toward Joey.
"Man, come on. You don't need to do this. Let's go before this shit gets crazy." He turned and headed toward the door, expecting that Ben would follow.

Suddenly, there was a loud thump and then a crash. Omar spun around to find the guy lying on the floor. Ben struck him so hard that he was dazed and bleeding from the nose.

"Oh shit, Ben!"
"Shut the hell up," Ben said, walking out of the store and grabbing a stick from the garbage pail near the curb. He reentered the shop and began beating Joey with it.

"Man, what are you doing?" Omar yelled.
"I said, shut the hell up!"
After breaking the large piece of wood on Joey's legs, Ben became more aggravated. He grabbed a large paperweight made of stone off the counter and bashed Joey in the forehead.

Omar ran back toward Ben. "What are you doing?"
"I'm not doing anything!"
"No, then what is this?" Omar pointed.

Joey was lying on the floor and bleeding from the nose and forehead.

"You want some more, get up!" Ben shouted. "I got your homo, faggot!"

Omar grabbed Ben's arm and pulled him toward the door.

"Get off of me!" Ben yelled, tearing away. He raced back toward the counter, kicking Joey a final time.

"Man, come on!"

"No, I'm going to get something from this fat prick," Ben said, snatching a flat screen television from the counter.

"Man, would you come the fuck on!" Omar yelled.

"Hold the door," Ben scoffed. "Hey Joey, I guess it's true, sticks and stones will break your mother fucking' bones."

He bolted out of the shop with Omar behind him.

CHAPTER TEN

That's What Friends Are For

On the way back to Brooklyn, Omar and Ben got into a heated exchange.

"What the fuck is wrong with you?" Ben snapped.

"What's wrong with me? What the hell is wrong with you?" Omar fired back.

"There's nothing wrong with me; I'm perfectly fine."

"Is that why that guy is lying on the floor back there with one less tooth and bleeding from the nose?"

"He's lucky I didn't stomp the rest of his teeth out," Ben scoffed.

Omar rubbed his forehead.

"Oh, so now you have a problem with the way I handle my business?"

"No. I have a problem with you pulling a stunt like that when I'm with you."

"Right, I forgot, you're a lover, not a fighter," Ben commented sarcastically. "Maybe I need to stop hanging out with you so much. You're starting to get soft."

Ben's comment brought about a sharp response from Omar.

"You know what, Ben? I've had just about enough of your passive-aggressive bullshit."

"Who are you calling passive-aggressive?"

"You!"

"Is that right?"

"Yes, first you drag me all the way to West Bubble-Fuck when I thought we were going someplace else. Now you're upset because I didn't join you in jumping on a guy just because he wouldn't sell you a camera!"

"I didn't need you to jump in, man. I can handle myself."

"You're not a hoodlum, Ben!"

"You don't know what I am. You've had your face buried so far up Asia's behind the past few days, you don't even recognize your own face."

Omar was unappreciative of Ben's tone. The respect he had for him was quickly becoming outweighed by a desire to hit him in the jaw.

"Look, all I'm saying is that we're too smart to be out here brawling like a bunch of knuckleheads."

"I know that but when it comes down to it, that's what friends are for."

"To be out brawling like hoodlums?"

"No, to have each other's back."

"What if that guy was strapped?"

"Then while he was aiming at me, you could've taken him down." Ben glanced at his fist. "Oh, I forgot; you were too busy walking out on me."

"I thought you were behind me!" Omar barked.

"Yeah, well, I wasn't. That motherfucker promised me something and didn't follow through. He deserved what he got."

"It was a damn' camera, Ben!"

"Fuck that, I wanted what he promised me!"

"Yeah, but instead you got a damn flat screen monitor."

"Whatever...just drive," Ben scoffed.

Omar couldn't take any more of Ben's lip service. He pulled the car into a gas station as Ben watched him pump the gas.

"Let's go!" he yelled. "I don't have all fuckin' day!"

Omar climbed back into the car, agitated. "You have to stop this!"

"Stop what?"

"You know what. You're acting like a-" He fought the urge to continue.

"Like a what, Omar?" Ben shot him an intense look. "You know what? Fuck it! Let's just drop it." Omar ended the dispute.

Ben sneered as Omar pulled out his cell phone and made a call.

"Who are you calling?"

Omar ignored him, turning toward the open window. "Hey, baby, it's me!"

Ben squinted as he listened.

Over the next few minutes, Omar spun a web of lies that would make Spiderman look like an amateur. Ben listened closely as he'd spun a lie himself. He wasn't meeting with Joey to pick up a camera, there was much more to the story he hadn't shared with Omar.

When Omar finished his call, Ben clapped.

"You did that in record time."

"Thanks."

"Do you think she'll buy it?"

"She has no other choice."

"You're the man."

"Well, I learned from the best."

Ben smiled, accepting Omar's flattery.

"Can you put this away for me?" Omar handed him the cell phone. Ben opened the glove compartment and his eyes popped. Inside were four other cell phones just like the one Omar had handed him.

"Man, you really take the game seriously, huh?"

"Don't you." Omar quickly replied.

"Yes, but damn, four cell phones?"

"What can I say; some men talk a good game. I live by it."

"Yeah, I can see that. Man, your game is as serious as cancer."

A light bulb turned on in Omar's head.

"What's up?" Ben noticed the look in Omar's eyes. He had seen it before.

"Nothing, I just..."

"Man, I'm sorry about earlier. I was just tripping because that fat fuck screwed me over. You know, I didn't mean the things I said, right?"

"It's all okay. I wasn't paying your crazy ass any mind, anyway."

Ben chuckled.

They shook hands.

"So, do you want to go for drinks?"

Omar nodded, turned on the music, and then stepped on the gas.

"Next stop, The Time Café."

CHAPTER ELEVEN

Laying Down The Law

She hadn't heard from him all morning, and now he was calling with some lame excuse. Asia listened to the message Omar had left on her answering machine. He claimed to have a good reason for missing their jog.

According to Asia, though, there was no good reason. She figured that Omar had probably found someone else to spend his morning with since his plans to romp around with her had failed. Now he was calling, hours later, expecting that she would buy into whatever lie he had conjured up. It was so typical.

Tai had left a few messages as well. He had been calling ever since they ran into each other at the concert.

Asia had been avoiding his calls, for fear of rehashing old feelings. She hadn't forgotten the way Tai left her without so much as a goodbye. Although she still had feelings for him, she wasn't sure she could ever trust him again. Besides that, she was too involved with trying to get to know Omar.

After listening to her messages, she decided that she had to lay down the law with Omar. She was a firm believer that a woman can teach a man how to treat her, but she must start training him from the door. It was also clear that Omar needed to be put in check, quick. First, she needed to make an important call-one that couldn't wait.

On the other side of town...

"Damn, man, you were incredible! I didn't know you could put it down like that. I'm ready to explode just thinking about it," Ben said, placing his arm around Omar's shoulder.

"You act like you're surprised."

"I am. I mean, one minute we're having drinks, the next you're banging the bartender in the employee's bathroom."

"She wanted it, so I had to give it to her."

"I'm glad you did. Those drinks were starting to add up."

"Did she clear our tab?"

"Clear it? She burned it." Ben giggled.

Omar cracked a half smile.

"Hey, what's wrong?" Ben noticed the serious look that had formed on Omar's face. "Is everything okay?"

"Yeah, man, I was just thinking about something Iris said to me that night at the party."

"What did she say?"

"She said that I should keep my Johnson in my pants and try to be a better man."

"To hell with Iris; what does she know about being a man?"

"My thoughts exactly, but I do feel bad about standing Asia up."

Ben rolled his eyes.

"What did you give me that look for?"

"It was just a jog; she'll get over it."

"That's not the point."

"No? Well, what is the point?"

"The point is, don't you ever get tired of the lies?"

"No," Ben said, walking toward the car. "You know as well as I do, if Asia knew what you were into, she'd never approve of it."

"That's just it-we're grown men. Why do we need anyone's approval? Since we're not hurting anyone, there shouldn't be any problem with what we do."

"Yeah, well, that all sounds good coming from you. Unfortunately, that's not the way the world is."

Omar unlocked the car. "No matter how liberal the world has become, some things will never be that simple."

"I guess you're right." Omar glanced at his watch.

"Of course, I'm right."

A buzzing sound filled the car.

"Hey, grab that for me, will you?"

"What?" Ben looked around as if he hadn't a clue where the sound was coming from.

"The cell phone in the glove compartment, remember?"

Ben opened the glove compartment and handed over the cell phone.

"It's Asia." Omar smiled. "She just left me a message." He stepped from the car while he listened to his voice mail.

Ben's mind burned with a prediction-Asia was about to become a problem.

CHAPTER TWELVE

As Serious As Cancer

After dropping Ben off, Omar raced home to change his clothes. Asia requested that he meet her for dinner around six o'clock. He could tell by the tone of Asia's voice that he was in for a scolding. He gargled and then headed out to meet her.

Omar arrived at the restaurant late, which wasn't in his best interest. Especially since he had stood her up that same morning.

Before entering the dining area, he glanced around to see if he could spot her. He did; she was sitting at a table in the center of the room. He played it cool as he walked in.

Asia's eyes were locked on him as he strode through the crowded dining room. The look on her face was hard to read. Omar couldn't figure out if she was happy to see him, or if she thought that he was the scum of the earth. He would soon find out.

As Omar approached her, she looked him square in the eyes. The fact that she was displeased with his tardiness showed on her face. She stirred a cup of tea as if she were conjuring a spell.

A passing waitress tried to draw Omar's attention by flashing a smile, but he ignored her. He didn't dare take his eyes off Asia for a second. He assessed from the slow and deliberate stirring of her tea that she was conjuring up something terrible for him.

Asia wore a stunning pink dress that had every woman in the restaurant feeling the sting of her presence. It was evident by the way they were clinging to the arms of their men and scowling at her from their seats. For most, it would have simply been easier just to acknowledge the fact that they were unequal to her in beauty, but women can be so catty.

He leaned in to kiss her cheek when he arrived at the table.

"Hey, babe, I'm sorry I'm late, but-"

She turned away.

Embarrassed, he glanced around to see if anyone else felt the chill of Asia's cold greeting. A few people had. He pulled out a seat, took a deep breath, and began to offer an explanation.

She interrupted. "You use that word '*but*' as if it's a get-out-of-jail-free-ticket."

"What are you talking about?"

She continued to stir her tea. "I'm talking about the night we met at the party. Clearly, I wasn't interested in meeting anyone that night, *but* you came over and introduced yourself to me anyway."

Confused, Omar's mouth tightened.

"I didn't ask you to drive me home that night after the party, *but* you insisted and like a fool I let you."

He tried to cut in, but she wouldn't let him.

"I asked you to slow down on the highway the other night, *but* you didn't, and you nearly got a ticket."

Omar sat back in his seat.

"I told you that you didn't have to go jogging with me, *but* you insisted...and then you stood me up. Now you walk in here fifteen minutes late with another *but* and I'm supposed to what? Be happy?"

Although slightly taken aback, he knew precisely where her scolding was coming from. It was the very reason he avoided relationships in the first place. Like most men, Omar hated drama, and to him, that's exactly what this was. At one point, he thought about walking out of the restaurant and heading back home but decided against it. Instead, he analyzed her every word and determined that the fact that she was so upset with him meant only one thing. She wanted him badly.

He sat quietly for the next few minutes, allowing her to vent.

"And another thing, Omar, I don't appreciate..."

At that moment, every word from Asia's mouth became muted. As far as Omar was concerned, she was full of hot air and only throwing a tantrum because she didn't get what she wanted. The fact that he had also shown up late to the restaurant was just another reason for her to fuss.

"Are you finished? Can I explain now?" he asked.

"Can you?" she spat.

He took a deep breath, exhaled slowly and began to explain.

"Wait, before you start, let me warn you; I already think you're a lying jerk, so anything you say that even remotely sounds like bullshit, is going to confirm my thoughts further and you might get this cup of hot tea thrown at you before this is all over."

He paused.

"As I was about to say, I got a call from my mom early this morning."

"And?"

He lowered his head.

Her eyes widened in anticipation of bad news.

"Omar?"

He took a few moments to respond.

"I just found out she might have cancer." He lowered his head farther.

Asia was shocked; she reached across the table and grabbed his hand. "Oh, my God, Omar, I'm sorry."

"No, I'm the one that's sorry. I didn't mean to drop this on you. Especially, since I've been so thoughtless."

"No, I'm the one that's been thoughtless. Here you are going through a tough time and all I could do is jump down your throat for something that wasn't even your fault. I feel like such a fool."

He smiled internally. He had successfully managed to transfer his guilt to her.

"It's not your fault either. I know I didn't handle things correctly, but I'm just trying to figure things out right now, you know?"

"Is there anything I can do, anything at all?" She stroked the top of his hand.

"There is something that you can do that will make me feel better." He raised his head slowly.

"What is it?"

"Well, you can…" He placed his hand on top of hers and began to stroke her fingers suggestively as he looked her directly in the eyes. "You can let me pay for dinner."

"You don't have to do that. I mean, I didn't have the right to be angry in the first place. It's not like we're a couple, you know?"

"Yeah, well, if I hope to change that one day, I have to start by being more accountable."

Omar knew that no woman could resist a man that insisted on being accountable. It meant that he would be responsible for his actions, his whereabouts, his faults, and his mistakes. Most importantly, it showed the willingness to do better and to be better. He had pulled that one straight out the playa's handbook. It was a smart move on his part, and he knew it. In fact, if Asia fell for that one, the next one would blow her straight out of her seat and right into his arms.

"I've been thinking about you a lot lately," he said leaning in a little.

"I've been thinking about you, too."

"Wow! That makes me feel a lot better." He held her hand.

"All day long I've been wondering where you were, what you were doing, and if I'd ever get the chance to take you out again. I wanted to call, but I didn't know if-" He hesitated, looking away in a dramatic show of restraint.

"If what?"

"Oh, nothing, I'm just being silly."

"No, you're not. I want to hear what you have to say." She studied him carefully.

"It's just that I didn't know if you felt the same way. I don't want to look like a fool by pursuing someone who is not interested in me."

"Well, you don't have to worry about that; I'm definitely interested.

His face lit up.

"What are you thinking?" she asked, taking a sip of tea.

"I don't know. It's just that it seems so unfair for me to feel this happy, knowing that my mom isn't well at all." He became choked-up.

The dramatic display of emotion sliced right through what was left of Asia's ice-princess demeanor. The thought of his mom being sick affecting him that way, opened a soft spot that she secretly held in her heart for him.

She walked over to his side of the table and wrapped her arms around him so tight that his face was pressed tight against her breasts.

"I know it's hard baby, but you have to be strong, for her and for yourself."

Omar sat with his face pressed firmly against her perky bosom, his eyes panning between them and his crotch, thinking, *you have no idea how HARD it is for me now. However, if you just glance down at my lap, you will get a great big idea.*

"You do know that she's going to be okay, don't you?" Asia did her best to encourage him.

"That's what she says, too, but she's in Georgia, and I'm here. Don't get me wrong; she's a strong woman, but I know she has to be very frightened."

"I'm sure she is, but she'll be okay. And you will too."

"I don't know that."

She placed a soft kiss on his forehead and began rubbing his back."

"I just don't know if I can do this alone," he said, sniffling a little.

"You don't have to; we can get through this together. If that's what you want."

His eyebrow rose and, in his mind, he, thought, *MISSION ACCOMPLISHED.*

He had managed to turn the tables on her; she was no longer concerned about being stood up; instead, she was concerned about him; nor did she care how tardy he had been. The only thing on Asia's mind was making sure that he was okay.

"I don't want you to worry. I know we've only known each other a short while, but I'm here for you." Asia continued to console him.

Meanwhile, he continued with his performance.

"Sweetheart, I can't ask you to deal with this; we've just met, and I don't want to burden you with my problems."

"That doesn't matter; I'm going to be here for you."

Like so many women, she had a soft spot for men in need, thinking if she helped him through a bad time, he'd see how much of a good woman she is and perhaps, well, just perhaps...She guided his chin upward and kissed him. The move was unexpected but desired. Omar closed his eyes and received her kiss. When their lips touched, it was everything he thought it would be, soft, sweet, and sensual. He wanted more-a lot more.

Unfortunately, the maître d' had noticed Asia standing and made his way to their table.

"Is everything all right, ma'am?"

"Yes, everything is fine," Asia said as she returned to her seat.

"Good, then I'll send your waiter over immediately." She smiled at him.

Seconds later, a young woman came to take their order. Asia recognized her as the waitress that had smiled at Omar when he arrived. She looked her up and down, paying close attention to her tight uniform and unkempt ghetto-girl hairdo.

Omar glanced across the table and noticed Asia's expression as the woman approached. When she arrived at the table, clearly, she had a bad attitude. The rolling of her eyes and the twisting of her lips were immediate indications of that.

Asia attempted to defuse the probability of a confrontation by being cordial. Her warm smile, however, was not returned. That's when she noticed the folded order pad shoved into the waitress' back pocket and that all her attention was focused on Omar.

Omar read the look on Asia's face and was about to comment but decided to let her handle things instead. He wanted to see if she was as feisty with other women as she was with him. Everything on the menu looked great; making a choice was hard. Asia's eyes rolled across the menu, pausing briefly on a dish made of scallops, tilapia, and red onions. She had a question about the accompanying side dishes and asked the waitress if she could explain. The rude waitress dismissed Asia's question, turning her focus to Omar instead.

At that time, he was glancing across the table at Asia. He could tell by the look on her face that she was fighting the urge to confront the waitress about her gawking, her lack of manners, and her need for a good perm.

Asia wasn't one for public scenes unless it was unavoidable. She inquired about the dish once more but was ignored a second time.

"That's it! Excuse me, but I'm inquiring about something on the menu. Do you think you can stop gawking at my friend long enough to answer my question?" Asia snapped at the waitress.

"Can you wait a minute?"

"What?" Asia stared across the table at Omar, as if to say, *Oh, no, this tacky-head heifer didn't.*

Omar interjected. "Miss, would you take my lady's order, please?"

The look on the waitress' face telegraphed her desire to do whatever he asked while rolling across the table at Asia as if she was the scorn of single women.

"Sure Sweetie," the waitress replied, batting her faux-fur eyelashes at Omar. She turned aggressively toward Asia, rolling her neck, "What was your question?"

"Do you have the creamed asparagus soup?"

"No."

"What about the German fried potatoes?"

"No."

"Lobster bisque?"

"No, we don't have that either."

"Well, Jesus, is there any side dish you do have?"

Asia chuckled.

"Look Ms. I have other tables to wait on. So, do you know what you want or not?" the waitress asked gruffly.

"No, but I know what you want!" Asia retorted, staring at her in disgust.

"Oh, girl, don't nobody want your man." She waved her hand at Asia as if dismissing her and her comment.

That was the last straw; Asia summoned for the maître d' to fetch the manager.

"So now you're going to call my manager, are you serious?"

"As cancer!" Asia replied. "Excuse me, Omar."

"It's okay," Omar gestured.

"Whatever! Sir, can I take your order?" The waitress turned her attention back to Omar.

He looked at Asia as if seeking a confirmation nod, which never came. Instead, he got the rolling of eyes as Asia shifted her glare from him to the waitress.

"First off, that 'oh girl' stuff doesn't work with me; I'm not one of your little nappy-headed girlfriends. So, you really need to leave that ghetto language in the hood where it belongs."

The waitress was embarrassed and immediately fired back.

"Wait a minute, who are you calling ghetto?" She took an aggressive posture.

"If the gold tooth fits, wear it," Asia taunted.

As their voices grew louder, a thin white male made his way over to the table, "Ma'am, is everything okay?"

"No, it's not; are you the manager?" Asia shifted her focus from the waitress briefly.

"Yes, I am. What seems to be the problem?

"The problem is that I came to this restaurant expecting to have an enjoyable meal and all I've gotten so far is attitude."

"I'm sorry ma'am, is there anything I can do?"

"Yes, you can tell this poor excuse for a waitress to stop gawking at my guest, refusing to take my order, and never again to address me with street slang."

"I wasn't gawking at anyone; it's just the way I look. If you have a problem with it, I'm sorry."

"Yes, you are. Not only that, but you insult beautiful black women all over this planet by walking around with your hair looking like something exploded in it."

The waitress' mouth fell open, as did Omar's and the managers. He cut his eyes toward the waitress as if it weren't the first time someone had complained about her.

"I apologize; please accept your meals on the house," he said, scowling at the waitress.

Omar smiled as he watched from across the table, but Asia still wasn't happy-she continued.

"Thank you, but we are perfectly capable of paying for our meals. However, I would like you to inform your wait staff, that is, if there's any more like her in the back, that they're in a customer service position, so they should serve."

"Wait a minute." The waitress tried to interject, but Asia wouldn't let her.

"No, you wait a minute! You need to understand that I am not your equal in age, in style, nor in class, and certainly not in earned wages. Which means you will respect me; and if I ever make the mistake of visiting this tired restaurant again and you make the mistake of disrespecting me the way you did earlier, the next time I raise my hand won't be to summon your manager."

Omar's mouth fell open. Asia had flipped the script on the waitress and on Omar's perception of her. Her words slit through the waitress like a sharp knife. By the time Asia finished with her, she was just standing there with her mouth hanging open, looking as foolish as she had behaved.

The manager's eyebrows rose. The next thing they knew, he angrily guided the waitress toward the back of the restaurant.

Omar was shocked. Asia had completely handled the situation without his assistance. Although he thought she might have been a bit rough on the waitress, he quietly applauded her.

"Way to go, champ," he joked.

Asia lifted her foot beneath the table, running her toes against the side of his leg, then between them, causing him to jump, nearly knocking the centerpiece from the table.

She laughed.

"Funny. We'll see who's laughing later," he playfully threatened.

She reached down to retrieve her purse from beside her chair.

"I'll get you back for that."

"What are you going to do, Omar?" She checked her makeup in a small mirror and through its reflection saw another waitress making her way over to their table.

"Good evening," she said, greeting Asia first and then Omar.

They greeted her warmly as she placed an ice bucket and a bottle of wine on their table.

"What's this?" Omar asked.

"The manager would like you to have this complimentary bottle of wine on the house."

"Wow, a lovely Riesling. Nice," Omar spoke softly.

"May I take your orders?" the pleasant waitress asked.

"Yes, you may," Omar replied, gesturing for her to take Asia's order first.

Asia smiled.

After placing their orders, they watched as waitress number two headed back to the kitchen.

"She sure is friendly," Asia said, placing her compact back in her purse.

Omar didn't respond right away; he just sat there enjoying how gorgeous Asia was; her fiery temperament stirred his curiosity. What would she be like in bed?

"What are you looking at?"

"I'm looking at you."

"I know that, but why are you looking at me that way?" Asia inquired.

"What way?"

"Like you want to eat me alive."

"I do; I want to devour you." He licked his lips, slowly undressing her with his eyes.

The heat of his stare caused her to shift in her seat, fiddle with the straps on her purse, fold and unfold her napkin-and his, to maintain her composure.

"Are you okay?"

"I'm fine," she lied, searching for a diversion. "So, does your mom also live in Brooklyn?"

"No, she lives in Georgia, but I told you that before."

"Right, you did. Does she live alone?"

"No, I have a nineteen-year-old sister who lives with her, but that's a whole other story."

"Nineteen? Wow, I remember those days."

Asia's sudden delve into idle chatter was a clear sign that she was uncomfortable. Being the gentleman that he is, Omar withdrew from his leering.

"Do you remember what it was like to be nineteen?" Asia asked.

"You act as though I'm in a wheelchair and wearing adult diapers. Yes, I remember what it was like being nineteen; it wasn't that long ago."

"Oh, I'm sorry, I didn't mean to imply."

"Yes, you did." Asia chuckled.

"Those were the good old days. The only thing I had to worry about then, was keeping up with the latest style of haircut."

"Oh, don't tell me you had a flat top." She laughed as she imagined him.

"That's right-a flat top, a carrot top, and a shag, too."

"I would give anything to have seen that."

"Well, if you ever come over to my place to visit, I'll show you some pictures."

Asia smiled at him.

"You know, you have the most beautiful smile."

"Thank you." She blushed.

As they sat spellbound, staring at each other across the table, the waitress returned with their orders - seared salmon with vegetables and a fresh artichoke salad. The servings were large enough to feed a small army.

Almost an hour later...

Asia dabbed her mouth with a napkin as the waitress returned to clear away their plates.

"Will you be having dessert?" she asked.

Asia and Omar looked at each other and shook their heads in unison.

"Our servings were more than enough, thank you," Asia answered.

Omar sat back in his seat rubbing his belly. He couldn't eat another bite. The waitress smiled, placed the check in front of him, and walked away. Asia savored the last of her wine as Omar reached for the check.

"Damn!"

"What is it?"

"My wallet; I must have lost it in haste to get here.

Asia removed the napkin from her lap, placed it on the table, sat straight up, and said, "Can I ask you a question?"

"Sure," he patted his pant pockets repeatedly as if patting them would cause his wallet to appear magically.

"Do you expect me to believe that you lost your wallet on the way over here?"

"I must have."

"What you 'must have' is eggs for brains if you expect me to fall for that one."

"What?"

"Oh, please, don't play naïve. I've seen this trick played on women many times before. A guy goes out to meet a woman for a meal, purposely leaves his wallet at home, claiming to have lost it on the way to the restaurant. That way he doesn't have to pay for the expensive meal. It's the oldest trick in the book."

"Is that what you think I'm doing?"

"Isn't it?"

"I don't even believe you would say something like that to me."

"Come on, I mean, really. This whole thing is a bit juvenile. First, you stand me up for a date, and then you arrive at the restaurant late and without your wallet. What am I supposed to think?"

"Hey, you know what? I don't really give a damn what you think. I'm telling you I had the wallet when I left home."

"Right." Asia mumbled as she returned to sipping.

Omar sat back in his seat...thinking. *Is this chick a descendent of Sybil? We just had a wonderful meal and now the check comes, and she decides to flip out?*

"Just give me the check, Omar; I'll pay it. I don't have time to be sitting in this restaurant looking like a bunch of broke ass crack heads trying to stiff out on the bill."

"Crack heads?"

She pulled a credit card from her purse and flagged for the waitress to collect the check.

"That's not necessary," Omar said, snatching the check pad away from her.

"So, if you don't have any money, how are you going to pay the bill, with your looks?"

"Perhaps," he replied, glancing under the table. Asia sat across from him with her face screwed up, thinking, *yeah, right you're not that cute.*

Just as Asia was preparing herself to get up and walk out the maître d' made his way over to them.

"Excuse me, sir, one of the guests found this on the way out. I believe you might have dropped it."

Omar's eyes widened in relief, as the maître d' handed him his wallet.

Asia was both astonished and embarrassed.

"Thank you so much," Omar beamed. He opened the wallet and checked quickly to see if anything was missing-nothing was.

Asia's face flustered with embarrassment.

"Omar, I'm sorry, I thought-"

"I know what you thought."

The maître d' sneered. After Omar paid the check, he escorted Asia from the restaurant. On the way out, he winked at the maître d', who nodded at him on the sly.

CHAPTER THIRTEEN

I'm Just Doing Me

Asia sat quietly in the car; Omar could tell she was embarrassed because she of her earlier assumption about him not wanting to pay for their meals. It was the perfect opportunity to introduce her to another side of him; it was all part of his plan.

"Hey, are you just going to sit there and not talk to me?" He placed his hand on her thigh.

She turned her face toward the window.

"What am I supposed to say?"

"I don't know; what do you feel like saying?"

"Just that I'm sorry and I will never doubt you again."

"Those were very powerful words, you know?"

"I know."

For the next few minutes, Asia beat herself up over her lack of faith in men. Omar treated her well and she was screwing things up royally. Had she become so rigid, so untrusting of men, that she thinks the worst of every man she meets? Perhaps she was scared to be wrong about Omar. Perhaps she expected him to be just like all the other guys she had met in the past. Her mind flashed back to her relationship with Tai and the way he had left her to pursue his career in music.

Omar noticed that her attention had drifted.

"Hey, it's okay, let's just forget it."

"It's not okay!"

"I don't want to talk about it anymore; it's forgotten." He gripped her hand.

The look on her face was one of disbelief.

"How come you're being so nice to me? Any other guy would have left me back at the restaurant."

"I don't know, maybe because I'm just a nice guy."

"Seriously, most guys would've pointed me to the nearest subway and never spoken to me again."

"Well, I'm not most guys."

"I can see that, Mr.-" She paused.

"What is it?"

"I can't believe it; this is the second time we've gone out and I don't even know your last name."

"Don't feel bad, the last woman I brought to dinner didn't know it either," he chuckled.

"Seriously, Omar, what is your last name?"

He hesitated.

She stared at him.

"Hicks; my last name is Hicks."

"Omar Hicks, that's a nice name." She looked at him with hope. He had paid for their meal and told her his last name. She was starting to let her guard down. "Can we talk seriously for a moment?"

"Sure, come on."

"I just want to know what you're looking for."

Omar's forehead wrinkled, "Looking for?"

Once again, he started playing stupid. He knew exactly what she meant, but like most men, he played dumb to avoid having to answer the question. Not because he was trying to be a jerk and not because he wanted to hurt her feelings; that would have been counterproductive to his goal of getting her in bed. Although most men probably would have told her exactly what she wanted to hear just for the sake of moving the conversation along, he wasn't about to. He didn't like being backed into a corner. Before he would answer Asia's question, he needed to get her to reveal her hand. Then he would play his cards accordingly.

"I want to know what your intentions are when you take a woman out."

"Wow! I've never been asked that question before. Do I get a kiss if I answer correctly?" he joked to distract her, but she was not going to be swayed. She wanted an answer.

"Come on, be serious. We're both adults, so we should be able to talk, right?"

Omar nodded.

She looked at him as if expecting him to blurt out a magical answer, which he wasn't about to do. How he answered was crucial. If he took the high road, she would clam up for the rest of the night and perhaps they'd never see each other again. If he took the low road, the conversation would at least become intense, but he'd still be the one in control.

"To tell you the truth, Asia, I'm just doing me right now. I'm not really looking for anything. I'm taking things one day at a time and enjoying each day as it comes."

Asia hated that line 'I'm just doing me right now.' What in the hell does that mean? You're just doing you while you're trying to do me and every other woman you meet, too?

"Oh, please." She folded her arms.

"What's wrong?"

"You want me to believe that you just go around starting conversations with women at parties with no intentions? How old are you again?"

"I'm twenty-nine. What does that have to do with anything and why do you find it so hard to believe?"

"Men these days are always looking for something, whether it's a quick lay or a place to stay, sometimes both.

So, you have to forgive me if I look as though I don't believe you."

"Baby girl, I have my own place, and as far as a quick lay, I don't know what that is. I've known you for nearly a week and the most you've given me is a peck on the lips."

"Stop playing with me."

"I'm not playing with you, yet."

As much as Asia tried to be serious, she enjoyed the back and forth flirting. She often wrestled between what her body was feeling and what her mind was thinking.

He reached for her hand, again.

She pulled away.

"Why do you keep doing that? Aren't you attracted to me?"

"Please, Omar, I'm attracted to cheesecake; that doesn't mean I want to sleep with one."

"Is that what this is about? Do you think I'm just looking to sleep with you?"

"All I'm saying is that I'm not looking to become another statistic. All my life I've watched women get their hearts broken because they mistook lust for love. I don't want to be that woman. I won't be that woman."

"I'm not asking you to be."

"Good, then answer my question."

"Right now, I'm just taking things one day at a time, as I said. I'd like to have a special woman in my life one day but finding one hasn't been easy."

Asia listened, but the look on her face telegraphed her skepticism.

"Oh, you don't believe me?"

"No, I don't."

"Why is that? Is it so hard to believe that a man would have a hard time finding a good woman?"

"That's not what I said. I said I don't believe you're having a hard time finding a good woman." Omar noticed that traffic was getting heavy.

"So, what is that supposed to mean, Asia?"

"It means that there are plenty of good women in the world and if you don't have one, it's probably because you don't want one."

Asia searched in her purse for a stick of gum.

"So, basically you're saying my being single is my fault."

"I'm saying if a man is single and he wants to change his status, all he has to do is avail himself to the possibilities."

Omar was great at playing chess, so he welcomed the game of intellect. He knew the way to win a debate was to make his opponent lose focus, which given Asia's relentlessness, would take some skill-luckily, he had lots of it. He couldn't care less whether women have a harder time finding a good man than men had finding a good woman. He just wanted a good lay and he was about to trump her statement.

"Okay, Ms. Know-It-All, why are so many women walking around single then? If all anyone has to do is avail themselves to the possibilities, shouldn't we all be running to the marriage chapels?"

"Well, I believe women want to be certain about who they are going to spend the rest of their lives with."

"Oh, please, you know good and well that you can never really know a person that well."

"I know, but there's no harm in taking the time to learn the basics about someone you're dating before sleeping with them."

"The basics...you mean like what brand of underwear he buys or if he snores?"

"No. I mean like does he want children, can he be a faithful partner, and is he a good provider."

"So, you think you should find that entire list out after a few dates?"

"It's possible."

"It's also possible for a guy to tell you what you want to hear just to get what he wants."

Asia sat pondering, "Are you trying to tell me something?"

"No, I'm just saying maybe the reason so many women are single is because they really don't know what they want."

"Omar, as good looking as you are, I think you would know a little more about women than that but since you don't, let me fill you in."

Asia began to ramble on about how men lie, cheat and mistreat women, and how there was an extreme shortage of good men in the world, particularly good black men.

Omar fought to contain his laughter but was unsuccessful.

"What's so funny?"

"I'm sorry, 'a shortage of good black men', Asia? Who the hell told you that, Terry McMillan?"

"No, it's a fact; I researched it."

"You researched it, huh?"

"That's right. I'm telling you at the rate things are going, the only way for a black woman to find a good black man is to build one or dig one out of the grave. Neither of which seems like a bad idea as of late." She glanced out of the window."

He let out a hearty chuckle.

"Oh, that's funny?"

"Yes."

"Really; so, you find humor in a woman having to consider dating an illegal alien to get a little affection?"

"You can't be serious?"

She looked at him as if to say, try me.

As intelligent as he knew Asia was, her statement was the most ignorant thing that he had ever heard.

"I'm serious, Omar, I'm actually thinking about it."

"Well, then, I think you should do it."

Asia stared at him, confused.

"Don't look at me like that. Go down to the Caribbean and marry one of those island boys, and next year when everything's interrupted, don't call me, call Terry McMillan; no, better yet, call Star Jones; she's a lawyer." He chuckled.

"You really think this is a joke, don't you?"

"Yes, I do. It's funny."

"What's funny, is the way you black men walk around grabbing your crotches and acting like you have it all together when you don't."

"Is that right?"

"That's right. The truth is, at least twenty-five percent of you are unemployed, another twenty-five percent is living with a woman who's taking care of you, and the other fifty percent is so relationship phobic that they can't commit to anything other than scratching their nuts."

"Wow!"

"Meanwhile, black women have been reduced to having to consider dating outside of our race to find even a little bit of happiness. That's what's funny."

Omar's laughter dissipated. She had struck a nerve.

"I don't know why I waste my time going out with black men. I should just find me a white man."

"You say that shit as if being with a white man is some prize," Omar snapped.

"Compared to going out with some of the black men I meet, it would be like living on Christmas Island."

Omar was pissed. He rolled his eyes and pulled the car over to the curb. "Okay, Ms. Jungle Fever, get out."

"Wait, What?"

He pushed a button that unlocked the passenger side door.

"Don't even think about it!" Asia said, the look in her eyes becoming tense.

"I'm just saying, since black men are no damn good, you shouldn't have a problem finding some random white guy to swoop down in a Superman outfit to whisk you off to Harlem!"

Her mouth fell open.

"You know, Asia, maybe black men are just waiting for black women to step up without all the strings and neediness."

"Pardon me!"

"All I ever hear about is what a black woman needs."

"So, you blame us for having aspirations?"

"No, I blame Oprah for that. The minute she told black women to dream big, you all lost your damn minds."

Asia grinned.

"I'm serious, what about what black men need?"

"You tell me; what do black men need?"

He gazed at a woman with a big ass as she crossed the intersection.

"Besides that!" She hit him on the arm.

He laughed.

The conversation had progressed just as he planned. They were no longer discussing her wants, but his. Little did Asia know, though, he was about to make her night, or as he says in his game of mental chess, take her knight.

"I can't speak for other men because this conversation isn't about them."

"Oh, it's not?" Asia replied, pulling a small bottle of lotion from her purse and applying some to her hands.

"No, it's about you and me."

Omar's being straightforward came as a shock.

"Go on."

"I'm a good man. I take care of myself and I make a good living. Just because I'm not dating anyone exclusively right now, most women I meet assume I'm a playa. Why is that?"

"I don't know; perhaps it's because of the car you drive. Or maybe it's because of the way you dress."

"So, you're saying if I drove a Toyota Camry and wore off the rack clothing, I'd be in a committed relationship by now?"

"No, what I'm saying is that men who drive fancy cars and dress like you do usually have a stream of women trailing behind them. If not on purpose, they become playas by default. If I were a guy, I'd probably have a slew of women trailing behind me, too."

His eyes lit up.

"Wait, that's not to say I condone the ill-treatment of women; I don't. It's just that some of us can be so stupid, but that withstanding, men should learn to keep their dicks in their pants and bring their black ass home to one woman. Then, we wouldn't have all the problems with cheating and infidelity."

"What if the man makes it clear from the beginning that he's not looking to commit to one woman; do you still consider that cheating?"

"Of course, I do."

"Why?"

"Omar, you know as well as I do that at least one of those women is going to believe that the relationship is more than it probably is."

"And you think that's the man's fault?"

"Yes, I do."

"Interesting; so, what's the responsibility of the woman in all of this?"

"Well, I think we women need to make better choices about who we share our bodies with; especially since so many of you men see us as nothing more than sexual conquests."

"So, now I'm included in that group?"

"Well, Omar, you are a guy."

"Yeah, but I've never let a woman believe that my association with her was anything other than what I said it was. I don't believe in stringing folks along."

"Good, then that brings us back to my original question. What are your intentions with me?"

Damn, she's good, he thought.

The traffic was getting heavier, so Omar used that fact to focus on the road and to buy some time before answering her question. He maneuvered the car slowly across the merging lanes.

"I'm waiting." Asia folded her arms and waited for an answer.

He thought about telling her what she wanted to hear, just to make her happy; which clearly would have meant foregoing his own happiness. Since that wasn't about to happen, he resorted to another trick from the playa's handbook.

Asia had made a big mistake by confronting him about his 'intentions'. He knew what she wanted to hear and sat quietly, plotting.

She watched and waited while he appeared to be mulling things over. She was convinced that she had him cornered again. What he would do next, however, would be one for the record books.

"Okay, Asia, you want an answer, here goes. I like you very much and I enjoy spending time with you. Do I know where things are going with us? No, but I'm hopeful things will progress with time."

She was stunned; she didn't know how to respond. In one breath, he had managed to flatter her, give her hope, painted her a world of possibilities and still hadn't told her shit. It was ingenious-the way he left her hanging.

"So, you're saying that you can have a friendship with a woman that's strictly plutonic?"

"Yes,"

"I don't believe you."

The look on Omar's face changed, reminding her of the promise she made never to doubt him again.

"Come on, Omar, you're a good-looking man. Women practically throw themselves at you."

"Yeah, but that's because of the way I dress. Isn't that what you said?"

"So, are you telling me that you never get the urge to sleep with any of the women you befriend?" She performed the quotation signs with her fingers.

"No, I'm telling you that if I make a choice to sleep with a woman, it's because we both understand the dynamics of our association."

"Really, so what are the 'dynamics' of our association, Omar?"

"That depends. Do you want to sleep with me?" Asia blushed. She was so overwhelmed by his forwardness that she abandoned her usual sense of logic. Any other time, she would have been insulted by such a flagrant invitation for sex. Deep down, she knew that a decent man would never ask a woman if she wanted to sleep with him for fear of coming across too strong. Yet, on the surface, she couldn't help smiling.

"Come on now, we're both adults, remember?" He mimicked her words from earlier.

She sat quietly.

"You know what, Asia? If you don't want to, it's fine. I'll only be heartbroken for the rest of my life."

Still no response.

He touched her leg. "You don't have to tell me now. In fact, I'd prefer it if you wouldn't. Think about it and when you're ready, let me know, okay?"

"Okay," she replied softly.

Meanwhile, Asia's loins were ablaze from the feel of Omar's hand on her thigh. She glanced out of the window thinking, Lord, please let this man take his hand off my leg before I go into convulsions.

"Oh, yeah, about the way that I dress; if it's not fair for a woman to be judged by her style of dress, then the same consideration should be given to men. Don't you think so?"

Asia gritted her teeth.

"Furthermore, I think men should start classifying women as we've been classified."

She started to get nervous. She checked her purse for a cigarette. His hand was still on her leg and it was driving her crazy.

"It's simple. Women are always classifying men as either good men or bad men, based on how much they can get out of us. So, I think we should start doing the same to them."

She looked at him as if he was speaking gibberish.

"Don't look at me like that. You know it's not fair that a man will go out and work a sixty-hour week; come home exhausted, and the first thing out of a woman's mouth is, 'where's my money?' If he gives it up, then he's a good man. If he hesitates, even for a second, then he's a no-good dog, a lying bastard, and his Mama should be ashamed to call him her son."

Asia chuckled.

"You're only laughing because you know it's true. As long as a man does what a woman thinks he should do, like paying bills, giving her money, taking care of kids even if they aren't his, then she has nothing to say, but the minute he's down on his luck, or between jobs, he becomes the topic of discussion amongst the girlfriends."

"That's not true." She grinned.

"Yes, it is. Hell, some of you would be ready to post our pictures on www.dontdatehimgirl.com."

She laughed heartily.

"Oh, you didn't think I knew about that, right? I have a lot of women in my family, Asia. I know things."

"Well, some men deserve to be put on blast."

"Yeah, well, some trifling ass women do, too."

Asia continued her search for a cigarette.

"What about all the men out there screwing around on good women, making babies all over the place, but not taking care of any of them? Are they good men, too, Omar?"

He flinched.

"Oh, now I've got your attention." She found a cigarette and lit it with precision, as if igniting a cannon "What about all the women who go out to work, mow the lawn, cook, clean, shop, perform tirelessly through sex that has either grown mundane or damn near funny, while some lame ass loser sits around playing video games and complaining that no one wants to hire his tired ass?"

Omar erupted in laughter.

"What about those men, Omar?" Asia's words were sharp and deliberate.

"Hold up, Asia, I'm not either of those men. So once again, I can't speak for them. What I can say, is that I can be anything to any woman; any fantasy, any daydream, any reality. That is, within the dynamics of our-"

Asia cut him off. "I know, 'Of your agreed association', blah, blah, blah!"

Asia was getting bored. The conversation had become predictable.

"So, it makes sense to you then?"

"Not really; it sounds a bit pimp-ish to me."

"Pimp-ish? Tell me something, Asia. If I want my woman to work, come home, cook dinner, and lay her paycheck on my dresser, does that make me a pimp or a bad guy?"

"Both!"

"Okay, well, if I go to work, come home, lay out money for food, clothes, shoes, hair, nails, bills and kids that probably aren't mine, who's the pimp then?"

Asia was quiet.

"All I'm saying is men deserve to have their needs met, too."

"So, are you saying that you want a woman to take care of you?"

"No, but I think I should be paid for my services," he replied facetiously.

Asia's forehead wrinkled; she didn't find him the least bit amusing.

"Hey, what's good for the goose is good for the gander."

"Well, I've never been fond of geese and for the record, I'm not taking care of any man." Asia rolled her eyes and flicked ashes from her cigarette out of the window.

The look on Omar's face read, we'll see about that.

For the next few minutes, there was no conversation; that is, until Asia decided that she needed to deliver a final blow.

"So, Pimp Omar, how much do I owe you for driving me home?"

"How much you got?" Omar retorted.

Asia found his comment to be crass, yet there was something about Omar that stirred the lioness in her. She taunted him.

"A few minutes ago, you said you weren't looking for anything; now you're charging for your services?"

"That's right, and you can pay me in kisses." Omar stopped for a light, leaned over, and kissed her.

Asia saw sparks. She felt a stream of emotion shoot from her heart straight down to her vagina. She hadn't felt that in a long time-not since "Oh, Tai."

Omar's eyes widened, "What did you say?"

"I said I'm tired; it's been a long day.

"I hear you. So, do you still want to get to know me?" he asked, strumming her face.

By that time, she was finding it increasingly hard to speak, especially since he put his tongue in her mouth right after he asked the question. Within seconds, they drifted into a faraway place, where making love was the only thing on either of their minds. For a few minutes, there was no one else in the universe. Their groove was all their own. That is, until the honking of horns doused their special moment.

"Oh shit!" Omar turned his focus back to the road.

"We're blocking traffic," Asia said, touching the corner of her mouth.

"I would block the entrance to heaven if it meant I could spend more time with you."

She blushed. Omar's words were syrupy but charming.

"So, can I get you to come?"

"Excuse me?"

"To my place," Omar said, clarifying his intentions as he grabbed her hand. "I'd like you to see where I live."

"I don't know; it's late and I don't want you to expect anything."

"Don't worry; I won't. I promise."

She smiled. Omar read the look in her eyes and headed into Brooklyn.

CHAPTER FOURTEEN

Bongs, Black Lacquer, and Marijuana

Ben had been calling all day, but Omar had been ignoring his calls. His plans were to spend as much time with Asia as possible. He clicked on the lights.

Asia's eyes widened.

"This is it."

"Wait; this is where you live?"

"Yes, this is where I live. Alone."

She looked around with her mouth open as wide as a window.

"Are you okay?"

"No. I'm floored." She admired the beautiful décor. "I didn't know that there were such nice homes in Brooklyn."

"You'd be surprised how many nice things you can find in Brooklyn."

She stepped farther inside as he turned on some additional lighting.

The size of his place fascinated her; the marble floors, high ceilings, expensive furniture, all of which defied the stereotype that she had come to believe about single black men.

"You look shocked."

"I am; I mean, there aren't any bongs, black lacquer, or marijuana plants anywhere."

"No, there aren't any of those, baby." He moved closer to her.

"Yes."

"Good, let me show you the bedrooms." He took her hand and guided her toward the staircase.

"Wait!" she backed up.

"Hey, I promised you that I wouldn't try anything, and I meant that."

He led her upstairs.

"This is really nice, Omar; I'm impressed."

"Thanks; there are three guest rooms, three full baths and of course, a master bedroom."

Omar led her inside.

"Wow! This is really something."

Omar's chest grew in circumference.

"Do you like it?"

"It's different."

"What do you mean?"

"You have rather eclectic taste," Asia observed, noticing the large paintings that hung above Omar's bed. The other walls were adorned with masks of African and Asian influence.

"When it comes to what I like, I can be a bit all over the place."

"I bet you can," Asia replied, making a mental note of his comment.

"Yes, but everything in my life has a place and so will you, Asia." He hugged her from behind.

"Do you really sleep in this room?" She slipped from his grasp.

"No, Will Smith sleeps here. Of course, I sleep here."

"I just asked because everything seems so untouched. Nothing is out of place." Her eyes rolled toward a chair near the bed.

"Well, almost everything." There was a black jock strap lying on a chair near the window. Asia's eyes fixed on it as though she was trying to imagine it on Omar.

"Sorry about that." He snatched it from her view.

"Don't apologize; this is your space. I'm just visiting."

Omar smiled as Asia continued to survey his bedroom. He watched as she admired all the little knickknacks he picked up along his travels. For the first time since they met, he viewed her as more than a potential bedfellow.

She walked over to the bed and rubbed her hand against the linen. "Ouch!"

"What happened?"

"Omar, don't take this the wrong way but until now, I thought there might be a slight chance that you were gay."

"What!"

"Okay, on the D. L."

Omar scowled.

She sat on the bed, crossed her legs, and grinned. "Come on now. All the fancy furnishings, the matching color schemes; the house is immaculate and you're single. You have to admit; it would raise a woman's eyebrow."

He smirked.

"Don't worry; thanks to these horrible sheets, all my doubts have been removed."

What was she talking about? He looked at her as if she was missing a screw.

"Quick, what thread count is this?" she tugged at the sheet.

"I don't know."

"Good, let's keep it that way," Asia said, bursting into laughter, again. In her mind, *a man who bought sheets ac-*

cording to thread count was gay. Either that or working in the purchasing department of a hotel.

Although she couldn't fathom sleeping with a man as fine as Omar on anything less than eight hundred thread count sheets, she steered the conversation far away from his bed.

Omar was curious, though, and wouldn't make it easy. "So, are you saying you don't like my sheets?"

"They're okay...for now," she answered, playfully. She began moving around his bedroom as if she belonged there.

Omar marveled at her shapely legs and tight derriere. The thought of seeing her out of her clothes caused him to become excited.

"I never liked these sheets either but since the housekeeper is away, I grabbed the first thing I saw."

Asia wasn't buying it. A person would have to have been colorblind to purchase those sheets. They were awful, multi-colored, and plaid; just an eyesore. She would have much rather walked in and saw a bare mattress rather than one covered with sheets that looked like a Skittles wrapper.

She glanced at a photo on the wall, "Are these your family members?"

"Yes, the woman on the left is my mom."

"Wow, she's beautiful."

"Yes, she is."

"Is this your father?"

"No, my dad left us when I was young."

"I'm sorry; I didn't know." She rubbed his arm.

"How could you? We never discussed it."

"Were your parents married?" Asia asked while further inspecting the photograph.

"No, but my mom always wanted to get married."

"What woman doesn't?" she mumbled

"What?"

"I said this is a cute picture. Who is this man that's sitting with your mom?"

"That's Earl, one of my many stepfathers."

Asia was confused.

"After my father left, my mom was worried that I'd grow up being resentful, lose my way, turn to gangs, and start hanging in the streets if I didn't have a father figure around to help me. She did what a lot of women do. She tried to replace him for my sake. At least, that's what she said. I would watch as her bedroom became a revolving door for fake uncles and potential stepdads. None of which ever stayed around. I read somewhere that not having a father around could cause a child irreparable damage. Funny though, seeing all those men coming in and out of our home did more damage to me than my father leaving ever could."

"I'm sorry," Asia said, realizing she might have overstepped. His comment struck a chord with her.

"You know, I've wanted to kiss you ever since we got here." He planted a kiss on her lips, "Now, is there anything else you want to know?"

She shook her head.

"Good, let's talk about you then."

He slid behind her and pressed his bulging crotch against her backside. "Do you find it hard?

She spun around. "What?"

"I mean, is it hard for you to talk about yourself?"

"No. Not really." She rolled her eyes playfully.

"What do you want to know?"

"Well, for starters, have you ever been arrested for stalking?"

"What?" Asia chuckled.

"I'm serious; have you ever broken into your ex's place?"

Asia stood on her toes, gripped his neck with both hands, and kissed him as if trying to steal his breath. After a few seconds, he pulled away.

"Damn, girl, I didn't know you could kiss like that."

"There are a lot of things you don't know about me."

She walked toward the closet. "Is this..."

"Yes, it is."

Her eyes lit up. She was tempted to ask if she could peek inside but fought the urge.

"Go ahead, take a look."

"Are you sure?"

"Yes, I'm sure." He swung the doors open, displaying a huge walk-in closet with track lighting, racks of suits, shelves upon shelves of shoes, ties, sweaters, fur coats and more.

Asia was impressed.

Omar owned over fifty suits, designer of course. All hung according to season and color.

"Nice." She closed the doors. "So, tell me, are you actually going to wear all of these clothes? Or are they just for show?"

"Just for show...usually I walk around naked."

Dodging Omar's flirts was becoming a dance. He reached for her, but she ducked his grasp again.

"That's a huge bed; how do you get into it?"

"Like this."

He scooped her into his arms and carried her over to the bed. It was a scene straight out of a romance novel.

He laid her down and lowered himself on top of her. His heart pounded with anticipation and so did hers. They kissed, but this time it was much more passionate. Amid their intimate moment, the phone rang.

"Aren't you going to answer it?"

"No," Omar replied, undoing her top.

She kicked off her heels and submitted to his advances.

The phone continued to ring.

"Someone really wants to talk to you," she managed to say between his kisses.

"It's not important; it'll stop."

"How do you know?"

"Trust me."

Suddenly, the ringing stopped.

"See, I told you."

They resumed their tongue dance, but the phone rang again. At that point, Asia had enough.

Her kisses grew cold.

She slid herself from beneath him and began straightening the wrinkles from her dress.

He laid there as twisted as a corkscrew.

"Baby, what are you doing?" he groaned.

"I think I'm ready to go, Omar," Asia said, slipping into her shoes.

"What? We just got here!"

"I know and I'm sorry. It's just that…" She started to make up an excuse but decided against it. "Can you just take me home, please?"

"Look, if I offended you, I'm sorry."

She checked her hair in the mirror, reapplied her makeup, and headed toward the door. A million thoughts were running through her mind. *How could he be so insensitive? Is making out with me more important than a potential call from his sick mother? What if something has happened to her?*

The fact that he refused to answer his phone sent up an immediate red flag. Was his mother even sick? She didn't know and she didn't care to find out. She wanted no part of the game he thought he was playing.

"Okay, I'll take you home. Before you go though, I want you to know that I'm sorry if I did anything to offend you. I really like you, Asia."

She fought the onset of a smile. Although she liked him, too, she was confused as to why he ignored the phone call.

"That call could have been from your mother."

"Asia, that wasn't my mom."

"How do you know?"

He didn't say a word.

"Okay, well, then there's some definite bullshit going on here and I don't want any part of it." She turned to leave the room.

"Come on, don't leave like this." He reached for her arm.

"Look, are you going to drive me home or should I take the subway?" Her eyes telegraphed her desire to get the hell out of there.

"Come on Asia, the subway? What type of guy do you think I am?"

You don't want me to answer that!" She mumbled.

Omar couldn't make sense of her sudden shift in disposition. No other woman had ever confused him so much. There was something about her besides her perky breast, shapely ass, and feisty attitude that drew him to her.

"Asia, the call was from a friend."

"You don't have to tell me who the call was from; I'm not your woman. So, you don't owe me any explanation."

Asia spoke as if she didn't care but the truth was in her eyes. Omar knew exactly where the attitude was coming from. He sat on the edge of the bed, staring at her. *Okay, I like you, but this shit is getting old and I'm getting bored with playing these fucking games. I've never worked so hard in my life for a piece of pussy and to tell the truth, I don't know if it's even worth it. One thing's for sure though, since we've come this far; I'm going to get what I'm after. You will not be the first woman to say she got away; that is for damn sure. So, you want to play a game, Asia, let's play!*

He leaped up abruptly and started toward her.

"Aren't you going to say something?" Asia phished.

"Yeah, let's go!" Omar replied, bolting past her.

Asia was shocked and followed him downstairs through the foyer.

The phone rang again.

They stared at each other.

"Go ahead and answer it." She waited.

He walked into the kitchen, glanced at the number, and then placed the call on speakerphone.

"Hello!"

"Omar, where have you been, I've been trying to reach you all evening?"

Asia was standing in the doorway; her expression changed immediately when she heard a woman's voice.

"Iris?"

"Yes. I've been trying to reach you all evening." A smug look settled on Asia's face. The call had confirmed her suspicions that it was another woman trying to reach him.

"I was out; what's wrong?"

"It's Ben. He's in trouble."

"What do you mean?"

"All I know is that I got a call from one of the bartenders at the Squeeze Bar and they said he's too drunk to drive home."

"Okay, I'll swing by and pick him up."

"You're a dream. Talk to you later."

Omar hung up the phone and joined Asia in the foyer.

Asia tried to apologize, "I'm sorry, I thought…"

"If you're about to apologize again, don't." Omar snapped, cutting her off in mid-sentence. "Let's just go!"

"Please...wait." She said, grabbing his arm.

"No, you wait. A lot of guys play games, Asia, but I'm not one of them. In time, you'll see that. Maybe then you'll even believe it."

He opened the door and held it for her to step out of his place.

CHAPTER FIFTEEN

Taken For A Ride

Asia had doubted Omar's sincerity three times that night, each time making an even bigger fool of herself than the last. It was so unlike her to make irrational assumptions- so unlike her to behave like a woman who'd go along with the games men play for fear of being alone. She had seen many of her friends fall into that trap and vowed that it would never happen to her. While trying to avoid becoming one type of woman, she was quickly becoming another, the kind that doesn't trust and who always thinks the worst. And although Omar was smart enough to understand her reasons for acting like an insecure fool, she knew that her constant lack of trust was enough to turn him off. She needed to redeem herself.

She watched from the corner of her eyes as Omar drove with a look of disappointment on his face.

"You know, even though I live in New York, I'll never get over how beautiful the city is at night," she said, trying to break the ice.

He didn't respond.

The ride back to her place was quiet and quick; twenty minutes to be exact.

She attempted to apologize a final time before exiting the car.

"Look, Omar, I'm really..."

"Beautiful."

"Huh?"

"You're even more beautiful than you were the night I first laid eyes on you." He leaned over and gently planted a kiss on her forehead.

Asia blushed.

"I'll call you tomorrow."

"Okay." She stepped out of the car and watched as he drove away.

She walked up the steps to her house, thinking, *what in the hell just happened?*

It had only been a few minutes...

Asia couldn't get him out of her mind. Although he was super macho and had strong opinions about the roles of women, she was still very attracted to him; which struck her as odd since she had all but called him a common slug by falsely accusing him of leaving his wallet at home on purpose.

As Omar's car cut across the intersection, his phone rang.

"Hello."

"The answer is yes."

"What?"

"I'm saying yes...to everything we talked about earlier. Yes, I want to see you again; yes, I want to sleep with you; yes, I'm willing to deal with you on your terms."

Omar was shocked and didn't respond.

"Are you there?"

"Yes, I'm here. Are you sure about this?"

"Yes, I'm sure. All that I ask is that you respect me, don't ever put your hands on me, and never come on to any of my friends. Okay?"

"Sure."

He could literally feel her smiling on the other end.

"Listen, it's late; get some sleep and we can talk about this tomorrow."

"Okay," Asia murmured. "Good night, Omar."

"Good night, baby."

He waited for her to hang up first.

Omar had an unerring knowledge about what women feel and although Asia played hard to get, her feelings were becoming more evident as the night progressed. He made another call.

"Hey baby, I'm downstairs; open the door."

CHAPTER SIXTEEN

His Way or The Highway

It had been a month since Asia had agreed to Omar's terms-thirty days of dating without any real commitment. Although she was the type of woman that wanted more out of a relationship, she thought that in time he would come around. She had seen his type before, men who were afraid of marriage, afraid of commitment, and afraid of the strength of a strong black woman. The world was full of them, but she was determined to prove to him that there was nothing to fear about loving her. Even if it meant following his rules for a little while.

Things were going good between them, for the most part. He would take her out and jog with her on the weekends; he even joined her when she shopped at the mall. Aside from the fact that they still hadn't slept together, he seemed content with the way things were between them.

Asia, however, was ready to take their association to the next level.

She had just finished washing her hair and gotten ready for bed when the telephone rang. She answered it reluctantly. "Hello?"

"Hey, baby, did I wake you?"

Her heart thumped; it was Omar. Even after a month, she still got goosebumps whenever she heard his voice.

"You didn't wake me. Are you okay; your voice sounds strange?"

"I'm fine; I just have a few things on my mind."

"Are you thinking about your mom?"

"Yes, and other things as well."

"Sweetheart, your mom will be fine, trust me. God is going to see to it."

"Yeah, well, you know how I feel about that."

Asia slid beneath her covers.

"You know, it's strange, but I trust you more than I've ever trusted any woman in my life."

She smiled.

"Why do you think that is?"

"I don't know; there's just something about you that makes me trust you. I can't put my finger on it. Anyway, it's late and I don't want to keep you up. I just wanted to say goodnight."

"Honey, are you sure everything is okay?"

"Asia, can I ask you a question?"

"Sure, what is it?"

"Do you think it's possible for a man to wake up one day and suddenly be in love?"

She stalled.

"Hello?"

"Um…I don't know. I guess it's possible." She stared across the room.

"Oh, okay."

"Why did you ask me that?"

He didn't respond.

"Hello, are you there?"

"Yeah, I'm here; I was just thinking." He cleared his throat.

"Well?"

"It's just that being in love is a strange thing, especially when it just happens out of nowhere."

"Okay." A chill ran up Asia's back.

"So, have you ever loved someone so much that you would do anything in the world to make them happy?"

Her mind began to race. *What was he talking about? Who was he referring to? Was it her?* She became so anxious that she could barely answer.

"I guess I have. Who are you in love with?"

"It doesn't matter. I'm probably just tired."

All at once, there was silence.

"Hello," Asia called out but received no response. Suddenly, she heard shallow breathing.

"Omar!" she squawked."

"Oh, I'm sorry, baby; I'm really tired. Can I call you tomorrow?"

"Sure." Her mouth fell into a frown. "But-"

"Thanks, baby, I'll call you when I wake up."

He yawned and then quickly hung up the phone.

ASIA'S BEDROOM

"Wait! Hello?"

The buzzing of the dial tone caused questions to ricochet through her mind. *What in the hell was that? What did Omar mean by calling me in the middle of the night with questions about being in love and then falling off to sleep in the middle of our conversation? What in the hell was he thinking?*

Asia couldn't sleep. She lay awake for hours, racking her brain over Omar's bold, but incomplete statement. There was no way she could rest without figuring out what he meant, so she called her girlfriends, Pam and Angela.

"He did what?" Pam asked.

"He hinted that he was in love with someone, but he didn't say who."

"Girl, you need to drop his tired ass," Angela added.

"Well, maybe not. I mean, if she thinks he was referring to her, maybe she shouldn't react so swiftly," Pam
attempted to reason.

"Oh, please, if he meant that he was in love with her,
he would have said so," Angela chimed in.

"That's true," Pam concurred.

"What is he doing for you anyway?" Angela asked
but before Asia could answer, she answered for her.
"Probably nothing!"

"Asia, you know you can do better than a man that
wants you to play guessing games."

"That's right; besides you two have only known each
other a little more than a month; that's too soon to be talking about falling in love. So, more than likely he was
talking about some other trick he's been laying up with."

Asia listened as her friends went on a tirade. She
couldn't get a word in edgewise. Neither one of them had
any luck finding a good man; so, when she called with her
problem, they were more than happy to attack Omar's intentions.

"I'm telling you; these black men aren't any good.
You just need to kick his ass to the curb now, before he
kicks you to the curb." Angela urged.

"I agree," Pam said. "The sooner you get rid of him,
the better off you'll be."

By the time her girlfriends finished adding their two
cents, Asia was more than convinced that Omar was in
love with another woman, and that he would be probably
be breaking up with her soon. So, she decided right then
and there that she would beat him to the punch.

"Thanks, girls. I'm going to call him back right now
and tell him it's over."

"Don't mention it. That's what we're here for."

"That's right. Call us anytime honey."

She hung up the phone and immediately called Omar. The phone rang about twelve times before he answered. When he did, his voice was stale and groggy.

"Hello."

"Omar?" Asia's voice blared through the phone.

"Yes."

"I'm sorry, but I no longer want to see you again. Don't call me again. Ever!"

CLICK!

She began pacing back and forth like a mental patient. *My friends were right; he was going to break up with me...that's why he hasn't called me back. It's been fifteen minutes and he still hasn't called me back! I'm glad I found out about him before it was too late. All that talk about not being able to find a good woman and about looking forward to building something with me in time was all hogwash. Why didn't he just call it what it was-an open relationship, where he got to screw whomever he wanted and I got to sit around twiddling my thumbs, hoping that he would one day see the value in the woman that I am. I can't believe those stupid lines. 'As long as you understand the dynamics of our association, baby, we'll be fine.' The dynamics of our association was that he was a dynamic asshole and I was a dynamic jerk for listening to that dynamic bullshit!*

She turned on the television.

I can't believe I thought he could be the one when he was probably just out for a quick lay. He never cared about me; if he had, he would have called me back.

She removed her robe and climbed into bed.

I should have known he was a loser by the way he was gawking at all those other women at the party. I saw him way before he even noticed me, and then he has the nerve to have the attention span of a grape. Of course, he's no damned good!

She turned off the television and pulled the covers up to her neck.

A tear rolled down her face.

"Damn you, Omar; I believed in you!"

She cried herself to sleep.

Thirty minutes later...

Asia was startled by a heavy pounding on her door. She leaped from her bed, slipped into a robe and headed downstairs; her eyes were still weighted with sleep.

"Who is it?" she called out as the pounding continued.

"I said who is it?"

She still received no answer, only more pounding. She eased her way to the peephole and then swung the door open.

"What are you doing here?"

There stood Omar, with his hand stuffed into his pockets, silent, not saying a word.

"I said what are you doing here, O-?"

Before she could fully pronounce his name, he stepped inside, grabbed her by the sides of her face, and began kissing her. She tried to pull away but couldn't. He held her tight, lifting her in his arms and stepping farther into the house. He kicked the door shut behind him as she squirmed in his arms.

"I told you I didn't want to see you again!" she said between his kisses.

He ignored her, moving through the house as if he owned it.

He walked over to the couch and laid her down on it, lowering himself on top of her. Asia's heart began to pound, hard.

"I'm a good man, Asia." He forced his tongue deeper into her mouth.

"How do I know that?"

"You have to trust me."

"How, when I don't even trust myself?"

Trusting a man was a huge issue for Asia. In the past, she had given her all to men, trying desperately to encourage, support and help them find themselves, all the while, losing herself. Until she met Omar, she viewed men as foes and not allies but not anymore.

She tore at his shirt, causing the buttons to pop from their place. She could feel her heart literally skipping a beat as she gazed at his thick, chiseled chest.

He slid his fingers into her robe.

"Wait." She stopped his hand.

"No more waiting. I want you." He reached farther into her robe, causing the belt to become undone.

Once again, she tried to resist, but couldn't. He wiggled his tongue around in her mouth and began squeezing her breasts. It felt so good that she threw her head back and allowed him to have his way. In fact, she leaned so far back that her breasts popped from their confinement.

He took one into his mouth, kissed it, licked it, and nibbled on it, gently.

She pleaded, "Omar, wait."

He ignored her.

Her hands gripped the back of his head.

"Damn, I want you so bad," he said, placing his hands between Asia thighs.

"Stop it!" she spat, causing him to freeze with agitation. She slid from beneath him.

"Not like this."

At that point, he tried to conceal the look of disappointment that had suddenly etched on his face. Her tone had caused the erection in his pants to quickly dissipate.

"I'm sorry," she said.

No, I'm sorry. Sorry, I came over here, he thought, keeling near the couch.

She read the look on his face as she walked toward him, dropping her robe to the floor.

Omar felt a sudden rush of blood between his legs, causing him to swell in his pants.

"What are you doing?" he asked.

She smiled at him with her eyes but didn't say a word.

The impact she was having on him wasn't just evident on his face, it was also evident beneath his clothes. He stood up and moved closer toward her.

"You are so damn beautiful, Asia."

"Don't speak." She placed her fingers against his lips. "Just take me upstairs-now."

She fell into his arms and allowed him to carry her up to her bedroom. He counted each step he climbed as he walked up the stairs that led to her bedroom.

"Nine, ten, eleven."

"What are you counting?"

"The number of orgasms you're going to have tonight. I'm going to see to it."

Asia grew warm inside.

He laid her down on the bed, staring directly into her eyes as he removed his shoes and pants.

Asia noticed the massive bulge in his boxer briefs and began to pray. *Lord, I know that I've often said that size doesn't matter, but I take it all back. I don't know if I can handle this, so I may need a little help. Oh, and Lord, please let him be a good man because after this. I'm going to need him to stay around for a little while.*

He lay on top of her, brushing her hair from her face.

"Be gentle," she urged.

"I plan to," he committed.

"I don't want to be hurt, Omar."

"I can't guarantee that you won't feel a little pain in the beginning but trust me it will soon turn into pleasure."

She stared up at him, "You know what I mean."

"I know and I promise, you won't be." He sealed his promise with multiple kisses to her forehead, lips and, breasts, working his way slowly toward her special place.

Within seconds, she was moaning and squirming as if she liked what he was doing. She lifted her pelvis slowly, slightly and deliberately.

Omar knew what she wanted him to do. He smiled as he licked her inner, upper thighs, blowing on them after each lick as if to cool her with his breath.

She began to moan louder. It was as though he had discovered the secret passageway to her heart.

Asia's reaction prompted him to go farther. His tongue slid across her body along her thighs, her breast and her neck, causing her to shiver. It was as if she had been doused with ice water.

"Your mouth feels so good," she stuttered, biting down on her bottom lip. She enjoyed the feel of his lips against her skin.

Lying there beneath him made her think about her life. She was a strong woman with a strong personality, had a good job and a good heart. The only thing missing in her life was a good man, one that she could call her own. For a long, time she wondered if she'd ever meet a man that didn't feel threatened by her beauty or her paycheck. Finding one hadn't been an easy task. Every guy she met fell short, physically or in personality and dedication. Many couldn't deal with the fact that she was financially independent and that she never asked a man for anything more than his time.

As his tongue swirled around her waist, she hoped that Omar was different. He was handsome, secure with himself and didn't fall short at all. He had his shit together. She didn't even care that he was a few years younger than her; age was just a number.

She threw her head back and accepted him wholeheartedly.

Omar crawled toward the top of the bed, his lips dripping with moisture. His appetite was unsatisfied. He wanted to devour her.

She watched as he moved slowly toward her, his dick coming more into focus with every second. Her eyes widened in disbelief, in fear, in excitement, and in anticipation of great pleasure. Her mouth began to spring water as he slid inside of her.

He whispered softly in her ear as his enormous extension caused her legs to tense up a bit.

"Don't worry; I'll be gentle."

She took a deep breath and wrapped her arms around his huge back, cooing as pressure shot throughout her body, from her thighs to her toes, from her vagina to the top of her head.

Omar buried his face into the side of her neck and did what he did best. "Relax, baby, I've only just begun. There are hours and inches more to come."

The contrast of their complexions as their bodies lay entwined was beautiful. His eyes scanned her body for places he'd yet to explore, to kiss, to touch, to lick, but none would go undiscovered that night.

"Oh, my God, Omar, this feels so-"

He placed one hand gently over her mouth, allowing her to suck on his fingers as he delivered short, calculated thrusts that scraped away all remnants of past visitors from her vagina, from her heart, and from her mind. She would recall no other moment, but the one she was currently engaged in.

He continued to kiss her passionately to relax her until her moans became more sedate. He massaged her leg as he sucked on the heel of her foot. His long, wet tongue traced her toes as he took each one into his mouth. She had never felt anything like it. Her screams were unexpected.

Omar was relentless in his pleasure giving, but he wasn't the only one.

After a while, Asia's confidence grew, and she began to twirl her hips.

Omar smiled and whispered in her ear, "That's right baby. Show me what you got."

The sound of his voice and warmth of his breath against her neck caused her to twirl her hips like she never had before. It had been a long time since Asia had allowed herself to be vulnerable with a man. In the past, every guy except for one, made her feel like she was expected to just lay there and take whatever they dished out, even if was a few minutes of unfulfilling sex. They made her feel as if they were doing her a favor, like she wasn't supposed to have any input, like her body didn't belong to her. Not this time though.

Omar made her feel alive, like an equal in their quest for ecstasy. She watched as licked every childhood scar, kissed every stretch mark on her stomach, gripped her thick ass, and without question, accepted all of her. He made her feel free, liberated and in control of her body. She knew right then what she wanted; she wanted him.

She began to work her stuff, her black girl magic. She rolled him over and mounted him, causing him to smile, not just with his mouth but with his eyes as well.

Omar's breathing changed as she rounded her back, curled her chin toward her chest, placed the top of her head against his chest, and began flexing her vaginal muscles.

"What the hell, baby, ooh!" Omar gripped her thighs in pleasure.

"Yeah, I know it's good; tell me how good, Daddy," she whispered, chuckling as she gyrated on top of him. "Who's in control now?"

"You, baby."

"Who?" she taunted, as she rode him like a pogo stick. "Say it again!"

The tension in Omar's fingers spoke volumes. She could feel how much he was enjoying her.

"Are you okay, Big Daddy?" she teased.

His eyes began to roll back in his head, which would have been a good thing, had he not seen the cocky grin etching on Asia's face. No woman had ever left him speechless or left his bed thinking that she was the one in control. As far as he was concerned, she wasn't about to be the first.

With a quick twirl of his legs, he tossed her over and thrust himself deeper into her vagina than any man or self-pleasuring device had ever gone before. She pressed her hands against his chest as tears sprung from her eyes. It was a feeling she had never experienced in her life.

Bolts of lightning shot across the heavens that night, not once, not twice, but many times. Asia was thrown for a loop as Omar repeatedly changed the rhythm of their exchange; she marveled at his skill in adjusting both the depth and speed of his strokes. She was no longer in control, not even a little bit.

The way Omar was making love to her caused a cataclysmic event to take place in her body. It was the merging of yin and yang, body and soul, mind and emotion. From that moment on, she would never think of him the same. *To her, he would no longer just be Omar.*

He was KING OMAR-Emperor of her vagina!

CHAPTER SEVENTEEN

After The Morning After

Asia awoke with a smile on her face and in her soul. She rolled over, stared at him, and in her mind relived the magnificent event. She kissed him softly on the shoulder. "Sleep as long as you like, my King." She tossed the sheets from her legs and swung them from the bed. When she stood up, she felt weak in the knees, but that was to be expected; it had been a long time since she'd made love, and never had she been twisted into so many positions.

On the way to the bathroom, she felt a jolt of electricity between her thighs and flinched.

"Ooh, gosh!"

She glanced back at Omar as he slept as if he had been the cause. In fact, he had. She took a deep breath, smiled, and once gain relived the extraordinary event.

In her mind it had all been worth it; the disagreement, the bad date, the sleepless night; all of it had led to her finding a 'good black man.'

Omar pretended to be asleep; meanwhile, he was watching as she moved slowly about the room. If she had taken anything more than baby steps, she probably would have screamed.

"I'm going to go downstairs and make you a meal fit for a king, baby. Right after I soak in some Epson salt," she whispered.

He fought the urge to laugh, peeking over the sheets as she left the room.

"Job well done," he said, glancing down at his crotch. He scooted over to the center of the bed, arrogantly etching his body into the plush mattress. He folded his hands behind his head as if he belonged there-in her life, in her bed, in his glory.

Once again, he stretched, gripped himself like a cocky son-of-a-bitch and then drifted back to sleep.

Asia hadn't seen her friends or Omar in weeks...

It was a beautiful day, the sky was clear, and the sun was shining brightly. The wind offered a breeze as slight as an infant's kiss, but clearly, Cupid had been making his rounds to everyone except her. She had been sitting around the house for weeks, waiting for him to call. At first, she thought that he might have been in an accident and was lying badly hurt in a ditch somewhere. Maybe he had taken a bad bump on the head and couldn't remember her number. Or worse, maybe something had happened to his mother and he didn't know how to deal with it.

Deep down, she knew that none of those were the reasons, but she thought she could convince herself that she hadn't been a total fool by trusting him.

She sat in the back seat of a yellow cab trying desperately to fight the sting of rejection. She couldn't help it, though. Everywhere she turned, there were couples holding hands, shopping, riding bikes, or strolling around with their children. She had once hoped that she and Omar would be so lucky but quickly checked her thoughts.

Who am I kidding? Even if something had happened, it's been a month. Omar could have called.

Asia conceded that Omar had managed to charm her out of her skirt and straight into the stereotype of women who don't think before spreading their legs. It was as much her fault as it was his.

As the cab approached the cafe, a tear fell from her eye. She wiped it away quickly. Her friends were standing outside and spotted her when the cab arrived.

They each gave her a tight hug.

"So, sweetie, how are you feeling?" Angela took her by the arm and led her to their table.

"Is everything okay?" Pam asked.

"I'm fine." She smiled at Pam. "Not that you two actually care."

"What do you mean?"

"Oh, don't play coy." She scooted around the sidewalk partition.

"Honey, of course we care," Pam said, touching her hand.

"Save it! The last time we went out you two were on the prowl and you left me to fend for myself, remember?"

"Oh girl, how long ago was that? We said we were sorry," Angela cut in.

"Is this table okay?"

"It's fine."

"You know we're only sitting outside because Angela likes to people watch."

"I know all too well, honey, but this is okay." Her eyes rolled toward a passing couple.

"Hey, is everything okay?" Pam glanced at the couple as well.

"Huh? Oh yeah, everything's fine; I'm just a little hungry, that's all."

Asia offered a quick excuse, but Angela wasn't buying it. They had been friends for years and she knew her well enough to know that she was covering up something.

"You know what? I figured you'd be hungry, so I took the liberty of ordering for you."

At that moment, a young, dark-haired waiter approached them. Angela flirted with him as he placed their orders on the table.

"What is this?" Asia sneered.

"A dieter's delight; I know how you're always watching your figure, so I ordered light."

Asia wasn't impressed with the low-cal, no-flavor entrée; she wanted real food, comfort food, and she wanted it now.

"Excuse me, do you have chicken livers?"

"Yes, we do."

Pam and Angela frowned.

"Good, then I'd like an order; fried crispy. A side of collard greens, some potato salad and a wedge of cornbread with butter, please."

Angela was livid; Asia never indulged in high-calorie foods. If it weren't clear before, it became more than obvious then that something was wrong.

The waiter nodded and then headed back to the kitchen.

Pam was also shocked by Asia's sudden change in eating habits.

"Damn girl, if I didn't know any better, I'd swear you were pregnant."

"Oh, please. not Miss-Goody-Two-Shoes." Angela giggled.

Asia dismissed their comments, turning her focus to yet another passing couple. They were giggling and making goofy eyes at each other as they walked by.

"Is all of that really necessary? No one wants to see all of that this early in the day," Asia scoffed.

Pam smiled at the couple, "I think it's cute."

"What's so cute about it?"

"Well, for one, I like to see people in love. Especially since I don't have a man. It gives me something to hope for."

"Oh, please." Asia waved her hand at the couple as if to dismiss Pam's statement.

Pam and Angela sat back in their seats, shocked at Asia's degrading disposition.

"Come on, we all know that eventually, that man is going to lie to her. So, why go through the motions? I think she should cut her losses now and save herself the heartache."

"What a minute. What has your panties in a bunch?" Angela asked, reaching for the salad dressing.

"Men, that's what; they're no good, they're dogs and they should all be destroyed."

Angela shot back, "Okay, Cruella de Vil, you go ahead and destroy all the dogs. When you need your pipes fixed, don't be looking at us."

"Angela, women are perfectly capable of fixing pipes," Asia said.

"Yeah girl, there are a lot of women plumbers in the world," Pam said.

"Right; and I don't want any of them fixing my plumbing, if you know what I mean." Angela chuckled.

Pam laughed.

"Joke all you want, but behind the smile of every smooth-talking man is a dog, just looking for the next place to bury his bone."

"Where is all of this coming from?" Angela questioned.

"All of what?"

"Asia, don't play stupid! Ever since you got here, you've been scowling and putting people down. Then you ordered chicken livers; what the hell is that about?"

Asia looked away.

"Okay, Asia, look, I know you were hoping that the situation between you and whatever-his-name-is would have worked out, but the days of men who are looking to settle down are over. Men just aren't looking for the wife, the house, and the commitment anymore. They're looking for a cold beer, a place to lay both of their heads and a warm body to lie next to that doesn't have an opinion, a brain, or a desire for a commitment."

"It's true, honey." Pam rubbed her arm.

"Yeah, well, I used to think there was a least one good black man left in the world."

"Oh, there is, but he's either sleeping with white women or other men." Asia chuckled.

As much as Angela's comment was unfair to black men, it made her laugh, something she hadn't done in a while.

"We know it's hard, but just be thankful that you had-n't slept with him; then it would really be a disaster," Pam said.

"Tell me about it," Asia mumbled.

"What?"

"Nothing. I said this place gets really crowded."

"I know. That's why we're sitting outside," Angela re-torted, watching Asia slyly.

Asia had done some fast maneuvering; she wasn't about to tell her girlfriends that she had slept with Omar. Not after they had warned her to kick him to the curb. If she had, the floodgates would have burst, and she would have never been able to shut them up. There would have been tons of questions, loads of bad advice and unsolicited opinions, none of which would change anything. Angela would be setting her up on blind dates with men she wouldn't even go out with. Pam would force her to watch Waiting to Exhale for the ten thousandth time. Lord knows, nothing was worth all of that.

She took a bite of food. "Mmm! This is good, have some?"

Angela's lips folded, "Oh, please, that's just nasty."

"No, nasty is that scavenger on your plate."

"Scavenger or not, I love shrimp, but you just lost your damn mind; who orders chicken livers for brunch?"

"Hillbillies," Pam said. She tapped Asia as she chuckled.

"I don't see what's so funny,"

"I do. With all the fine men running around in New York City, all you can think to put in your mouth is chicken liver? Girl bye!"

Asia burst into laughter. They all did. For a few moments, she had forgotten about Omar.

"Is sex all she ever thinks about?" Asia queried, tapping Pam on the knee.

"Pretty much," Angela retorted, becoming distracted by a guy who had parked his car a few feet from where they sat. Her face lit up as though someone was shining a light on it.

"Girl, what's wrong with you?" Asia asked.

Pam joined Angela in gawking at the guy as he stepped onto the sidewalk.

Angela's heart thumped.

They watched a guy with a beautiful muscular build make his way toward them. He wore a pair of fitted sweats and a sleeveless shirt that showed off his body.

Pam fanned herself.

Angela licked her lips.

Asia folded her arms.

Angela pushed her breast up.

"Uh, uh, Angela, stop that, or I'm leaving!" Asia warned.

"Girl, please, he's fine." Angela shifted in her seat.

Asia smirked. As far as looks go, no one was as fine as Omar in her eyes and since he turned out only to be after one thing, she was unimpressed.

"I don't see anything so special about him."

"Yeah, well, that's you. I think he's hotter than gravy and I could just sop him up with this biscuit." Angela licked her lips.

"So, now you're on the prowl again?"

"I'm not prowling, honey. If I were, you two would be sitting here alone."

Angela dabbed her mouth with a napkin, opened her purse, and began searching inside.

Pam grinned.

"I know she's not about to, Pam..." Asia stared at Angela in disbelief.

"She's been doing it since college."

"That's right and it works every time...whoops!"

She purposely let a small compact slip from her hand. It fell to the curb.

"Oh, I don't want anything to do with this." Asia covered her face with one hand.

"Relax, Asia, it's all in fun." Pam chuckled into her hand.

"Listen, you should be helping me talk her out of this."

"Ssh! Here he comes."

"I don't believe you. What if he's married?" Asia spoke softly.

"Look, if he's married, that's not my problem. Let the woman wearing his ring worry about what he's doing." Angela rolled her eyes.

Pam and Asia watched as she undid the top button on her blouse.

"Besides, I don't want to marry him; I just want to sleep with him once."

"What?"

"Excuse me, I believe you dropped this."

"Oh my, thank you so much." Angela said, batting her eyes as she pretended to be shocked

He handed Angela back her compact.

"I'm Charles, by the way."

"Hi, Charles, I'm Angela."

"It's nice to meet you."

"No, it's nice to meet you. This is my favorite compact. Had I lost it; I would have just died."

Angela was piling the shit so high, she forgot that Pam and Asia were sitting at the table.

"Well, in that case, I'm glad you didn't."

"Charles, do you work out?"

"Yes, I do. How'd you know?"

Asia nearly threw up. It was obvious the guy worked out; hell, he looked like he'd been injecting steroids since he came out of the womb.

"Can I touch your arm?"

"Sure."

Angela began squeezing his arm as if trying to activate his penis.

Asia couldn't believe it. He just stood there, letting her, as if he was auditioning for the cover of a fitness magazine. Meanwhile, Angela's only concern was the muscle in his pants, not his arm.

"He is cute," Pam whispered.

Asia disagreed. She thought he looked like a recent parolee pining for a lay. She became annoyed watching him whisper in Angela's ear.

"What type of man whispers in public?" Pam said.

"What type of man whispers period?" Asia commented with a look of disgust on her face. She cleared her throat.

"Oh, I'm sorry, I'm being rude; these are my friends Asia and Pam."

"How are you ladies doing today?"

"Fine," Pam responded.

Asia didn't bother.

"Charles, please forgive my friend's rudeness. She's not feeling too well today."

"It's all right. Listen, I left my cell in the car; I'll be right back."

"You do that." Angela smiled.

They watched as he trotted away.

"Okay, what did he have to say that was so private that he needed to whisper in your ear?" Asia squawked.

"Lower your voice, he'll hear you."

"Girl, I don't care if his mother hears me. I know you're not taking this guy seriously."

"Why not?"

"Look at him; he's not your type."

"Honey, every man's my type," Angela replied, watching as he returned.

Asia leapt up.

"Where are you going?"

"I just remembered...I left something on the stove; I have to go." She pulled twenty dollars from her purse and flung it on the table

Pam was stunned. "Asia, wait!"

Asia ignored her, stepping around the partition.

"Girl, you know how Angela is. She didn't mean anything by it."

"I know." Asia flagged a cab. "I'll call you both later."

Just as Asia was about to step into the cab, her cell phone rang.

She ignored it.

"Thanks for lunch, Angela, we'll talk later."

Angela ignored her. She was too busy giggling, while having her ear nibbled on by Charles.

The cab driver mumbled, impatiently.

"One minute, sir. Angela, did you hear what I said?"

"Girl, I heard you. Call me when you get home."

Yeah, right! Asia thought. *The way that guy is nibbling on your ear, you'll be lucky to still have one when you get up.*

She lowered herself into the cab and waved goodbye to Pam.

"Where to?" the driver asked.

"Someplace where there aren't any men."

"Hell, if I knew where that was, I'd be there myself."

Suddenly, a feeling of sadness overcame Asia.

"Ma'am, I said where to!"

"I'm sorry; West 122 street, please."

As the cab made its way through the streets of Manhattan, her heart filled with emotion. She fought the urge to cry but was unsuccessful.

The driver watched from his mirror.

"Hey, lady, are you okay?"

"I'm fine, just drive, please."

Asia was strong. She wasn't going to crack-not yet. She reached in her purse to silence the buzzing of her cell phone. It was annoying her. "All right, all right, I have a message, I know!"

She flipped her hair to one side, opened the phone, and began listening to her messages.

Dressed to kill...

Asia slipped into a pair of black Jimmy Choo five-inch stiletto heels and a little black dress with invisible spaghetti strings; they were ingenious, and she looked perfect.

Traffic was heavy, so she arrived at the restaurant late. She didn't care, though; he deserved to be left waiting.

I'm going to order the most expensive dish on the menu and then I'm going to get up and leave, just like he left me.

She stepped inside the glass elevator and was whisked away, high above street level. When the doors opened, she was immediately floored by the spectacular view.

"Welcome to the View Lounge," a maître d' greeted her. "Will you be dining alone this evening or with guests?"

"I'm meeting someone, and I think I see him right over there," she replied.

"Great. I'll show you to your table then."

Asia was impressed. The restaurant was named appropriately, boasting a breathtaking modernist design, and was filled with intimate tables beside large glass windows. It was paradise in the sky. As they made their way through the dining room, she noticed that the room was revolving, another neat feature.

Following the maître d', she couldn't help thinking about how long it had been since she'd seen him; also, about how hurt she felt the day he left. She thought about retreating but decided against it. No, not this time; they had unfinished business.

Their eyes met as she approached the table. Her heart swelled with emotion, and her mind with questions that simply needed to be answered. He stared at her as he pulled out her chair.

"You look incredible," he said, reaching across the table to strum the back of her hand.

"Thank you," she replied, sliding her hand away quickly. *'Incredible,'* she thought. *Hell, I'm dressed to kill.* It was not the time, nor the place to relive the familiarity of a touch. Sure, they had a moment after the concert, but that was just to save face in front of Torrey and Camaron. She had a bone to pick with him and she was prepared to pick that bitch dry.

"You know, for a minute, I didn't think you were going to show up."

"Why is that?" she asked, glancing down at a menu.

"Well, because of the way things went down between us."

She looked him straight in the eyes and said nothing.

"Okay, Asia, I know I was wrong, but I'm here to make it right."

"And you think it's going to be just that easy; why is that?" she retorted, perusing the menu as if uninterested.

"Well, because I'm sorry and because I know you have a forgiving heart."

"Is that right?" She turned to the waiter. "I'll have the rosemary duck, the mango shrimp, the beef short ribs, a side of asparagus and a coke, please."

"Wow, you're really hungry, huh?"

"No, just hitting you where it hurts."

He chuckled. "Okay, well, I'll have the usual, Antoine. Oh...and bring us a bottle of Pinot Grigio Santa Margarita, please."

"You know, when you left me, my whole world changed," she said.

"I made a mistake."

"Call it what you want; I woke up one morning and you were gone. Do you have any idea how much that hurts?"

He leaned in to console her.

She moved away.

"Baby, let me make it up to you, please."

"How can a man ever make up for breaking a woman's heart? A glass of wine and a cheap dinner doesn't fix shit."

The waiter returned with their wine.

"Oh no? So, why did you come here tonight?

"I don't know; maybe I needed closure. Maybe I needed to look you in the face and tell you how much I hate you."

"Is that how you really feel?"

"I don't know how I feel anymore. Do you?" Asia snapped.

"Okay, I deserve that, but I'm here now; doesn't that count for something?"

She lowered her head.

Tai stared at her from across the table. At that moment, he regretted his decision to leave her. Although he loved his music, he loved her, too.

"Asia, if I could take away all the pain I've caused you I would, without any hesitation. I'd give up everything I have for you-all the money, all the fancy clothes. All you have to do is just say the word. Tell me that you will take me back and I'll walk away from it all."

"It's too late for that!" She stood up to leave.

"Wait!" He grabbed her wrist.

"Let go of me, Tai."

"Please, give me a second chance."

"Why, so we can pick up where we left off?"

"Yes."

"I'm sorry; I'm not willing to do that!" She turned to walk away.

He reached for her arm.

She pulled away.

"Asia, marry me!"

"What?" She froze in her tracks. "What did you just say?"

CHAPTER EIGHTEEN

A Woman Forgives, She Doesn't Forget

She sat in the passenger seat in his car, nestled in his arms.

"I can't believe this; it doesn't seem real," she said, resting her head on his chest.

"It's real." He kissed her. "I'm back, baby."

Tears fell from her eyes.

"Tell me those are tears of joy," he said, wiping the moisture from her eyes.

"They are."

"Listen, it's getting late. Why don't I let you go, and we can talk about things tomorrow."

She nodded in agreement.

He pulled her close and held her like he didn't want to let her go, ever.

"You're making this so hard for me," she said.

"It's hard for me, too, baby."

They looked into each other's eyes and shared another kiss.

"Asia, please, think about what I said; I promise if you take me back, I'll never do anything to hurt you again."

"I said I'll think about it."

She stepped from the car.

"Damn, I've missed those sexy legs!"

He watched as she walked away.

"Good night, Tai."

"Good night, baby girl. I love you," he said as he drove away.

"I love you, too, Tai."

Just as she spoke those words, another car pulled up curbside.

"Asia!"

"Omar?" She ran up the stairs to her house.

"Wait, baby, please; let me explain." Omar leaped from the car.

She fumbled with her keys.

"Honey, I just want to talk." He headed up the steps behind her.

She opened the door and stepped inside quickly.

"Baby, listen, I know what I did was wrong and I'm sorry."

"Yes, you are sorry, Omar. Goodbye!"

She slammed the door shut in his face. At that moment he didn't know what was worse, the slamming of the door or the sound of the lock clicking.

On the other side of the door, Asia made the decision to put both of their asses on ice for a while....

FIVE MONTHS PASSED QUICKLY.

He sat on the edge of her bed, unrolling a pair of dress socks, glancing around the room at her things; her photos, her reading lamp, her pillows; he began to chuckle.

Talk about sacrifice. He had given up a lot to be with her.

He removed a shirt from her closet, smiling as he dressed. Asia had been spending a lot of money on him. He read a note she had left on the nightstand asking him to pick her up at Maroon's Restaurant, a neat little Caribbean/Soul bistro in the heart of Chelsea. He knew it well. They had dined there a few times before. He slipped into a pair of black Kenneth Cole loafers and headed out to meet her.

Whaddup Dawg?

The birds were chirping, the sun was beaming, and all was fair in Asia-Ville. Her girlfriends noticed it immediately.

She walked into the restaurant wearing a pair of black Manolo Blahniks and a beautiful cerulean silk dress that made her look like a fashion model. Her makeup was flawless and her accessories, perfectly matched. The purse she carried was small and clutched beneath the arm of her three-quarter silver fox coat.

"Sorry I'm late, ladies." Asia joined them at the table.

"Oh, my goodness, look at you." Pam's eyes widened. "You look incredible."

"Yes, you do," Angela agreed, approving of the glow on Asia's face.

Pam rolled her eyes over Asia's outfit. "Wait a minute, girl; you do realize that we're going shopping today, right?"

"Oh, was that today?" She pulled a pack of gum from her purse. "Care for some?"

Angela playfully snapped. "Did she just?? Heifer, we don't want no gum. Now tell us where you've been and why you're walking in here dressed like you're going to Cinderella's ball?"

"What do you mean?"

"Pam, if she says that one more time-" Angela gritted her teeth.

"Asia, you look nice, honey, but do you think it's a good idea to go shopping in such high heels?"

"Who says I'm going shopping?"

Angela's head swung to the side. "Did she just-?"

"Oh yes, she did." Pam frowned.

Angela folded her arms and stared across the table.

"Okay, listen, I can't go shopping with you two, today."

"Oh. Why not?" Pam pouted

"I'll tell you later," Asia whispered.

"Asia, if you think you're just going to walk up in here looking like you're about to audition for America's Next Top Over-the-Hill Model and not tell us where you're going, you are sadly mistaken, "Angela scoffed.

Asia chuckled.

A waiter brought over a menu.

Asia halted him. "No thanks...just tea, please."

Something was up and Angela knew it. She scooted over to the seat next to Asia.

"If you don't tell us what's going on right now, I'm going to start screaming in here at the top of my lungs."

"You better do it, girl. You know she has a big mouth." Pam laughed. Asia knew Angela well. If she said she would start screaming, she meant just that.

"Okay, I'm going shopping with my boyfriend."

"Right, you have a boyfriend and we haven't met him yet?"

"Asia, are you making this up?" Pam chuckled.

"No, I'm not making it up."

"Then why haven't we met him?" Angela pried.

"I wanted to make sure he was the one before I started showing him off, okay?"

"Okay, well, is he cute?" Pam asked.

"He's beyond cute; he's hot."

"Ooh, girl, is he hotter than Idris Elba?"

"Hotter!" Asia sipped from her tea.

Angela leaped up. "Okay, first off, Pam, you need to stop it with the Edris Elba fantasy. You wouldn't even know what to do with him." She spun around to Asia. "And you, if this guy is so fine, why haven't you introduced him to your best friend? You know I need to check him out before I give my approval."

Pam rolled her eyes at Angela.

"What? I am her best friend."

"Pam, don't listen to her. You are both my best friends."

Asia pinched Angela's arm.

"Ouch! All right, I'm sorry, Pam."

Angela leaned across the table to give Pam a hug.

"Okay, now, give us the dirt. Is he married, bisexual, or an illegal alien?"

"Excuse me, he's none of the above, thank you very much."

"Well, that's a switch. Which kennel did you say you got him from?"

Pam giggled.

"First off, Angela, he's not a dog, so I would appreciate it if you'll stop referring to him as such."

"Wait, this can't be the same person that sat across a table from us months ago; complaining about how much she hated men, and that they were dogs that needed to be destroyed?"

"Yeah, that's her." Pam nodded.

"I know what I said, but I was wrong. My man is different; he holds me, he kisses me, makes me believe in little girl dreams. You know, like happily-ever-after is actually possible."

Pam listened attentively.

"A dog did all that?" Angela joked.

"Yes, I mean, no. I mean, stop calling him that!" Asia was growing tired of her friend's taunts and she was about to lay into her.

Angela glanced at Pam. "Now, why can't I call them dogs? They call themselves dogs. 'What's up, dawg?' 'Hey, dawg.' 'Where are you going, dawg?' Asia, men are just dogs, D.O.G.S!"

Pam chuckled like a hyena.

Asia wondered how she ever became friends with such clowns. Angela was a bitter, but beautiful, man-basher who had been hurt so much in the past, that now she only used men for sex. Pam was a black woman trapped in a white woman's body who, for some reason, had a problem finding a man of any race to settle down with her.

"Hey, has anyone heard from Keisha?" Asia queried.

The look on Angela's face could cut through steel.

"Uh oh." Pam lowered her head.

The waiter returned to their table carrying a kettle of hot water and a tray of fresh fruit and pastries.

"Did you think that was funny?" Angela asked.

"What?"

"You know I don't like that heifer, so I don't know why you brought her name up?"

The waiter refilled their cups.

"I was just asking. Besides, she is my cousin."

"Yeah, okay. Anyway, finish telling us about your new friend. Is he any good in bed?"

Angela's comment caused the waiter to scatter away.

"See, I told you. They're all dogs; woof, woof!"

They all laughed.

"Angela, you are so bad."

"So, how long have you been seeing this mystery guy?"

Pam passed Asia a pack of sugar.

"A while."

"How long is a while, Asia?" Angela cut in.

"Five months," Asia mumbled.

"What did you say?" Pam moved closer.

"She said 'five months'."

Angela dropped her fork and stared across the table. "Asia, you've been seeing some strange man for five months, and we're just finding out?"

"I guess that's why we hardly see you anymore, huh?" Pam sneered.

"No, I've been busy putting in a lot of hours at work, so I can send some money to Austin. It has nothing to do with him."

"I bet," Angela mumbled.

Asia noticed the look that had settled on Angela's face.

"All right, I'm sorry, okay. As I said, I just wanted to be sure he was the one before I started introducing him to my friends."

"And it took you five months to be certain?" Angela smirked.

"Honey, you know how these men are; they're here today and gone tomorrow," Asia replied.

"I had to be absolutely sure."

Angela sat quietly for a few minutes. "So, you really believe this guy is the one?"

"Yes, I do."

"Well, then I'm happy for you." Angela hugged her.

"Me too." Pam hugged her as well.

"So, it's been five months and I bet your stuck-up behind is still holding out on him, huh?" Angela teased.

Asia reached for a Biscotti.

Angela's mouth immediately fell open and so did Pam's. They gasped.

Asia's eyes shifted between her two friends as the Biscotti dangled from her lips.

"Pam, did you see that?" Angela gawked.

"I saw it," Pam said, dunking a piece of pound cake into her coffee.

Asia was stumped.

"You did it, didn't you?" Angela repeated.

"Did what?"

"You know what!" Angela's stare intensified. "What? No," Asia tried to dodge their interrogation but was unsuccessful.

Angela persisted, "You did it; I can tell. Tell the truth!"

"Yeah, tell the truth, honey, and shame the devil," Pam said, continuing to dunk her cake.

"Okay, okay, we did it and it was explosive," Asia said.

Angela and Pam cheered.

"Oh girl, you have to tell us all about it," Angela insisted.

"Yes, tell, tell, tell," Pam added. "When you say explosive, do you mean explosive like in firecracker, or explosive as in weapon of mass destruction?"

"Girl, he nuked me!"

They all burst into laughter.

A few seconds later, their chuckling was interrupted by the ringing of Asia's cell phone. She answered it. "Hello?"

"Hey Baby."

Asia smiled.

"Oh, girl, is that him?" Pam scooted over in her seat. Angela leaned in as well. What's he saying?"

Asia motioned for them to be quiet.

"Yes, baby, I did miss you." She spoke softly, "Did you get my note?"

Pam and Angela listened closely.

"Yes, I'm ready for you. Where are you?

"I'm right outside; turn around."

Asia spun around, glanced out of the large window in the front of the restaurant, and spotted him leaning against his car.

"Damn!" Pam said.

Damn was right. The outfit he was wearing made him look like he had fallen out of a men's fashion magazine.

He licked his lips then blew her a kiss.

"Oh my God, is that him?" Angela asked, dropping an unopened packet of sweetener in her coffee.

"Yes, that's him."

Pam dropped her cake on the floor. She would have dropped her panties had she been wearing any.

Angela tried to speak but couldn't.

"Damn, Damn, Damn...he's fine!" Pam squealed.

"I know." Asia smiled.

She lifted herself from her seat, placed her phone back in her purse, and then stepped away from the table.

Angela halted her.

Girl wait; aren't you going to introduce us?"

"Yeah, girl, why don't you tell him to come in?"

Asia twirled around dramatically, tucked her purse under her arm and gave a quick reply.

"No!"

Angela rolled her eyes as Asia sashayed out of the restaurant like a model; and why not, she felt like one. The hem of her dress swayed with every step that she took.

"Can you believe her?" Angela asked, watching as Asia skirted out of the restaurant and into the arms of a man that made Tyson Bedford look like roadkill.

Meanwhile, Pam was sitting there like a block of ice, not moving, not even blinking-just frozen.

"Pam, snap out of it!" Angela said.

Pam began to shake as if in need of a dose of Ritalin. Angela rubbed the back of her hand to calm her nerves.

"I can't believe how fine he is," she said.

"I can't believe it either."

Angela watched as they drove away.

"I'm telling you, Pam, I take back every bad thing I've ever said about black men."

"Me, too," Pam said.

Angela rolled her eyes. "You know what, Pam? Just eat your damn cake."

CHAPTER NINETEEN

A Spread In The Linen Department

Asia skirted around the store as if it were her own personal runway. Her beautiful complexion drew stares from every man she passed. Within seconds, she had an audience, but Asia couldn't care less. The man she wanted was right behind her. She stopped in front of the escalator, watching Omar as he made his way through a horde of male onlookers. He moved confidently through the crowd, unaffected by their obvious gawking.

Asia and Omar stepped on the up escalator.

"You do know that you could have any of those guys you want," Omar observed.

"You do know that I'm ignoring you, right?" Asia said, moving to the step above him.

"Why? It's true."

"Yeah, well, why would I want any of them when I have you?"

Asia positioned herself in front of Omar resting her back against his chest.

"Besides, you know what I call men who stand around in malls, gawking at women."

"No, what?"

"Losers!" Asia replied, chuckling.

Omar noticed a woman was staring at him from just an arm's length away. She was on the down escalator. She smiled at him; he smiled back. Her eyes followed him lustfully.

"I'm really glad you decided to let me take you shopping, baby. Do you like the gift I bought you?" she asked.

"Yes, I do." Omar hugged her from behind. He stole one final look at the woman on the down escalator before she vanished from his view.

Asia turned around, threw her arms around his neck, and kissed him.

"What was that for?"

"No reason." She smiled. They stepped off the escalator.

After they stepped off the escalator, Asia held Omar's hand as they strolled through the electronics department. She noticed Omar's eyes were fixed on a large flat-screen television.

He held her by the waist, "So baby, you were really serious about taking me shopping, huh?"

"Well, you're always complaining that the television in your bedroom is too small and Christmas is in a few days."

"Excuse me. Can we get some help over here, please?" He flagged a salesperson.

She smiled. "Listen, sweetie, here's my credit card, pick out the television you want and then meet me in the bedding department. I have to pick up some sheets for a new client." She tickled his stomach before walking away.

Twenty minutes later...

Omar joined her in the linen department.

"Hey, what took you so long?"

"Ah, you know me. When I see something I like, I want to know everything about it."

"Yes, you do." She kissed him.

"Listen, baby, I'm going to be a few more minutes and I know how you hate shopping for stuff like this. If you want to wait for me in the electronics department, it's okay."

Omar considered doing just that, but that was before he realized just how vast the inventory in the bedding department was. There were wall-to-wall sheets, spreads, pillows, blankets and WOMEN.

There were so many colors, so many sizes.

"Come to think of it, I'm going to look around; I've been thinking about picking up a new spread anyway."

"Okay, I'll help you; just let me finish with this."

"No, I'll be fine. Take your time."

"Okay."

Asia turned her attention back to the huge display of brand name sheets.

Omar's attention swung to a woman who had been watching him from across the room. She wore jeans that looked like they had been painted on, a blouse that showed off her belly and a look in her eyes that said, *come hither.* She jotted down her number on a small piece of paper. She began to flirt.

Damn, she's hot! Omar thought. A smile settled on his face.

He watched as she reached for a pack of sheets that were stacked high on a shelf.

He made his way over, "Can I help you with that?"

"Can you?" She undressed him with her eyes as he reached for the package of sheets and handed them to her.

She was just about to hand him her number when Asia walked over.

"Collette?"

"Asia?" They rushed toward each other.

Omar's eyebrows rose.

"Girl, you look different."

"You think so?" Asia flashed a confident smile.

"Just a little bit, how have you been?"

"I'm great. How's your sister and the baby?"

Omar watched from a safe distance.

"Everyone is fine, girl. So, what are you doing here?"

"Oh, I'm just here with my-"

"Friend!" Omar cut in. "Hi, I'm Omar."

The look on Asia's face changed immediately.

"Hey, don't you work at Skyscrapers?" Collette asked.

"Yes, I do." Omar smiled, showing all his teeth. He loved when folks recognized him, particularly attractive women.

"One of my close friends works there. I've stopped by a few times but never joined. I remember seeing you there a few times."

Asia was steaming. *What in the hell did he mean, "friend"?*

She bit her tongue while Collette played groupie, but Omar was going to get it.

"It's nice to meet you, Omar," Collette said, moving closer. "Listen, I've been thinking about hiring a trainer; maybe you can refer me to someone who can give me a good workout."

"I'm sure I can; why don't you call me, and we can set something up." Omar reached in his wallet and passed over his business card.

Asia was shocked. She didn't even know Omar had business cards. She was ready to go. First Omar had referred to her as his *friend*; now he was handing out business cards.

"Uh, excuse me, Omar, we have to go," she said.

"Oh, okay. Listen, Collette, it was nice meeting you. Don't forget to give me a call."

"Believe me, I won't, Collette said suggestively before turning to Asia. "Girl, it was nice seeing you again. Listen. Here's my number. The next time we run into each other, we have to do lunch."

Asia flashed a phony smile, thinking, *please, the next time I run into you, I hope I'm driving a bus.* She cringed when Collette gave her a hug and then made a beeline toward the cashier counter.

Omar trailed behind her.

"Baby, hold up!"

Asia ignored him.

"Sweetheart, wait!"

"Wait for what, Omar?"

"What's wrong with you?"

"There's nothing wrong with me. What's wrong with you?" She continued to walk ahead of him.

He grabbed her arm.

"Get off of me."

"Okay, just tell me if I did something wrong?"

"You know exactly what you did." she snapped, turning toward the cashier.

"Hi, how are you today?"

"I'm fine. Will this be cash or charge?"

Asia placed her things on the counter.

"Charge."

"Honey, if I did something wrong, let me know."

"You referred to me as your friend." Asia scowled.

"Is that what this is all about?" He stared at her.

"Yes."

"Baby, I didn't mean anything by it."

"Then why did you give her your business card? I didn't even know you had business cards."

"Asia, trainers give out business cards all the time; it's how we get our clients."

"Yeah, well, I still don't like it."

"Come on; Ben gives out fifty to a hundred cards a day,"

"Yeah, well, Ben isn't a saint, and he's hardly the defense you should be using right now."

Omar didn't appreciate Asia's comment. What did she mean by defense? He didn't feel that he had to defend his actions to anyone.

"What is this really about, Asia?"

Asia did what she always did when she's upset, ignored him.

"Baby, people are going to say hello to me; I'm a trainer in one of the hottest gyms on the east coast. What do you want me to do? Walk around with a bag over my head?"

"That might help."

"Oh, I get it. You're jealous," he said.

She looked off.

"That's what it is...you're jealous, admit it." His voice elevated.

"Stop it, you're making a scene." She searched her purse for her credit card.

"I don't care. You want people to know we're more than friends, right?" He moved into the middle of the room. "Listen up everyone; my lady friend wants to have me all to herself; is that okay?" he yelled.

Asia turned as red as a tomato.

"See, no one cares, Asia. So, you shouldn't care. We know what we have; that's all that matters." He handed her back her credit card.

"Yeah, but what about your flirting?"

"What about it?"

"What?"

"Asia, you don't have anything to worry about." He grabbed her by the waist. "You want me to be successful, right?"

"You know I do."

"Good, then give me a kiss and stop treating me so badly."

She smiled and gave him a quick kiss on the cheek. After paying for her items, they headed toward the escalator-this time, together. Omar felt it was the least he could do, being she had just paid for his brand new 60" HD television.

They were stepping off the escalator when the sound of a woman's voice caught Asia's attention.

"Keisha?"

"Asia?"

They raced toward each other, screaming.

"What are you doing here?"

"No, what are you doing here?" Asia said.

Omar stood there thinking, *No, what am I doing here?*

Once again, Asia had left him holding her bags, while she played catch up with a woman who looked like a video vixen.

"Girl, I haven't seen you in so long." Keisha looked her up and down before hugging her again.

"Showing off that body of yours."

"Well, you know me girl."

Omar watched as Keisha broke into a Wonder Woman spin to give Asia a closer look.

"You go, girl,"

"Oh, I'm going, baby, believe that."

"So, you still didn't tell me what you were doing here."

"Oh, I work here."

"In the cosmetic department, I hope?"

"Where else?"

Asia chuckled.

"I'm on break right now, so I stopped by my friend's counter to pick up some fragrances."

"Are you still wearing men's cologne?" Asia frowned.

"That's right, honey, the men love it." She looked past Asia. "And who is this?"

"Oh, where are my manners? This is Omar, my friend."

"Hi."

"It's nice to meet you, Omar. I'm Keisha, Asia's cousin." She flirted with her eyes.

Omar extended his hand to Keisha while simultaneously shooting a cutting look at Asia.

Asia didn't seem to care. That's how Keisha was. Besides, she wanted to prove a point to Omar; that how you introduce someone does matter.

"Tell me, Omar, do you like the way this fragrance smells on me?" She hoisted her breasts toward his face.

Omar flinched.

"What's wrong?"

"Honestly, it comes on a bit too strong. I'm into something a little more subtle." He wrapped his arms around Asia.

Keisha didn't seem to care about his comment, especially since she wasn't wearing any perfume in the first place. She continued to flirt.

"Well, it's still nice to meet you, Omar. I'm sure I'll see you around."

"I doubt it, but it's nice to meet you, too," he said, cracking a half smile. He quickly looked away. Omar hated overly forward women. He couldn't care less about Keisha, her breasts or her imaginary perfume. All he wanted to do was take Asia home to re-introduce her to the goliath in his pants so she can give him some much-needed personal attention.

When Keisha realized that Omar wasn't immediately bowled over by her outstanding features, she quickly turned her focus back to Asia.

"So, cousin, when are you going home to Austin, girl?"

Asia glanced at Omar.

"Sweetheart, would you mind waiting for me in the car? I'll be out in a minute."

"Sure."

Omar was glad to oblige. The scents radiating from those little bottles of perfume the salesgirls were spraying on everyone who passed by, was starting to sicken him.

He gently patted Asia on her behind and headed out to the car.

"Don't take too long."

"I won't."

"Way to go, girl. He's fine," Keisha commented.

"Yes, he is."

"So, is that yours?"

"Is what mine?"

"You know, Mr. Tall, Dark, and Handsome."

"Well, I don't own him, but if you're asking if we're together, the answer is yes."

"Really... So, how long have you two been together?" Keisha wrapped her arms around Asia and guided her closer to the perfume counter.

"Five months, but it seems like forever."

"Okay, that's still pretty new, but he seems to be into you."

"Do you think so?"

"Are you kidding? I threw these babies in his face and he didn't even blink. So, either he's very into you or he's gay." She chuckled.

Asia snickered as well.

"Excuse me?" A voice spilled from behind the perfume counter.

Asia blushed with embarrassment as a tall, wiry, and obviously gay male gawked at them. He stood with his arms folded, leering at them over the counter with arched eyebrows and a painted-on Cindy Crawford mole.

"We're sorry. We didn't mean anything by it," Asia said.

Keisha sucked her teeth.

Asia nudged her, "Girl, don't be rude."

"Oh please, girl, don't apologize to him." Keisha wiggled her finger as she pointed in his direction. "Jerome, shouldn't you be getting my order together?"

"You know him?" Asia whispered.

"Girl, this queen has been doing my makeup for years. Now he's working behind this perfume counter and he had better hook me up, too." Keisha playfully cut her eyes at him.

Asia forced a smiled.

"So, when are you going back to Texas? You know, Austin hasn't been the same since you left."

"I know, but I've been so busy with work; I barely have time right now."

Keisha sneered.

"Don't look at me like that. I've thought about this long and hard."

"So, you've basically made your decision?"

"Yes."

"Well, okay. If you like it, I love it," Keisha said, handing Jerome her credit card. She turned back to Asia, "So, tell me, have you and Omar slept together yet?"

"I'm not telling you that." She started smelling perfumes samples to avoid Keisha's prying.

"Asia!"

"What?"

"Girl, we've been close for years. You know good and well that there aren't any secrets between us."

Keisha knew that Asia was known for holding out on guys, but Omar was fine. She was curious if Asia had, for once in her life, caved into temptation.

"Okay, okay, let's put it this way; on a scale of one to ten, he's a twelve-literally!"

Keisha gasped and so did Jerome.

"You know, Kareem was built like that, too."

"Kareem?" Asia snapped.

Keisha read the look on her cousin's face and quickly corrected herself. "I mean... that's what I heard."

Asia wasn't buying it though. When they were in college, Keisha was known for sleeping with men who belonged to other women. She and Angela had fallen out over that very thing. Rumor had it that Keisha was seeing Kareem, Angela's boyfriend at the time. However, when Angela confronted her, she denied it. Days later, Angela had caught her coming out of Kareem's dorm room. They got into a huge fight, which broke up their friendship. Although Keisha has always denied sleeping with Kareem, Angela never believed her. Since that day, they had been sworn enemies.

"Don't look at me like that, Asia. I'm telling you it was a rumor that went around campus, remember?"

"No, the rumor that went around campus was that you and Kareem were messing around behind Angela's back; that's why you two fell out, remember?"

"Yeah, well, I told her it wasn't true."

"That's your story and you're sticking to it, huh?"

"That's right. Anyway, let's exchange numbers before we forget; we have a lot of catching up to do."

Keisha pulled a small cell phone from between her size Double-D breasts.

"Uh, uh." Asia chuckled.

"Oh, please, honey, nothing's changed."

"Don't forget to call me," Asia said before heading toward the exit.

"I won't."

Keisha watched as she vanished through the revolving doors.

"Damn, did you see that? Her guy is fine."

"Oh, yes, he was," Jerome said. He fanned himself as he handed Keisha back her credit card.

"I swear if Asia wasn't my cousin, I'd be all over him."

"Yeah, me too, girl." Jerome licked his lips.

Keisha spun around. "See, that's the damn problem now. It's not enough that she has to worry about other women trying to take her man, now she has to worry about your ass!"

"Oh, Keisha, please; I was just saying."

"I know what you were just saying. Just give me the damn perfume so I can go!" She snatched the bag from his hands and strode away.

Jerome stepped from behind the counter.

"Keisha, you know you don't have to act like that."

"Yeah, you don't either." Keisha snapped her fingers in a circular motion before she also vanished through the revolving doors.

Meanwhile, a crowd of their peers was watching from across other counters. They were staring at Jerome as if he had a pair of dragon wings growing out of his back.

"What the hell are you all looking at? Haven't you ever seen two friends joke around? Get back to work with your nosy asses!"

CHAPTER TWENTY

If Men Are Pimps Then What Are Women?

When Asia exited the store, she noticed that Omar was standing across the street from the main entrance. He was leaning against a parking meter with his hands tucked deep into his pockets. She waited for the traffic light to change, then scurried quickly across the intersection.

"Sorry I took so long."

"No problem; I'd wait for you forever," he said, opening the passenger side door to help her into the car.

"Thanks."

"So, that's your cousin, huh?"

"Yes." Asia tossed her purse onto the back seat. "Do you know, I haven't seen that girl in two years."

"Why so long?"

"It's a long story."

"Money?"

"Nope, a man."

He switched the subject, immediately. "So, is she always like that?"

"Like what?"

He looked askance, as if to say, come on. You know exactly what I'm talking about.

"Oh, you mean the flirting?"

He nodded.

"Keisha's harmless."

"I don't know; if I were a woman, I wouldn't trust her."

"Well, thank God, you're not a woman."

She slid her hand along his thigh.

"Hey, don't start something you can't finish right here."

"Don't worry...if I start it, I'll finish it."

"Yeah, right." He smiled.

"Anyway, I'm just saying, you don't have to worry about it."

"Oh, I wasn't worried; I just thought it was strange that you had a problem with Collette, but you didn't mind your cousin being so flirtatious?"

"Did you enjoy it?" Asia joked.

"Please!"

"I saw the way you were staring at her."

"Yes, I was staring at her because she's built like a Mack truck."

Asia punched him playfully in the arm. "So, that's what you want...a woman with big breasts and a big ass so you can gawk at her all day?"

"Asia, stop it."

"No, just admit it; you like her."

"Please, she's too aggressive for me."

"I thought most men like forward women."

"Forward, yes, but she's the type of woman that doesn't respect boundaries."

"I don't know what you're talking about."

"Come on, you saw her. She was practically throwing herself at me even though she knew that you were my lady."

Asia froze.

"Men aren't like that; we respect each other's territory. At least, when we know the guy is around. For instance, if a man sees a good-looking woman with another guy, he might take notice, sneak a glance or two, but that's about it. It stops there."

"And your point is?"

"My point is that women don't respect boundaries." Any other time, Asia would have been all over that comment, but not this time. She was too caught up in the fact that he had indirectly referred to her as his lady. She unfolded her arms and thought about what her next words should be. While she agreed that Keisha was a flirt, she had things that were more important on her mind.

"I agree with you."

Omar nearly lost control of his steering.

"What did you just say?"

"You're right; she's a huge flirt."

He couldn't believe it. For the first time since he's known her, she was letting him make a comment without having to prove him wrong. The change of direction pleased him.

He grabbed Asia's hand and kissed it.

"What's that for?"

"Just because you're you. Tell me, what do you want to do now? Whatever you want to do is fine with me."

She glanced out of the window at a boat that was sailing across the Hudson.

"The city is so beautiful around the holidays."

"Done!"

"What? No, Omar, wait, you don't even know what I was going to say."

"Yes, I do." He stepped on the gas.

Asia was shocked.

"Where are we going?"

"You'll see."

She started reading the traffic signs and deduced that they were heading for the South Street Seaport.

"Oh, my goodness, are we going for the moonlight cruises?"

"You know, a good man knows what his woman wants even before she says it." He stopped for a light.

"So, are you happy?"

"Yes," she replied softly.

He kissed her hand again.

In the past two minutes, Omar had referred to her as his lady and his woman. She was dumbfounded. Both of those titles were a big jump from previously being referred to as his *'friend'*. She wanted to ask him if he knew what he was saying but feared she would ruin things. Besides, she had been waiting to hear those words for months.

For the rest of the ride, she sat quietly, feeling like Sophia from The Color Purple. All she could do was smile and think, *I's got a man now!*

New York City is beautiful at night...

The view of Manhattan was spectacular. The way the tall buildings lit up the sky made every moment with Omar more magical.

"I could sail all night," Asia said.

"You know I would make that happen for you, too, right?"

"Would you?"

"Yes, I'll give you anything your heart desires if I can; even the moon. Just ask.

Asia melted with every word Omar spoke as she stared into his beautiful eyes. She could have swum in them, they were so deep and full, but as the boat neared the dock, he received a call and the look on his face changed.

"Is everything okay?" she asked.

"Yeah, I just remembered I have a meeting tonight." He folded her into his arms.

"I'm sorry; I didn't mean to keep you out so late."

"Don't be, you didn't know about my meeting. The thing is when I'm with you, I lose track of time." He looked down into her eyes.

She had hoped to spend more time with him, but her aspirations were being quickly doused.

"I want to give you something." He reached up as if snatching something from the sky.

"What are you doing?" she chuckled.

"Just close your eyes."

"Omar?"

"Close them," he demanded.

She did what he asked.

"Okay, open them."

"Oh, my goodness, what is this?"

"I know I said I'd give you the moon, but will you settle for a locket for now?"

She blushed. Although the line sounded like something stolen from a decade long before her existence, she melted.

"Omar, this is beautiful."

"I'm glad you like it."

"Like it?" She turned away from him to give the pendant a quick scan, noticing that it was from Tiffany. "I love it."

"Read the inscription."

She read it aloud.

"To my favorite girl." Her eyes began to tear.

The expression on Asia's face was clear; Omar had more than made up for having to cut their evening short.

He held her by the waist as they left the ferry terminal. "So, will you take a rain check on the moon?"

"Yes. This has been the best night of my life."

"You're a good woman, Asia. Good women deserve the best." He glanced at his phone as they exited the boat.

They walked swiftly toward the car.

"If I don't get you home and get to my meeting, the only moon I'll be able to afford to buy you will be a moon pie."

He helped Asia inside and then hopped in himself. He put the key in the ignition and quickly pulled out of the parking space. They didn't even get three blocks before they had to stop for a red light.

Asia began to sing as they waited for the light to change.

"Wow, you have a beautiful voice."

"You're just saying that."

"I'm a lot of things, Asia, but I'm not a liar."

"Yeah, okay, so what do you know about music?"

"Come on, I'm a poet. I know a lot about music."

"Oh, so now you're a poet, too?"

"That's right."

"Well okay, Langston Hughes. Recite something for me right now, and it better be original."

Clearly, Asia had forgotten whom she was dealing with. If Omar said he was a poet, then he was a poet. He licked his lips and started to recite...

"Like diamonds in the sky, I hang on the blue of the night; sparkling in your distance and so you dance in my light.

And while the wind blows - whistling a song so melancholy, I realize it's just for me.

For you, and I will never be.

Even as much as I can, I have reached down, gently stroking your velvet way.

My fingers have danced across your endless back, but still the sun chases me away.

But tomorrow, I'll be back

And the night after that, and the night after that, and the night after that.

But until then, my dear, I hope to see you soon and for now, its love always...Your Melancholy Moon. "

Asia was completely blown away. Omar's flawless delivery of "*Melancholy Moon*" made her moist. She sat silently, basking in the many layers of his personality. She was amazed that after so many months there were still things she didn't know about him.

When they arrived at her place, they sat in the car for a few moments fighting the urge to strip naked and have sex in his car.

"You know I want to drop everything and accompany you upstairs, right?"

"I know, but you can't."

"No, I can't. I'll call you later, though." He kissed her hand.

"Are you sure you can't come in for a little while?"

"I can't, but I'll call you when I get in, okay?"

"Okay."

Omar's phone was buzzing like a bee. He blew her a kiss and sped off.

As Asia made her way up the stairs to her house, she noticed a package lying in front of her door. She read the label as she carried it inside. It was from her grandmother. Kicking off her shoes, she headed into the kitchen for a knife.

She set the box on the countertop, grabbed a glass of water, and began checking her messages. There were twelve.

"Hi, Asia, it's me, Grandma. I'm just thinking about you. I hope you got the package I sent. Call me."

Beep!

"Hey, girl, it's Pam, and me, Angela; give us a call if you want to go see a movie tonight."

Beep!

"Asia, it's Tai. I know it's been a while, but I'm not giving up that easily. Call me."

Beep!

"Hey, girl, it's me, Keisha. Give me a call when you get in, okay?"

Beep!

She smiled as she listened to Keisha's message; it was good seeing her cousin again.

"Hey, Asia, it's me again, Keisha. I guess you're not back yet. Give me a call when you get in."

Beep!

"Hey, A, it's Keisha. Are you still out with that fine man of yours? Give me a call when you get in."

Beep!

Asia's smile started to dissipate.

"What's up, Asia? Listen. Call me no matter what time you get in. I want to talk to you about something; it's important."

Beep!

Asia freaked; she immediately returned Keisha's calls.

"Hey, Keisha, what's up?"

"Oh, Asia, hey, hold on a sec, let me clear my other line, okay?"

"Okay."

Two minutes passed.

"Okay, I'm back."

"Keisha, is everything all right?"

"You mean outside the constant requests for late night booty calls? Yes." She chuckled.

Asia didn't find it funny; she wasn't the type to engage in either late night booty calls or idle phone chatter at such a late hour.

"So, what's up, Keisha, your messages sounded urgent."

"Oh, it was nothing, girl. I was just anxious to catch up with you; that's all."

Asia was relieved. "I'm anxious to catch up, too. But why didn't you call me on my cell phone?"

She used a knife to open the box. Inside was a beautiful bouquet of flowers with a note, some photos and a badly handwritten card that read, *From Austin, with love.*

For a few seconds, Asia had forgotten that Keisha was on the phone. Her eyes filled with tears. She wiped them away quickly.

"Asia, are you there?"

"Yes, I'm here." She carried the flowers up to her bedroom, turning off the lights along the way.

"Okay, well, I was saying, I did call your cell phone, but you didn't answer."

"I'm sorry; I was having so much fun with Omar, I didn't even hear your call come in." She placed the flowers on the nightstand near her bed.

"So, what did you guys do this evening?" Keisha pried.

"Girl, it's late. I'm not about to get into all of that with you." Asia noticed how beautiful the vase was.

"Oh, please, you know you can tell me anything. Remember how we used to stay up late nights, talking on the phone for hours?"

"Yes, I remember." Asia smiled.

"Hey, how's Pam doing? Is she still on the hunt for a Mandingo warrior?"

"She's fine and yes, she's still interested in black men."

Keisha found Pam's obsession with black men hilarious, "Why doesn't she just date someone from her own ethnic background? She'll probably have better luck."

"Keisha, Pam has the right to date whomever she wants. Besides, it's not easy to find a good man no matter what race he is. I'm just thankful that I've found Omar."

"Yeah, well, God did have your back with that one. So, does he know that you..."

"No, he doesn't!" Asia snapped. "I really wish you would stop bringing it up."

"I'm sorry."

There were a few seconds of silence between them. "Anyway, did I tell you that I'm on the choir at my church?"

"Really; why?" Keisha asked sarcastically.

"Well, because I enjoy singing and church helps me to clear my head, believe it or not."

"Not." Keisha joked.

"Well, we're having a concert at the church in two weeks and I'd like for you to come."

"To church?" Keisha snarled.

"Yes, to the church! You do still remember what a church is, don't you?"

"Yeah, I remember. That's the place where all the hypocrites go to learn how to cast stones at their friends."

"Oh no, you didn't?"

"Oh, calm down; I'm just playing."

"Good, then I'll get you a ticket."

"Oh, okay," Keisha replied blankly.

"And don't you even think about backing out later, Keisha; once I pay for your ticket, that's it."

Keisha hesitated.

"Hello?"

"Girl, you know I don't get along with church folks."

"I know, but church will do you some good."

Keisha switched gears. "So, what did you say you and Omar did tonight?"

"Here you go with that again." Asia yawned. "Listen, it's late and I have to get some rest."

"Okay, well you have a good night. Is Omar coming to the church, too?"

"No, he isn't. Why do you keep asking about him?"

"No reason."

"Okay, well, good night then!"

"Good night, Asia."

After her conversation with Keisha, Asia headed into the bathroom. She chuckled as she ran the tub full of water. Immersing her body in a warm bubble bath, she thought about the fact that she had finally found her 'good black man'. She was happy; she had good health, a good job, a good man, a fabulous home, and some great friends. She still missed   Austin so much; leaving was the hardest thing she ever had to do. Her mind flashed back to her conversation with Keisha to prevent her from bursting into tears.

"Church is really going to do that girl some good," she muttered.

Keisha had some issues that kept her from the church. They all did at one time or another. What worried her most was not whether Keisha would show up, but what Angela would do when she does.

ACROSS TOWN AT KEISHA'S

"Hello, Jerome?"

"Yeah."

"Hi, this is Keisha."

"I know who it is. What's wrong?"

"Nothing, I just got off of the phone with my cousin Asia, and do you know what she had the nerve to ask me?"

"What?"

"She asked if I would come to her church to hear her sing."

"Ooh, she must really want the saints to do a Hallelujah dance."

"I know that's right. Asia knows good and well that I don't get along with church folk. Why would she invite me there to hear her sing? Hell, I've listened to her sing since we were kids; I don't need to go to church to hear her sing."

Jerome didn't reply.

"Hello, Jerome!"

"Yeah, I'm here."

"What are you doing?"

"Girl, I have company."

Jerome began to moan.

"Uh, uh. Jerome, I know you're not getting your cakes smashed while I'm on the phone with an emergency."

"Keisha, girl, it's late. Get to the point; are you going to the church or not?"

"Not."

"Good, then I'll see you at work tomorrow, bye."

"Bye!"

Keisha hung up the phone and paced around her apartment.

"Huh, it will be a cold day in hell before I set foot in another church."

CHAPTER TWENTY-ONE

Trust me, You're the Only One

Omar parked in front of an apartment building on East 72nd Street. While he waited, he thought about Asia. He even phoned her a few times in hopes of hearing her sweet voice, but unfortunately, she never answered; this bothered him.

He noticed a woman approaching his car. She was dressed in a pink tweed suit; it fit her well. She was pretty and apparently well-conditioned; just the way he liked. The closer she got, the more aroused he became; still he couldn't help thinking about Asia.

He removed his jacket from the passenger side and flung it onto the back seat. He licked his lips, checked his face in the rearview mirror, and tried to shake the thought of Asia from his mind.

A sharp tap on the window broke into his thoughts.

"Are you going to open the door, or should I ride on the hood?" the woman flirted, although never displaying a smile.

He grinned and opened the passenger door.

"Gee, thanks. It's good to know chivalry isn't dead." She reached over to touch his face.

He intercepted her hand.

"Don't!" he warned. His face bore a stern appearance. "Ooh! Aggressive; I like that."

"Yeah, well, the less you talk tonight, the more enjoyable this will be for both of us."

"You're the boss!"

The woman folded her hands and smiled.

Omar started the car.

She glanced at his arms and at his crotch then mumbled, "This workout will be worth every penny."

Straight to the bouquet

Asia had seen Mahogany a dozen times and she always cried at the same parts. Before Omar, Asia didn't think God made men like Billy Dee Williams anymore. He was a good black man, strong, confident, and always on time.

Speaking of which, she noticed that her 'good black man' hadn't called her as promised. Until that moment, he had been a man of his word. Although she tried to fight it, she was beginning to worry. She never got over the fact that Omar had left her in the past; she still had a fear of him doing it again.

She pressed the rewind button on the remote control and tried to focus on pleasant thoughts.

Her phone rang.

"Hello."

"Hey, did I wake you?"

She beamed.

"No, I haven't been to sleep yet."

"Why is that?" he questioned.

"I don't know; I'm not sleepy, I guess." She was being evasive. She didn't want him to know that she had been thinking about him the entire time.

"Did you go out?"

"Nope, I've been right here since you dropped me off."

His silence caught her off guard.

"Hello."

He still didn't answer.

"Omar are you there?"

"I'm here. Are you sure you didn't go out?"

"I told you...I was right here the whole time." She chuckled.

"I called you and you didn't answer the phone; did you have company?"

She decided to tease him.

"You know what, Omar? I did have company; he was tall, dark, and handsome. In fact, he's here right now."

CLICK!

Omar gasped; she had hung up on him. He tried calling her right back but got no answer.

Seconds later, Asia's doorbell rang. She leaped from her bed and glanced out of the window.

"Who is it?"

No one answered.

"Who's there?" she called out.

Still, there was no answer.

"I said who's there?"

She slipped into her robe, reached into the closet for an aluminum baseball bat, and then headed downstairs. She approached the door with caution as the ringing continued.

"You better get away from my door!" she said nervously.

"Asia, it's me...open the door!"

"Omar?"

She unlatched the door and swung it open.

"What took you so long?"

"What are you doing here?'

"Were you expecting someone else?" he asked.

"No, I thought someone was trying to break in on me."

"Oh really, and what were you going to do with that bat?" He glanced at the Louisville Slugger and smirked.

"I was going to hit him with it."

"Where, on the knees?"

"Actually, I thought a little bit higher than that."

"Yeah, whatever!"

"Whatever yourself!" She closed the door.

He glanced around.

"So, what are you doing here? I thought you had a meeting."

"Okay, let's get some things straight!"

Asia drew back.

"When I dropped you off tonight, I was under the impression that you would be in for the night."

"I was."

"Yeah, well, why didn't you answer your phone?"

"What phone, Omar?"

"The house phone, the cell phone, the pay phone, the phone in the sky, Asia, take your pick!"

She was as shocked at Omar's tone as she was about his calling upon her at such a late hour. She could smell liquor on his breath.

"I was here all night. What are you talking about?"

He studied her as he slipped out of his jacket.

She had joked about having company, and boy, did that start a fire! One she was having a hard time extinguishing.

"So, is your company still here?" Omar started toward the steps.

"What? Come on, Omar, get serious."

"I am serious." He headed to her bedroom.

"You actually believe that I would have another man in my house and in my bedroom, Omar?"

He ignored her and began searching her bedroom like a madman. No one was there.

"Are you finished?" she asked.

"Not yet." He looked under the bed.

"Are you going to check the flowerpots, too?" Asia laughed.

Unfortunately, that was the wrong thing to say because he turned his attention straight to the bouquet of flowers on her nightstand.

"What's this?" he asked, making his way across the bed to examine the arrangements.

She didn't respond.

"Who the hell is Austin, Asia?" he asked as he read the card.

"My grandmother sent those to me from Texas."

"You expect me to believe that?"

"Yes."

"I don't believe you!" He grabbed the vase and prepared to smash it.

"Wait!" She pressed the play button on her answering machine. Her grandmother's voice filled the room.

As Omar listened to the message, he sat on the bed and lowered his head.

Asia moved toward him.

"I'm sorry. I thought…"

"Baby, what is this all about?" She removed the vase from his hands and returned it to the nightstand.

He grabbed her hand and pulled her closer.

"Asia, I'm sorry; I tried to fight this, but I can't anymore!"

"Fight what; what's going on?"

"I think about you all the time, probably too much. I get crazy when I think of you with another guy. You're on my mind constantly."

Her eyes widened. She never thought she would hear those words coming from his mouth. Her heart felt a jolt as well. "Trust me, baby, I'm not seeing anyone else. You're the only man I'm interested in."

"I don't even know why I flipped out like this. All I know is that I love you."

She stared down into his eyes, abandoning all sense of reason and resistance. She felt wanted and that was good enough reason to forgive his juvenile display.

"I love you, too."

He wrapped his arms around her legs, gripping them tightly.

"Do you want me?" he asked, using his face to part her robe.

"Yes."

He pressed his face against her thighs.

The feel of his facial hair against her skin tickled her senses.

"Omar, wait." She stopped his hand from moving up her leg.

"I thought you said you loved me."

"I do!"

"Then let me do this." He placed multiple kisses on her thighs. "Let me make you feel like you've never felt before."

She gripped his head, pointed her tits into the air, and then guided him toward her pleasure zone.

As Omar explored her, she remembered their first time. She had never experienced such pleasure, not before him, not since him.

He buried his face between her legs. The coarse hair from his goatee lent an added sensation as he licked, kissed, and sucked her.

"Omar, please, if I get hurt again, I don't know what I'll do."

"Ssh! I'm not him, and I'm not going to do anything you don't want me to do."

His tone was comforting. His hands seemed to massage all her inhibitions away.

She spread her legs and allowed his entry.

"Make love to me," she said.

Her eyes met his as he crawled closer to her. Suddenly a strange look appeared on his face.

"What's wrong?"

"Before we do this, I have to tell you something." He looked down into her eyes. "I want you to know everything about me."

"I know all that I need to know...for now," she said, pushing him over to straddle him.

"I know that you're a gentleman." She kissed his forehead.

"I know that you're a Scorpio." She kissed his nose.

"I know that you love me." She kissed his lips.

"I know that you would never hurt me." She kissed his chest.

"And I know that I want to make you feel as special as you make me feel." She kissed his belly.

"I know that it's time, Omar." She attempted to go lower.

He stopped her. "Asia, don't!"

He placed one hand between them.

She looked into his eyes.

"Am I your lady?" she asked.

"Yes, you are."

"Do you love me?"

"Yes."

"Then let me do this...let me make you feel like no other woman can."

She placed her hands around his wrists, pinned his hands to the mattress, and then lowered her head between his legs. The warmth of her mouth caused his eyes to roll back in his head.

"Asia!" he called out. His fingers gripped her hair. His toes began to curl and every muscle in his lower extremity flexed.

For nearly an hour, he moaned with satisfaction. That night, they made love to each other, repeatedly. He loved her and she loved him, and it was all that mattered, for now.

CHAPTER TWENTY-TWO

You Must Have Me Mistaken

Ben's note said to meet him at the Marriott Marquis at 9 o'clock. Omar sat in the hotel lobby, tossing back shots of Patron. He thought about Asia while he waited for Ben to arrive. He hated feeling helpless. The fact that Asia wouldn't return his calls, made him feel vulnerable and exposed - like he made her feel when they had their first big fight. They had been together for a year and a half and as much as it hurt, he remembered that evening as if it were yesterday...

> *"Love painted a picture for me; upfront it*
> *was in black, the background too. She said*
> *that it was of roses and of children dancing*
> *along a creek, of the wind spiraling through*
> *fields. She said, imagine love being anything*
> *in the world that I want it to be, and so, I im-*
> *agined you- "*

Asia loved that poem. It reminded her of how deeply one person could feel for another. Being able to share it with Omar was an epic moment in her life. She had been writing since she was a child, but not since her breakup with Tai, had she been willing to share such an intimate part of herself with a man.

She stroked the side of Omar's face, as he rested his head on her lap. "Wasn't that beautiful, baby?"

She smiled, hoping he appreciated her willingness to share.

Omar didn't respond, causing her mood to shift.

"Omar, are you happy?" she asked placing the worn copy of *"Like Leaves on a Poet Tree"* down beside her.

"Yeah, why do you ask that?" he questioned, while playing with the straps on her nightgown.

"I don't know. Sometimes, I feel like you're not here, like you're preoccupied."

He rolled over, removing himself from her arms. He grabbed the remote control and began flicking channels on the television. It was something he always did whenever he wanted to avoid a conversation.

They were having a pretty peaceful evening until that point. She didn't want to spoil things by asking a bunch of questions, but she couldn't help it.

She watched as he lay on the opposite side of the bed with the sheet pulled up to his chest, as if he were in bed alone.

"See, this is what I'm talking about. I ask you a simple question and you run to the other side of the bed."

"What are you talking about, Asia? I'm trying to watch a program."

"Really, and since when did you become so interested in QVC?" She glanced at the TV and then back at him.

All at once, he pressed the off button on the remote control and sat up in the bed.

"Okay, what is it, Asia? What's on your damn mind?"

"Excuse me?"

"You want to talk, right? Now, the television is turned off. You have my undivided attention, so shoot."

At that point, he had no idea how much Asia wanted to do just that. Shoot him.

His tone of voice had become so increasingly sharp over the past few weeks that she couldn't help taking notice. Whenever she would bring up a subject that he was uncomfortable with or that he didn't feel like discussing, he'd snap, and she didn't like it one bit.

She propped herself up on two pillows and stared at him.

At that moment, lying next to him was like lying next to a stranger. She had no idea who he was anymore.

"If we can't talk like two adults who are supposedly in a relationship, then forget it!"

"Baby, look, I'm sorry. I had a long day at the gym. Folks hire a personal trainer and think that we're supposed to turn into magicians suddenly. It's like they expect us to wave a magic dumbbell and instantly, all the years of unhealthy living and bad eating habits will just disappear. It's been crazy."

"I know your job is hectic, baby. That's why when you're here, I try to do everything I can to help you relax."

"I know you do." He rubbed the back of her hand.

She leaned forward to kiss him, but the message alert on his cell phone sounded, cutting that intimate moment short.

He moved away to check his phone.

Asia's mouth was fell open allowing her tongue to feel the frost from the air conditioning.

"You know, Omar, I don't even believe you," she spouted.

"What did I do now?"

"You pay more attention to your cell phone than you do to our relationship."

"Come on, now you're exaggerating." He moved his fingers swiftly across the screen on his phone as if playing a handheld video game.

"Oh, I'm exaggerating, huh? How many times did your phone ring since we've been in bed?"

"I don't know, once, twice maybe."

"Try six times, Omar." She smirked. "How many times did the text alert go off after that?"

"I don't know, Asia."

"Yeah, I lost count too."

He was getting annoyed with Asia's questioning. The look on his face said, I wish you would just be quiet and drop it. He knew better than to say it though, because she was seconds away from grabbing his phone and slinging it out of the window."

"What do you want me to do, Asia, turn my phone off?"

"Yes."

"Yeah right. Stop playing." He chuckled.

"Then why did you ask?"

"Just to see what you were going to say."

"That's a bit childish, don't you think?"

"No more childish than your complaints about calls that are coming from my job."

"Oh, so, you expect me to believe that every time your phone rings, it's your job calling?"

"That's right, ninety-seven percent of the time it's business."

"So, what about the other three percent, is that pleasure?" she asked.

He glanced at the clock; it was 1:00 a.m.

"Baby, can we just have a peaceful night and not argue over something that makes no sense?"

He slid over in the bed to kiss her. She closed her eyes and once again, prepared for a long, passionate, kiss. Once again, they were interrupted by the chiming of his cell phone.

He rolled over to check the message window.

Asia rolled over, too, in the opposite direction.

He climbed from the bed.

"Excuse me, but where are you going?" She asked.

"I have to run out, but I'll be back." He grabbed his watch from the nightstand.

"You'll be back?"

"Yeah."

"Where are you going?" she scoffed.

"Out."

"How much longer do you think I'm going to put up with this?" She asked, swinging her legs from the bed. Although she was Christian she was getting tired of his shit.

"What are you talking about?"

"I'm talking about the fact that you run out of here every time your phone rings, like it's okay."

He retrieved his underwear from the foot of the bed.

"I'm talking about the fact that it's one o'clock in the morning and you're still getting text messages."

"I have to meet with Ben," he said, slipping into his pants.

"Right...I forgot. Are you fucking Ben, too?"

He looked at Asia and shook his head.

"Shake your head all you want. I'm shaking mine, too."

He headed into the bathroom.

She followed him.

"You know, you walk around here as if I should be glad that you're with me."

He gripped his crotch and smiled. The look on his face telegraphed the words, you should be!

Asia scowled as she watched him dress in the clothes she bought him.

"I know you're going to see another woman, Omar. I'm not stupid."

"No one said you were."

"What are you going to do...take her to dinner like you took me? Are you going to give her the song, dance, and poetry, too?"

The more questions she asked, the more he ignored her.

"You're not slick, you know; you're going to get caught in your shit, sooner or later."

He blew a kiss at his reflection in the mirror.

"Look at you. Do you know what they call men who spend hours primping and staring in the mirror?"

"No, what?"

"Faggots, Omar; they call them faggots!"

He cut her a quick look.

"No, you're not a faggot; you just think you're God's gift to women, right? Well, you're not!" He headed out of the bedroom. She followed him, angrily.

"You know what, Omar, you're no better than the rest of those lying ass men out there. You're a damn dog, too!"

He continued to ignore her.

"Do you hear me, Omar? You're a dog!" she yelled.

He spun around.

"You know, I've always known you were a desperate woman, but I never actually pegged you as a stupid one, until now."

Her eyes widened.

He grabbed his jacket from the closet.

"Do you think starting an argument with me is going to make me stay here?"

She stared at him.

"Well, it's not. I'm leaving whether you take your black ass to bed or stand there screaming for the next two hours. So, you might as well save your breath."

Asia couldn't believe her ears; Omar had never spoken to her that way. Tears began to form in her eyes.

"Oh, don't start that crying shit now. Not after you've done all that yelling and name calling. Let me ask you this, how long do you think I'm going to put up with *your* shit?" He continued down the stairs.

She followed him into the foyer.

"Oh, so now you're disrespecting me?"

He grinned.

"I don't even know why I wasted my time with you," she said.

He paused. "You know, I could have any woman I want, but I'm here with you. That's not enough for you, right?"

"No, it's not. I want you with me all the time, Omar. Not just when it's convenient for you, or when your damn cell phone isn't ringing."

"What are you talking about? I can't remember the last time I slept in my own bed for more than three days in a row. I'm always here with you; I'd thought you'd be happy."

"What do you mean? I thought you were here because you wanted to be, and because you were in love me."

"Not quite."

"Oh, so, now you think you're doing me a favor by being here with me, Omar? Believe me, you're not putting up with anything more than I'm putting up with!"

"No? What about the constant bickering, the jealousy, and the snooping through my things?"

She drew back.

"Yeah, you didn't think I knew about that, right?"
She didn't respond.

He moved toward her. "I should get a goddamn medal just for putting up with that immature bullshit. Never mind the fact that you've put on weight since we first met."

"Five pounds, Omar; I put on five pounds in a year and a half, big deal!"

"Try twenty-five pounds and it is a big deal because I'm the one that has to sleep next to your big ass!"

Her mouth dropped open. She couldn't believe the things Omar was saying to her.

"So, are you telling me that you run out of here every night because I put on a few pounds?"

"No. I'm telling you that I run out of here every night because I can. I'm a grown ass man, Asia. You can't tell me what to do."

"You're not the same man I fell in love with." She lowered her head.

"Yes, I am. I'm just not putting up with the same bullshit. I told you a long time ago that I wasn't looking to get serious. You're the one who kept pushing the issue."

"Yeah, well, maybe I shouldn't have. It's not like I need the drama."

"Come on man, go ahead with all that."

"Oh, I see you must have me mistaken for one of your friends. That's your first mistake. I'm not a man Omar, I'm a woman or have you forgotten the difference?"

He ignored her rant as he headed for the door.

"I'm not going to be your victim, Omar!" she jeered.

"My victim?" he repeated, turning around slowly. "Do you know why I kept pursuing you after that night you slammed the door in my face?"

"No, I don't," she replied, folding her arms.

"Well, let me tell you. It was because I felt sorry for you. I knew if I hadn't, you would have ended up being just another bitter, black woman that hated black men. God knows we don't need any more of those in the Universe."

She tried to cut in, but he wouldn't let her.

"I took pity on you. I stuck around; tried to make you happy. I gave you the best loving you ever had in your life; and what do I get; a bunch of bullshit from your nagging ass!"

She attempted to slap him but missed.

"Oh, don't act surprised. It wasn't a secret then and it's not a secret now. You're a nagger. The only reason I put up with it this long, is because you were buying me things to pacify me; as if buying me things would really make me stay with you."

"Well, you're still here."

"What can I say...you give great gifts."

"You ungrateful bastard; I did those things because I care about you!" A tear fell from her eyes.

"No, you did those things because you thought you could buy me."

"That's a lie. Those things came from my heart, Omar."

"Exactly; no one twisted your arm. Now you want to cry, victim!" He patted his pocket for his keys.

Asia was livid. The things he said to her hit her like a ton of bricks.

"Do you really think I'm desperate? Do you really think I need you?"

"If you could do better you would. Then again, who's better than me?"

"If I'm so desperate and needy, why are you here, huh? Why don't you just leave?" she asked. Her voice cracked with emotion. "I don't need this shit, Omar, and most of all I don't need you!"

He sneered.

"Asia, I'm the one who doesn't need you. Hell, you should be glad that I put up with you this long. Any other man would probably have been gone by now."

"Any other man would know how to love a good woman, the RIGHT way, not run every time Ben summons him like some punk!" she shot back.

Her words landed like a dagger in Omar's chest. This time he felt the sting of her insinuation, but he wasn't about to show it. He winked at her and then opened the door.

"I should have gone out with my ex!" she yelled.

"Maybe you should have," he replied, letting the door slam shut behind him.

Asia immediately fell to her knees, crying. She loved him, but he was a different man than she had fallen in love with. That man would have never said those things to her. He would have never walked out on her.

As tears brimmed her eyes, she thought about leaving the relationship, but how could she?

Omar had been part of her life for nearly two years and now she couldn't imagine life without him. Unfortunately, she would have to, though, for the night.

Thirty minutes later...

When Omar walked into the apartment, the sender of the text message greeted him. His eye lit up and so did his face. He grabbed his crotch as if in need of reinforcement.

"Come in," his solicitor said.

Omar smiled.

"Sorry I'm late."

"It's okay. I've just been waiting on you, forever."

"Yeah, well, I'm here now."

"Yes, you are."

Omar removed his jacket and tossed it over the arm of a chair. He was wearing a powder blue shirt that showed off his huge chest and thick nipples.

His suitor began to purr like a cat.

"Why do you do that every time you see me?" Omar asked.

"Why do you think?"

"I don't know." Omar beamed, lowering his pants and revealing the part of his anatomy that he was most proud of.

"Damn!" his petitioner exclaimed.

"What?"

"You must be from Africa."

"Why do you say that?"

"Well, the last time I saw a man so endowed, I was on sabbatical in Angola researching the Yoruba tribe.

Omar smiled. He tugged at his jock strap as he stepped out of his pants, tossing them over the arm of the chair as well.

"Do you want to hang those up?"

"No, it's fine."

Omar licked his lips as he was led into the bedroom.

CHAPTER TWENTY-THREE

Two Can Play That Game

Asia sat at a small makeup table in her bedroom. She was wrapped in a large white towel. Omar had left her reeling. It was true that she had become somewhat of an insecure, whining nag, but he had changed as well. He was hardly the respectful gentleman who she had come to know and love. She hadn't seen him in a while. He seemed taller, more muscular, happy. How was it possible for someone so good-looking to become even better looking in such a short amount to time? Could he really be happy without me? Was another woman responsible for the look of content in his eyes? He even smelled differently. It's as though she didn't know him at all. Still, she loved him and hated him all at once.

She brushed her hair as if trying to brush him from her mind.

'I'll be back. I have to go meet with Ben.' She mimicked.

"Bullshit!"

In Asia's mind, there's only one type of man that would leave a woman as fine as her lying in bed to go chase after his male friend.

She thumbed through her makeup drawer.

"Need him? I don't need him." She painted a deep red coloring across her lips.

"Needy is for women who are too afraid to believe that they can do better."

She applied eyeliner.

"He called me, 'desperate.' Well, *desperate* is a woman that will do anything to keep a man. I'm not that woman." She batted her eyes as she spoke.

She stood up slowly and tugged at her towel, causing it to fall to the floor. She slipped into a pair of black heels and a lace undergarment that made her look like a Playboy centerfold. She looked in the mirror and for a few seconds more, reflected on her argument with Omar.

So, you want to go out in the middle of the night? Okay, well, two can play that game and someone should have told you that women are much better at it.

She sprayed on some perfume.

"He has no idea what he just started," she said aloud and then headed downstairs.

She slipped on a black, patent-leather trench coat that hung just below her mid-thigh. It was short and exposed the length of her legs and the fire in her strut.

She grabbed her purse and keys from the counter and headed for the door.

On her way out the telephone rang. She stopped briefly to glance at who was calling and saw that it was Omar. She smirked and then left the house.

Somewhere in Queens, Omar sat on the edge bed, wiping the sweat from his forehead. Time had quickly slipped by. He glanced at his watch. It was 3:00 a.m.

"So, was it worth it?"

"Was what worth it?" Omar replied.

"You know, traveling all the way over here in the middle of the night to see me," the person lying in bed said with a hint of mischief.

"I guess so," Omar replied as he headed into the bathroom.

"You guess so?"

"Okay, it was fine," Omar growled.

"Gee, thanks!"

"Don't mention it."

"You know, I've never been with a man as well-endowed as you. It was a bit of a stretch for me."

"I bet it was." Omar chuckled, rubbing a large amount of soap between his hands, and then turned on the faucet. He scrubbed himself as if trying to wash away any evidence of his indiscretion.

Suddenly, he felt a soft kiss on the back of his neck. "What's the rush; I wasn't done yet."

"It's late," he replied.

"I know, but I hoped I could show you how long I could hold my breath underwater."

The shower was turned on Omar was escorted inside.

"What are you doing?" he asked.

The next thing he knew, he was moaning, again.

Meanwhile at Smokey's...

Asia was sitting at the bar having a drink when she noticed a handsome gentleman staring at her from the opposite end. He was tall with black, wavy hair and perfectly groomed facial hair that outlined his chiseled jawline. The salt and pepper accents in his beard made him look really distinguished.

She noticed him checking her out and she was doing the same. She admired how fit and well-dressed he was.

She flirted with him playfully, by twirling a straw around in her drink and licking her lips as if to beckon him.

It wasn't like Asia to be so forward, but she was on her second apple martini and feeling a bit uninhibited.

Smokey's Bar was a neighborhood establishment, about a ten-minute walk from her house. She decided it would be the best place to go since she knew everyone there, and because if she found herself getting too inebriated, she could quickly dash home.

She briefly turned her attention to one of the waitresses when a husky voice spilled from behind her.

"Are the men in this room crazy?"

She glanced over her shoulder to find the handsome gentleman from the other end of the bar standing behind her.

"I don't know, are they?"

"My guess would be yes. Otherwise, there's no way you would be sitting here, drinking alone."

"But I'm not alone, right Alex?" She addressed a middle-aged bartender that was collecting empty glasses from the counter.

"That's right," he nodded.

"Oh, I'm sorry. I didn't mean to be presumptuous. "

"There's no reason to apologize. How would you have known?"

He smiled.

"What are you having, buddy?" the bartender asked. "Johnny Walker Black, please. Oh, and give the lady another of whatever she's having."

"No, that's all right, really. I'm fine."

"Are you sure?"

"Yes. Besides, I'm not in the business of accepting a drink from a man whose name I don't even know?"

"If that's the only thing that's stopping you from joining me in a drink, then my name is Melvin. What's yours?" He extended his hand.

She glanced down at his hand and recalled something she had read in a book once, about a man with large hands. She quickly crossed her legs.

"Hi Melvin, I'm Asia."

"It's nice to meet you, Asia."

She stared into his mocha-colored eyes as she spoke. As she slid her hand from his, she caught a glimpse of a large ring he was wearing. She cast her eyes on it, discreetly.

"So, you're a Mason?" she asked.

"Yes, I am."

"Wow, that's interesting."

"You really think so?"

"Yes, I do."

"Why, what do you know about Masons?"

"Not much, but I heard they're upstanding men."

"Yes, we are." He glanced down at himself.

"Mysterious men have always fascinated me."

"Oh, you like a little mystery?"

"Yes, when the time is right," she replied.

"How's my timing?" he flirted.

"I think it might be." She warmly smiled.

"Good." He leaned in closer." So, tell me, Asia. Will you have that drink with me now?"

"Yes," she replied, finding it hard to tear her eyes from his. The smell of his cologne sent chills up her spine.

"Great. Bartender, another Apple Martini, please." The bartender didn't respond; he just stood there staring at Melvin.

"Alex!" Asia flagged him.

"Sorry, I was lost in the effects of this guy's brassy voice."

They all shared a laugh.

"It's only for the ladies, man, only for the ladies."

"Aw, that's too bad!" Alex joked.

Asia chuckled.

"Do you mind if I sit next to you?"

"Not at all." She gestured for him to sit.

The bartender placed their drinks in front of them and left them to their private conversation.

A few hours later...

Melvin's Cadillac rode like a dream. Asia sat in the passenger seat, laughing all the way back to her place. She hadn't laughed so much in a long time. For a while, Omar wasn't even a thought.

Melvin was handsome, charming and had a wonderful sense of humor, but it was getting late, and Asia needed to get some rest.

"Melvin, I had a good time. Thank you so much."

"It was my pleasure." He kissed her hand.

She blushed as he pulled onto her block. As they got closer to her house, she noticed Omar's car parked out front.

"Melvin, listen...you can let me out right here," she said nervously.

"I thought you said the number of your house was 367. This is 361."

"I know, but I can get out here. My brother is home and he's very protective, and I don't want him to get the wrong idea."

"Oh, your brother?"

"Yes."

He pulled the car over immediately.

"I'm going to sit here until I know that you're in-side."

"You really don't have to. Really, I'll be okay."

"Are you sure?"

"Yes. I'll be fine. Thanks."

Melvin smiled. He knew all too well the game Asia was playing. He had been around long enough to recognize when a woman was stepping out on her man.

She stepped from the car.

"Asia!" Melvin called out.

"Yes." She turned around.

He handed her a card with his phone number on it.

"What's this?"

"It's my number."

"I don't think I should take that."

"Come, on. If you and your brother don't work out, give me a call."

She blushed with embarrassment.

"Believe me, I understand." He winked at her.

At that point, she couldn't say a word. She accepted his number and the kiss he blew her and then watched as he drove away thinking, damn I should have fucked him.

She headed toward her house, hoping to slip past Omar without him noticing. The closer she got, she could see that he was sitting in his car and that he had been watching the entire time.

She sped up.

"Hey, hey, hey wait a minute. Where were you?" Omar asked, leaping from his car like a jealous hus-band.

"Excuse me?"

"You heard me; where were you?"

"Why are you so concerned; I thought you had business with Ben?"

"I asked you where you were, Asia."

"I don't have to tell you that." She stepped to the side.

"The hell you don't!" he barked, standing in front of her to prohibit her from walking away. "You better tell me something."

"What do you want to hear, Omar?"

"I don't know, tell me you were out emptying the trash, or that you were walking around because you couldn't sleep; something."

"No, I don't have to lie to you. I'm a grown woman." She walked around him and headed toward her house.

"Asia!" he scoffed.

"Okay, Omar, I was out. Okay, now what?"

"You went out on a date?" He stared at her in disbelief.

"Yes, I was on a date."

"Where did you go?" He slammed his hand on the hood of his car.

"That's none of your business!"

"What do you mean, none of my business? It's five o'clock in the morning, Asia."

"I know what time it is, and if you don't mind, please keep your voice down. I don't need you waking my neighbors."

"I DON'T GIVE A DAMN ABOUT YOUR NEIGHBORS! I want to know what you're doing coming home at this hour." He grabbed her by the arm.

"Take your hands off of me," she demanded.

"No, not until you tell me where you've been."

"I don't have to tell you anything!" she snapped, staring him straight in the eye.

He gritted his teeth.

She pulled away from him.

"Okay, then whose car was that you just got out of. Was that old guy your father?"

"No, he wasn't; Melvin isn't old either. He's a distinguished gentleman that knows how to treat a woman."

"Well, he looked old enough to be your father!"

"If that's true, then why are you so worried about him?"

"I'm not worried about him; I'm worried about you."

"Why? Why would you suddenly be worried about desperate, stupid, nagging Asia? She's nothing but a headache, remember?"

"I don't care; you're still my headache."

"Your headache? I don't belong to you, Omar. Just like you don't belong to me...you made that perfectly clear earlier."

"So, what are you saying?"

"I'm saying there's not a woman in this world that needs to put up with some disrespectful ass man that doesn't know how to appreciate her, myself included. So, you can take that fake jealousy act and run it on someone that's not hip to it. I'm done with you." She started up the stairs to her house.

"Oh, so it's like that?"

"Yes, it's like that...Oh, and Melvin doesn't think I'm fat at all." She glanced back at him.

"What did you say?" His eyes stretched wide with jealousy.

"You heard what I said."

"Yeah, I heard you. Asia, don't make me hurt your little boyfriend, okay? You better tell him to step off before I do something all three of us will regret."

"Like what?"

"Put it like this, I would really hate to go to jail for assaulting a senior citizen."

"Whatever!"

"Yeah, whatever!"

"You know, you should try talking to Melvin, baby; he can teach you a thing or two about how to treat a lady."

"If Melvin or Grandpa...or whatever his fucking name is, knew how to treat a lady, he would have brought you home at a decent hour. I mean, what type of man keeps a woman out till five in the morning?" His voice was full of insinuation.

"I don't know. Perhaps the same kind that leaves his woman in bed because he got a text message."

Omar's face cracked as Asia headed up the stairs.

He followed her.

"Uh, where are you going?" she stopped in front of her door, pulling out her keys.

"What do you mean? I'm coming inside."

"No, you're not."

"Asia, stop playing; I'm tired and it's late."

"That's right; you are tired, and it is late-too late to be playing this little game with you. So, you can go home and try calling me when you think you can start respecting me again."

"I do respect you, but you are not going to say the things you said to me and not expect me to fire back, Asia."

"Well, maybe you should try being honest with me for a change."

"Maybe you should learn to trust me for a change!"

"You know what? Maybe we both need just THAT, a change." She unlocked the door.

"When are you going to stop going against the grain and just be happy with what we have?"

"When donkeys learn to sing but until then, I'm going to always question a man that leaves me in bed to go traipsing around in the street at one o'clock in the morning. Good night, Omar." She stepped inside her house.

Asia, don't walk away from me!"

"Goodnight!"

She slammed the door shut.

CHAPTER TWENTY-FOUR

Deja Vu

The sounds of a large entourage invaded Omar's thoughts as they made their way into the hotel lobby. There were scores of women wearing slinky dresses, nearly a dozen photographers, and a group of guys surrounded by body-guards.

"Great show, guys," he heard someone say.

At that moment, he repositioned himself for a better view.

The hotel manager greeted the large crowd as if they were royalty.

After a few moments, two familiar faces came into view-Reb-732 and Camaron from the group.

Damn! Omar thought. *What is the fuckin' chances?* He watched as they made their way to the private eleva-tors.

Seconds later, the lead singer strolled into the hotel with a string of personal security guards and a slew of screaming fans trailing behind them.

Tai was dressed in his usual flashy manner, and wear-ing so much ice, he looked like he had robbed the Orapa diamond mine in Botswana.

Omar's face contorted.

He never thought he'd never actually see Asia's ex again but there he was, in the flesh, standing just a few feet from where he sat. The fact that he had a cell phone pressed against his ear and was distracted, presented the perfect opportunity for Omar to pounce on him.

He stood up and prepared for the attack but noticed that Tai had a deep look of concern on his face. Out of respect for whoever was on the other end, he decided to wait and listen. "Baby, I got your message; I just got to the hotel and I'm worried about you; call me. Oh, and Asia, I love you," Tai said.

Omar scowled. *Was Asia back in contact with this clown?*

He stared across the room with his blood boiling, planning exactly how he would break Tai's neck.

Before he could make a move though, he spotted Ben gliding through the crowded lobby as if he were on a pair of skis. On his arm were two women, a blonde and a fiery redhead. From where Omar sat, they looked like twins and Ben was sporting them like matching cufflinks.

"Sorry I'm late." Ben grinned.

Omar glanced at his watch and then at the women; they had very tiny waistlines and magnificently altered bust lines. It was difficult not to notice them immediately.

"You know I don't like to be kept waiting, Ben."

"Yeah, I know." Ben made the introductions.

"Ladies, meet the man that's going to make Thigh Scrapers a household name."

"How are you this evening? I'm Catalina," the blonde said, extending her hand.

Omar rose from his seat and extended his.

"It's nice to meet you, Catalina. I'm Omar."

Her icy blue eyes scanned him immediately. He turned toward the other woman.

"Hi, I'm Omar and you are?"

She ignored him.

"Okay," Ben interjected.

"Omar, this is Natasha; she and Catalina are sisters."

"I should have known seeing how they're both so beautiful."

Catalina swung her head to the side, tossing her long blond locks from her face, smiling as she accepted Omar's flirt.

Natasha, however, seemed unimpressed; she stared at Omar and declined to shake his hand.

"What's wrong with her?" Ben whispered to Catalina.

"She noticed him ogling us when we arrived. She thought it was rude."

Omar observed her guardedness. He took it as more of a challenge than an insult and drew back coolly.

"Shall we sit?" he said, pulling out a chair for Catalina.

Ben helped Natasha to a seat.

"So, Ladies, as I was telling you, if you're really looking for a good workout, Omar is your man. He's a master trainer and if you want to sweat, he's the one to turn up the heat."

"How tall are you and how much do you weigh?" Natasha asked, staring at Omar as if he were beneath her.

Omar wasn't used to being spoken down to by a woman. He replied slowly. "six-three, two hundred and forty-five pounds."

She smirked.

Omar glanced at Ben and commented with his eyes; this is bullshit!

The waiter returned with Omar's drink. He swallowed it immediately.

Natasha removed a gold-plated cigarette case from her purse, placing it between her fingers, parted her silicon-injected lips and began to smoke.

The way she pulled on the cigarette gave Omar the impression that her lips might be her best asset, especially given her nasty attitude.

"Let me see the contract!" she demanded and then rolled her eyes as if meeting with Omar was a burden.

Ben slid an envelope toward her.

Omar glanced at Catalina, who was flirting with him from across the table.

Ben watched anxiously as Natasha blew a ring of smoke into the air. For a few moments, there was complete silence and then she dropped her cigarette into Omar's drink.

At that moment he experienced déjà vu. Asia had done the exact same thing to a guy the night they met.

"So, when do we start?" Natasha asked.

Omar smiled.

Ben cut in. "Well, just sign and we'll contact you in a few days to work out the schedule,"

Omar cast his eyes across the room and noticed that the crowd had thinned. Tai had vanished and so did the hotel manager.

"Listen, Ben, I have to make a quick phone call."

"Right now?" Ben muttered.

"Yes, right now! Catalina, it was nice meeting you. I'll see you real soon." He kissed her hand.

She blushed.

Natasha sneered; she was arrogant and extremely temperamental.

Omar noticed the look on her face and whispered in her ear before stepping away from the table.

"I'm going to give it to you so hard that you're going to scream politsiya before it's over!"

He brushed his crotch along her arm as he passed her.

She smiled.

Catalina did, too.

Natasha slid the contract back to Ben, who was grinning like the Cheshire cat.

"I hope you ladies have been doing your Palates," Ben said, escorting them through the hotel lobby.

A few minutes had passed...

Ben was standing outside the Marriott Marquis, staring at Catalina and Natasha as their black Mercedes disappeared in traffic.

"Forget Palates, you two had better have painkillers and crutches on deck. Hell, you might need an epidural." He chuckled as he lit a cigarette.

Omar stepped through the revolving doors. Ben turned around, "You know you're the man, right?"

Omar didn't respond.

"Did you hear what I said?"

Omar was distracted. He stood with his cell phone pressed against his ear. "Baby, listen, I know you can hear me; it's been three days and I really need to talk to you. Please call me."

Ben lit a cigarette. "So, you're begging now?"

"Don't start, Ben. Please."

"No, you just don't make the mistake of letting your feelings for that woman come between what we're trying to build!"

Omar didn't comment.

"Look, let's just try to keep things in perspective, okay? That woman was never supposed to be anything more than a one-night stand; we agreed to that, remember?" He coughed as he blew a puff of smoke in the air.

"Yes, I remember, Ben!"

"Good; then don't go wasting all your energy on somebody that shouldn't have been in the picture in the first place; save it for the one that really cares about you."

Ben patted him on the shoulder and then walked away.

Omar headed for the parking garage where he had parked his car. Even though Ben's comment laid heavily on his mind, he was determined to reconcile with Asia.

Omar knew that he needed to pull out the big guns on this one. A simple apology wasn't going to do this time. He racked his brain, trying to come up with a plan to get back into her good graces, but kept coming up empty-handed.

Oh, how easy it used to be...

After their first fight, they hadn't seen each other for two weeks. Omar knew he needed to do something to get back into Asia's good graces. After work, he made a few stops, picked up some lingerie, a bouquet of flowers, a gigantic card and a stuffed teddy bear with the words, "I miss you" inscribed on its belly.

He drove over to Asia's place, showered her with gifts, and then promised never to treat her poorly again. It was that simple. They spent the rest of the day in bed.

The next morning Asia slid out of bed quietly, gathering her clothing for church service. She glanced back at Omar as he rested peacefully. Her heart was filled with happiness as she tip-toed through the bedroom.

"Where are you going?" he asked, rolling over in the bed.

"I have to go to church today. Go back to sleep."

"So, you're just going to leave me here like this?"

"Like what?"

"Like this." He tossed the sheets away from his body, revealing the stiffness of an early morning erection.

She blushed.

"Omar, its Sunday."

"I know what day it is. Come over here and let me bless you."

"Oh, no. You'll make me late for church."

"I won't, I promise. Come here." He gripped himself.

"No, Omar, I'm serious. Today is the Lord's Day."

She moved closer to the bed. "Besides, I'm singing today, and I don't want to be late."

Omar reached up and pulled her down on top of him. "Oh really; well, hit a note for me before you go."

He kissed her on the neck and face.

She tore away from him and quickly moved toward the door. "I'm sorry, baby, I have to go."

"Are you still upset about our fight? That was two weeks ago. I thought you forgave me."

"I did. My taxi should be here in a few minutes, so I don't have time to make you breakfast. There's plenty of food in the kitchen if you get hungry. Oh, in case you need to go out, I'm leaving you a set of my keys."

"You really believe in me, don't you?" He flashed a boyish smile.

"What do you think?" She blew him a kiss and then left the bedroom.

Twenty Minutes Later...

Omar stood, watching from the window while she waited for a taxi. He played with the short hairs on his stomach, allowing them to slip between his fingers as quickly as her taxi slipped from his sight.

After a few minutes of being home alone, his inquisitiveness kicked in. She had never left him in her house alone before. He glanced around her bedroom, noticing the many large and oddly shaped bottles of perfume that lined her dresser. He sniffed them one by one, curiously. Through the corner of his eye, he noticed the light blinking on her answering machine. It read six new messages. He was tempted to listen to them but decided against it. Instead, he searched through her things, hoping to find out something new about her; something that he didn't already know.

While looking through her drawers, he came across her underwear collection. She owned many styles and colors; boy shorts, thongs, and lace bikinis. She had them all. He lifted a pair of purple, lace panties from the drawer and imagined her wearing them.

The flashing light from the answering machine was nagging at him. He continued to ignore it.

He made his way over to the nightstand where he found an envelope lying in the top drawer; he opened it and read the note inside...

Dearest Omar,
    By now, you've probably snooped through my things and found this letter. (His eyes widened.) *It's okay, pick out the piece of lin-*

gerie you'd like to see me in, and I'll wear it for you when I get home. (He blushed.) *Last night was so special that I don't think anything in the world will ever compare to it.* (He groped himself.) *I love you and I'll see you later, baby.* (He smiled.) *Don't forget-close my drawers.*

Omar smiled from ear to ear as he returned the letter to its rightful place. While doing so, he noticed a greeting card; it was lying beneath a small notepad. He read it as well.

To the Love of My Life,

I've been trying to find the words to tell you how much I love you. Every moment that we're apart, feels like an eternity. I hope one day that you'll be able to forgive my selfishness. I just want what's best for you. I've written this poem just for you. It's called I LOVE YOU:

We lay together, silent, sharing a moment where words only exist through brief utterances. With each breath, I am transformed, and we are no longer separate but equal in existence. I feel like I have died and come alive again. I breathe and feel God holding me, holding us. I have learned to love again, and I am not ashamed. Forever you will always be a part of me, and I am a part of you. I'll love you forever, for always, from the inside.

The note tugged at his heart. He sat on the edge of her bed, and for the first time, realized how much he cared for her, too.

"What are you trying to do to me, Asia?" he mumbled.

He placed the card back into the drawer. At that moment, he began to reassess Asia and their relationship.

He closed the drawer to the nightstand and began flexing his muscles in front of the mirror. He thought about all the ways he was going to make love to Asia that night.

As he danced in the mirror, the phone rang; the answering machine clicked, and a man's voice spilled through the room.

"Hey, baby, it's me, Tai. I just called to say I love you. Call me, Asia; I'm waiting."

Omar became outraged. The sound of Tai's voice made him extremely jealous; his nostrils flared, and his temples began to throb. It was clear what Tai wanted and he wasn't about to let Asia's ex worm his way back into her life; not after the night they had, not after the notes she had left him.

Omar knew he needed to stay three steps ahead of the game, which meant staying in control of Asia's mind, body and her messages.

He erased them all.

CHAPTER TWENTY-FIVE

The Devil Isn't The Only One Who Wears Prada

Asia stood in front of the church waiting for Keisha to arrive. Pam and Angela joined her.

"You did tell her what time service starts, didn't you?" Angela asked, sharply.

"Yes,"

"Yeah, well, I don't know why you invited her to come to church with us in the first place," Angela said, leering at every car that passed. She despised Keisha with a passion. Although they were once close friends, it was a long time ago and she hated the ground Keisha walked on.

Asia nudged her, "Angela, will you be nice?"

"No, I will not. I don't like her, and she'll be lucky if I don't sock her one when I see her."

"Just let me know," Pam coached. "We might be in church, but I have a jar of Vaseline in my bag."

Asia rolled her eyes. "Pam, will you cut it out?"

"Don't tell her to cut it out! You need to tell that trick to keep it cool when she gets here, or else!"

"Or else what?"

"I'm just saying this is a black church, anything can happen. Who knows, she might accidentally get hit in the head with a tambourine, or trip and fall face first into the baptismal pool."

Angela's sarcasm caused Pam to burst into laughter.

"Pam, stop laughing." Asia spun around.

"Angela, is this how mature, professional women behave?"

"When someone sleeps with your man, maturity and professionalism go out of the window, and ghetto and straight razors come into play."

Asia stared at Angela in disbelief.

"Okay, okay, but she better not make one comment about Kareem."

"She won't," Asia insisted.

"Okay, we'll call the trick and see what's taking her so long to get here."

Just as Angela spoke those words, a candy-apple red Lexus pulled up in front of the church. The music from the car was blasting so loud it nearly drowned out the church bell. Angela scowled, sensing it was Keisha. She was right.

Pam's jaw dropped.

Asia's eyes widened in unbelief, "Oh, my goodness,"

"Is she serious?" Pam added.

They watched as Keisha stepped out of the car wearing a bright red dress, five-inch heels, black shades, no stockings, and from the way she was jiggling, probably no underwear. Her dress was cut low in the front, low in the back, high at the thigh, and was so tight-if she sneezed, it would have probably popped off.

"Where is she going dressed like that?" Pam mumbled.

"I don't know, but she's not sitting next to me," Angela turned and headed into the church.

"Come back here, don't be rude!" Asia demanded, casting her eyes at Angela as she walked away.

"Hey, Asia," Keisha cried out as she made her way up the walkway.

"Hey, Keisha," Asia smiled. They hugged; Pam was still gasping at Keisha's truck-stop outfit.

"Girl, was that Angela I saw out here a few seconds ago?"

"Yes, she went inside to hold a few seats."

Keisha sneered. She didn't believe a word Asia said. As they headed into the church, Asia quietly asked God to forgive her for telling that little white lie and to forgive Keisha for wearing that little red dress that showed more flesh than anyone cared to see on a Sunday morning.

"Keisha, you remember Pam?" Asia asked.

Keisha spun around. "Of course, how are you, Pam?"

"I'm fine. I was just admiring your dress."

Keisha flipped her hair, "Thanks girl, it's Prada."

"Well, I was just telling Asia-"

Keisha turned her attention back to Asia.

"So, girl, are there any single men in this church?"

She dismissed Pam entirely, grabbing Asia by the arm and headed through the church foyer.

Pam rolled her eyes.

"All right, you two...go find some seats. I'll see you later."

"Where are you going?" Keisha asked.

"I have to get ready for my solo"

"All right, you always wanted to be Miss Ross; now you're going solo, huh?"

Asia drew back.

"I'm just playing girl, go get 'em." She kissed Asia on the cheek and then headed into the sanctuary.

Every eye in the church watched as Keisha made her way down the aisle. It was as though Satan's daughter had put on a little red dress and came to service.

She drew the attention of every man, young and old, as she made her way past row after row of pews; causing a few people to drop more money into the collection plate than intended. Her presence was so shocking that the usher lost his footing and nearly tripped into the aisle while escorting her and Pam to their seats.

Keisha spotted Angela and made her way over. "Hey girl, I thought that was you."

Angela nearly swallowed her tongue when she looked up and saw Keisha entering the row, scooting past her to get to a seat.

Keisha's backside gave Angela flashbacks of how she must have flaunted it in front of her ex.

She gritted her teeth, clenched her Bible, and began reciting the Lord's Prayer.

Pam had hoped Keisha would take the seat furthest away from Angela, but was quickly disappointed when she sat down, right next to her.

As the service opened, the Pastor made his way to the pulpit. He was a handsome man; dressed in a blue suit, grey shirt and matching tie. As he spoke, Keisha lowered her shades, leaned toward Pam and said, "Damn, the Pastor is fine!"

"Oh, my goodness," Pam whispered. "Are you serious? We're in church!"

Keisha smiled as she slid her glasses into her purse.

The Pastor began his sermon by speaking about forgiveness, a topic that seemed to move everyone in the congregation except for Angela. He instructed them to turn to the person sitting next to them and say three simple words, "I forgive you."

Asia was watching from the choir loft and had noticed the pensive look on Angela's face. She started to worry.

Pam leaned to the woman seated next to her and said, "I forgive you."

The woman said the same to her.

Angela looked across toward the center aisle and said to an older gentleman, "I forgive you."

He responded in kind.

Keisha, however, leaned over to Angela and whispered, "Look, I know you're still mad about what you think happened with Kareem, but I just want to let you know that I forgive you."

The sound of Keisha's voice and the mere mention of Kareem's name sent shockwaves through Angela's body. As much as she tried to resist, she couldn't help firing back.

"What do you mean you forgive me? If anything, you should be begging my forgiveness."

"For what?"

Keisha responded snidely.

"For sleeping with Kareem, for being a lying two-faced trick, and for walking in this church dressed like you're looking for customers."

Keisha's mouth fell open.

"You're just mad because you think I took your man."

Angela leaped from her seat.

"Bitch, are you crazy?" An immediate hush fell over the congregation, the organist stopped playing, the Pastor's eyes widened, the Mother of the Church passed out on the front pew, Asia shrunk to the size of an ant and Pam just sat there in shock.

The Pastor's voice resonated from the pulpit. "Excuse me, sister, but we don't use that type of language in the house of the Lord."

Angela froze with embarrassment. Her lips tightened as she slowly descended to her seat.

"Now, sisters, it's obvious that there's something bothering you. I want you to bring it up to the altar, lay it here, and leave it here."

Angela hesitated.

"Go on up there! You need some Jesus in your life," Keisha taunted.

"Yeah, and you need some penicillin in yours," Angela snapped.

To avoid any further embarrassment, Angela stood up and stepped into the aisle. She glanced at Keisha with a menacing look as they continued their exchange.

"You better be glad we're in church," Angela threatened.

"Oh, please, go up there and get your blessing. No one's scared of you."

Keisha waved her hand as if to shoo Angela away. She was unbothered by her juvenile threats.

"Jezebel!" Angela scoffed.

"Loser!" Keisha snapped.

"Trick!" Angela fired back; her tone had once again become heightened.

By that time, Asia had left the choir loft, made her way down the aisle, and proceeded to escort Angela up to the altar.

Keisha chuckled from her seat.

"I don't know why you're laughing; you're coming, too." Asia reached for her hand.

"What? No, I'm not. I'll leave first."

"Keisha, either you get up now or lose my number."

Keisha didn't take kindly to ultimatums. She and Asia were close, but she was not going to be bullied.

The congregation watched as she reached into her purse, placed her shades back on her face, and through their dark tint, watched as Angela and Asia made their way to the altar.

Keisha turned to Pam as she pressed her hand into her purse and pulled out a cigarette, "Girl, do you have a light?"

Pam turned the color of a beat. "Oh my gosh, put that away. You know what, you need to go there and repent and when you're finished do it again. You God in yourself."

"What?" Keisha returned the unlit cigarette to her purse and began waving her hand in the air, "Hallelujah Pastor, won't He do it!"

Pam was mortified, "Repent and Repeat, that's what you need to do. Repent and Repeat!"

Repent, Repeat and then go eat.

After the service, Asia could tell that Angela was still upset.

"Are you okay?" She touched Angela's arm.

"I'm fine."

"Are you sure?" Pam asked, concerned as well.

"I said I'm okay; I just need to take care of something."

Angela headed toward her car.

"Where are you going?" Pam followed.

"I'll be back!" Angela said, jumping in her car and speeding away.

Asia turned to Keisha. "Did you have to start with her?"

"I didn't start anything; all I said was simply

"Keisha's explanation was abruptly interrupted by a high-pitched voice calling out.

"Now, I know the devil is wearing snow boots and eating popsicles. Is that Ms. Keisha I see over there?"

"Jerome!" Keisha's eyes widened

"In the flesh, honey." He twirled around.

"What are you doing here?"

"Never mind that; what are you doing here?"

"Well, my cousin really wanted me to come so I decided that it wouldn't hurt if I popped in for a little while."

"And popped in you did, honey." He surveyed Keisha's outfit, snapping his fingers up and down.

"Ooh, Miss Thing, the devil really does wear Prada."

"Stop it, Jerome."

They laughed.

"So, what are you doing here?" she asked again.

"Girl, my new boo asked me to come with him to church, and I couldn't say no."

Pam leaned toward Asia and whispered, "Did he just say his new 'boo' is a man?"

Asia nodded

"Oh, really? Where is he?" Keisha inquired. Jerome turned around and summoned for his friend, who was shaking hands with the Pastor. He noticed Jerome beckoning him and made his way over.

As he approached, the women did a collective gasp. "Ooh, he's fine," Pam muttered. She couldn't believe her eyes; neither could Keisha. Asia, however, had a different reason for not believing what she saw.

Jerome placed his arm around the guy's waist.

"Keisha, this is my new boo."

"Boo is just a pet name he calls me, but you can call me Charles. It's nice to meet you, Keisha." He extended his hand.

'Boo' was right. Asia's mouth fell open as if she had seen a ghost. She recognized Boo, Charles, or whatever his name was, as the guy who stood sucking on Angela's earlobe when they were out to lunch.

Pam was clueless.

"It's nice to meet you, Charles. These are my friends, Asia, and-" Keisha began snapping her fingers as if unable to recall Pam's name.

Pam knew she was being catty and introduced herself.

Asia didn't bother; she just waved.

"Okay, Keisha, I'm not going to hold you up," Jerome said. "I just wanted to tell you that you are working those shoes, Ms. Lady," He chirped, snapping his fingers in a circular motion.

Keisha's lips parted into a huge smile. She spun around as if she was a member of Team-Twirl. "Thank you, sweetie; do you really like them?"

"Like them? Honey, they're fierce! If Ms. Dorothy were wearing those when she clicked her heels, she would have landed in Paris, instead of wretched Kansas." He snapped his fingers again and dramatically strutted away with Charles in tow.

Keisha burst into laughter.

"What was that?" Pam whispered.

Asia once again shook her head.

"Listen, Asia, I'm going to run home and change, so I can get back to your place before you-know-who eats up all the food." Keisha said, cutting her eyes at Pam.

Asia hugged her. "Okay, just hurry up."

Keisha leaped into her car, turned on the music and pulled quickly across the intersection.

Asia waved at her as she crossed at the light.

"I guess it's just me and you, honey," Pam said, grabbing her by the arm and heading toward the street.

Gypsy cabs frequently appeared in front of the church. They caught one quickly. Asia climbed in first; Pam followed.

"Where to?" the driver asked, looking through the rearview mirror.

Pam marveled at how handsome he was. She was instantly swept into a trance by his thick accent, jet-black facial hair that framed his jawline, and the warmth of his stare. Her legs immediately parted.

"I don't know where she's going, but I'm going to 1410 East 86th Street, apartment 9F. If you're not doing anything later, you can stop by for dinner. I make a mean falafel."

Asia's eyes widened; she couldn't believe how forward Pam had become. "Please excuse my friend; she hasn't eaten all morning and I think her blood sugar is low."

Asia pinched Pam on the knee as she informed the driver of their real destination.

"Ouch! Girl, if my blood sugar is low, he just might be the complex carbohydrate I need to bring it up," Pam whispered.

"He's a cab driver!" Asia retorted.

"So? Cabbies need love, too."

"Oh, God, I feel like I'm in an episode of Sex in the City," Asia mumbled.

"Say what you want, girl; I think he's fine."

The driver overheard their conversation and chuckled.

"I think you're fine, too," he said, staring at Pam through his rearview mirror.

Asia froze. Pam did as well, but only for a second; her next few words were straight to the point.

"So, what time do you get off work?"

CHAPTER TWENTY-SIX

What She Doesn't Know

Omar knew he needed to step his game up. His first thought was to meet her at church and take her out to lunch but decided against it. Instead, he would plan an extravagant lunch and an afternoon of back-to-back lovemaking. First, he would need to hit the supermarket and a few other places.

He called Ben to accompany him, and because he wanted some advice. Unfortunately, it wasn't long before he started to regret asking his friend for advice. As they went aisle to aisle, he endured the bothersome and unsupportive buzz of Ben berating his decision to make things right with Asia.

"So, tell me again why you're going through all of this?" Ben asked.

"I told you; I want to do something nice for her."

"Man, we have to get out of here," Ben said, growing more annoyed with every second.

Omar ignored him, sniffing melons, squeezing cantaloupes and trying to decide how large of a pineapple he should buy.

"Look at us, two single good-looking men walking around a super-market squeezing melons on a Sunday afternoon. How do you think this shit looks?"

"Cut it out, Ben." Omar said, as he selected two ready-to-eat pineapples and placed them in his basket.

"I'm serious man." Ben pointed. "Look at all of these women. I think they're talking about us."

"What?" Omar grinned. "They might be just looking for the next unsuspecting victim."

"Or they might be thinking we're gay."

"What the hell are you talking about?"

"I'm talking about the way they're looking at us. I'm telling you man; they think we're gay."

A portly woman made her way over. "Excuse me; do you know which aisle I can find the condiments in?

Ben looked at Omar as if his head was about to explode, "See what I mean? How the fuck would we know where the condiments are?"

Omar grinned and pointed, "Aisle six."

The woman smiled as she walked away, "Thanks sweeties."

"We need to get the hell up out of here, man."

"Ben, would you cut it out?"

"No, and you better listen to me. Do you really think she didn't know where to find the ketchup?"

"Possibly."

"She looks like she's won a few frank-eating contests in her day. Trust me-she knows where the ketchup is."

Omar giggled.

"I'm telling you, Omar, the supermarket is no place or a single man to linger around. We need to get in and get out."

"It's not about lingering; you just don't like shopping. You think its women's work."

"That's right."

"So, if shopping is women's work, how is a single man supposed to eat?"

"There are a lot of nice restaurants that deliver in the city." Ben reached into the basket and removed one of the pineapples.

"Would you stop that?"

"No, this is woman's work. I told you."

"Oh, yeah, well what else is women's work?"

"The three F's."

"What?"

"You know, the three F's...feed, fuck, and fuss at us. That's all."

"You're sick."

"No, you're sick; sick in the head for being out here shopping like you have a show on the cooking channel."

Omar checked his list as he continued to ignore Ben. He made his way over to the berries.

Ben just stared at him.

"I'm joking! When do you think we'll hear from the guy about the place?"

Before Ben could reply, he became awestruck by a beautiful woman making her way down the aisle. His heart thumped as she walked toward them.

She was wearing a low-cut blouse that showed off her tiny waist and huge breasts. The curves of her hips careened through a tight black miniskirt that was so tight, she looked as if she had leaped off a diving board to get into it.

"Excuse me, do you work here?" the woman asked, as she and her large breast were just inches away from Ben's face.

"No, I'm sorry, but I'll be glad to help you with whatever you need bae," Ben replied, licking his lips as he spoke.

She blushed and then glanced over at Omar, "Haven't I seen you before?"

Omar looked up and away, "I don't think so."

"Yeah, well, you look familiar."

At that moment, Omar looked over at Ben to signal that he was ready to check out another aisle but found himself gawking at the woman's bosom as if he'd lost something in her cleavage.

Omar and the bodacious woman made eye contact. She did look familiar, but he couldn't recall where he'd seen her.

After checking his mental database of quick, meaningless romps, he drew a blank. Which usually happens when he's unimpressed with a woman.

"So, do you work here?" she asked, stepping closer to him.

"No, I don't."

"Oh, that's too bad. I was looking for a ripe melon and I hoped one of you could help me find it."

The woman's flirting was an immediate turn-off.

Although she was extremely attractive, Omar smirked.

Ben did the same.

She walked past Omar brushing her breast against his back. "You know, you look familiar, too. Have we met before?"

A warm feeling filled Omar's crotch as the woman stood nearby. "I don't think so; I'm sorry, baby."

"No, I'm sure we have. It was a while ago, but I never forget a face." Her eyes lit up as if she had remembered something.

Ben watched anxiously as the woman flirted with Omar. Any other time he would have been annoyed too, but now, he thought it was a good thing. He hoped she would cause Omar to forget about Asia.

"I'm sorry, I don't remember you, excuse me." Omar stepped away from her and moved over to the melons.

"So, you like melons?"

"Yes, I do. My lady likes them, too."

Omar intended for his comment to be a deterrent but was unsuccessful.

"Are you sure you don't remember me?" She asked, leaning over the melons while licking her lips invitingly.

For a moment, Omar was distracted by Ben's laughter. He reached out, not paying attention to what he was doing and inadvertently squeezed one of her breasts, instead of a melon.

"Oops." She giggled.

Omar drew back.

"I'm sorry, I didn't mean to do that; it was a mistake." He stumbled over his words.

Ben laughed hysterically as he watched from the sideline. He found Omar's lack of composure amusing.

"Omar, man, calm down."

"I didn't mean to bother you. I'll just be on my way." She glanced back repeatedly as she walked away. "It was a pleasure meeting you."

"Nah, the pleasure was entirely his, sweetheart." Ben laughed.

Omar proceeded into one of the aisles.

"Man, you should have seen your face."

"Please, Ben, it took everything in me to keep from doing her right there on top of the melons."

They heard a voice behind them.

"Excuse me, I'm sorry to bother you, again." The woman made her way back down the aisle and over to Omar. "I know that you said you have a lady, but I wanted to give you my number, anyway. You know, just in case."

She handed Omar a business card with her name written on back of it.

"Call me, if you ever want to...talk." She licked her lips and strode away.

"Damn!" Ben gripped his crotch as if he could explode at any second. "I'm telling you man, that girl is ready for da pole. Not the pole, but, DA POLE."

Omar sized her up as she walked away. "See, this is the type of shit that I'm talking about."

"What?"

"Men are always getting labeled as dogs, but did you see how quickly she came back for the bone?"

"I told her that I have a lady and you'd think that would have sent her scurrying into another direction. Instead, she comes back and hands me her number."

"So?"

"So, if I call her, then I'm a 'no good' man. I'm a cheater and I'm not fit to walk the earth. Meanwhile, she knows I have a lady and she came on to me anyway. Shit is so one-sided in the world today."

Ben trailed behind Omar as they made their way to the register. "You know, Omar, men have been sleeping with more than one woman since the beginning of time. What do you think Adam was doing when Eve was out talking to that damn snake?"

"I don't know. What?"

"Come on, man. I know you don't think Eve was the only woman God made for Adam. You know, God hooked that brother up."

Omar stared at Ben in disbelief, he didn't believe in God, and he didn't believe Ben's logic.

"Man, God knows no man can ever truly be happy with one woman, that's why he said, 'go for it' and multiply homey!'"

Omar shook his head.

"Do you really think all these people really came from Eve? Come on, there had to be some other women involved."

"You know you're stupid, right!"

"Hey, watch your mouth!" Ben snapped.

"Look, Ben, all I'm saying is that woman did not give me her number because she was attracted to me."

"No? Then why?"

"She gave it to me because she was attracted to what another woman had. It's like my mom always said, 'a woman never wants a man unless she knows another woman wants him first'."

Ben flipped through a magazine near the counter as if uninterested in Omar's comment. Deep down, he had his own reasons for pushing Omar on women.

"Anyway, how is your mom?"

"Oh, man, she's fine. I'm thinking about taking Asia to meet her."

"What!" Ben scowled.

"Okay, now you're taking this shit too far."

"Gotcha!"

Omar's face lit up. He placed his arm around Ben's shoulder and headed for the register. He placed his basket on the conveyer belt.

"Man, don't play like that. I thought you had lost your mind."

"Oh yeah, and what were you going to do about it?"

"I was about to bust you in the head with one of these pineapples to help you get it back." The woman behind the register chuckled.

"So, are you going to call?" Ben asked.

"No, I'm not; things between Asia and me are good right now, I'd like to keep it that way."

"You know as well as I do that nothing's guaranteed. Who knows if you and Asia will even be dealing a month from now? After all, she's just for show, remember?"

The cashier listened closely.

"Man, I don't care, remember there's an art to the shit we do."

"Exactly, and it's time to start painting Asia out of the picture.

Omar handed the cashier his credit card.

"Do you have to be so harsh?"

"All I'm saying is...don't let that high-yellow heifer get you sprung."

"Watch your mouth, Ben."

"Omar, you know as well as I do that the thing between a woman's thighs can cause men to do some silly shit." He glanced down at Omar's groceries. "That's why I stick and move."

"What are you saying?"

"I'm saying...there's no way I'm going to get stuck in a relationship with somebody that can't deal with who I really am."

"Yeah, well, you and I are different."

"You're right about that. No woman will ever have me out buying up a bunch of fruit that looks like guerilla nuts! What are these, anyway?" He lifted a bag of greenish-brown fruit from the counter.

"That's kiwi, now put it down."

Omar snatched the plastic produce bag from Ben's hands and tossed it on the scale.

The cashier stared at them as if she were annoyed.

"You know, Ben, sometimes you act like you're my wife or something."

The cashier raised a brow.

"Whatever! So, you're going to sleep with this woman or not?"

"No, I'm not."

"Come on, Omar. You and I both know that you're thinking about it."

"What makes you so sure?"

"Well, probably the fact that you haven't tossed away the number yet."

"You think you know me that well, huh?"

"Yes, I do."

He reached into his pocket and tossed the number to the floor, grabbing his bags and headed out of the store. Ben retrieved the number and followed him.

"Hey man, this might be a dynamite piece of ass you're throwing away."

"You're right...the kind that will blow up in my face if I'm not careful. No thanks!"

Omar placed the groceries in the trunk.

Ben climbed into the passenger side, baffled by Omar's newfound loyalty to a woman who started out as nothing more than a common lay.

"Fasten your seat belt," Omar said, climbing into the driver's seat.

"I'm telling you, Omar, you're starting to worry me."

"Would you stop looking at me like that and buckle your seat belt!"

"I don't know when it happened, but some fucking aliens must have come down here and cloned my buddy and left your punk ass here to torment me."

Omar grinned as Ben complained.

"Man, would you just drop it," he insisted. "Put your seat belt on, please."

"I'll put my seat belt on if you say you'll use the number; at least think about giving her a call."

"What type of bullshit is that? We're not in third grade; put on the damn seat belt!"

Ben ignored him, "Man, she wants you."

"Put your seat belt on!"

"Man, she wants you to spank her and make her call you daddy."

"Put your seat belt on!"

"She's practically throwing the ass at you. Ooh, Omar, ooh, Omar," Ben teased.

"All right, give me the damn card, and buckle your seat belt!"

Ben chuckled.

"You know you're an asshole, right?"

"I know and you love me anyway," Ben replied, fastening the seat belt around his waist.

Omar was barely out of the supermarket's parking lot when all at once something slammed into the back of his car.

"What the hell!" Omar glanced through the rearview mirror as he released his seatbelt."

"Ben, are you all right?"

Ben nodded.

Omar leaped from his car.

"What are you, fucking blind?"

A woman rushed toward him.

"I'm so sorry; I wasn't looking where I was going." Omar stared at the women who had assaulted his vehicle. She was beautiful.

There she was standing in the middle of the street, wearing a tight yellow two-piece suit. The skirt was extra short, and the neckline of her blouse was plunged so deep into her midsection she looked as though she was wearing a pair of men's suspenders. She stepped past him to assess the damage to his car.

Omar's eyes followed.

"I'm so sorry, I wasn't looking where I was going and-"

"That's okay, there doesn't seem to be much

damage...just a little chipped paint.

Ben stepped from the car.

"I can pay for the damages. How much do you think it will cost?" Her lip gloss glistened in the sunlight as she spoke.

Ben listened from a non-intrusive distance.

"It's okay; you don't have to do that, really." Omar tried to halt her.

What? Now it's time to step in, Ben thought. "Wait a minute, bro, this isn't a Hyundai...it's a Mercedes S Class and the color is custom; it's going to cost a fortune to have it matched."

Omar's forehead wrinkled.

"Okay, well how much?" the woman asked.

"I'd say about a thousand dollars." Omar immediately pulled Ben aside.

"Can I talk to you for a minute?"

The woman stared at Ben as if he had lost his mind.

"What are you trying to do? It's just a little chipped paint," Omar questioned.

"I know, but you're about to let this woman walk away without getting a red cent."

"Maybe I feel like being nice for a change."

"Or maybe you're just being stupid."

"Does everything come down to money with you?"

"Does Condoleezza Rice look like that mouse from Pinky and the Brain?"

Omar chuckled.

"Look, I'm not letting you leave here without the cash or the ass, so you decide."

"Don't start that shit, Ben. I'm telling you." he glanced back at the woman.

"Start what? She's hot."

"Yeah, she is."

"I bet she's a freak, too."

They watched as she leaned over to check out the damage to her car. Her backside was perfectly shaped and calling out to their animal senses.

"Okay, I'll wait here; go make your move," Ben said.

"Man, do you ever stop?"

"No. You shouldn't either. Now get over there."

"Alright, I'm going. Hey, you know she reminds me of Asia."

"Good, then that should make it even easier." Omar left Ben standing by the car.

"Listen, we can split the cost; I could probably get it fixed for about four hundred dollars." Omar glanced at his watch.

"Okay, great, I'll write you a check." The woman opened her purse and accidentally dropped it. The contents spilled into the street.

"Great!" she spat, bending down to retrieve her things from the ground, giving Omar and Ben a bird's eye view of her beautiful bosom.

Omar was quick to help.

"Lord, what else can go wrong?" she asked.

Suddenly they heard the roar of sirens approaching.

"Fuck!" Omar said.

Fuck is right! She thought, staring at Omar's crotch.

Neither one of them wanted to make a big deal of things.

"Listen, my checkbook isn't here. Can you follow me home and I can give you the check and something extra for your trouble?"

Omar pondered.

"It'll only take a few minutes," the woman insisted.

Omar hesitated, glancing at Ben.

"Okay, how far do you live from here?"

"I'm just across 8th Avenue and 139th Street."

"Okay, I'll follow you." Omar glanced at his watch and then jogged back to his car where Ben was standing on the passenger side, smiling.

"How am I supposed to do this? I can't go with this chick, drop you off, and then get back to Asia's in time to prepare a meal?"

"Don't worry about me. I can catch a cab back to my car and Asia can eat cake."

Omar scowled at Ben.

"You're wasting time."

"What's going on, man? Is this some type of sign?" He watched as she pulled her car in front of his.

"Yeah, it's a sign that you need to stop thinking about Asia so much."

"You think so?"

"I know so; why else do you think the Universe is throwing all this pussy at you?"

Ben hoped Omar would take advantage of the situation. At that point, he'd do anything to keep Omar's mind off Asia.

"So, what are you going to do, buddy?"

"I don't know, man."

"Yeah, well, what you don't know won't hurt you, and what Asia doesn't know, is none of her damn business."

It was in that moment that he did what every man does, weighed his chances of getting away with it.

In a split second, he decided.

Ben watched as the two cars pull away. He made a mental note...Stay away from supermarkets and women driving Corollas!

CHAPTER TWENTY-SEVEN

Well, Don't Just Stand There

Omar hesitated as the elevator door opened on the fourth floor. Asia was due home soon and he needed to make it home before she did. A million thoughts began to run through his mind. So fast, that he thought about bolting down a stairwell as they walked through the hall.

"Don't just stand there, make yourself comfortable." She slipped out of her shoes, turned on some music and headed into her bedroom.

Omar looked around.

"You know, I really can't stay too long."

"I'll be with you in a minute," she called out.

"Okay," Omar replied, noticing a picture on a shelf on the other side of the room. He moved toward it. Before he could get a good glimpse of it, she called out again.

"Hey, can you do me a favor?"

Omar spun around. "Sure, what is it?"

"Can you come back here, please? I need your help with something."

He headed slowly toward the back of the apartment.

"Where are you? I really need to be going."

"I'm back here."

He followed the sound of her voice.

"Where are you?"

"I'm here."

Omar glanced in a room and found the woman naked on the bed; she was staring at him and purring like a cat in heat. His first instinct was to turn and run out of the apartment, but like most men he was led by his dick and the sight of her naked glory enticed him.

"Close the door," she said.

"Listen, I just came here for the money, that's it."

"I know and I'm going to give it to you." She spread her legs and revealed four, crisp one hundred-dollar bills dangling from her vagina.

Omar began to undress. The way his endowment sprung from its confinement made her eyes widen. He walked over slowly and mounted her. She smiled as he cupped her breast. Her lips parted in anticipation of a kiss. None came.

He used his knees to part her thighs, she could feel his manhood growing between her legs. He began slapping it against her inner thighs, causing her to have second thoughts. It was too late though. Before she could say a word, he pressed himself into her. She had never experienced anything like it. Within the first few strokes she had determined that Omar wasn't just a well-endowed man, he was a god.

He entered her, drawing tears from her eyes. He could feel her heart flutter as his rigid monstrous endowment plowed through her thighs.

Omar glanced at himself in a mirror on the wall. As he jabbed his fleshy shaft inside of her, he thought of Asia and of Ben.

She seemed to lose a little breath with each stroke. Omar rolled his hips in a circular motion, dipping into her with force and frequency. She screamed at the top of her voice in pleasure, in pain, in ecstasy.

He pulled away from her as she lay there shivering. It was what she wanted, what she expected, and what he feared. She grinned, slyly.

He took a deep breath, crawled from the bed, and dressed quickly.

"So, how long have you two been together?"

"What?" his face wrinkled as he slid into his pants. He tucked himself, to conceal his still rigid member.

"What you have must be really special."

"I don't know what you're talking about."

"You don't remember me, do you?"

He cut his eyes toward the bed. "You know what? I'm not into fucking games; just keep the money and let's just act like this never happened. We'll never see each other again anyway."

"Are you sure?" she asked.

"Yes, I'm sure," he replied snidely.

She rolled from the bed as well. "Well, if you're absolutely sure about it. You can at least let me show you out."

She smiled as she brushed her naked body against him.

He shoved her away.

"That's okay; I can find my own way out!"

As Omar was leaving the apartment, he caught another glimpse of himself in a mirror near the door and for the first time in a long time, he hated what he saw.

While he was waiting for the elevator, Omar slammed his fist repeatedly against the wall, bruising his knuckles. Still, he knew the pain that he was feeling was nothing compared to the pain Asia would feel if she ever found out. If it were left up to him, she never would. He dashed down the stairwell and headed back to her place.

Caesar salad and shade

The cab ride from the church back to Asia's was short, but it seemed like it took forever. When they pulled up in front of Asia's house, she paid the driver and jumped out.

"Are you coming?" she stared at Pam, who was staring at her newfound friend.

The ride had been filled with ogling and sexual innuendoes between Pam and the cab driver. Asia had been caught in the crossfire.

"Girl, just give him your number and come on!" she said, shutting the taxi door and headed toward her house.

Pam took her advice, wrote her number on a piece of scrap paper, and flicked a hand-kiss goodbye.

"I'll see you later, Habib."

"Bye, baby." He smiled before pulling off.

Pam was beside herself with joy as she made her way up the stairs of Asia's home.

"Okay, so now that you've thrown yourself at the Maharajah, now what?"

"Well, now you won't be the only one with a good black man."

"Girl please, he's not black."

"That's okay; he's close enough."

"What am I going to do with you?" Asia shook her head and knocked on the door.

"Wait, I may have issues, but you live alone and you're outside knocking on the door?" Pam twirled her finger around her ear as if Asia was crazy.

"Oh, cut it out."

"Do you have some type of secret knock that will open this door automatically?" Pam asked.

"No."

"Then I suggest you use your key."

Asia was disappointed. All day she had been thinking about arriving home, knocking on her door, and having her man greet her when it opened. She pulled her keys from her purse.

"Omar is supposed to be here."

"You gave him a set of keys already?"

"No, I gave him a spare key in case he needed to run out for something."

They stepped inside.

"Omar!"

Asia called out repeatedly but received no answer.

"I guess he isn't here," Pam said, glancing around. "Girl, you really took that interior design course seriously, huh?"

"Yes, I did," Asia said, kicking off her shoes.

"I can see that. I must get you over to my place to do some decorating. I need a change."

"Please, Pam, you haven't changed a light bulb in your place since you moved in. Now I'm supposed to believe you're ready to redecorate?"

Asia looked toward the staircase.

"Well, you never know. Now that I have a boy-friend, I'm thinking about getting my place together."

"Oh, now the maharajah is your boyfriend?" Asia headed into the kitchen; Pam followed.

A few minutes later, Asia stood at the counter cutting up vegetables.

"What are you making for us?" Pam asked.

"Caesar salad and-"

"Whoever heard of putting cucumbers, tomatoes, and black olives in Caesar salad?" Pam popped olive after olive as she spoke.

"This salad is for Omar and it's the way he likes it."

"Oh, this is Omar's salad," Pam mimicked.

"Maybe one day, I'll be able to say this is Habib's salad."

"Don't you mean Habib's couscous?" Asia joked.

Tears welled in Pam's eyes.

"Pam, what is it?" Asia walked over and grabbed her hands.

"I guess I'm just tired of waiting for my knight in shining armor to make his way up Eighty-Six Street to sweep me off my feet. Maybe I'm not even worth it."

Asia listened attentively.

"Ever since Tony and I broke up seven years ago, I haven't found one man that's willing to take things slow and get to know me, you know? If they're not trying to sow their wide oats, they're looking for me to sew the holes in their socks. Say what you want, but I'm just not willing to play Suzy Homemaker to a guy that doesn't want anything more from me than a quickie, a hot meal, and someone to tag along to functions when it's convenient to him."

"And you shouldn't be, none of us should," Asia said, rubbing the back of Pam's hand to console her.

"Maybe Habib will be different; he's from Pakistan you know?"

"Uh, yeah, I assumed that." Asia gave her friend a paper towel and some words of advice. "Look, Pam, you know I'm the last one to ever tell another woman to let her guard down. Lord knows, I've had mine up for a long time. However, if you really want a good man in your life, you must believe you're worth having one. Quit doubting yourself, girl."

A tear fell from Pam's eyes.

"Most important, Pam, you have to keep smiling. So, when that good man does come along, he can see the strong, beautiful woman you are."

They hugged.

"Now get out of my kitchen, before you have me crying in Omar's salad."

KEYS, CHEESE, AND FLEAS

An hour had passed and neither Keisha, Angela, nor Omar had arrived.

"I wonder what's taking everyone so long to get here." Asia glanced at the clock.

"I don't know; Angela should have been here already."

"Keisha, too," Asia added.

"I hope those two haven't gotten into trouble."

"I don't know about Keisha, but Angela's not the get-into-trouble type," Asia said.

"I guess you're right, but she was upset when she left the church."

"Well, I hoped that she just needed some time to breathe and then she'd be right over."

Just as Pam spoke those words, they heard keys jiggling outside of Asia's door.

"Hold that thought." Asia leaped up and ran to open the door.

"Omar?"

"Now girl, I've been mistaken for a lot of things, but never a man."

Keisha walked in carrying a large plastic bag.

"I'm sorry. Come in. I heard keys jiggling and I thought it might have been Omar."

"No, it's just me." Keisha jiggling a set of keys, "You left these in the door."

"Oh gosh, girl, thank you." She snatched the keys from Keisha's hand as they headed into the living room, "So, what took you so long?"

"Well, I didn't want to come empty-handed." She handed Asia a plastic bag.

"You didn't have to do this," Asia said, opening the bag.

Pam watched in anticipation as she reached in the bag, pulling out a large basket filled with imported crackers, Italian cheeses, cold cuts, fruit, and chocolates.

"Keisha, thank you; this is so thoughtful." Asia kissed her on the cheek.

Pam sneered.

"Well, it's my way of apologizing for that scene at church. It was wrong and I'm sorry."

"See, Pam, I told you Keisha was cool."

Asia smiled, placing the basket of food on the coffee table.

Pam flashed a spurious smile.

"Well, since we can't touch the food in the kitchen until Angela gets here, let's crack the basket," Pam said, reaching across the large coffee table.

"Touch it and you die," Asia said, slapping her hand away.

"I'm already half dead from starvation so I'll take my chances."

"You could stand to lose a few pounds," Keisha mumbled while fingering through her purse.

"What?" Pam snapped.

Keisha turned her attention to Asia. "Ooh, cousin, your place is really laid out. When are you going to give me a tour so I can see the rest of it?"

"Keisha, you're not a stranger, look around. The bedrooms are upstairs but stay away from my perfumes."

Keisha tossed her purse on the couch and swished her way up the stairs.

"Don't forget what she said about the perfume, either!" Pam yelled.

Asia nudged her.

"What? You know she steals," Pam joked.

Asia laughed, "Stop it!"

"No, she should have taken this ugly purse with her, too."

"It is ugly, isn't it?" Asia chuckled.

Keisha soon rejoined Asia and Pam in the living room. "Girl, I really like what you've done to the place. It's so big, though, aren't you afraid to stay here alone?"

"No. At the most, it gets a little lonely, but hopefully, that's all about to change."

Asia's tone insinuated that she and Omar were considering taking their relationship to the next level.

"Are you saying you're considering marrying Omar already?" Keisha clutched her pearls.

"No, I'm saying I lent my man a key this morning and I'm thinking about letting him keep it."

Keisha breathed a visible sigh of relief.

"I was about to say you're not ready for all of that."

Pam couldn't believe her ears.

"Well damn, Keisha. Don't hold back your opinion."
Keisha snarled at Pam.

"Excuse me, but was I talking to you?"

Pam and Keisha began to bicker. Asia tried to referee. They were all cackling so loudly that they didn't hear that someone had walked in.

Asia heard someone clearing their throat. She turned around to find Omar standing there, watching them.

"Oh my God, Omar, I didn't even hear you come in, I'm sorry." She rushed over to him.

He set the bags on a table near the door.

"I'm sorry; I didn't know you were having company. I can come back later," he gestured toward the door.

Asia wrapped her arms around his waist and then kissed him. "Oh, stop it; what's in the bags?"

"I wanted to do something special just for you, but it looks like that's not going to happen."

Omar noticed the large basket sitting in the middle of the coffee table.

"I'm sorry, I should have told you I was bringing company home."

"No, I should have checked with you before buying all of this."

"You don't have to check with me before you do anything."

"Yes, I do, this is your place."

"Okay, you know what? Let's just forget about all of that. I want you to meet my friends."

Omar was hesitant; he didn't want to meet her friends. He slipped out of his jacket thinking, *Damn, I've avoided meeting her friends all this time and now today of all days she has a house full of them.*

He took a deep breath, placed his hands around Asia's waist, and followed her into the living room.

"Omar, you remember my cousin Keisha, from the mall?"

"Oh yeah," he smirked while extended his hand.

Keisha was sitting with her legs crossed. As she shook Omar's hand, she uncrossed her legs and then crossed them again. From where he stood, he could see that she wasn't wearing any underwear either.

They shook hands.

"It's nice to see you again, Omar." *It's nice to squeeze you again, Keisha*, Omar recalled. He turned away quickly.

"Baby, this is my friend, Pam."

Omar extended his hand. "It's really nice to meet you, Pam."

Pam sat there, staring at him as if she had seen Jesus.

Omar's face wrinkled with laughter.

"Is she okay?"

"She's fine. Girl, close your mouth!" She tossed a pillow in Pam's direction.

Asia chuckled.

"Baby, I wanted to make one more introduction." Just as Asia spoke, the doorbell rang. "I'll be right back."

"Okay," Omar said, quickly kissing her before she headed out of the living room.

Keisha stared at him.

There were a few seconds of silence before Asia returned. When she did, things got drastically worse.

"Hey everyone, look who's here!" she said, escorting Angela into the living room.

Omar turned around.

"Baby, I want you to meet one of my best friends in the whole world, Angela." Asia beamed with excitement.

Omar took one look at Angela and his mouth dropped open.

Asia noticed that he was speechless for the first time since they'd known each other. In fact, for a few seconds the entire room was still. Angela was staring at Omar, Omar was staring at Asia, Asia was staring at Angela, Angela stared at Pam, Pam was staring at Keisha, and Keisha was staring at Angela. It was one big mess until Angela decided to break the awkwardness.

"It's nice to meet you, Omar." She gazed at him as she extended her hand.

Omar felt a lump form in his throat.

"Have we met before?" Angela asked.

Omar didn't respond.

"Baby, is everything okay?" Asia asked.

"Everything's fine. Listen, I'll be upstairs."

Angela smirked as Omar scurried upstairs. She removed her coat and flung it over the side of the couch.

"What took you so long, Angela?" Pam asked.

"Well, I had a little accident."

Asia and Pam ran to her side.

"Are you okay?"

"Did you get hurt?"

Keisha didn't flinch.

"I'm fine, really."

"So, where's the car?"

"Oh, I dropped it off at the mechanics and took the bus over."

"You took the bus over here dressed like that?"

Angela was wearing a very revealing outfit.

Pam checked it out as well.

Angela started strutting around as if her sole purpose for being there was to taunt Keisha. Keisha,
however, was paying her no mind. She was too busy
watching Omar spying down from atop the staircase.

Omar noticed her watching him and slid back from
her view. She fixed her eyes on Angela.

"Honey, I'm glad you're all right. Listen, let's head
into the kitchen. I have the food all laid out," Asia said.

Pam and Angela started toward the kitchen.

"I hope you didn't cook anything too heavy. I need
to look good when my mechanic takes me out next
week."

"Girl, you met a mechanic and Pam met a maharajah," Asia joked.

"What?" Angela giggled.

"Keisha, aren't you coming?" Asia asked.

"Oh, I'll be there in a minute."

Angela grabbed Asia by the arm and guided her.
Asia couldn't help noticing the peculiar look on her
cousin's face as she headed toward the kitchen; Keisha
was in deep thought.

"Would you come on, I'm hungry."

"Girl, that Omar is fine. You better keep your eyes
on him; some jealous trick might try to slip up under
him when you're not looking," Angela said, as she followed Asia into the kitchen.

"That's right cousin, because if he lays down with a
female dog, he will definitely get up with fleas."

Angela glanced back and cut her eyes at Keisha.

Keisha was unbothered. When it comes down to it,
she knew she could kick Angela's ass all over Asia's
apartment. Instead, she sat quietly, with her legs and
arms crossed, thinking about the awkwardness between

Angela and Omar. Something was up, and she was going to find out what it was. She could hear Angela's
hyena-like laugh coming from the kitchen and thought,
*you can laugh now bitch, but you're going to slip up
and when you do, I'm going to be right there to call you
out.*

    She got up and joined them in the kitchen.

CHAPTER TWENTY-EIGHT

Oh, Don't Get It Twisted

After her friends left, Asia decided to spend the rest of the night with Omar, undisturbed. It had been a long, eventful day for them both, and neither of them could wait to be in the other's arms. She could hear Omar speaking to her as he finished up his shower.

"You know, I saw your friend, Keisha, in the supermarket earlier today."

"Oh yeah, did she flirt with you, again?"

"What do you think?" he asked, stepping out of the bathroom.

When he entered the bedroom, he couldn't believe his eyes. Asia was wearing a red lace panty that he had laid out for her earlier.

He removed the towel from his waist, leaped into bed and pulled her over on top of him. The reflection from a mirror near the bed revealed the curve of Asia's ass. He loved it. He began kissing her, his lips moved from her ear to her neck. For some reason, though, Asia seemed distracted.

"Are you okay?"

"Yeah, I'm fine, but can I ask you something?"

"Sure, what is it?"

"Well, earlier when I introduced you to my friends, it seemed like something was bothering you. What was it?"

"Nothing, now kiss me!"

"Are you sure? I mean, I've never seen you so lost for words before."

Omar folded his hands behind his head.

"So, I was a little quiet, so what?"

"If something made you uncomfortable, then I want to know."

As Asia spoke, Omar closed his eyes as if to block out any further questioning. "I told you...there's nothing wrong. Why don't you just drop it!

Asia glanced at the message display on her answering machine and realized that there were no messages waiting.

"So, are you saying that I don't have the right to ask questions?"

"I'm saying, don't you think it's a little too soon for you to be acting like this? It's not like we're married."

She paused for a moment and then rolled off him. "You know what, you are right!" She slipped into her slippers and a bathrobe. "Where are you going?"

"Oh, I'm not going anywhere."

"So, what? Are you angry?"

"Angry? No, I've just been giving you the best that I've got, sharing everything with you and you have the nerve to tell me 'it's too soon' to ask you a question?"

"What are you saying?"

"I'm saying if it's too soon for me to ask you questions, then it's too soon for you to be laying your black ass up in my bed every night. Get up!"

Asia walked over to the bedroom door and held it open.

"Are you serious?"

"Are you?" she snapped.

Omar couldn't believe that she was acting in such a way. He dressed quickly and headed downstairs. She followed him.

"What is this about, Asia, huh? Do you have something you want to tell me?"

"What are you talking about?"

"I'm just saying, are you sure this isn't about your ex-boyfriend?"

"What?"

"I heard his message, Asia."

"You did what?"

"That's right; I know that you're still in contact with him. That's why I deleted your messages."

Asia was stunned; she had no idea that he would stoop so low as to listen to her messages. The look on her face had turned very serious. Omar had never seen such a look of contempt in her eyes.

"Get out, Omar! I never want to see you again."

"You don't mean that."

"I can show you better than I can tell you. Get out!"

Omar was floored; he never thought he would hear those words from Asia's mouth, but clearly, she meant them.

"I said get out!"

"This is what you wanted to do all along, right?"

She didn't answer. As far as she was concerned, he had no right deleting her messages or being in her house after she asked him to leave.

"I'm telling you right now, if I leave here tonight, I'm not coming back."

"Oh, don't get it twisted; you're leaving here tonight because I'm putting you out, not because you want to go."

"So, that's what this is about-power?"

"Yeah, pussy power. Now, please leave."

"Okay, I can see that you're a bit emotional; you don't really know what you're saying. What is it...that time of the month?"

"What?"

"If it is, tell me. I'll understand. If not, then you better change your attitude before this shit gets really serious and you regret it later."

Asia stared at him, thinking, *You are one arrogant son of a bitch! How dare you!*

Omar's statement sounded more like an ultimatum than a plea for forgiveness. She reached past him, unlocked the front door, and swung it open. The chill in the evening air hit him in the face like a frozen brick, and so did the reality that things between him and Asia had drastically changed.

Omar was barely out of the door before Asia slammed it shut behind him. The gust of wind from the slamming door nearly blew him from the steps.

She stood at the door, watching through the peephole until he left. Although she was upset, she was firm in her decision; she would not be played for a fool any longer.

She opened the door, glanced down at the welcome mat he bought her, and sighed. He was no longer welcome in her house or in her heart. In fact, no man was. She picked up the mat and flung it to the street.

She turned off the light in the foyer and then headed back to her bedroom-alone.

CHAPTER TWENTY-NINE

Tasha and The Black Bunny Mask

One of the bartenders at The Squeeze Bar had called Ben several times, annoyed at the ruckus Omar was causing in the establishment.

The Squeeze Bar was an adult dive lounge known for its cheap drinks, busty waitresses and secluded location. It had become a meeting place of men looking to escape the drama of a tumultuous relationship. Ever since he and Asia fell out, Omar had been hanging there.

When Ben arrived, he immediately read the look of frustration on the bartender's face.

Omar was standing on the far end of the room banging his fist against a pinball machine.

"It's about time you got here." The bartender grimaced.

"How long has he been like this?"

"Three hours and if he breaks that machine, I'm going to beat his ass for three hours."

"Okay, relax!" Ben shot the bartender a firm look. "Don't worry, I've got him."

"Yeah, well, get him then."

Ben walked coolly across the room.

"Hey, Omar, what's up buddy?"

Omar glanced around. "Great, what the fuck are you doing here?"

"Wow, is that any way to speak to your other half?"

Omar threw him a look of warning.

"Man, I just stopped in to get a drink, but hey, listen; the bartender said if you break the machine, he's going to break your ass."

"Yeah, let him try it; I could use a good workout right about now." Omar glanced at the bartender as if daring him to say a word.

"So, did you see the game tonight? Ben asked, attempting small talk.

"No, I didn't see the damn game. In fact, I haven't seen a game since I started messing with that crazy heifer on 122nd Street."

He lifted the front of the pinball machine and began slamming it repeatedly against the floor.

The other patrons in the bar watched nervously. The bartender pulled a bat from beneath the bar.

"Omar, come on. What are you doing?" Ben asked,

"I'm trying to get the fucking ball in the hole!"

Omar gave the machine a swift kick. Ben pulled him over to a nearby table.

"You want me to believe that all of this is about you trying to get that little silver ball in a hole?"

"What else?" Omar fiddled with the buttons on his cell phone.

"Come on, you know this isn't about that."

"What is it about then, Mr. I-have-all-the-damn-answers?"

"This is about your balls."

"What?"

"That's right; your balls are twisted because you can't handle that woman you got. Now, you want to take it out on a damn pinball machine."

"You don't know what you're talking about."

"Oh, I don't?"

"No."

"So, what is it then?"

"Nothing...I'm just not going back, that's all."

"Oh, now you're not going back?"

"That's right."

Ben analyzed the expression on Omar's face. "When I warned you about that woman, you told me you could handle yourself. Now you're in here acting like somebody else is responsible for your screw up."

"You know what? I don't need to hear this shit right now, Ben."

Omar attempted to walk away, but Ben halted him. "Sit down!"

Omar paused.

"I told you before, never show a woman your hand because she'll turn on you like a dog."

Omar listened.

"When you started going out with Asia, I didn't say a word; when she started spending nights at your place, I bit my tongue; when you started shopping for her, I tried to warn you. Now, you're in here acting like you don't have any sense because what I said would happen, happened."

Ben gestured for the bartender to send over a round of drinks, lifting a shot glass to his mouth.

"If you don't comply with what a woman wants, she'll stomp all over your nuts; especially black women. Didn't I tell you that?"

Ben spoke to Omar like a child. Ordinarily, he wouldn't have gotten away with it, but he knew that Omar was too preoccupied beating himself up, to lay a hand on him.

"So, what happened? Did she find out that you were sleeping around?"

"No."

"Okay, then what?"

"She put me out!"

"What?"

"She told me not to come back to her place." Ben fell into laughter.

"So, you're acting like a teenage boy whose mom found his Vaseline under the bed because she asked you to leave her house?"

"I don't see what so funny."

"I'm sorry man, but don't you see she did you a favor. Now you don't have to break up with her. She did it for you." Ben continued to laugh.

Omar didn't appreciate Ben's humor.

"Did you at least do what you promised you would do?"

"No."

"Okay, well, now what?" Ben's voice was layered with disappointment.

Omar looked away.

"Man, what am I going to do with you?"

"Hey, are you okay buddy?" the bartender asked. He decided to deliver the shots himself.

"Yeah, I'm fine, man. Listen, I'm sorry about the pin-ball machine."

"It's okay; it's a piece of shit anyway." They all laughed.

"Listen, why don't you guys head to the back? We have a couple of new girls dancing tonight."

That was right up Ben's alley; he stood up quickly and led the way.

Behind the velvet curtains...

They entered the lounge.

"So, you really think I should just leave her alone?" Omar asked.

"Yes," Ben replied.

While they were waiting to be seated, Omar caught a glimpse of a woman leaving the stage. For a moment, he thought he recognized her, but quickly passed it off as an effect of the liquor.

The room was full of smoke, which hindered Omar's vision as well. A topless waitress escorted them to a table near the stage.

"Okay, Ben, you've been right so far; so, I'm going to do as you say."

"Good." Ben checked his jacket for cigarettes. "So, what's our next step? Did you find a place for us?" Omar asked, swallowing the shot of liquor like it was air.

"We should have one in a few days," Ben replied, lighting a cigarette as he spoke.

"I swear I hate that I let a woman get to me like this. I feel like going over there and boning the hell out of her right now."

"That's what she wants you to do. Omar, you've been going back and forth with this charade for a while now; it's time to let it go and move on. Besides, she's probably back with her ex by now."

"Don't even say that."

"It's a possibility."

"When I left, Asia was so mad, I don't think any man will get next to her for a long time."

"Man, listen, a hurt woman is a scornful woman; she'll do whatever she has to, to rid herself of the pain of a relationship gone bad. Even if it means taking up with an ex-lover, which in this case happens to be the lead singer of a group whose album just went double platinum."

"I know he wants her back, but I don't think she would actually go back to him."

"Whatever! Either way, Asia's not sitting around waiting for you to make things right this time. She's moved on, and so should you."

"Maybe you're right; I don't need the distraction."

"Exactly, you're already distracted enough." Ben rubbed his shoulder.

"Man, I have to get back in the gym. I need to clear my head."

Ben tapped Omar on the belly. "Yeah, you need to tighten this up, too. I don't want it getting in the way."

Omar slapped his hand away. "I'll be fine."

"I know you will." Ben raised his glass and looked Omar in the eyes. "Hey man, I'm glad that I got you back."

"I'm glad, too."

Suddenly the lights dimmed, and the music started up. Omar flagged a waitress to come over. While he was ordering a drink, Ben's eyes were fixed on the stage. His manhood nearly ripped through his pants when a sexy dancer somersaulted onto the stage wearing a black bunny mask, fishnet stockings, and a pair of heels that looked like they had been sculpted from a block of ice.

He tapped Omar's leg repeatedly.

"What's up, man, what is it?" Omar turned around and found he was staring directly between the woman's thighs.

"Oh, shit!" He bit his bottom lip.

"Brother, somebody up there is really fucking with you." Ben patted him on the shoulder.

The dancer crawled toward them.

"She's coming this way." Ben started searching his wallet for single dollar bills.

Omar watched as the woman rolled into a handstand and then spread her legs like a human goal post.

"Is this some type of joke?" Omar gripped himself.

"I don't know, but the shit isn't funny. I don't have any singles." Ben patted his pockets.

The woman leaped into the air, grabbing hold of a pole that was affixed to the middle of the stage. She flung herself upside down and slid down the pole, slowly, like hot chocolate dripping down the handle of a spoon. She sensed Omar's excitement and dismounted the pole.

He watched as she crawled toward the edge of the stage approaching their table.

"Oh shit, she's coming this way, again. Give her a dollar," Ben said.

Omar hesitated.

"Come on; give her a dollar, quick!"

"Man, I don't give women money; you know that!"

"Then give it to me. I'll give it to her for you." The next thing they knew the woman flipped off
of the stage and landed directly on Omar's lap, with her legs straddled on each side of him.

The crowd roared.

"I get off in ten minutes; how long does it take you?" she whispered in his ear.

The cheers grew louder.

Omar wasn't impressed, though. His first thought was to shove her away, but it was quickly abandoned as she began gyrating on his crotch.

"Damn it, Asia, do you see what you're about to make me do," Omar muttered.

"What did you say, baby?"

"Nothing."

The drinks started to kick in. Omar was buzzing and so was his cell phone. He reached for it, but Ben snatched it away, "I got this; you handle that."

Ben turned his back, pressed a finger into his ear, and answered the phone, "Hello."

"Hello, Omar?"

"No, sweetheart, this is not Omar. Who is this?"

"This is Asia,"

"Who is it?" Omar asked.

Ben covered the mouthpiece. "Man, it's some chick named Tasha."

Omar didn't know anyone by the name of Tasha, so he shrugged his shoulders as if to signal Ben to dismiss the call-which is exactly what he did.

"I'm sorry, baby. Omar has his hands full right now; you're going to have to call him back later, better yet, don't!"

Omar leaned back and enjoyed the lap dance. It had been a while since he was on the other side of one. Ben erased the call history and slid the phone back into Omar's pocket.

Omar leaned forward and whispered, "Do you want to get out of here?"

The woman nodded.

"Meet me out front in ten minutes."

She smiled and then headed backstage. Omar watched as she walked away; her backside shook like jelly.

"Hey, man, what's going on?" Ben asked.

"I'm just taking your advice, buddy; just taking your advice."

"Now that's what I'm talking about." Ben grinned. Outside, in front of the Squeeze Bar, Omar decided to check his messages.

"You have no new messages and no saved messages." For a moment, Omar felt sad. The fact that Asia hadn't called nor left any messages was proof enough that she had moved on. The irony was that he finally knew how she felt when he left her after the night they slept together. "Hey, baby. Are you ready to party?" A voice dripped seductively from behind him.

He turned around and nodded in agreement.

Good," she smiled as she snatched the keys from his hand, "and don't you worry daddy, I'm going to take good care of you."

Omar gripped himself as they headed for the car.

He smiled, watching her bouncing bosom as she walked around to the driver's side.

"All right, so what's our destination?" he asked. She glanced at him as she started the car, cracked a smile, and replied, "Ecstasy, baby, ecstasy!"

A few hours later...

Omar woke up to the glare of a neon sign hanging in a paint-stained window in the *Don't Tell Motel.*

He rubbed his eyes to gain focus and quickly learned that he wasn't alone. There was a beautifully built, nude woman standing near the desk opposite the bed; she had just hung up the phone.

"Hey, sleepyhead; are you ready for round two?" she asked.

It took a few minutes, but he remembered her.

"How long was I asleep?"

"Not long, tiger."

He smiled as she walked over to the bed and straddled him.

"Don't tell me you never took that mask off?"

"Okay, then I won't tell you."

His eyebrows rose. He couldn't believe that he had slept with a woman without seeing her face. He reached up to remove it. She wouldn't let him, playfully dodging his hands.

"Take it off!" Omar demanded.

She hesitated but decided to remove it after reading the look on Omar's face.

"Wow, you're pretty."

"Thanks."

Omar had no regrets.

"See, that wasn't so bad, was it?"

"Not at all, baby." She massaged his chest.

"You were an animal last night. I never experienced anything quite like it."

"Is that right?" Omar blushed.

"Yes."

"So, I take it you were satisfied?" he asked, pretending not to know the answer to that question.

"Yes, we both were."

"Both?" His eyes rolled toward the bathroom door as someone stepped out. He leaped from the bed in shock. "Keisha?"

"Omar, wait, it's not what you think!"

Omar grabbed his clothes and started to dress. Keisha reached for his arm as he slipped into his pants.

"Don't touch me! I told you before that I'm not with this shit!"

He buttoned his shirt.

Just give me a minute, please!"

"Why; so you can stab your cousin in the back again?" He slipped on his shoes. "Y'all are some real trifling ass bitches."

"Y'all?"

"That's right; you, Angela, and that bitch over there!" Keisha threw herself between Omar and the door.

"Wait! You slept with Angela, too?"

Omar searched his pocket for his wallet and keys. Keisha's eyes widened and she tried to contain a sly grin. She knew something was up with Angela all along; she just couldn't put her finger on it.

"So, does Asia know this?"

"She knows as much about that as she does about this." Omar scoffed.

Keisha stepped toward him.

"You know, we could keep this just between us."

She tried to kiss him.

He stepped around her and headed for the door. "Where are you going?" she grabbed his arm. Before she knew anything, Omar grabbed her by the throat and shoved her against the wall.

"Don't you ever put your fucking hands on me again; do you hear me?"

Keisha's eyes bulged as she nodded.

He shoved her aside and proceeded to open the door.

"She doesn't have to find out, Omar!" Keisha yelled.

Omar stopped, looked back at her, and then let the door slam shut behind him.

Keisha locked the door, checked her neck in the mirror and through the reflection, noticed that a third person was standing behind her.

"Bravo! That was a great performance."

"Thanks, hope it doesn't leave a bruise."

"You'll be okay. At least you'll be getting what you want."

"We both will."

Keisha watched through the mirror as Ben and the other dancer exited the room.

She smiled as she stared in the mirror and muttered before heading back into the bathroom.

"Well, well, well, Angela, I told you I was going to get you!"

CHAPTER THIRTY

Judge Him by His Heart

That same night...

Asia was sitting in a chair by her bedroom window, watching every car that entered the quiet street, hoping each time that it would be Omar.

Although she knew she had every right to be upset, she wasn't certain that she had handled the situation in the best way. She tried calling a few times but received no answer-only voice mail. Although she missed him terribly, she refused to leave a message.

Later she decided that she needed someone to talk to, not Pam, not Angela, or Keisha. She was in desperate need of someone who could help her make sense of the mess her life had become. As she selected the number in her phone, she thought about her relationship with Omar and all the mistakes she had made.

A soft voice cracked through the phone.

"Good evening."

"Hello, Grandma."

"Asia? Baby, is that you?"

"Yeah, it's me. I just called to see how things are going."

"Oh, that's nice; is everything okay?"

"Everything's fine."

"Are you sure?"

"Yes. Why'd you ask?"

"Well, because it's 3:30 in the morning and I'm your grandmother. I know when something's bothering you." Her warm and compassionate voice caused tears to fall from Asia's eyes.

"Baby, tell Granny what's wrong."

Asia hesitated, noticing something lying on the floor near the foot of her bed. She reached down to pick it up.

"Grandma, have you ever made a decision that you regretted and didn't know how to fix it afterwards?"

"Yes, what's wrong, Asia?"

"Oh, Grandma." Her voice cracked.

"Come on, baby, you can tell Granny."

"I can't keep making these mistakes."

"What mistakes, sweetheart?"

"When I met this man, I was strong, secure with my life, and now I feel like I can't control anything."

She began to cry a little harder.

"Listen, honey, women have been making decisions since the beginning of time, some of them good, some of them not so good."

Asia's mind immediately flashed to an image of Eve and that apple. She listened intently.

"The thing is, whenever you make a huge decision like this, you have to be woman enough to stand by it because you made it for a reason. If he's a good man, he'll make things right."

Asia was stumped; how did her Granny know she was having problems with a guy? She hadn't talked to anyone in her family about Omar.

"What makes you think this has to do with a man, Grandma?"

"Asia Marie Chapley, your grandfather and I were married for forty-five years before he passed away. I can't tell you how many times I've stayed up late talking to my girlfriends, my mom, and to my own Granny, trying to figure out if I made the right choice picking that man."

"What do you mean?" Asia questioned.

"I mean, no one is perfect; people make mistakes all the time. You're not the first and you won't be the last woman that has to buckle down and ask herself if you're judging him by the same standard in which you wish to be judged."

Asia's curiosity was peaked.

"What did granddaddy do that made you feel like you needed to make a choice?"

"Honey, that's between me and your grandfather, may God rest his soul. I've made amends with that a long time ago. The question is...what are you going to do, now?"

"I don't know." Asia took a deep breath.

"Well, think about all the things he's doing right and weigh them against the things he's done wrong; the answer should be simple."

"That's just it, he's hasn't done anything wrong, he's perfect."

"So, then what is this call about?" Granny cleared her throat.

"Grandma, Omar's not like any other man I've ever met. He's kind, compassionate, and attentive...and he makes me feel alive."

"Well, it sounds like he's a keeper, darling."

"That's just it. I don't know how to judge that. A few days ago, I asked him a simple question and he blew me off as if I didn't have the right. I don't know how to feel about that."

"Oh, baby, that's how men are; they want to do what they want, when they want, and how they want. Usually, they don't know what they want."

Asia chuckled.

"Like I said, you aren't the first woman that got upset because her man didn't tell her what she wanted to hear, when she wanted to hear it, and you won't be the last."

"So, you're saying that I should have just backed off and not insisted that he answer me?"

"I'm saying you have to choose your battles wisely or you can lose a good man."

Asia listened closely.

"If he's a good man, give him time and he'll answer all the questions you have and more."

Granny began chuckling as if she knew something that Asia didn't. Perhaps something that only comes with the wisdom of age.

"You really think so, Grandma?"

"That's right baby, he'll tell you things you never thought he'd tell, but you have to give him time."

"See, that's the thing, we've been together for so long and I don't know how to judge whether he's coming or going. How can I be sure?"

"Just do what smart women have been doing since the beginning of time; judge him by his heart, baby, not by his mistakes."

Asia's Granny always gave the best advice. Her old-world wisdom was so empowering. The women in her family had always been strong, intelligent, and capable. She was not about to prove them otherwise.

"Well, Grandma, I'm going to turn in now; it's late."

"Okay, baby. Are you sure you're okay?"

"I'm fine. Have you been keeping up with your doctor's appointments?"

"Yes, I have. In fact, I have one later today."

"Good, so then you better get off this phone and get some rest. I'll be waiting to hear a good report from you tomorrow."

"Yeah, I'll be expecting the same from you. Don't forget to call me and let me know when that man is back. What did you say his name was again?"

"His name is Omar, Grandma-Omar."

"Oh, that's a nice name." Asia could hear her granny's voice fading; it was indeed late.

"Grandma, you know I love Austin, right? It's just that I can't come back to Texas right now."

"Oh honey, I know. You just make a good life for yourself there in New York. You got a chance to start over; you'll come back to Austin when it's time."

Tears welled in Asia's eyes. "I love you, Grandma."

"I love you too, honey, and so does Austin." Her grandmother said softly, "Oh and baby, I made the right choice sticking with your Grandfather, and you will make the right choice about that Oscar and about coming back to Austin."

"Grandma, his name is…"

"Goodnight baby." Her granny hung up the phone.

A tear ran down Asia's face.

After the conversation with her grandmother, she felt like a weight had been lifted from her shoulders. She climbed into bed, glanced at the Tiffany locket Omar had given her and allowed her heart to fill with joy.

She weighed her options that night; tomorrow she would apply them.

CHAPTER THIRTY-ONE

Cold Hard Confessions

Omar stood at the top of the steps, recalling the last time he saw her; the chipped paint on the door frame reminded him of just how angry she had gotten. He hoped time had calmed her down.

He had been sitting on her steps all night, trying to work up the nerve to face her again. He took a deep breath, then rang the bell.

While waiting for an answer, he studied an ant that was crawling along one of the steps. It was dragging a large chunk of bread toward a hole in the concrete. He was amazed by the ant's strength and determination. The fact that something so tiny could manage such a huge task gave him the confidence to see his decision through. He was going to get back with Asia no matter what it took. Although he didn't believe in God, he took it as a sign.

He pressed the bell again, this time hearing footsteps in the distance. His heart thumped as they grew nearer. A voice called out,

"Who is it?"

"Omar. Asia, can we please talk?"

She didn't answer. For two minutes, he stood there waiting in the cold. She didn't respond. She didn't open the door or make a sound for the entire time that he was standing there. Growing discouraged, Omar began to think, maybe it wasn't a sign.

Perhaps the ant was just a damn ant.

Omar started down the stairs, but before he could reach the halfway point, he heard a lock being undone. He turned around and saw Asia standing there in a pair of pajamas with one hand on her hip and the other holding the door open.

"What do you want, Omar?"

"May I come in?"

"No, you may not." She backed up to close the door.

"My mom died!" Omar blurted out.

"Oh no," Asia's heart dropped.

"I got a call early this morning." Omar's voice cracked.

"I can't do this alone. Asia, please."

Although the brisk air chilled her body her heart melted for Omar because of his loss. "Come inside."

Omar glanced around the house as if it were his first time being there. As much as Asia felt bad about his mother's passing, she knew she still couldn't show weakness.

"I'm so sorry to hear about your mom, are you okay?"

"Not really, but I'm trying to be strong."

"What about your sister; how is she?"

"She's okay, but I don't know if I'm going to be."

"What are you saying, Omar?"

"I'm saying, I've had a lot of time to think and I'm ready to answer your question"

Her heart smiled. Granny was right; time had done precisely what she said it would.

"Fine, you have five minutes."

"Well, I'm sorry; I've been a fool. When you asked me, what was wrong that night, I should have told you."

"Yes, you should have." Asia replied snidely.

He lowered his head.

Asia tapped her foot as a sign of her impatience. "Four minutes," she said, making it clear that he didn't have much time left before she would once again put him out in the cold.

"Asia, the day that I met your friends, the reason I looked so shocked was because Angela reminded me of someone I had slept with."

"What?"

"Wait, let me finish."

Asia folded her arms and began to brood.

"The woman was my ex and a crazy one at that. She stalked me for nearly six months after I broke up with her. She busted out the windows on my car; spray painted the sidewalk in front of my house, and even showed up at my boss' party in lingerie making a scene. It was crazy. So, when I saw Angela and she looked so much like her, I guess I just freaked."

"Why didn't you just tell me that, Omar?" Asia's tone was starting to change.

Omar sensed that the ice was melting and decided to make a plea for her forgiveness.

"Baby, I was scared. Please forgive me."

"Scared of what?" Asia folded her arms again and slid back in her seat.

Uh oh. Omar thought. Scared was the wrong word. No woman wants a scary man. He quickly maneuvered to bring clarity to his words.

"I was afraid that if you found out that I had a crazy ex-girlfriend, you would see it as baggage and that you wouldn't want to see me again."

Asia's iceberg facade had suddenly melted to the size of an ice cube. The fact that he wanted to protect her from a potentially psychotic ex, made him even more desirable to her. He wasn't out of the doghouse yet, though. She had a few more questions.

"So, that's it?"

"Yes."

"What about the girl you took home the other night?"

Omar nearly swallowed his tongue.

"What?"

"Don't bother lying, Omar. I heard everything!" Asia stared at him, just waiting for him to say the wrong thing.

"What are you talking about?"

"I'm talking about the woman from the club."
Omar's face cracked.

"That's right, I heard everything; and you can tell your ignorant ass friend that my name is Asia, not Tasha!"

Omar began putting two-and-two together and came up with Ben. Asia had been the one who called that night; Ben had misinformed him. Ben also must have forgotten to end the call before closing his phone, which is how Asia overheard everything. At that moment he wanted to kill Ben, but that would have to wait. He had bigger problems, like just how much had Asia overheard.

"Okay baby, I did meet a woman. Ben and I had gone out to a bar and this woman started coming on to me."

"I know and I could tell by the way you were moaning that you were enjoying it."

Omar became flustered with embarrassment.

"Did you take her home?"

"You know I wouldn't take another woman to my place, Asia."

"I didn't ask you that; I asked you if you took her home."

Asia's mouth tightened. Omar knew he needed to tell the truth.

"Yes, I did."

"Did you sleep with her?"

"Baby, please don't do this!" Omar crawled from his chair and gripped Asia's knees.

"Well, did you?"

He stared at her. "No, we were just or-"

Before the words could fully depart from his lips, Asia slapped the shit out of him. "You put your mouth on her?"

Omar saw stars. Asia had slapped him so hard; she nearly loosened a tooth. The thought of him putting his mouth on another woman sickened her and the slap to his face was only the beginning.

"Honey, wait."

Asia slid away from him. "So, is that what you do?"

"What?"

"Do you just go around dropping your face between the legs of every woman you meet?"

"No. Asia, I promise you."

Asia started pacing. "You know, right now your promises mean just about as much to me as a snowsuit in hell. Get out of my house!"

She headed for the door.

"No, I'm not leaving until you listen to me." He grabbed her arm. She pulled away.

"Look, I'm telling the truth. It didn't happen that way!"

"You expect me to believe that?"

"Yes!" Omar's voice elevated.

"Don't raise your voice in here; you don't have the right to raise your voice in here," Asia snapped.

"Of course, I don't," Omar mumbled.

"What?"

"I'm just saying, you asked me to tell you the truth and when I do, you don't believe me. What do you want me to do, Asia, lie or tell you the truth?"

"I want the truth, Omar; the truth!"

"Can you handle the truth, Asia?"

"Yes, about as much as I can handle all the bullshit you've been feeding me all this time."

Asia's words cut through Omar like a knife; he folded his bottom lip into his mouth to prevent firing back. He was unsuccessful.

"Okay, Asia, you want the truth? Here's the truth. You don't have the right to slap me nor get angry at me because we weren't even together at the time, remember? You had put me out!"

Asia knew what Omar was saying was true; she had put him out.

"When I left that night, I didn't think we'd ever see each other again. Hell, I'm sure you felt the same way. So, as hard as it may be to swallow, the fact that I was with another woman is as much your fault as it is mine."

Asia stared at Omar and thought about what her granny had said. She had made a bad decision, so in that moment she needed to decide whether to end the relationship or judge Omar by his heart.

"Are you sure that's all you did with her?" Asia took a seat on the opposite end of the couch.

"Yes," Omar replied quickly. He moved closer to her. "I don't want to lose you over this, Asia."

Asia didn't want to lose him either, but she saw an opportunity to find out more and she took it.

"Omar, do you love me?"

"Yes. You know I do."

"Then I want you to do something for me."

"Anything, just name it."

"I want you to admit that you're a cheater."

"Okay, I'm a cheater."

"Good, now I want you to tell me everything."

"I have told you everything, Asia."

"No, I mean, I want you to tell me everything that cheating ass men like you have been keeping from women like me since the beginning of time."

Omar looked at her as if she were crazy.

"That's right; I want to know where you guys hang out, where you shop, why you call us from blocked numbers, and where you really are when you say you're out with the guys. Where is out with the guys, Omar?"

He reached for her hand. "Baby, you're kidding right?"

Asia stared at him with a blank look on her face.

"Asia, you're asking me to betray the trust of millions of men across the world; I can't do that." He stood up.

"Then you have to go; get out!"

"Baby, wait."

"No, you should have been so adamant about not wanting to betray my trust, but you weren't, were you?"

Omar reached for her hand.

She pulled away.

He grabbed her, pulling her from her seat with force.

He wrapped her tight in his arms and kissed her.

"I'm sorry."

"I'm sorry, too," Asia replied coldly.

Omar turned and headed toward the door.

An hour later...

Omar was sitting in his car outside of Asia's house. What she had asked him to do was unthinkable, but he was cold, tired, thirsty, and his stomach was growling. He reluctantly returned to Asia's doorstep. She sneered as she let him in.

He studied her body language as she poured him a cup of hot coffee, hoping that she wouldn't suddenly have the urge to toss it at him.

The look on Asia's face showed that she was confident that he'd return. She continued with her inquiries.

"So, you're telling me that a man will actually purchase a second cell phone just so his woman will not be able to track his calls?"

Omar nodded.

"What else?"

"Well, usually if a guy phones his lady up and says that he's spending a night over a friend's because it's too late to drive home, it's a lie. Most men would rather drive in a blizzard just to sleep in their own beds, rather than spend the night out. If he does, there's a big chance there's another female in the equation."

Asia's eyebrow rose.

"What about when we ask you guys if you think we're getting fat?"

Omar sipped from the cup. "Well, usually if you have to ask, then you are. We say no just so we can have peace after the fact."

Asia took mental notes. "So, what about sex?"

"What about it?"

"Why do so many men just want to jump right in...no communication, no romance, and no intimacy, just sex?"

"Well, some men feel like intimacy is a sign of weakness. Most guys aren't willing to appear weak for the sake of pleasing a woman; that would be too much like turning the authority over to her. So, if he jumps right into things, then he's the one in charge. Usually, until he gets a nut; afterwards he couldn't care less."

Asia's top lip rose on one end.

"Why do men who have good women at home, still feel the need to go out and cheat?"

Omar took that question as a personal stab; he paused before answering. "Most men know when they have a good woman and there could be a million reasons why a man would cheat."

"Like what?" Asia asked, listening attentively. Omar sighed.

"Okay, well, one reason might be sexual incompatibility. If a man feels like he wants to try something new in the sexual area of his relationship and his woman isn't

willing, he might be inclined to go out and seek fulfill-
ment elsewhere."

Asia gritted her teeth. "Go on."

"Another reason could be, he really does love the
woman that he has at home, but he is no longer sexually
attracted to her. Rather than leave her, he gets his sexual
needs fulfilled away from home. He still comes home to
her."

At that point, Asia was utterly disgusted, and it
showed on her face.

"I know what it sounds like, Asia, but it's the truth.
Most men are dogs. We're always looking for a place to
bury our bones. We don't care if it's at home or outside in
the trash, as long as we can get away with it."

"So, you admit that you go around preying on unsuspecting woman?"

"Come on, women aren't stupid. They know when a
man is cheating on them."

"How do we know, Omar?"

"You know because you feel it every time, we do
something out of the ordinary, like breaking our call pat-
terns, or not accompanying you to important functions, or
starting fights just to get out of the house."

Asia's eyebrow rose. Omar had said the wrong thing.
She recalled the many times he pulled that stunt on her.
She remained cool though; she grabbed a pen and started
to take notes.

"What are you writing?" Omar asked.

"Don't worry about that, you just keep talking," Asia
snapped.

"Okay, another way a woman can tell if her man is
cheating, is by observing him during the holidays. If he
always misses family gatherings or dresses up and leaves
her at home, chances are there's another woman in the
equation."

Asia was boiling; the fact that any man would consider a woman to be so stupid made her sick and Omar was going to pay for it.

"Continue," she said, tapping the counter with her pen. "What else do you want to know?"

"When men enter a relationship, do they have a hidden agenda? Do they purposely manipulate? Do men know that they are frightened of permanent commitment beforehand? Does that fear make them expect and provoke the termination of a relationship by finding excuses as to why it shouldn't continue?"

"Damn, what are you going to do, write a book about it or something?" Omar chuckled.

She rolled her eyes and continued. "Why do men move in with a woman, become afraid of the commitment, and respond with rage and feelings of entrapment? Do you guys behave this way on purpose to distance yourselves? Do you do it to distance yourselves so that the woman can call it quits?"

Asia's tone sharpened; she was asking so many questions that Omar couldn't keep up.

He began to stutter.

"Come on, why does a man wine, dine and charm a woman into thinking that she has a future with him, when in essence, no one woman stands a chance of ever really getting all of his affection?"

"Well-"

She cut him off.

"Why does a man screw up a relationship whenever a good woman gets too close?"

Damn! In just a few seconds, Asia had managed to unmask his entire life. He had been running games on women for so long that he didn't know any other way to be. What started out as basic juvenile behavior literally became his reality. Before Asia, he had convinced himself that no one woman was worth committing to. He wasn't alone in his reasoning, either. Many men shared the same reasons for concocting elaborate rationalizations and reasons for not fully wanting to commit to a woman, Ben especially.

Asia rolled her tongue around in her mouth as she wrote in shorthand. As much as she didn't like the things Omar was telling her, she knew that they were true and there was a lot more to the bullshit men pull on women. He was going to give it to her no matter what.

Omar stared at her with the sincerest look in his eyes. "Asia, you've asked a lot of questions, most of which you already know the answers to. I'm going to keep the next few short and to the point to avoid being thrown out in the cold again. Is that okay?"

"Fine." Asia folded her arms and listened.

No matter what Omar said, she assumed a percentage of it would be a lie.

"If a man doesn't fully want to commit to a woman, when she starts to get too close, he'll start to act out."

"Oh, you've got to explain that one."

"Well, he will look for excuses and faults in a woman to help him feel better about his behavior; he'll complain about her hair, her clothes, the way she cooks, her friends, her family, her job, the laundry, her children, if she has any, and to really bring it all home, he'll comment on her weight."

Asia shot him a sullen stare. She recalled a time in their relationship when Omar had made disparaging comments about her weight.

"Most men know deep down that their constant emphasis on a woman's weaknesses is only a means of rationalizing that allows them to avoid looking too deeply at their own major flaw-the inability to commit."

"So, you admit that you're a two-timing dog that manipulated me from the beginning?"

"No. I admit that in the beginning, I didn't know what I wanted and that I was just like so many other men who feared commitment. But that's in my past; I know what I want now."

"You know, I've been thinking about getting a dog."

"Asia, did you hear what I said?"

"I heard you. Listen, what type of dog should I get?"

"What? I don't know." Omar was growing agitated. He could see past Asia's bullshit but, he couldn't deny his feelings for her.

Asia ignored his sighs.

"So, tell me, if you were a dog what kind would you be...a Beagle, a Rottweiler?"

Omar shook his head.

"Baby, please."

"Answer the question, Omar."

"What does that have to do with anything?"

She opened a book that was lying on the coffee table. She had picked it up from the library a few days earlier. It was a book about dogs and their different characteristics. She started flipping through the pages, "You know dogs are really quite amazing, Omar. In fact, it wasn't until I picked up this book that I realized how much you actually have in common with a dog."

Omar had no idea where Asia's comments were leading. She began to read.

"Interesting...this book says that Beagles have a warm, friendly disposition and that they're both loyal and brave. Beagles are lively, playful, and curious, which combined with their pleasant personalities, makes them excellent family pets." She looked at him.

"So!"

"So, do you think you're a Beagle?"

"What?"

"It also says here that they love company and affection, and they get along well with other dogs. They have a very independent and determined streak, so they may not always be easy to train. That could be you, Omar."

Omar was starting to become insulted. He sat across from her thinking, *Is she actually comparing me to a real dog?*

"Boxers, on the other hand, are very energetic and playful with a friendly and cheerful disposition. Although they can be willful at times, they are generally very happy, keen, and alert dogs with a high level of intelligence and the eagerness to learn and to please. The Boxer is a pleasant combination of playfulness, alertness, loyalty, affection, and intelligence. Now Labs-"

"Okay, okay," Omar cut in. "I guess if I had to choose, I'd say a Rottweiler."

Asia smirked.

"That's funny; the Rottweiler is known to be very brave, loyal, and protective of the things it loves. They will fight till the end to keep the ones they love from harm. They are very loving and make good, reliable companions when properly socialized and trained."

"Okay, so, that's a good thing, right?"

"Wrong!"

His eyes widened.

"The fact that you would even look me in the face and compare yourself to a damn dog, tells me just what type of man you really are!"

A look of disgust settled on her face.

"Baby, wait...please!"

"Wait for what, to hear more about your sickness?"

"Asia, you asked me to tell you these things."

"Oh, please, I don't have time for this."

"Come on, hear me out."

"Actually, I've heard enough."

"But-"

"But nothing! If I had known that you were going to turn out to be such a liar, I would have never wasted my time with you."

She tossed the book on the table.

"So, are you saying that you don't love me anymore?"

"I'm saying I do love you, but I love myself more."

She stood up and walked across the room.

The nervousness showed in Omar's posture. Time was running out. He was desperate and needed to do something quickly.

"Asia, I know I messed up, but give me a chance. You're a church-going woman; can't you find it in your heart to forgive me?" Omar's voice was layered with desperation.

Asia just stood there staring at him.

"I promise on all I have left in this world; I've changed."

She headed over to the door, stood there for a moment, and then locked the door. Omar smiled.

"Baby, I did this for you. No other woman could have made me confess those things."

Asia read his eyes as he spoke. He wrapped his arms around her.

"This might sound strange but contrary to what you might be thinking right now, some men are actually capable of telling the truth and falling in love."

"What about you? Are you capable of falling in love?"

"I already have."

He kissed her gently, reaching his hand up as if pulling something from the air.

"What are you doing?"

"Close your eyes and open your hands."

"What?"

"Please."

Asia did what he said and felt something cold in hit her palm. When she opened her eyes, her mouth fell open.

"These are the keys to your house."

"I know. I want you to have them."

Her heart skipped a beat.

"Baby, you don't have to do this."

"I know, but I want to." Omar lifted her hand to his mouth and kissed it.

They embraced.

"I'm really sorry about your mother and I'm glad you're back."

"Me too, baby."

He looked up at the ceiling and gave the God, he didn't believe in, a silent *thank you*.

She grabbed him by the hand and guided him upstairs, where she took her time to undress him.

"Wait, I just thought of something."

"What is it?" Asia asked.

"You know if this ever gets out, every guy in this world will have it out for me."

"Don't worry, baby, your secrets are safe with me." She shoved him down on the bed and they began to make up for lost time. As he lay moaning beneath her, she thought, *that's right, baby, your secret is safe with me, if you don't fuck up again!*

His eyes rolled to the back of his head as he began to moan with pleasure thinking, *I can't believe she fell for all that bullshit. Women are so fucking naïve.* He chuckled on the inside. *Anyway, she's happy now and I am out of the damn doghouse, again. That's all that matters.*

No More Secrets, No More Lies

A month had passed since they had gotten back together. Asia was extremely happy that their relationship had taken a turn for the better and things were finally good between them. There were no lies and no secrets. He called from his hotel room while he was away on business.

"Good morning, baby."

The sound of Omar's voice sent ripples through Asia's body.

"Good morning, sweetheart; how's Georgia?"

"Hot, but you're hotter."

Asia blushed.

"I just called to say I love you and I miss you, baby."

"I miss you, too." She blew a kiss through the phone.

"So, what do you have planned for the day?"

"Well, first I'm going for a quick jog and then I have an aerobics class at noon."

"You're really trying to keep that body tight for me, huh?"

"Of course; you're walking around here looking like a god. I have to keep up with you."

"That's right." Omar chuckled.

"So, how's everything coming along with your sister?"

"It's coming along. She misses my mother, but she'll be okay; we both will."

"That's right, baby, God will see to that."

"Asia, you know I don't believe in God."

"I know, but I'm just saying-"

"Anyway, she'll be stopping by here in a little while with the baby."

"Oh, that's nice."

"Yeah. Hey, do you think my abs look okay? Maybe I should try to find a gym while I'm out here." Omar glanced at himself in a mirror.

Ironically, Asia was doing the same thing; she was also concerned about the sudden expansion of her waistline.

"Stop it, you look amazing."

"Thank you, sweetheart, so do you. Listen, I have to run now; love you." Omar hastened off the call.

"I love you, too."

Asia had never been happier in her life. Her relationship with Omar was better than it had ever been. They trusted each other, they loved each other, and that was all that mattered.

Omar flexed his abs in a mirror

"Wow, that quick three hundred crunches really made a difference." He spoke to his reflection in a full-length mirror.

Time had passed quickly; he glanced at his watch before his guest's arrival.

A knock fell upon the door. He opened it and when he saw who was standing in the hall, a huge smile appeared on his face.

"Good morning."

"Good morning to you." Omar smiled.

"So, how is the most handsome bachelor in the world?" Ben said, almost flirtingly.

Omar's eyebrow rose. "I'm fine."

"Yes, you are. So, are you nervous?"

"What do you think?"

"I don't know; that's why I'm asking."

"I'm nervous as hell, man. I've never done anything like this before."

Ben moved toward him. "I know, but this is what we've been working toward. We've been sneaking around for a long time."

"I know, but-"

"Don't tell me you're having second thoughts."

"No, I'm ready." Omar looked him straight in the eyes. "Let's do it."

Ben smiled as they left the hotel room.

CHAPTER THIRTY-THREE

The Irony of It All

Omar slid the latch on the gate to his front yard, breathing a sigh of relief as he proceeded up the walkway. He was happy to be home. It had been a long trip, a long week, and a long time since he had seen her.

He opened the door, dropped his luggage, and immediately called out to her. "Baby, where are you?"

A few seconds passed and then out of nowhere she came rushing toward him, leaping into his arms and covering his face with kisses.

"I've missed you so much, baby," she said.

Omar's eyes lit up, "I missed you, too!"

"Good, then you can show me how much tonight," she said, flirting as she led him into the house.

"Mmm," Omar moaned, "sounds good, just like your kisses."

"There's more where that came from. Hey, you know I tried to call you, but I couldn't get through."

"I know and I'm sorry. The signal on my cell phone was low."

Omar's honesty meant the world to Asia. He offered a response to her concern quickly and she liked it.

"Believe me, it won't ever happen again; I promise." He pulled her closer and planted a multitude of kisses on her face, her neck and forehead; each one was sealed with the promise to be faithful to her.

"Why don't you go upstairs and get out of those clothes? I'll be up in a minute," she said, in a suggestive tone.

Omar winked at her, lifted his bag, and then headed upstairs. When he walked into the bedroom, he dropped the bag and sat on the edge of the bed. As much as he wanted to forget what had happened, he started replaying the events of the trip in his mind. He couldn't believe that Ben tried to take their friendship to that level. *When he kept pressing me to do a threesome, I should have known that something was up*, he thought, staring down at his bruised fist. He was surprised that Asia hadn't noticed it. Ben had crossed the line and things had gotten out of control.

He flashed back to the events that took place once he and Ben left the hotel...

Something's brewing

He stood looking at himself in the mirror and gave himself a mental pat on the back; he had become so good at lying that he amazed himself sometimes. He could hear her moving around downstairs and quickly slid the duffle bag under the bed; he would put it in a safer place tomorrow.

He kicked off his shoes, lowered his pants and realized that he was wearing a pair of boxers that Asia had bought him. He shook his head.

The trip that he and Ben had taken together had propelled their relationship to the next level. Although he had lied to Asia about where he was, it had all been worth it.

The next morning...

Omar decided to head to the gym early. Asia had asked if he could drop her home for a change of clothes because she wanted to go for a quick jog in the park before heading back to his place.

She had only been in the house for a few moments before someone knocked on the door.

"Who is it?"

"Asia, it's me."

"Keisha?" Asia swung the door open, "Girl, what are you doing here this early in the morning? Don't you know you're lucky you caught me at home?"

Keisha didn't respond.

"Honey, what's wrong?"

"Are we alone?" Keisha asked, glancing around Asia's place.

"Yes, why, did something happen?"

"Asia, we need to talk...about Angela."

Asia rolled her eyes, "Keisha, I know you didn't come all the way over here to talk about Angela; I mean, really."

"Listen, I think you should know some things about her."

"I know everything there is to know about her," Asia chuckled, "She's my best friend, remember?"

"Yeah. Right."

The look on Asia's face was one of disinterest, but she tried to hide it by smiling and offering Keisha something to eat, "I guess since I'm not going to make it to the park, I should have some breakfast; you want some?"

"No."

Asia removed a carton of eggs from the refrigerator. She sat them near a bowl on the counter.

"What about some fresh-brewed coffee?"

"Asia, how much do you know about Omar?"

"Excuse me, what do you mean?"

"He's been lying to you."

Asia halted her. "You know what? I don't even want to hear it. Omar and I are fine. So, don't come here with that nonsense, Keisha."

Keisha tried to continue, but Asia wouldn't let her.

"You know, Keisha, you really need to drop this vendetta you have against Angela. I mean, really it's gone on too long, don't you think?"

"Asia, Angela slept with Omar!" Keisha retorted, blurting out the words with no subtlety.

Asia pretended she didn't even hear Keisha. She started mumbling.

"Asia, did you hear me?"

"I heard you!" Asia yelled. "I heard you and I don't believe you. You've been out to get Angela ever since she found out about you and Kareem."

"Asia, I never slept with Kareem. The night when Angela saw me coming out of his place, I was there to talk to him, that's all."

"Right!"

"It's true. I went there to confront him about the rumors. When I got there, he told me that he had caught Angela messing around with another guy and how it wasn't the first time that she had done it."

"You are such a liar." Asia chuckled.

"Asia, I'm not lying, it's the truth!"

"It's not the truth! Just like what you're telling me about Angela and Omar isn't the truth!"

"I know it hurts, but I'm not lying."

Asia slammed her hand against the counter.

"You know, Keisha, I've seen you do some low things in your life, but this is the lowest. I can't believe you came all the way over here with these lies about my best friend and my man. Girl, this is even low for you."

"Asia, I'm your cousin; why would I lie to you?"

"I don't know, you tell me," Asia said as she began cracking the eggs, one by one.

"I know you don't want to believe it, Asia, but Angela's been lying to you the whole time."

"Okay, prove it, Keisha. Where's your proof?" Keisha hesitated.

"Right; you don't have any because Angela isn't that type of person. Sleeping with a friend's man has always been more your style."

Keisha could tell that she was going to have a hard time convincing Asia, but she still felt she needed to know. "Remember that day I came to your church?"

"How could I forget?" she said, recalling the terrible scene Keisha and Angela made during services.

"When I left you, I bumped into Omar at the supermarket."

"I know; he told me."

Keisha paused; she hadn't expected that. Asia, on the other hand, was waiting to hear something she didn't already know.

"He told you, huh?"

"Yes, he did. We don't have any secrets, Keisha." Asia felt empowered in that fact.

"Well, did he also tell you that he bumped into Angela that same afternoon?"

Asia's eyes widened.

"Angela had an accident that day; she was talking on her cell phone and accidentally ran into another car, remember?

"So?"

"So, the car she ran into was Omar's." Asia's legs nearly dropped out from under her.

As Keisha spoke, Asia recalled the look on Omar's face when she introduced him to Angela.

"I asked Omar about the dent on his car; he said he hit something while talking on *his* cell phone."

"Oh, he hit something all right, but it wasn't a car."

"What are you saying, Keisha?"

"I'm saying if he ran into another car, the dent would be on the front, not on the rear fender."

Asia sat down as Keisha continued.

"After the accident, Angela lured Omar to her house and slept with him; that's why they were both late getting to the house, remember?"

"How do you know all of this?"

"Let's just say a little bird told me."

Asia's heart sunk. She pressed her hand against her belly as if growing sick. "I can't believe this; Angela is my friend. How could she have done this to me?" she said, shaking with anger.

"I'm sorry, Asia, but you needed to know," Keisha said. "Listen, I need to get to work; are you going to be okay?"

"I'm fine," Asia said as she rocked back and forth in her seat.

"Okay, I'll give you a call later to check on you. Okay? Keep your head up, girl."

"What about you, Keisha?" Asia said.

"What?" Keisha quickly spun around.

"What about you? Did you sleep with Omar, too?" Asia's tone burst with insinuation as she rose from her seat.

A lump formed in Keisha's throat. "No girl, why would you ask me a thing like that?"

"I found one of your cards in my bedroom, Keisha."

"Oh, okay, it must have dropped out of my purse a long time ago; when I was looking around, remember?"

Asia's face tightened.

"Yeah, that's exactly what I thought, too, until I remembered that you had left your purse on the couch that afternoon."

"Are you sure?"

"Yes, I'm sure. I remember because Pam and I were talking about how ugly it was."

Keisha was busted.

"Did you really think I wouldn't find out?"

"Asia, I...I thought-"

"You thought what?" Asia walked toward her. "That poor gullible Asia would be too busy refereeing your cat-fights with Angela to notice that you were coming on to her man?"

"I'm sorry, Asia, let me explain..."

"Don't even bother. It doesn't even surprise me; you've always been a big slut, Keisha. The thing that gets me, though, is how you had the nerve to come over here to dish dirt on Angela, knowing that you had stabbed me in the back as well."

"Asia, Omar came on to me, I tried to avoid it."

"You're a lying, two-faced, conniving bitch! Get out of my house, Keisha!"

Keisha tucked her purse under her arm and started toward the door, but decided she wasn't finished. She spun around. "You know, you're no better than me. You might walk around here acting all high and mighty, but the truth is your hands are dirty, too."

"I told you to leave, Keisha."

"Oh, I'm leaving, but not before I get this off my chest. All you do is turn your nose up at people, judging everyone you see as though you're holier than thou. You're not without flaw you know? Maybe that's why Omar found comfort in someone else."

"Oh, please. He didn't find comfort in you, bitch. He found a quick corner-store lay with no probability of being anything better. You're a whore, always have been, always will be."

"And what did he find in you, huh? An insecure, relationship-hound that has to manipulate a man into believing she's something that she really isn't?" Does Omar even know why you were really in Texas for two years?"

Asia's eyes grew in circumference.

"I guess not," Keisha said. "When do you plan to tell him, huh?"

"I don't have to explain anything to you or Omar," Asia scoffed.

"I guess not because you're holier than thou, right? You're such a fucking hypocrite."

Asia couldn't believe Keisha's audacity. She leaped toward her, locking her hands in Keisha's long, black hair. A tussle ensued. Asia slung Keisha across the living room, causing one of her shoes to fly off as she tripped over a chair.

Keisha jumped up and although only wearing one shoe, forced Asia back into the kitchen. She was swinging like a wild woman. Keisha had a street edge to her, so she was not going down without a fight. For nearly ten minutes pots slammed, pans flew, and so did everything else they could get their hands on.

After a while, and a few hard licks to the face, Keisha grew tired and decided to retreat but not before Asia doused her with the entire pot of hot coffee. She raced out of the house wearing only one shoe and a torn blouse. The huge knot Asia put on her head preceded her. It was so large that she raced out of the house looking like the last black unicorn.

Asia picked up the scattered dishes and tossed them into the sink. The thought of so many people betraying her at once sickened her. She recalled Angela's words, *"Every man is my type."*

"We'll see about that!"

Asia grabbed her keys and her cell phone and headed toward the door. She called Angela before leaving.

"Hello?"

"Hi, Angela, it's me."

"Hey, girl, is everything okay? You sound upset."

"Oh no, everything's fine. Listen, can you meet me a little earlier?"

"Sure," Angela replied immediately.

"Good, I'm on my way now; I'll meet you in front of your job in twenty minutes."

Asia hung up the phone, grabbed the aluminum bat from the closet near the front door, and headed out to meet with her frenemy, Angela.

Later that afternoon...

Omar had finished with his customers early and had decided to surprise Asia by coming home early. He thought she'd enjoy spending some quiet time together.

He made a few stops and picked up a dozen pink roses, a box of her favorite chocolates and some wine. He knew how much Asia loved wine.

It had been a beautiful day and he was excited about spending the evening with Asia.

When he arrived home, the pleasant aroma of his favorite meal cooling on the stove-vegetable lasagna, met him. He lifted the foil from the large pan that was resting on top of the stove and inhaled deeply. Asia was a great cook and he couldn't wait to dig in, but first, he would head upstairs to surprise her.

When he walked in his bedroom, he found her sitting on the bed staring at the television screen.

"Hey, baby, I have a surprise for you." He smiled. Asia didn't respond, though; she didn't move, she didn't blink. Nothing.

"How's my favorite girl, today?" He leaned over to place a soft kiss on her face. She turned away.

"You know, Omar, it's funny that you would use the term favorite; especially when you know it implies that you have more than one."

"What are you talking about? Come here." Omar attempted a second kiss but got the same results.

Asia's eyes were growing colder by the second.

"Oh, I see, you want to play hard to get? Then your gifts are going to be hard to get, too," he said, placing the flowers behind his back.

Asia still had no response. After a few seconds, he realized something was wrong.

"Baby, is everything okay?"

"You know what else is funny? The fact that you actually believe that you're some type of gift to women, when the truth of that matter, is you're a fucking joke."

Omar was baffled; he set the flowers down on the bed. Asia glanced at the flowers and smirked.

"Asia, what's going on? Did something happen while I was gone?" He glanced at himself in the mirror as he removed his jacket.

Asia scowled at him.

"Baby, talk to me." He reached for her hand.

She moved away.

"What happened to you?" he asked, noticing a large scratch on her forearm.

"Oh, I had a little run-in with two of your bitches today," Asia replied, rolling down her sleeve.

Omar's forehead wrinkled.

"Asia, please, what are you talking about? Let me see your arm." He reached for her again.

"Don't touch me!" Asia dodged his touch.

Omar didn't know how to react. Just a few hours prior, they were laughing and joking, and everything was fine. Now she was acting as though he had the plague.

Asia stood up and wiped away the tears that had begun to form in her eyes.

"When you should have been pleasing me, you were out pleasing someone else."

"Baby, I haven't been with anyone. I've been at work all day."

"Work," Asia sneered. "Is that what you're calling it now?" She began gathering her things.

"What are you doing?"

"You're a smart man, figure it out."

"Why are you packing?"

Asia ignored him; she began tossing her things into a large duffle bag that she had brought from her place.

"Would you stop packing and tell me what's going on!" Omar demanded. He might have well been talking to the wall because Asia didn't acknowledge a word that he said.

"Asia, would you stop?" he snapped, snatching the bag with one hand and her arm with the other. "What's going on with you; why are you acting like this?"

She pried herself from his grip.

"Babe!"

Asia tore out of the bedroom and raced down the stairs. He followed her into the kitchen.

"Leave me alone, Omar, I just want to leave."

"No, you're not leaving until you tell me what's going on. I thought everything was fine between us. What happened?"

Asia tried to push past him, but he was too big. Omar literally towered over her.

"Baby, can't you see that I'm trying? I love you."

"Love me? You don't love me; you love yourself!" She scoffed, then grabbed a bottle of preserves from the counter and threw it at him.

"What the hell are you doing? You're messing up my place!"

"Oh, I'm sorry, I forgot; this is your bachelor's pad. Who gives a damn?" She flung another bottle toward him, this time narrowly missing his head. It busted against the foyer wall. Omar angered.

"You know what, go! When you're ready to stop acting like a crazy person, call me." He picked up the broken
glass in the foyer.

"Just like that, huh?"

"What do you want me to say, Asia? I'm not going to
stand here and let you fuck up my place when I don't
even know why you're doing it."

"You mean the way you fucked up my life, fucked my
friends, and FUCKED MY COUSIN!"

Omar spun around.

"That's right, I know all about it," Asia said, staring at
him. "How long, huh? How long were you sleeping with
Keisha?"

Omar was at a loss for words.

"I'm talking to you!" Asia shouted.

"Asia, I'm sorry; I made a mistake!" Omar pro-
claimed, lowering his head like a wounded puppy.

"Yes, you are sorry. I thought you were a man, but
you're not. You're no good punk! I'm leaving."

"Asia, wait!"

"No, you wait! Better yet, forget it; you make me
sick."

"Okay, I was wrong!" Omar yelled. "I slept with Keisha, but it was a mistake. I was drunk and this girl tricked
me!"

Is that supposed to make me feel better? You knew
she was my cousin, Omar!"

"I know, baby, but you have to understand how it
happened. That night when I left the *Squeeze Bar*, I was
really, really drunk. I didn't know what I was doing."

"Whatever." Asia retorted. She put the palm of her
hand up in front of his face, in a show of dismissal. She
didn't want to hear anything else he had to say.

"It's like that now, Asia?"

"Yes, it's like that. You slept with my cousin; then you had the nerve to bring your lying ass to my house talking about how much you love and missed me."

"I do, Asia; it true."

"Yeah, well, SURPRISE, Omar! I don't believe you." She leered at him. "But you want to know what's even more surprising?"

"No, but I'm sure you're going to tell me."

"You're damn right," Asia's tone was sharp and deliberate, "What's more surprising is that you never noticed that I had set some of your clothes on fire before you got home that night."

Omar stood there with his mouth agape.

Asia giggled, "Surprise, mother fucker!"

"Asia, please...let's talk about this."

"No! You should reserve your conversation for God, seeing how He is the only one that will ever be able to forgive you for this shit. Oh, wait, I forgot; you're so screwed up you don't believe in God. I should have dumped your atheist ass the first time those words came out of your mouth."

Omar was speechless. Every word that Asia spoke was the truth; he had slept with Keisha and a host of other women she didn't know about. He read the look in her eyes and knew she was through with him.

"Asia, I deserve everything you're saying to me, and I know I'm going to pay for what I've done. Hell, I'm paying for it right now."

Asia's mouth tightened as she listened.

"I don't know why I did what I did; perhaps it's because I'm stupid. Perhaps it's because I'm crying out for help."

"I'd go with the first one," Asia said, sarcastically.

"Okay, I'll accept that. Maybe it's a little bit of both. All I know is that you're the only woman I've ever loved. Losing you would be like losing my breath. I don't want to lose my breath, Asia. I can't live without you.

Asia rolled her eyes, "Really!"

Omar lowered his head, "Yes."

"You don't think you could live without me, Omar?"

"No," he said, stepping toward her.

"You're such a fucking liar!"

"I'm not lying!" Omar barked, growing agitated with Asia's demeaning disposition.

"Okay, then tell me this; do you think you could live without Angela?"

His eyes widened.

"Better yet, how about that nasty pole-dancing stripper from the bar?"

His mouth fell open.

"What about the woman on the escalator at the mall or the one you picked up on 72nd Street, Omar? Can you live without them?"

Omar's pulse began to elevate; how did Asia know about all of them?

"Baby, please, I-"

"Wait, what about the woman you met outside of the hospital the night I saved your ass from getting a ticket? She was attractive; she should be hard to live without. What about the woman that asked you to help her reach a pack of sheets? Did you ever reach her sheets, Omar? Can you live without Collette?"

Omar had flashbacks of having slept with all the women Asia had mentioned and there were a lot more secrets he hoped she didn't know about. He began to sweat.

"Oh, let's not forget about the twins. Can you live without the goddamn twins?"

Omar's breathing became more rapid.

"You know what, don't answer that; you'll just lie about it anyway. I'll pick up my things tomorrow when you're not here."

Asia started toward the door. "I'll leave your key in the mailbox."

"No, you won't. You either take this shit out of here now or you won't get it."

Omar's words stopped Asia in her tracks. She played the words over in her head and quickly determined that Omar had lost his damn mind. She let the door close and walked back into the foyer.

"Let me tell you something, Omar. I know you're stupid because you've thrown all of this away." She outlined her body with her hands. "But you'd be a damn fool to try to keep my things. I'll make your life a living hell."

"You already have," Omar fired back. "And believe me, I don't want your things!" At that point he had enough of Asia's bitching. He raced through the house, grabbing everything of hers he could see and then tossed them into a pile in front of her.

"You want to go? Go!" he said, tossing anything that even reminded him of her into that pile.

Asia couldn't believe her eyes. The tables had turned again; now she was the one being tossed out and her things tossed out with her. Although she had planned to leave, she preferred it be on her terms, not his.

"You don't have the right to treat my things like trash, Omar. You're the one that fucked up!" Asia screamed.

Omar bolted up to his bedroom and returned with the large duffle bag Asia had filled, as well as two large plastic bags. He tossed them all onto the pile of her things.

Asia began to cry.

"Oh, don't cry now; it's too late for that. You messed up my house, told me that I'm useless, and said you don't need me. You don't believe me when I say that I'm sorry, so here's your shit; take it and go!"

Asia's heart shrunk to the size of a grain of salt. She felt lower than any man had ever made her feel before.

"I hate you, Omar. You're a manipulative, selfish, uncaring asshole!"

"Yeah, well, you're a stuck-up, bossy heifer, so I guess that makes us even; now get your shit and get out of my house!"

Tears streamed down Asia's face as she began stuffing her things into the empty trash bags. She couldn't believe what her life had come to. She looked up at Omar as she lifted a broken picture frame from the pile. "You keep this; I want you to remember what you destroyed."

Omar grabbed the broken frame and stared at the photo. They had taken it during their trip to the South Street Seaport. While staring at it, he recalled a time when their relationship was simple, uncomplicated, and without drama; but that was long ago. He tossed the broken frame aside.

"Would you hurry up; I'm expecting company," he said, kicking the scattered items closer to her.

Asia charged toward him, slamming her hand against his face. She wanted to hurt him as badly as he had hurt her.

Omar backed away, but Asia kept charging toward him. She clawed at his face, scratching him above the eye.

Bad move.

Omar acted out of reflex, shoving her against the wall. The impact from her body caused a picture frame to fall to the floor. Standing against the wall Asia glanced down, noticing the cracked frame and the shards of broken glass surrounding a photo of the two of them. For a split second she recalled how happy they were back then. She also realized the irony of the moment and how their once beautiful relationship was as broken as the picture frame. Suddenly her mind drifted back into the present moment. Her eyes telegraphed a look of shock, *Oh hell, no!* She ran into the kitchen.

"Asia, wait!" He ran behind her and bumped right into the barrel of a 45 Caliber handgun.

"Oh, shit!"

"You lied to me, you cheated on me, you humiliated me, and I dealt with all of that. Now you think you're going to put your damn hands on me?"

"Baby, please, put the gun down! I didn't mean it."

"No! I will blow your fucking head off, Omar!"

The look in Asia's eyes was deadly. Sweat sprung from Omar's body and he began to tremble.

"Asia, please baby, don't...don't do this!"

She fired a single shot between his legs, which just missed his scrotum. Omar fell to his knees, gripping himself.

"Oh my God, Asia, please!" He began sobbing uncontrollably.

"Oh, now you believe in God; isn't this some shit!"

"Yes, baby, I believe in God and I believe in us. Please, baby, let's talk this out!"

"You mean like we did before?" Asia cocked the pistol.

"Yes, I mean...No! Asia, please, I'm about to piss on myself; God!"

Tears ran down Omar's face and into the sides of his mouth.

"What will you do to save your life, Omar?"

"I'll do anything you say; I'll get counseling."

"Counseling, huh?"

"Yes, baby, please, I'm sick; I need help."

At that moment, Omar was sick. Not because he had cheated on Asia so many times, but because he had never had a gun pointed in his face. He was practically ready to defecate on himself.

"Asia, please, I feel sick!" He began to shake hysterically.

"You really think counseling will help you?"

"Yes, baby, I do." Omar said, crawling toward her. He wrapped his arms around her legs, "I never meant to hurt you. I love you, but I just don't know how to stop. I'll do anything to be with you. Don't do this, please!" Omar's bawling began to pierce Asia's heart.

"Baby, if you kill me, I'll never have the chance to make it right. Please let me make it right, baby, please!"

Asia was weakening; she still loved him and deep down, she knew there was some truth to what he was saying. She began to lower the gun.

Omar pressed his face against her leg, using his chin to raise her skirt a little. He placed one hand around the barrel of the gun and began kissing her thighs.

The feel of Omar's face against her leg caused chills to run up Asia's spine. She tried to back away, but something inside of her wouldn't let her.

Omar moved his hand slowly over the barrel of the gun, extending his fingers to hers.

"No, Omar; I'm not going to let you hurt me again." Asia began to cry.

"Baby, I won't; I promise you. Please, Asia, you must believe me. I'm going to do better; help me to do better, please?" Omar said, as he continued to move his hand slowly up the side of her leg toward her special place.

Asia's grip on the gun was loosening a little; she was beginning to melt. Suddenly the phone rang.

He pressed his lips against her panties, causing her to let off a low moan. He fought to contain a smile.

She closed her eyes and grabbed his head with one hand, guiding it closer to her special place. He willingly allowed her to have her way. The phone continued to ring.

After a while, the grip she had on the gun was almost non-existent. He slowly began to work the gun from her hand as he swished his tongue back and forth between her legs.

All at once, they heard the clicking of the answering machine and a voice spill through it.

"Hi, Omar, it's Mom. Give me a call when you get in. Your sister and I just got back from our cruise and we want to tell you all about it. It was great. Next year you should come with us. Okay, call me, baby; bye."

His eyes stretched as he felt Asia's fingers tighten around the gun. He looked up and screamed.

The End

EPILOGUE

Omar leaped up, panting and sweating as if he had been chased by the devil.

"Hey, are you okay?" Asia asked.

Omar scooted over in the bed and wrapped his arms around her.

"Honey, do you want to talk about it?" she asked, stroking the side of his face.

Omar looked up and kissed her, "No, I'm okay."

"Are you sure?"

He gripped her tightly, "Yes, baby, I'm sure."

Omar was confident in the fact that Keisha hadn't told Asia about their little run in. Nor had Asia found out about him and Angela. He didn't give a damn about the nightmares. If he was able to wake up from them he was okay. Besides, he and Asia were back on good terms again and he had gotten over like a fat rat.

"You know I love you, right?" he asked.

"Yes," Asia replied, "and I love you too, baby." She leaned over and kissed him on the forehead.

Much later that night...

Asia had gotten up for a drink of water; when she returned to the bedroom, she smiled at Omar as he slept. A week was too long to be away from him. She couldn't believe how lonely she had been without him, without his touch, without the warmth of his strong body against hers. All the arguing and jealousy had been a waste of time, and all because of her childish insecurities. When she thought about the way she had written the message on his bedroom mirror, she chuckled with embarrassment. "I must have been crazy," she muttered. "Everything I was thinking was all in your mind."

Asia had decided at that moment to no longer question Omar or accuse him of doing things that he wasn't doing. From that point on, she was determined to trust him. After all, he was there with her, that's all that mattered. She wasn't worried about him hanging out with Ben anymore, either; they were just friends and she was certain of it.

She continued to stare at him lying next to her. He was such a handsome man and she loved him so much. They had been through some tough times, but things were finally moving in the right direction and she was happy now.

She snuggled close to him; the warmth of his body made her feel secure. She yawned and readied herself for sleep. Or so she thought; her cell phone began to vibrate. Her first thought was to ignore the buzzing, but it was incessant. She picked it up, and against her better judgment, listened to the voice message.

After listening to the mysterious voicemail message, Asia slid out of bed and began searching through Omar's things.

She opened the bedroom closet and found his travel bag behind a large suitcase. She also noticed a brown carry-on in the back of the closet. It was exactly where the person on the voicemail said it would be. Inside was a pair of men's socks, a white handkerchief, a picture of Omar and Ben dressed in black tuxedos, and another of Ben in bed wearing only a pair of underwear.

Her eyebrow rose and her mind drifted for a second, but she quickly shook away the thought. She continued to look through the bag and found a DVD; her curiosity peaked. She quietly placed the disc into the DVD player, turned the volume down low, and sat on the edge of the bed, watching as the words *Thigh Scrapers: The Work Out - Part One* appeared on the screen.

She turned the volume up as the movie began to play. At first glance, she thought it was a fitness video, but that notion was quickly done away with when the camera panned to a man lying on a bed wearing only a jock strap. It was Omar.

Asia's shuddered as she watched two women enter the scene, they were naked, white and begin to perform sexual acts on Omar. She was immediately overcome with emotion. Tears fell from her eyes as she sat watching her man do things with other women, she thought he only did with her. Suddenly it felt as though her heart was about to leap from her chest. The room seemed to be closing in on her. She began to experience feelings of hurt, sadness, shock and anger all at once. Fear also crept up on her, like a thug in a dark alley it leaped out and stifling her. She had spent a great deal of time loving, fighting and believing in Omar, how could he do such a thing? She became flustered with shame, guilt, and extraordinary disbelief. It was clear she didn't know him at all.

As the movie continued to play, Asia closed her eyes and began to pray. As if praying would somehow cause the video to disappear and she could forget she ever saw it. When she opened her eyes, Omar was still there, in the video, twisting the white women into positions she would have never thought humanly possible.

The sound of their moans sent chills up her spine. She glanced at Omar as he slept, and tears began to stream down her face.

Asia sat in a chair near Omar's bed for nearly four hours; from where she sat, she could smell the stench of lies and infidelity on his body. She didn't know what to do or what to say. She just sat there, looking at him and thinking.

Thigh Scrapers huh? So, you've been running around with your twisted friend, sticking your dicks in every pair of open thighs in this city. How many has it been Omar? How many were my friends, you bastard! You know what, forget it, you'll probably lie about that too because that's what sick men like you do, and what kind of stupid fucking name is Thigh Scrapers anyway!!! You know what, never mind Fuck Thigh Scrapers, fuck Ben, and fuck you, Omar. Fuck you!

As dawn marked the first light of the day, Asia planned for life without Omar. She had been up all night, thinking and crying. What Omar had done to her was un-forgivable.

She walked over to her side of the bed, grabbed her purse from the nightstand and glanced at him as he slept. Seconds later, she lifted her gown and then mounted him.

"Wake up, baby," she said in a low whisper, but Omar was sound asleep.

She leaned over and pressed her lips against his ear.

"Sweetheart, wake up," she said.

The sound of Asia's voice summoned him from his sleep-that and the fact that he felt the warmth of her thighs straddling him.

He smiled with his eyes shut.

"Is it time to get up?"

"Yeah, it's time," Asia whispered, nibbling on his ear. "You know, baby, I'm so glad we don't have any secrets anymore."

Omar stretched, "Me too."

"So, there's absolutely nothing you're keeping from me, now?"

"No." He spoke with his eyes still shut.

"Well, I have to admit that there's something I've been keeping from you," she said, kissing the side of his face.

"Really, is it bad?" Omar questioned, smiling as he played along.

"Yes, very bad."

"What is it?"

"Let me whisper it in your ear."

She leaned over and placed her soft lips against his neck and then slid her tongue into his ear."

Omar moaned, gripping himself before their early morning session.

She began whispering in his ear, causing his forehead to wrinkle. He waited for a punch line to her joke. None came.

When he opened his eyes, he felt something cold pressed against his face. Asia was in tears, her hands were trembling, and the nozzle of a forty-five-caliber handgun was pressed right between his eyes.

"Baby, no!" he shouted, attempting to grab the gun.

They tussled and the gun went off.

A cold feeling raced through Asia's body as Omar lay beneath her with his eyes widened. In the distance, she could hear the faint sound of a woman screaming, "politsiya, Politsiya, POLITSIYA!"

Omar reached up to touch her face. She could feel every emotion in his body. She knew then that he really did love her and that he was sorry for what he had done, but it was too late.

Asia's body went limp and fell to the mattress as Omar tried to speak but couldn't.

She moved swiftly around his place...

She used her gown to wipe her prints from the gun, carefully placed it in Omar's hand, and then climbed from the bed.

While waiting for her cab to arrive, every second felt like an eternity. As a black four-door sedan pulled up, she breathed a sigh of relief. Asia sat in the back while the driver placed her things in the trunk. As they drove away, she opened her pocketbook and true to form, applied a fresh coat of lipstick. She was on her way back to Harlem. Still Asia couldn't help but think about her friends.

They were right; there weren't any good black men left in the world.

Made in the USA
Monee, IL
11 November 2020